Praise for

SISTERS AND SECRETS

"Jennifer Ryan's *Sisters and Secrets* should win an award for being the most unputdownable book of the whole year. The drama will keep you on the edge of your seat, and the emotional roller coaster will touch every emotion."

—Carolyn Brown, *New York Times* and *USA Today* bestselling author

"Sibling rivalry comes to a head in a masterpiece of family and secrets." —Fresh Fiction

Sisters
and
Secrets

By Jennifer Ryan

Standalone Novels
LOST AND FOUND FAMILY • SISTERS AND SECRETS
THE ME I USED TO BE

The Wyoming Wildes Series
CHASE WILDE COMES HOME

The McGraths Series
TRUE LOVE COWBOY • LOVE OF A COWBOY
WAITING ON A COWBOY

Wild Rose Ranch Series
TOUGH TALKING COWBOY • RESTLESS RANCHER
DIRTY LITTLE SECRET

Montana Heat Series
TEMPTED BY LOVE • TRUE TO YOU
ESCAPE TO YOU • PROTECTED BY LOVE

Montana Men Series
HIS COWBOY HEART • HER RENEGADE RANCHER
STONE COLD COWBOY • HER LUCKY COWBOY
WHEN IT'S RIGHT • AT WOLF RANCH

The McBrides Series
DYLAN'S REDEMPTION • FALLING FOR OWEN
THE RETURN OF BRODY MCBRIDE

The Hunted Series
EVERYTHING SHE WANTED
CHASING MORGAN • THE RIGHT BRIDE
LUCKY LIKE US • SAVED BY THE RANCHER

Short Stories
"Close to Perfect" (appears in *Snowbound at Christmas*)
"Can't Wait"
(appears in *All I Want for Christmas Is a Cowboy*)
"Waiting for You"
(appears *in Confessions of a Secret Admirer*)

JENNIFER RYAN

Sisters and Secrets

A Novel

AVONBOOKS
An Imprint of HarperCollinsPublishers

SISTERS AND SECRETS. Copyright © 2020 by Jennifer Ryan. All rights reserved. Printed in the United States of America. No part of this book may be used or reproduced in any manner whatsoever without written permission except in the case of brief quotations embodied in critical articles and reviews. For information, address HarperCollins Publishers, 195 Broadway, New York, NY 10007.

First Avon Books mass market printing: May 2022
First William Morrow paperback printing: June 2020

Print Edition ISBN: 978-0-06-307181-0
Digital Edition ISBN: 978-0-06-294447-4

Designed by Diahann Sturge
Chapter opener image © Irina Mos / Shutterstock, Inc.
Cover design by Mimi Bark
Cover photographs © Susan Fox/Arcangel Images (women); © ILINA SIMEONOVA/Trevillion Images (woman); © Shutterstock

Avon, Avon & logo, and Avon Books & logo are registered trademarks of HarperCollins Publishers in the United States of America and other countries.

HarperCollins is a registered trademark of HarperCollins Publishers in the United States of America and other countries.

22 23 24 25 26   QGM   10 9 8 7 6 5 4 3 2 1

For all of you out there who need to rebuild or renovate your life, this one is for you. Let go of the past and anything that doesn't bring you joy. Fill your life with laughter and love. You deserve to be happy.

Chapter One

Flames burned bright orange and red on both sides of the two-lane road as they consumed and destroyed everything in their path. Homes, businesses, multimillion-dollar vineyards. Nothing was spared as the fire climbed over the Napa Valley hills, unrelenting in its destruction. Sierra prayed it spared everyone on the road leading out, especially her sons.

She drove, heart pounding, fear amped to infinity, with her clammy palms locked on the steering wheel. Bumper to bumper, traffic moved at a snail's pace. Like her, the other residents had been notified too late to gradually evacuate. The sheer number of people trying to escape all at once down a single lane prevented them from racing away from the flames. The other lane was left open to emergency vehicles that occasionally sped into the belly of the beast. Everyone had to feel exactly like her: desperate to flee before this dark and dangerous road became their grave.

She loved watching the flames dance in her woodburning stove, but driving through a wildfire made her feel like she was inside an inferno. Trapped. A wave of terror shot through her, cold fear dancing down her spine. She wanted out. Now.

Sierra glanced at her two small sons in the back

seat, danger inches away outside. Helpless to eradicate it, she sucked in a breath to calm the fear and focus on getting them out of here as safely as possible. Every instinct told her to stomp on the gas, jump in the other lane, speed past everyone, and get them to safety no matter what. But like everyone else, she tried to stay orderly and calm.

Noxious fumes, unbelievable heat, and fire surrounded them. Nothing and no one was a match for Mother Nature's firestorm. Ash, smoke, and sparks blew all around them while the satellite radio cut in and out, the signal blocked by the thick smoke obliterating their view of the night sky. Fear knotted her gut and rising panic sped up her heartbeat. Every second trapped within the blaze raging on both sides of them made it harder to keep it together for her two little boys.

She thought about their lives, how they'd already suffered a great loss when their father died, and all they had ahead of them. She didn't want it to end this way. She wanted to see them grown, happy, healthy, living the life they chose and thriving.

"Mom." Danny's voice shook. "The window is hot."

"Don't touch it." She'd flipped the vent system to recirculate, but the smoky stench permeated the car along with the immense heat. The acrid scent turned her stomach and left a sour taste in her mouth.

Oliver held his favorite blanket over his mouth and nose. His eyes held a world of worry, too great for one five-year-old to face and understand beyond the fact that the scene outside was scary as hell and he wanted to be far away.

So do I.

Frustration got the better of the guy in the pickup truck behind her and he laid on the horn. Where did he expect her to go? The line of cars had only moved ten feet in the last two minutes. At this rate, they wouldn't get out of the fire zone before dawn.

At least, it felt that way.

A rush of adrenaline shot through her again, signaling the flight-or-fight response she'd felt when she'd seen the smoke and fire headed toward their home. She could neither fight it nor flee from it when it literally surrounded her. And so she tried her best to stay alert, remain calm, and pray this all worked out.

Three more fire engines sped past in the opposite lane. Reinforcements for the dozens she'd passed on the tedious and exceedingly dangerous trip out of here.

We'll make it out. We have to.

She'd worked too hard the last eleven months to keep her head above water after her husband's tragic car accident to have it all end like this . . . in a car, on a dark road, consumed by fire.

It felt too eerily close to how they lost David.

Sierra gripped the steering wheel even tighter to stop her hands from shaking and focused on the car in front of her, following it around another curve, not getting her hopes up when their speed increased even marginally, but telling herself *steady as she goes* was good enough, so long as they got out of this alive.

The thought of anything happening to her babies . . . She couldn't go there. It stopped her heart. But that fear drove her to keep her head and do everything possible to get them out of this situation even as thoughts of their home, her job, and the future swamped her mind. She'd barely made it by these last many months. If she lost everything . . . What then?

How would she support herself and the boys?

More flashing red and white lights glowed against the thick smoke ahead. She inched her way toward the emergency vehicles, the cars slowing ahead of her as they approached what must be an intersection. Fire trucks and police cars blocked the cross street, drawing everyone's attention and slowing them down as everyone stared to the side to see if the fire had destroyed everything down that road. Ahead, cars shot forward as if they were racehorses released from the starting gates as they passed the commotion and the open road broke free of the fire border.

Relief hit like a crashing wave.

We made it.

Now what?

She didn't really have a plan for where to go. She ran out of her house with the clothes on her back, her purse, an armful of personal files, and her two sons in tow with the stench of smoke heavy in the air and flames devouring the houses only six streets away. By now, for all she knew, her house and all those on her block were gone.

Bile rose to the back of her throat, the thought so terribly upsetting, their future left uncertain.

Right now, though, she'd take the thirty-five-mile-an-hour speeds, the open land and road ahead of her as she outran the fire and smoke and spotted the sign for Yountville and the acclaimed restaurant the French Laundry.

"Is the fire gone?" Oliver asked.

She wished. "We're getting farther and farther away from it."

"Where are we going?" Danny leaned toward his brother so he could see through the windshield.

Now that the flames weren't licking at the sides of the car and bearing down on them, Sierra took a moment to think about her next move. She needed a place to put the boys down to bed tonight. In the morning, there'd be news of the firefighters' efforts to stop the massive blaze and whether or not her home had been spared. She hoped, but her heart sank with the realization it didn't seem likely and they'd lost everything.

Chapter Two

A wasteland of ash and blackened trees spread before Sierra. It looked like an apocalyptic scene from a movie. But this was her neighborhood, the site where her home used to stand, its welcoming garden inviting you to the front door and the safe place she used to love.

Nothing stirred but the wind. The quiet unsettled her.

An officer escorted her into the fire zone and dropped her off, just as he had with some of her neighbors.

Driving through the eerily empty neighborhood, having to try extrahard to decipher where she was and where she used to live, left her stomach clenched in a knot. The park where the kids used to play was nothing more than a few burnt trees, their empty blackened branches reaching for the bright blue sky from barren ground. Many of the trees had burned to ash. The play set was nothing but some metal bars sticking out of the sunken cement rectangle with pools of melted plastic from the slides, seesaw, and swings.

Tears stung her eyes as memories of her boys playing and laughing with their friends assailed her.

It was nothing compared to standing in her driveway and seeing nothing but her blackened washer and dryer shells, twisted metal from her stove vent hood, and half her chimney standing, the top part in a heap of brick where the hearth used to be. She remembered hanging stockings from the thick wood mantel every Christmas and dashed a tear from her cheek with her finger.

The loss felt like a sledgehammer to what was left of her broken heart.

The boys' photo albums from birth to now, gone. She had the digital photos stored in the cloud, but she'd painstakingly put the albums together with other mementos. The hospital bands they wore when they were born. The ticket stubs from their first movie. The armbands from their first visit to the zoo. The pictures they colored on their first day of preschool. The colored and stained kids' menu from breakfast with Mickey at Disneyland. The prayer card from their father's funeral.

It killed her when they asked if all their father's things were gone. She'd promised them she'd find everything she could.

She thought of the cuff links he wore at their wedding. She'd hoped that one day the boys would wear them when they married the person of their dreams. She'd kept his golf clubs, despite how many times she'd resented him taking off for eighteen holes of solitude and fun when she barely got an hour to herself each day. But she'd hoped her boys would give the sport a try and find some commonality with their father. She pictured them standing on the course and taking a moment to think about him every time they played.

David died so young. It wouldn't be long before the boys lost the sharpness of their memories of him. She feared Oliver would forget him altogether.

She'd kept as much as she could of David in the house to remind them, despite how those reminders triggered her resentments and anger.

Sierra reminded herself that she didn't need the things in the house to remember all they'd shared under that roof. The good times. The bad. She still carried them with her.

David's sudden death left her the keeper of his memory for the boys. She tried to keep him alive for them, but the fire took everything of his, all the mementos the boys needed to help them remember their father.

His stuff may be gone, but he'd left her with suspicions and doubts about the many months leading up to his death. Those didn't burn up in the fire. But anything that might have revealed the truth was gone.

Sierra didn't know if she could live without knowing, but what choice did she have now?

The fire had wiped the slate clean of every possession and tie to the past. She had to rebuild from the ground up.

No home. No job. A dwindling savings account.

It had taken hours to complete her claim with the insurance company, but a payout was weeks if not months away.

Rebuilding could take years with all the government red tape. But the cost of rebuilding . . . The insurance probably wouldn't cover it.

Added to her worries, she no longer had an income. The property management company she worked for had burned down, too, along with many of the properties they oversaw.

She faced a long journey ahead of her to figure out what to do with the home she no longer felt a connection to.

It felt like one more thing David had left for her to deal with on her own.

What am I doing here?

There's nothing left.

But she had promised the boys she'd take back anything she could salvage. She hoped to find at least one thing for each of them. The stuffed fish David won Oliver at the fair knocking down milk jugs with a baseball wasn't even worth consideration. Neither was Danny's science fair certificate he was so proud of winning. The memory would have to be enough for both of them. But maybe something survived.

She walked toward the property site and slid the respirator mask she'd been given over her head to cover her nose and mouth. She didn't want to breathe in all the soot, ash, and toxic chemicals from everything that had burned and melted.

With the layout of the house ahead of her obscured by debris and simply unrecognizable without the walls defining the space, she started at the cement porch steps that led to where her door used to be. She stepped up to what used to be the entry and surveyed the destruction with a lump in her throat, tears in her eyes, and a very heavy heart.

Nothing in the living room, kitchen, dining room, or bathrooms was worth sorting through all the wreckage to find. She visualized the house and made her way to where the boys' rooms were located, her rubber boots crunching over the remains of what used to be their home.

She tried not to think too hard about all they'd lost. Dishes, furniture, TVs, computers, clothes— all of it could be replaced, she reminded herself. That didn't help ease the ache in her chest or the wanting to have it all back. The baby clothes she'd saved. The crib she'd stored in the garage just in case one day they had another baby.

Not possible for them now.

But she'd liked knowing it was there if she needed it.

Just like her grandmother's quilt wrapped in tissue and stored in a box in the hall linen closet.

With the destruction spread out before her, it seemed ridiculous to even think something survived the flames and heat.

Sierra found what she thought was Danny's room and where his desk and bookshelf used to stand. She pulled on thick work gloves and dug into the debris, hoping to find something recognizable. Ten minutes in, her fingers brushed something hard. She picked up the disk and stared at it, not believing her eyes. The outside of the pocket watch had blackened, but when she opened it, the inside wasn't that bad off. The glass had cracked and the clock mechanism didn't work, but Danny would love to have it, anyway. She and David bought it for him at some downtown antique shop on their vacation up to Jamestown where they took the kids gold panning in an old abandoned ghost town turned into a tourist attraction. The kids had even made candles.

The memory along with finding the pocket watch eased her heart a bit. She had something to give to

Danny besides the metal frame of what might be a Ford Mustang Hot Wheel with no tires and the paint melted completely away.

She spent ten more minutes rummaging through what was left of Danny's room before working on Oliver's space. She didn't find much until she made it to where his toy box had sat below his window. There, she found a treasure that brought tears to her eyes. His marble collection had survived inside a tin that had once held Hershey's chocolate they'd bought at the chocolate factory they'd toured in the Central Valley.

Oliver would be so happy.

She lifted a half-burnt board and found two dirty but perfectly intact plastic dinosaurs. How they didn't melt escaped her, but she'd take the little guys back to Oliver. The mound of burnt plastic ten inches away had to be the bin that held all the others. She didn't even bother trying to pull it apart to see if anything in the middle survived. She just moved on, brushing things this way and that hoping something else caught her eye.

Even though her thighs and ankles hurt from crouching, she moved on to her bedroom, strategic in where she looked. She started where she thought the closet used to be, hoping that even if her wooden jewelry box hadn't survived, some of her jewelry had, especially the pieces she'd put into a metal lockbox.

Metal hangers told Sierra she was in the right place. But she didn't find anything resembling the few pieces of jewelry she owned until she started backing up toward where the bed used to be. Her foot kicked something and the metallic thump of it hitting something else made her heart pound and hope rise. She shoved debris aside to get to the blackened rectangle with the lock still intact. She hugged the box to her chest and heard several things inside rattle. She didn't have the key to open it, but with some tools, she hoped to bust it open and find her and David's wedding rings, along with her pair of diamond studs, and a couple other rings and a diamond heart pendant David gave her their first Christmas as a married couple.

"Find something?" the officer who dropped her off asked from the road as he stood outside his patrol car.

She stood, pulled her mask off, and found a smile. "Yes. I did."

"It's getting late. We'll close the neighborhood off to visitors for the night soon. It's time to head back. You can return tomorrow if you'd like."

They'd closed off the neighborhood to keep looters from trying to sort through homes looking for anything that survived the fire.

Some people suck.

It wasn't bad enough the people who used to live here lost everything; someone wanted to profit off them.

Which made her think of all the paperwork and hoops she'd had to jump through to file her insurance claim and put in for federal assistance.

It sucked that the process was so hard and convoluted.

She put the metal box into the bucket she'd brought with her that now contained her treasures, planted her hands on her knees, and pushed herself up. Her legs ached, but her heart felt lighter. She'd found what she'd come here for, and Danny and Oliver would be so happy to have a small piece of their past to hold on to when everything had been taken away, including the school they used to attend.

They couldn't stay here much longer.

She needed to get the boys somewhere they could settle in and go back to school.

She also needed to call her mom and have the talk she'd put off because immediate concerns took precedence to actually making decisions that extended beyond their need for a roof over their heads and dealing with the aftermath of the fire.

She'd done what she needed to do with the property.

There truly was nothing left for her to do here.

Overwhelmed by what came next and the abundance of decisions that had to be made to start a whole new life, Sierra trudged through the wreckage, walked down the porch steps one last time, her heart heavy that this was probably the last time she'd ever come here, and headed for the police car. She opened the back door, set her bucket on the seat, then turned back and looked at what used to be.

Emotion flooded her, sending tears down her cheeks. She pulled off a glove and brushed them away with clean fingers.

"You can rebuild," the officer assured her.

Yes, I will. Just not here.

Her boys were counting on her.

But she had to face reality and listen to her heart. She didn't want to be here anymore.

She wanted to go home to Carmel.

* * *

"Hi, sweetheart."

"Hey, Mom." Sierra stood outside the motel room door on the balcony overlooking the pool with her cell phone to her ear, so happy to hear her mother's reassuring voice.

"It's been a couple of days. I worried."

The days since the fire had left Sierra drained. "I'm sorry. I went to the house yesterday. There's nothing left but ash and burnt trees. Everywhere I looked . . . there was just nothing."

"I can't imagine." Emotion tightened her mom's soft voice. "We spoke about this the other day, but I'll say it again. I'm happy to help in any way you need."

"I appreciate that."

"Just tell me how much you need and I'll get it to you."

She didn't want to rely on her mother for financial support. That was more her little sister Heather's MO. "Right now I need something besides money."

"Anything."

"I want to come home, Mom."

"I've got your old room and the spare bedroom all ready for you."

Relief swept through her. Her mom offered the second she found out the house was lost. Overwhelmed in the moment, and since, Sierra hadn't been able to really think or plan.

"When will you be here?"

"Tomorrow?" She hated to impose, but she also wanted to get the boys settled.

"I can't wait." Her mother's excitement eased Sierra's mind.

"Thank you for this. I'm out of options." At least it felt that way.

"I'm always here for you, Sierra. This is still your home no matter how old you get."

Tears clogged her throat, but she pushed the words out. "I love you."

"I love you, too, sweetheart. Everything is going to be okay."

She really needed to hear that right now.

Sierra outlined her plans for the trip home, thanked her mom one more time, and said good-bye with a lighter heart and a belly full of anticipation.

This felt right. With everything of her old life literally left in ashes, she needed a fresh start.

So did the boys. They'd been through so much this past year, losing their father and now their home.

She walked back into their latest rented room and stared at her boys sitting on the queen bed in the fourth motel they'd moved to in the last three weeks. Their treasures she'd found at the house yesterday sat on the nightstand beside them. They'd been so surprised and excited to get them, but also sad that the few items had been all that was left of their belongings. She felt the same way.

One of the guys at the fire victims center took a hammer and screwdriver to the lockbox and popped it open for her. David's cuff links had survived. So had their wedding rings. The jewelry hadn't come out unscathed. The metal had turned black and tarnished, but the diamonds were eerily bright and sparkly. Maybe one day she'd have them reset into new men's rings for the boys. They could wear a piece of what bound her and David together.

Backs against the propped pillows, Danny and Oliver were deep into a cupcake baking show on the Food Network. Eventually, they'd ask to go to the local grocery store to pick up some treats.

They deserved something sweet for being such troopers. They missed their friends, their own things, and even school.

Sierra pressed her hand over the stack of papers sitting on the small table by the window. They were all she'd managed to grab on her mad dash out of the house to beat the fire. All these months after David's death, she still couldn't account for the personal loan he'd taken out without her knowledge.

Fifty thousand dollars.

This past year, she'd struggled on her income combined with David's Social Security to pay the bills and keep a roof over their heads. And now she didn't even have the house or a job.

She had this motel room for the next two days, another lined up for one night, but she needed something more permanent. The boys needed stability. They needed routine.

And so did she.

All this uncertainty left her a live wire of anxiety, sadness for all they'd lost, and uncertainty about how she'd get them all back on track and thriving again.

As a mom, she thought she could do it all. She tried.

Most days, until the fire, she did a pretty good job.

You can't have everything. Something's gotta give. But right now, overwhelmed by their circumstances and uncertainty about the future, she needed help.

Her family knew of their troubles. They wanted to help. She appreciated it, but until now she'd gone from hour to hour, day to day, trying her best to deal with the aftermath of the fire and keep the boys entertained.

But she needed to start thinking of the bigger picture. Especially because she was running out of money and racking up credit card debt. Yes, there was help out there for the fire victims. She'd taken advantage of the free clothes, everyday necessities, like toiletries, and even a few toys for the boys to take their minds off all they'd lost.

Truly, when she thought about all the *things* they needed to replace, it overwhelmed her.

And yet, she had moments where she embraced the fact that this was a chance to start over, start fresh.

But there was so much of the past still left unsettled.

While the community had come together to provide free meals and assistance to navigate the process and red tape involved in a disaster, it was still so overwhelming. All she wanted to do was hand the whole job over to someone else. She wanted to turn back time and go back to her life before the fire destroyed everything.

That thought only reminded her that life hadn't been happy and carefree for a long time. Certainly not since her husband's death and, if she was honest with herself, it started before that. There'd been a distance building between them for some time. The more she thought about it, the more she realized that she'd never get the answers she desperately wanted from David.

Right now, that didn't matter.

Her boys deserved better than dingy motel rooms and another takeout meal.

Sierra glanced around the messy room. Plastic shopping bags with their meager belongings on the floor and dresser, discarded takeout containers scattered across the small table by the window, the boys' bath towels on the tile floor by the vanity with the dripping faucet, both beds a mess of tangled sheets littered with toy cars and stuffed animals, and her boys sitting among the chaos eating a bag of chips instead of a healthy snack.

The untidy room reflected the current state of her life.

She needed to clean up the mess, clear her mind, and come up with a plan for their new life.

"What do you guys think about going to visit Grandma and Aunt Amy and Aunt Heather?" Asking for help had never come easy, but Sierra really needed some right now. She'd reached that point where there was so much to tackle she didn't know where to start.

The boys rolled up to their feet and jumped up and down on the bed. "Yes!"

Danny bounced and landed on his butt. "When can we go?"

"Now!" Oliver begged.

Yep, they needed family. Stability. Something familiar.

Truth be told, so did she, but that meant going home. It felt like the right decision, but sometimes going home was easier said than done.

She hoped she wasn't trading one drama for another.

Chapter Three

Heather pulled onto the shoulder and parked the car next to the mailboxes. She checked the car seat behind her and found her daughter, Hallee, still slumbering, her face soft and sweet. Every time she looked at her little girl, she saw a glimpse of the man she'd loved and lost.

Cars drove by on the main road. She climbed out and inhaled the slightly salty scent in the air, though they were a ways from the beach. She loved it here in Carmel Valley. So much so, she'd never left.

Not like Sierra.

She couldn't imagine all her sister had been through these last weeks.

Her mother had called an hour ago, said she'd heard from Sierra, and asked Heather to stop by after work to talk about Sierra and the boys.

She missed her sister. But as much as she wanted to help, she dreaded Sierra's return. Everyone would start asking questions about Heather's daughter again.

Family. They wanted all the details about your successes and mistakes.

Hopefully, Sierra's troubles would keep them all occupied and off her back.

Life had always been about her older sisters. This time would be no different.

Amy seemed to have a new crisis every week. If you could call motherhood a crisis. Amy seemed to think everything had to be perfect in her perfect life.

Heather rolled her eyes at that. Sometimes the messy things gave you the most satisfaction and joy. She glanced at her sweet sleeping angel. Yep. The mess, the pain, the bad choices . . . totally worth it.

Even if she had to live with the consequences and secrets.

A Mercedes pulled in front of her car as she retrieved the mail from her mother's box. It had been a long time since she'd seen the sexy man who climbed out and stopped short when he saw her.

Mason Moore. Superhot next-door neighbor. Now a successful divorce attorney. They met him the day they moved here after their mom married husband number four. As teens, at one time or another, she, Amy, and even Sierra had a crush on him.

He had an odd profession for a guy who didn't seem to enjoy other people's drama. But Mom said rumor had it he'd helped an old flame out during a nasty divorce, managing to get her full custody of her kids from an ex-husband who liked to hurt the people he supposedly loved.

Mason would want to be the guy who protected people like her and the child.

He was just a good guy.

Maybe if she'd gone for someone like him instead of the bad boys she preferred . . . Well, that's what happened when your heart wanted what it wanted.

Her heart sped up just looking at him.

"Heather. Hey. What are you doing here?"

Thinking about getting out of this rut and dating again. God, you're gorgeous.

It had been a long time since she'd enjoyed a night out with a guy. She missed the flirting, listening to a man's deep voice, having all his attention focused on her.

No offense to her sweet girl, but Mama needed some affection, too, sometimes.

She held up the stack of envelopes and catalogs. "Grabbing the mail for Mom on my way to see her."

"How is she?" He unlocked his box and pulled out his mail, his focus more on the bills than her. Unfortunately.

"Fine. Getting the house ready for company."

One eyebrow raised above his dark sunglasses. "Company?"

"Sierra and the boys."

The eyebrow went up again. "Sierra's coming home?" A hint of anticipation and hope filled the question that sounded way more like a statement he needed to hear to believe it.

She couldn't see his eyes, but she felt his interest in the answer, not her. "They'll be here tomorrow."

"How are they? I mean, they must be devastated after the fire."

"It's been difficult. They've been moving from one hotel or motel to the next while Sierra sorts out the mess with the insurance and government assistance. There's not much left up there for them. Sierra's job is gone along with everything else they owned, so . . ." She shrugged. "I guess this is her only choice right now."

Mason tilted his head. "She's smart. Resourceful. I'm sure she'll be back on her feet in no time. But it will be good to have her home."

Heather wasn't so sure about that. She loved her sister, but when they got together, they fell back into childhood roles. Heather wanted Sierra to see her for who she was now, not the impulsive spoiled brat Sierra used to call her. Of course, her sisters and mom never let her forget her mistakes and missteps. "I'm looking forward to seeing the boys." That at least was wholly true.

"Please tell Sierra, if there's anything she needs, I'm happy to help."

Yeah, everyone had scrambled to help Sierra after David died. They'd do the same now after the fire. She'd be everyone's priority.

Mason glanced at the back of her car. Hallee gave him a bright smile and waved. Mason waved back, smiling for the first time. It made him even more handsome, and Hallee ate it up, covering her face with her stuffed elephant, then moving it away and smiling at him again.

Mason turned his attention back to her. "She's really sweet."

"Growing like a weed."

"She'll probably love having the boys around."

Heather wished she could see his eyes. Something in his voice hinted at an underlying message she couldn't decipher. "Uh, yeah. We haven't seen Sierra and the boys in a while."

He leaned his weight on one leg in a casual stance, but she felt his focus. "How are you getting on all by yourself? It can't be easy being a single mom."

"I'm doing okay." It sucked. She wished she had a loving husband. Hallee deserved a father who loved her and showed her what a good man looked like.

Hallee's father had loved her. He had wanted her. It just wasn't meant to be.

"Good to hear it." That same edge she'd heard before came again. "Well, it's been a long day and I have to get home and check on the horses. Say hi to your mom for me. Maybe I'll stop by to see Sierra and the boys once they've settled in."

"I'm sure she'd love to see you."

The innocuous statement made him pause for a second. "She's been through a lot. I hope she finds some happiness here."

Why did she hear a deeper meaning in the things he said?

Heather held up the mail. "I better get going, too." She stopped him just before he opened his car door. "It's nice to see you, Mason. It's been too long. We've known each other forever, yet we hardly take the time to say hi anymore."

"It's been a long time since you girls were jumping fences and begging me to ride the horses."

"Maybe I'll make a point to stop by and do just that."

She got another of those stares from behind his glasses that she couldn't see or read. "Tell Sierra if the boys need a distraction, I'm happy to saddle up a couple horses for them." With that, Mason slid into his car, started the engine, and pulled back onto the road, taking the long driveway just past her mother's.

"He's a strange one. But sexy as all get-out." Maybe she would take a chance and stop by for a *ride*. The images that evoked made her warm all over.

Definitely time to get back in the dating saddle.

But first she needed to meet her mom and Amy about Sierra. Because just like Mason's comments, everything right now for everyone was about *her*.

Chapter Four

Sierra pulled into the driveway.

Dede's stomach fluttered with anticipation. She hoped she, Amy, and Heather had gathered everything Sierra and the boys needed to settle in here.

With four marriages under her belt, Dede feared the only thing she'd taught her daughters about love and marriage was that neither lasts. With Amy on the verge of a divorce she wouldn't see coming with her blinders on, Heather a single mom with zero interest in finding a partner, and Sierra a widow with two young sons, it didn't look like any one of them would find the kind of love that lasts.

Despite not finding it for herself, she wanted her daughters to find their soul mates—if such a thing even existed.

But, oh, those daughters of hers!

Amy held on so tight to her husband and the image she showed the world—perfect marriage, perfect kids, perfect life—that she didn't enjoy any of it. The moments were lost, despite how much she loved to share the perfect pictures. She didn't seem to savor the memories or reflect on how lucky she was to have a man who really loved her and the kids. Amy was so busy creating a moment, she didn't share it with her husband and kids. Her family was perfect without all the fuss and polish Amy heaped on them. And Rex was getting tired of feeling like he didn't matter as much as the Instagram-perfect meal Amy set in front of him each night.

Dede rolled her eyes at a memory of their last family meal together, a moment when Rex had tried to lean in and kiss his wife. Amy had nudged him out of her way so she could get the star-shaped cucumbers out of the fridge. They needed to go on top of the salad or it just wasn't finished. Rejected for cucumbers. Dede sighed. No wonder Rex was frustrated and feeling underappreciated.

But Amy would say no one appreciated all the fuss and bother she put into everything.

Dede had tried to tell her to relax and stop taking on so much. Of course, her oldest wouldn't listen. She had to be right about everything.

And maybe she got that from Dede, too.

Heather, on the other hand, just wanted to be with her little girl and soak up Hallee's bright smiles and joyful giggles. She loved being a mother. And yet, for all the happiness Dede saw in Heather when she and Hallee were together, Dede sometimes caught moments when that joy was replaced by a look of deep sadness and regret Dede wished she understood.

But Heather had always liked her secrets. As a kid she'd spy on Amy and Sierra. She knew which one of them ate the last of the cookies without permission. As a teen she knew who snuck in late. Heather relished knowing her sisters' secrets and letting you know she knew.

She loved sneaking around and listening in when she shouldn't. Those little things she knew were fun.

But withholding the name of Hallee's father—and not letting everyone know—seemed to wear on Heather. Still, she refused to divulge the information. And things didn't quite add up. She said the man knew about Hallee but wanted to remain in the background. In the beginning, he provided for Heather and Hallee, but lately it seemed evident by the number of times Heather asked to "borrow" money he wasn't even peripherally involved in their lives anymore. And that sadness she saw in Heather seemed to grow.

Dede didn't mind helping her daughters out when they needed it. But Heather relied on it a little too much. Her fault for spoiling the baby of the family.

And poor Sierra. How much could one young woman take? David had died tragically and unexpectedly nearly a year ago and now she'd lost everything in that devastating wildfire.

Dede barely heard from Sierra these last many months since David's death. She hadn't wanted to pry or seem to hover. Sierra thought herself capable and invincible. Dede agreed. But even someone as strong as Sierra could only take so much.

Though she suspected Sierra would come home to evaluate her options, the vulnerability she'd heard in her daughter's soft voice when she called asking to come home had made Dede's heart ache. It actually made her pause and think about all the times Sierra swore she was okay, she could take care of . . . whatever, but maybe she'd just been putting on a good front. Sierra always stood on her own two feet, ready for anything. But though she got through it, Dede wondered if she'd let Sierra down by not noticing that deep down Sierra needed her help and support.

Not this time.

This time I'm going to make sure Sierra feels safe and protected and that this new beginning is what she truly wants.

Because Dede suspected Sierra had settled in the past for what she thought was enough instead of reaching for what she really wanted.

Amy came up behind her and glanced out the front windows. Her two children, P.J. and Emma, ignored the plate of sliced apples slathered in almond butter in front of them. Instead, they devoured a second cupcake each.

"Mom, seriously, you couldn't have gotten something better for them to eat?"

"You don't have to be the sweets police all the time. A cupcake once in a while doesn't hurt. And I'm their grandmother. It's my job to spoil them."

She'd made the cupcakes for Danny and Oliver, hoping something sweet would make them feel welcome. They hadn't visited since they stayed a couple of days after David's funeral. The time before that had been during her own husband's funeral. She never thought to have that in common with her daughter, but life happens. Tragedy strikes. She wanted to give her grandsons something good to associate with visits with her, something besides death.

And all kids love cupcakes.

"I'm trying to teach the kids to make healthy choices."

Dede shrugged, wishing Amy would loosen her

rigid control over her kids. "You can feed them qui-noa and kale all you want. When they're here, let them be kids instead of organic-health-nuts-in-the-making and enjoy the simple pleasure of a sugar rush."

Amy turned to P.J. and Emma, who'd been av-idly watching to see if Grandma won this argument. "Put the cupcakes down and eat the apples."

Loud and upset groans punctuated the kids dropping the treats and pushing the plate of apples away.

Dede rolled her eyes. "Moderation, Amy. Teach them that, so they can find balance and not feel like you're taking things away from them."

"You never let us gorge on cupcakes before dinner."

"Unless it was a party or holiday. You know, there's a time and place for everything, including letting kids be kids."

Amy needed to ease up in every part of her life. She was wound so tight, she was bound to snap and unravel. Dede pushed because she didn't want to see that happen. Amy needed to have some fun and relax. No one could be that anxious and obsessive about things and not suffer some consequences.

Amy clearly swallowed a retort when the front door opened. Her eyes went wide at the sight of Sierra and the boys standing there. "Poor thing. She looks worn out."

Of course Sierra heard the not-so-subtle stage whisper.

Instead of responding to Amy's comment, she simply said, "Hello, Amy," and stroked a hand over Danny's head, nudging him inside with his bundled blanket, backpack, and several overflowing plastic bags. Like a mini vagabond, he held his precious few belongings.

Oliver followed his brother in, his arms not quite as full, but still the five-year-old held what little belonged to him, including a cute stuffed brown puppy.

Dede rushed to greet them and make them feel welcome. "Oh my, you boys have grown so much."

"I have to pee," Oliver announced.

"The bathroom is this way." Amy held her hand out toward the hall.

Sierra smiled down at her littlest. "Go ahead. Aunt Amy will take you. Say hi to Grandma first."

Oliver gave her a shy smile. "Hi, Grandma."

Dede brushed her hand over his dark head. "Hey, sweetie. I'm so happy you're here."

Oliver glanced at the cartoon on the TV. "Motel TVs are hard." With that, he ran after Amy to get to the bathroom.

Danny looked up at Dede. "The remotes are weird." He leaned into her for the hug she wrapped him in.

"Well, soon your mom will have a new place for you to live maybe with a TV easier for you to use. Until then, I'm so happy to have you here with me." She released Danny, noting how much he reminded her of his father. "Your room is up the stairs. Second door on the right. You'll find a surprise on the bed for you and Oliver."

Danny gave her a smile, glanced briefly at his mom for an approving nod for him to go ahead, and he dashed up the stairs with a speed Dede could no longer achieve in her advanced age. But it did her heart good to hear him squeal with delight when he found his gift.

His shouted "No way!" made Sierra raise an eyebrow.

"I got him and Oliver new tablets. The nice boy at the electronics store said they're exactly what kids are using these days."

"Mom, you didn't have to do that."

"I wanted to give them something familiar. They lost everything, and you said it was the one thing they were missing the most."

"They read these online graphic novels and the newest one came out last week and they've been dying to see it."

"There you go, they're reading."

"Oh, they play their fair share of games and watch videos, too." Sierra hitched up the laundry basket she carried under one arm before it slipped off her hip and she dropped it.

"Your room is ready upstairs. Set your stuff down. Take a breath. When you're settled, come down for lunch . . . or a cupcake."

Sierra smiled. "Thanks, Mom." Weariness shadowed her eyes. "It's been a long few weeks."

"And now you're here, where help is just a request away."

Momentary relief shone in Sierra's eyes.

"I set up an appointment with the elementary school for tomorrow morning at ten. They have a terrific after-school program you can look into when you find a job and are back to work. Until then, I'm happy to watch them after school while you go on interviews."

Sierra nodded. "I'll see what I can find and what makes the most sense."

Dede put her hand on Sierra's shoulder. "There's no rush, Sierra. Take your time. Figure out what's best for *you*."

Sierra raked her fingers through her long dark waves. "I've just been trying to get through each day and do whatever needs to be done right now." That was Sierra. Make a list, check the box, keep moving forward. "I haven't had time to really process."

"Then take the time."

Sierra set the basket on the floor and hugged her. "Thanks, Mom." She held on like she hadn't done since she was young.

Dede teared up and held on to her little girl who had grown up and had the problems to show for it. This couldn't be fixed with a bandage and a kiss on the owie. No, this required thoughtful planning and a lot of hard work to create a new life for her and the boys.

Dede had done it after each of her divorces. It wasn't easy to face things alone. To know that your children were counting on you for their happiness and the stability they needed.

Sierra carried the load well, but it would take time for her to find solid footing again when so much was up in the air right now. Once she found a job, settled with the insurance company, sold or rebuilt her place up north, and found a new place here to make a home, she'd find happiness again.

Sierra slipped free and went to the sofa, leaning over to hook her arms around P.J. and Emma. One at a time, she nuzzled her nose into both their necks. "Not even a *hi, Auntie*."

"Hi, Auntie," they said in unison, both giggling.

"You better save me a cupcake."

"Mom won't let us have any more." P.J. fell back into the sofa with a dramatic sigh.

Emma looked up at Sierra and snagged a handful of her long hair. "It's so pretty." She brushed a lock against her cheek.

Sierra smiled down at her and tugged Emma's caramel-colored straight hair. "You got the better color. Mine's just plain brown. Yours is shot through with sunshine."

Emma beamed.

Amy led Oliver back into the room and went right to Sierra and hugged her. "Look how skinny you are." Amy squeezed Sierra's middle. "Two kids and I still haven't lost the baby weight." She stepped back and rubbed her hand over the barely there belly pooch.

Sierra had a matching one, even if her sister was kind enough not to point it out.

Dede saw it as a badge of honor. A sign your body had done something amazing. And it had. Her daughters had created life and given her beautiful grandchildren.

Amy rolled her eyes. "The last ten pounds are the worst."

Fit. Toned. Amy worked out and ran after her kids nonstop. But Amy always found fault in something about herself. Dede worried that sometimes Amy put too much pressure on herself for no reason, battling her insecurities by trying to be perfect all the time.

Sierra looked her sister up and down with a frown. "You're right. You're fat. More cupcakes for me."

Amy pursed her lips. "I'm sure you're ready for something better than sweets and takeout by now."

"You have no idea. I never thought I'd say this, but I miss cooking."

Amy shrugged. "It's all I can do to get a decent meal on the table some nights. The kids' schedules are so packed. Dancing. Baseball. Swimming. Music lessons."

"Stop signing them up for everything under the sun," Dede remarked. She didn't understand why Amy thought the kids needed to be occupied every second of the day. It left no time for them to be creative and use their imaginations without it being a planned activity.

"They enjoy it. And it makes them well-rounded kids."

"So does riding their bikes with their friends on the street and playing in the backyard." Dede wrapped her arm around Oliver. "Head up the stairs and find your brother. There's a present up there for you."

Oliver carried his bundle of things and ran up the stairs.

Amy sighed. "I wish I had his energy." She turned to Sierra. "How are they doing after the fire and everything?"

"They miss the house and are sad we moved away from their friends. They're heartbroken that all of David's things are gone. It's like they lost him all over again." Sierra took a second to compose herself. "They seem to have an easier

time getting through the day and accepting whatever we have to do in the moment. To be honest,
they were getting bored and restless. Living in a
motel room lost its shine about four days in. They
just wanted to go home, but they knew there was
no home to go back to and that made it even harder.
The uncertainty about what we were going to do
got to them. And me." Sierra shifted from one foot
to the other. "I had to make up my mind and get
them settled either up there or here. Long term, this
seemed like the best choice with you all here." She
let out a huge sigh. "No more moving around every
couple days."

"I'm happy you're back." Amy brushed her hand
down Sierra's arm. "It'll be nice for the kids to
spend time together. And Mom won't be rattling
around this house all alone."

Dede took exception to that. She had a very full
life. "I'm not alone. I have my clubs and friends.
There's something to be said about being solely responsible for only yourself." She'd finally learned
after four marriages how to be alone and be okay
with it.

Oliver's little feet pounded on the hardwood
upstairs seconds before he shouted down to them.
"Mom! Look!" He held up his new tablet.

Sierra smiled for the first time since they'd arrived. "Awesome!"

Oliver ran back to his brother and Sierra turned
that smile on Dede. "Thanks, Mom."

"You're welcome, sweetheart."

"Mom took care of keeping the kids occupied. I
took care of the basics." Amy pointed to the bags of
clothes sitting one after the next going up the first

four steps. "I got three outfits for each of you, plus a couple basics. Socks. Underwear. I know you'll do a big school spree soon, but I thought you'd like something to tide you over."

"Amy, you didn't have to do that." Sierra's eyes glassed over at her sister's generosity.

Amy took it in stride. "Of course I did. I just hope I got all the sizes right. I can't have you wearing a Tweety Bird sweatshirt to school drop-off." Amy wrinkled her nose, hip cocked; she wore her designer yoga pants and workout top that made her look chic and casual.

Sierra looked like she'd just stepped off an eight-hour bus ride with no air conditioning and a dozen screaming kids from Disneyland.

Someone knocked three times, then opened the front door. Heather walked in with Hallee. The eighteen-month-old toddled next to her mother in a pair of purple tennis shoes that lit up around the bottom with every step.

Emma scrambled over the back of the sofa.

"Hey, we don't do that," Amy scolded.

That didn't stop Emma one bit. She ran for Hallee, took both her hands, and helped her walk into the living room area. Hallee smiled up at her older cousin and babbled some nonsense.

Heather sidestepped the laundry basket Sierra had left in the entry and stopped short of hugging Sierra. "Hey, sis. How are you?"

Dede wondered why Heather didn't embrace her sister, but she didn't say anything.

Sierra glanced at Hallee. "Look at her, Heather. She's walking."

"You were right. It goes by way too fast. Before I

know it, she'll be dating bad boys with rock T-shirts and leather boots."

"So she'll take after you," Amy teased. "I'm guessing that's the description of the father-who-shall-not-be-named."

Of course Amy was teasing, but the menacing tone and mocking grin only made Heather glare at her older sister.

Heather dismissed Amy and turned to Sierra. "Where are the boys?"

"Upstairs glued to the new tablets Mom got them."

"How are they doing?"

"It's been hard, but they're resilient. Once they're in school making new friends, I think they'll be happy here."

"This isn't just a visit to figure out what to do next? You're staying for good?" Heather's surprise and disbelief mixed with a hint of disapproval didn't set off anything obvious in Sierra, but Dede wondered why Heather might not want her sister moving home.

What was with her odd behavior?

A bad day? Feeling that Sierra would get all the attention instead of her for a while?

Dede hated to admit that as a romantic at heart she'd sometimes gotten caught up in finding love and spending time with the men in her life, leaving the girls to jockey for her attention. She'd sometimes been selfish and distracted.

Sierra became self-sufficient early on. She reasoned things out and solved her own problems. She knew what needed to be done and got to it.

Amy turned into a perfectionist, hoping Dede

would notice how excellent she was at everything. She craved acknowledgment and accolades for making things pretty, or getting the best grades, or having the perfect family.

Admittedly, because Heather was the youngest, Dede always found time for her. Sierra and Amy picked up the slack when Dede wasn't around. Basically, Heather thought anything and everything she wanted would be handed to her.

"The fire put a lot of things in perspective. It's been hard since David's death, trying to do everything on my own. The expenses . . . the bills piling up . . . I feel like I've been treading water for so long. The boys need to get back in school. And I'm tired. I have no time to myself." Sierra's eyes filled with defeat. "I need some help. Or at least to know you guys are around if I need you. Over the last year, I've lost friends simply because I didn't have time for anything but work and the kids."

Dede put her hand on Sierra's arm. "You're here now. You don't have to do it all alone anymore. You've always been so independent."

"Is that a nice way of saying stubborn?"

Dede squeezed Sierra's arm. "Yes." Dede shared a smile with Sierra and a moment of remembrance for all the memories they shared where they clashed or disagreed. Not in anger, but in that natural way young girls want to prove themselves to their mothers. "It's that inner strength and determination that will see you through this, too." She gave her daughter a reassuring smile.

Heather pressed her lips together. "What about your house? Your life in Napa?"

Sierra scoffed. "There's nothing left. Rebuilding could take years. The insurance might not even cover it. And my boys can't be displaced and their lives left up in the air that long. I don't have the luxury of waiting to see what happens up in Napa. I need to have a plan to get things back to as normal as possible for Danny and Oliver. That means finding a job, a new place to live, and getting them back in school and on a routine."

"I guess it makes sense, I just didn't think you wanted to move back *here*, that you liked your life up there away from us." Heather shrugged one shoulder, a hint of pain in her eyes.

Dede brushed her hand down Heather's back. Maybe she had missed her sister and wished she'd moved back sooner.

"I've wanted to move back for a long time. David didn't want to leave his job and connections he had up there. It was a good job with great benefits, so I couldn't really complain. I understood why he didn't want to give that up."

Heather's eyes went wide. "Really? I didn't know all that."

Sierra tilted her head. "It doesn't matter now."

Heather frowned. "I guess it doesn't. Not anymore." Sadness clouded Heather's usually bright eyes.

David's death had had a huge impact on all of them. Dede missed him. And more than that, she, along with Amy and Heather, wished David, Sierra, and the boys had lived out the promise of a happy life together everyone wants when they get married and start a family.

"Anyway, we're here now, and we're going to stay." Sierra went to pick up the basket she'd left in the entry. "I'll take this upstairs, then come back for the clothes Amy bought us." She settled the basket against her hip. "I've got more things in the car."

Amy headed for the door. "On it. We'll get you settled in no time."

Dede hoped everyone would settle into this change in their lives.

The girls had always been close but competitive with one another. Amy and Heather had both seen Sierra's life up in Napa from the outside looking in, only seeing what they wanted to see and thinking she had an ideal life. They admired her for it and were jealous because of it.

Heather had the child, but not the loving husband.

Amy had the loving husband—at least for now—and children, but still thought the grass was greener in Sierra's world.

From a distance, things may seem greener, but look closer and you'll find the weeds.

Dede hoped the girls would set aside comparisons and past hurts and insecurities and come together now to help Sierra and the boys start this new chapter in their lives.

Chapter Five

Sierra stood with her sisters on the porch, hands braced on the railing. She stared out across the yard to the wide pasture beyond that belonged to the Moore family and her thoughts turned to Mason. She remembered the last time she'd seen him. Husband number four's funeral. Poor Charles. Dead of a heart attack far too young. Mason came to pay his respects to her mother at the house. He'd done the whole cordial neighbor thing, saying hello, asking about the family, making sure everyone was well.

He and David had once been close friends. And that day, as they reminisced about the past, David jovial and teasing, most people watching them might've thought that closeness remained. Not her. While Mason joined in, he didn't have the same enthusiasm or level of engagement David displayed. Mason held back and didn't rise to David's teasing about the new lady in Mason's life.

Carrie. Christie. Something like that. Sierra didn't really pay attention because she didn't want to know.

She hadn't been able to keep her gaze from straying to Mason when he was in the same room. She watched him as he actively avoided her. Not that it was hard when she was rushing around trying to keep her then three- and five-year-old in line. David opted to socialize anywhere the kids weren't demanding his attention, which had left her frustrated and looking like a frazzled maniac.

When she finally got a second of nearly a private moment to speak to Mason, he'd kept it short, asked about her, the kids, then gracefully departed with an "I'm happy you're happy," and walked away like they hadn't been friends for years. The whole time they talked she'd been assailed by memories. Them riding horseback out to the creek, racing across the fields on the way home. Summers out at the pond sitting on the dock talking, teasing, and having fun. Watching the Fourth of July fireworks in the pasture his dad set off every year. Holiday parties. Summer barbecues. School events. Though he was two years older than she, they still managed to see each other a lot.

When her sisters were running late for school, she'd rush out to the road, hoping to hitch a ride with him. He never said no. Not to the ride to school or when she showed up in his barn asking to go horseback riding. Mason always saddled a horse for her and let her ride. Most of the time, he went with her. Sometimes when he could tell she just wanted to blow off steam from a bad day, a fight with her sisters, or an argument with her mom, he'd let her go alone, but he'd always watch her from the stables to be sure she never got hurt.

And in the end, she'd treated him badly one night at a bar by holding back what she really wanted to say in an awkward exchange that ended with mixed signals and hurt feelings.

"Daydreaming about our hunky neighbor?" Amy

bumped her shoulder, bringing her back to the here and now. A mischievous grin tilted her lips, and an *I-know-I'm-right* look lit her eyes.

"I never heard whether or not he got married." Of course he didn't invite her after . . .

"They broke up before they ever set a wedding date." Of course Amy knew. She was hooked in to the Mommy Grapevine in this town.

No doubt every single mother wanted a sexy, successful husband, and the last time Sierra saw Mason he certainly fit the bill to a T.

Heather fell in beside Sierra, leaning the opposite way on the railing and looking at her sideways. "I saw him at the mailbox yesterday when I visited Mom. He looks good."

Amy leaned back and met Heather's gaze. "Did you score a date with your dream guy?"

Heather tried to contain a soft smile as her cheeks pinked. "We had a nice conversation."

"I bet." Amy took on a far-off look. "We all had a mad crush on him at one point or another."

Sierra eyed Amy, surprised by her admission. Maybe it was inevitable back then. Amy and Mason were the same age and in the same high school class. But Sierra spent the most time at his place because she loved to ride.

Heather stared down at her feet. "As usual, he was nice. Hallee loved him."

"I think every female who sees him falls a little in love with him." Amy patted her heart, her eyes wistful with a touch of mirth.

Heather didn't let it go. "He's a good guy. I could use one of them."

"He's definitely a better choice than the dead-beat dad you picked." Amy sometimes didn't know when to keep her thoughts to herself.

Heather glared. "He wasn't a deadbeat dad. You don't know what happened, so shut up."

Amy held her hands up in surrender. "Okay. Touchy subject. Got it. But one of these days you're going to have to spill the beans about your baby daddy."

Heather bounced off the railing and headed for the front door. "Leave it alone." She walked in and slammed it behind her.

Sierra would have gone after her, but she wanted a little while longer out on the porch in the peace and quiet of a beautiful starlit night while the kids watched a Disney movie. "You shouldn't badger her about Hallee's father."

"Don't you want to know who it is?"

"I'm curious, but I also know it's none of my business."

Amy bumped shoulders with her again. "Come on. You know you can't stand not knowing. I think she keeps it a secret because she had a one-night stand and doesn't even know the guy's name."

"Why not just say that then?" It would suck not to know. People would judge. But in this day and age of swipe right Sierra bet there were a few thousand kids out there with moms who didn't know their hookup's real name.

"Too embarrassed. Who wants to admit that?" Amy stared up at the night sky. "Maybe the guy is married or a serial killer."

Sierra laughed. "A serial killer who left Heather

pregnant and alive? There's a few holes in that scenario."

"Maybe she slept with one of her friend's boyfriends and now she can't say anything because she doesn't want to lose her friend."

Sierra shrugged. "Whoever it is, he isn't in the picture. Maybe she doesn't say anything about him because she and Hallee are better off on their own. Maybe the guy turned out to be a real shit. Maybe he hit her. Maybe he's a total loser with no job and no prospects and Heather did the grown-up thing for her kid and shut *him* out so she didn't have to take care of two children."

Amy frowned. "You're better at this than me. That sounds exactly like the kind of guy Heather used to like, only out for a good time, sponging off others, and never taking anything seriously."

Sierra could imagine it. "She discovers she's pregnant and grows up fast. You have to be an adult sometime, and expecting a baby will put your life into a whole new perspective."

Amy braced her hands on the rail, much like Sierra stood. "Poor Heather."

"What about me? I'm a single mom to two boys. I'm outnumbered."

"Yeah, but you've always had your shit together. Heather's a dreamer, always looking for someone to take care of her and looking in all the wrong places."

"*We* always took care of her."

"What are big sisters for? I'm still helping her out. I watch Hallee when she's sick and can't go to day care. I've come through with the school treats for holidays, taken her late-night calls when Hallee is sick and she doesn't know what to do, and generally been her go-to help the last few years you've been away."

"I've taken my fair share of what-do-I-do phone calls. Though she hasn't done much of that since David passed." A lot of people stopped calling, asking her for things or her time. They didn't want to bother her. They didn't know what to say to the widow. "Well, I'm back and happy to help with the load." She wanted to be part of her sisters' lives in a real way now.

"I'm surprised you came back."

Sierra glanced at her sister. "Why?"

"You seemed happy up there, just you and David and the kids living your picturesque life."

"Napa Valley is beautiful, but expensive."

"So is Carmel."

True. But Napa lost its shine. Carmel still held a wealth of happy memories and you couldn't beat the beautiful valley and gorgeous beach. "There's too many memories and nothing left up there. You know?"

Amy pressed her lips tight. "Yeah. I know. I'm real sorry, Sierra. It sucks that you lost your husband and your home all in one year. One's bad enough, but both." Amy shook her head in dismay.

Sierra changed the subject. "How's your hunky husband? How come he didn't stop by? And don't give me that shit about him working late."

"I asked him to give me tonight with you and Heather. It's been too long since it was just us with Mom. Plus, he'd be the odd man out, so he was happy to steer clear of the estrogen party."

"The boys would love to see him."

Amy nodded, her lips pressed tight. "They miss their dad."

"Every day. I try to be there for them and give them what they need, but I know there's a huge hole in their hearts and lives without him here with them."

"Have you thought about dating again?"

It had been almost a year. And Sierra really hated being alone. "Who has time to think of such things with two kids and a job? It's all I can do to keep up with them, work, the house, the bills." And dating after all these years seemed scary. She was out of practice. She couldn't remember the last time she'd even flirted.

Amy grew quiet for a long moment. "Don't lose yourself taking care of everyone else. You deserve to be happy, too." With that, Amy walked back into the house to check on the kids, leaving Sierra alone on the porch.

As she looked out across the land and saw a glimpse of light across the way that could only be a light from Mason's place, Sierra felt as alone as she'd ever felt after David's death and wondered how long she'd feel this way before she did something about it.

Chapter Six

Sierra peeked through the ajar door into the boys' dark room and smiled at them sleeping. Her mom had redecorated, swapping out the neutral "guest-room" quilts for blue-and-red-striped comforters. She'd added stained wood toy boxes at the foot of each twin bed. The comforters and toy boxes were for the boys to keep when they moved into their next home. They'd get to take something familiar with them, instead of another round of entirely new things.

New was fun and exciting to a point. Then, you just wanted to be around the things that made you feel comfortable, that made you feel like you belonged there because they were your things. You saw them, surrounded yourself with them and the memories they held.

With the boys settled for the night and happy to be here with their family, Sierra headed downstairs for the talk she knew her mother wanted to have about what came next.

She found her mom in the living room on the sofa, feet tucked up beside her under a blanket, and a mug of tea in hand. Sierra rounded the sofa, picked up her mug off the table, sniffed the fragrant apple cinnamon tea that reminded her of Big Red gum, and sat in the corner of the sofa, facing her mom.

"It can't be easy to go through what you've been through this past year. Losing your husband . . . Well, I never thought you'd go through something like that so young. I know the fire took everything you owned, but you still have what's important. Those boys. Your family."

"Really, that's all that matters, Mom. Getting the boys to safety . . . It was scary." Even now, thinking about it made her heart race. "For a little while there, sitting in the car, surrounded by the heat, caustic smoke, and flames so close . . . I really thought . . ." She swallowed back the fear and took a sip of tea to calm her nerves.

Dede leaned forward and put her hand on her thigh. "You made it out. Now what? You as much as told Heather you're planning to make a life here. Is that what you really want?"

Sierra sighed. "I don't have many options."

"That's not an answer."

Sierra had made up her mind the second she called home and knew that's where she belonged. "Yes. I want to live here. I think the boys would be happy here. Going back to Napa . . . Well, there are too many memories."

"Good memories that make you sad, or memories you want to escape?"

Leave it to Mom to dig deep.

"If we still had the house, I'd want the boys to be there, so they'd have an easier time remembering their father. But without the house, there's only the ghost of him and our life there. It's going to be a long time before everything's rebuilt. I've been told it could take more than two years. That's too long to make them wait. I don't want them to settle in here then uproot them again. It's too much. We're staying put."

"Okay, that's settled. You'll enroll them in school here, find a job, and once the insurance settlement comes through, you can buy your own place and start fresh."

"I'm afraid the insurance settlement won't be enough for me to buy a house here. At least not right away."

"What do you mean?"

"There's the outstanding mortgage and—"

Her mother eyed her over her mug. "And?"

"Before David died, he took out a large loan."

One eyebrow shot up. Her mother carefully asked, "Were you having financial difficulties?"

"No. Everything was fine until he took out the loan."

Questions lit her eyes. "What did you use the money for?"

"*I* didn't use it for anything. I only found out about it after he died." Her gut tightened just thinking about that huge sum and the daunting task ahead of her to pay it off.

Dede sat up straighter. "You have no idea what David used the money for, do you?"

"No."

"An investment of some sort?"

"Not that I could find."

As always, her mother went the direct route. "An affair?"

Sierra shrugged and tried to stave off the ache in her chest and the anger that wanted to surge. "That would have been my guess, too, but I can't find any evidence of one." She couldn't prove it one way or another. Which left her in a constant state of wonder and suspicion and second-guessing everything she knew and thought about her husband.

Sure, they'd had their problems.

But she didn't think they'd had secrets.

She'd been wrong.

"Did you find anything in his office when you cleaned it out? In any of his papers?"

"After he died, I glanced through the boxes that arrived from his office."

"You didn't clean it out yourself?"

She shook her head. At the time, she simply couldn't deal with the mundane task. Not when she had two heartbroken kids at home missing their father and wondering if she'd die, too. Oh, the questions they'd asked. Hard questions like *Where did Daddy go?* Easier ones like *Can I put my toy truck in his casket?*

Sierra didn't need to ask why Oliver wanted his father to have his favorite truck. He'd wanted his father to remember him wherever he went.

It broke her heart.

And as sad and overwhelmed and lonely as she'd been those first few weeks, she'd also felt extremely guilty. Her mind spun a million things she wished she'd said to David. They carried on a hundred imagined conversations in her head that she wished they'd had in person. Ever present was the nagging feeling that the distance and silence she felt from David those last few months leading up to his death were fraught with his indecision. And she didn't even know the questions he pondered. She'd catch him about to say something to her, then he'd stop himself and turn away or say something mundane about dinner or Danny's homework. Once he'd even commented on the weather when it had been warm and sunny for days so there wasn't much to say about it.

Why didn't I just ask him what he wanted to say?

She'd asked herself that question a thousand times.

She'd been scared of the answer, afraid that her suspicions were true. Either he was having an affair, or he simply didn't want her anymore.

There'd still been love there, especially for their children, but they hadn't truly connected in a long time. They went through their days and lived together, but the intimacy in their relationship suffered. They didn't put their relationship ahead of everything else.

And frankly, at the end of a long day, she hadn't been all that receptive to his needs. Switching from mom to wife when she walked through their bedroom door hadn't been as easy as flipping a switch.

She saw the marriage suffering, but she hadn't made a real effort to fix it. She blamed the distance he put between them, the sneaky way he'd shut down his computer screen when she walked into his office and covered by saying he was done with his work email, and the way he explained away overnight trips he had recently started taking when his company had never asked him to travel in the past.

She made excuses for him. He didn't have a lot of time to himself. Neither did she. She got it. Maybe he shut down his computer because he didn't want work to interfere with their home life. Maybe his company really did need him to visit a customer here and there to make them happy or seal a deal.

Maybe he snuck away to recharge so he could be better for them. Lord knows, she'd thought about a weekend retreat, maybe a few days with her sisters in Carmel and a long day being pampered at the spa where Heather worked.

He didn't mean to snap at her, he'd had a long day.

He didn't want to miss Danny's soccer game, but work needed him to be out of town.

Dinner out wasn't an option because he had a call with a client and would be home late.

"The last thing I wanted to do after the funeral was pack up his office and go through his things. I took what they sent me and put it in the garage. He was gone and I missed him and I was angry he left me and the boys. I know that's terrible to say because it was an accident, but that's how I felt. I had two little boys who missed their father and grieved for him and I blamed him for taking that last-minute trip instead of being home with us."

Her mom leaned over and squeezed her hand. "Grief is a lot of different emotions all balled up and tangled into a mess. Don't fret over the fact your marriage wasn't perfect. Whose is? People make mistakes, they tell lies, they drift apart, but all that can be forgiven when there's love. Maybe you two hadn't gotten to that point in the particular valley you found yourselves in at the time of his death, but that doesn't mean that whatever was going on couldn't have been fixed. You just didn't have the time to do it. That's not your fault, Sierra. And yes, it's a shame you had doubts and suspicions about your husband. I wish he was here to answer your questions and account for that money. But he's not.

But that doesn't mean you can't get some answers another way."

Sierra cocked her head. "What do you mean?"

"Ask Mason to help you."

The answer surprised her. "What can Mason do?"

"He's a divorce attorney. He has investigators who uncover everything the opposing spouse is hiding, including hidden bank accounts and such. Perhaps he can figure out why David took out the loan and what he did with the money. If it's sitting in a secret bank account, that money belongs to you. It would go a long way to getting you back on your feet."

Sierra hadn't thought of that. But the idea gave her hope that maybe she could recover the money, or at least part of it, and that she could use it to help take care of the boys.

Although asking Mason for help sounded easy, it was anything but.

A long time ago . . . A lifetime ago, they'd had a moment. There'd been a spark. But she was with David. She'd chosen him.

And maybe a time or two she'd asked herself if she'd made the right decision.

"Sierra." Her mom snapped out her name like it wasn't the first time she'd said it.

"Huh. What?"

"I said you could go over and see him tomorrow. Take the boys. You know how much they love to see the horses in the pastures. An up-close look might take their mind off everything else going on."

"I can't ask him to look into their father's past with the boys right there."

"Be discreet, of course, but ask Mason all the same."

"Maybe I'll call his office and make an appointment."

Dede rolled her eyes. "You've known him since you were thirteen. You don't need an appointment."

Sierra sighed. "Mom, it's been a long time since we were friends and neighbors. I'm asking him to do something that isn't exactly his job. I think approaching him with the request as a business arrangement—"

"Pishaw. This isn't business. It's a friend asking a friend for help."

"It's a business transaction. I don't expect him to have his investigator do the work for free."

"I'm not saying you shouldn't pay him, but you don't have to make the request so formal."

"Mom. Let me handle it my way." If she even asked him. Seeing him again . . . Well, he might not want to see her at all.

Her mother conceded with a wave of her hand.

Sierra went on, "Besides, depending on the cost, I may not be able to afford his services." Mason was one of the best divorce attorneys around. Wives loved it when he stuck it to their husbands. Husbands loved that he kept their wives from taking them to the cleaners.

She knew Mason. He'd always been fair-minded, honest, and a great negotiator. He'd settled more than one dispute between her and her sisters back in the day.

She wanted to believe he'd been a little more on her side than her sisters', but that might be her teenage heart locked in a crush on the boy next door talking.

"You know I'm more than happy to help you through this difficult time." Dede hadn't exactly taken her exes to the cleaners, but she'd come out of every divorce with a hefty payout. She could afford to help Sierra. But she had taught her girls to be independent and never rely on others when you were perfectly capable of taking care of yourself.

Well, Sierra had taken that to heart, unlike Heather, who sponged off Dede all the time.

"I appreciate you letting us stay here until I find a job and a place of our own, but I need to take care of the rest."

"Sierra, honey, I love you. It's never been easy for you to accept financial support, but I want to help. I have the means."

"I know. I appreciate it." But it made her feel guilty and a little bit like she couldn't take care of herself and the boys on her own when she'd worked so hard to do that alone this past year.

The possibility of discovering what David did with that money gave her hope that she might get out from under at least part of the debt. "If I can't afford to pay Mason for the investigation myself, I'll let you know, so long as it's not too much." If she found the money, she'd have no trouble paying her mom back.

"Peace of mind is worth the cost."

Careful what you wish for. "What if I discover something I don't want to know?"

"Sometimes knowing the worst is still better than being in the dark. Maybe it will allow you to put your relationship with David to rest. You deserve that, honey. Then you can move on with a clear heart and mind."

She hoped so, because the questions swirling in her mind sometimes grew quiet, but they never went silent.

Right now, though, Sierra settled into the sofa and finished her tea and thanked her lucky star to have a mom who loved her and welcomed her home with open arms.

She soaked up the warmth of home, her mother's steady and familiar presence, and knew that though things may be difficult the next days, weeks, and months, she and her sons had a roof over their heads, the love and support of her family, and everything, eventually, would be all right.

Chapter Seven

Sierra leaned back against the hood of her SUV and watched Danny and Oliver playing on the playground at their new school. She'd gotten them enrolled and taken them to meet their new teachers. They were hesitant at first about a new place and new people. She saw it in their little faces when they realized that leaving their old life behind meant losing friends and the familiarity of all they'd known.

Since the fire most of the families they'd known had also scattered to find new homes while they dealt with the aftermath of losing everything. They all had to start over.

She explained that to the boys just before setting them loose on the playground. They seemed to get it, but it didn't make it easier. And she wished they didn't have to learn so many hard lessons or suffer so much tragedy in their young lives.

"Look at me, Mom!" Oliver plopped down on the slide and whooshed down, his feet hitting the thick pad at the bottom before he jumped up, gave her a huge smile, and ran to climb back up to the platform and do it again.

For the first time in a long time, her heart felt lighter seeing the boys simply play and have fun.

Amy pulled in next to her car in her white mini-van. The side door slid open the second the car stopped and P.J. and Emma leaped out and ran to the playground.

"I want to slide, too." Emma climbed up the wide steps behind Oliver.

P.J. grabbed a swing, scooted into the seat, and pumped his legs to get going. Danny took the swing next to him. It only took a second for them to see who could fly higher. Their smiles and delight as they tried to outdo each other made Sierra grin.

"We used to be them." Amy copied Sierra's pose against the front of the SUV with her arms crossed as she stared out at their four kids playing together.

They were them. Competition and trying to one-up your siblings never changed. At least in Sierra's experience. As the oldest, Amy always wanted to be the best at everything. She wanted to have everything first.

"How are you, sis?" It had been a long time since Sierra had a good long catch-up with her sister. Dinner the other night had been fun, but they spent most of the evening trying to corral the kids and get them to eat.

"Good. Great." That was Amy's way of saying "Fine" when she didn't really mean it.

"I got the boys enrolled in school. Oliver and Emma are in the same class, but Danny is with Ms. Franks's class."

"She's good, but Ms. Simms is better. She knows how to command the classroom. She pushes the kids. Their test scores are higher than the other teachers' classes."

That might be true, but Ms. Franks seemed kind and understanding of what Danny had been through. She'd promised to focus on making sure

Danny felt accepted and found new friends so he settled in and felt welcome. She understood that was important for kids starting over at a new school. If he didn't feel connected to school, he wouldn't put the work in to getting good grades.

Sierra let it go because convincing her sister that good grades weren't the most important thing was pointless. She wouldn't change Amy's mind.

"Does P.J. like his teacher?"

Amy scoffed. "No. He hates her. He thinks she's mean. He hates all the homework."

At this age and especially during this difficult time the last thing Sierra wanted was for the boys to hate school. With so many years left to go, she didn't want them turned off and checked out because of a bad experience. Sierra believed school should be fun and engaging, not just a chore.

"Danny and Oliver liked their teachers. Once they make some friends, they'll settle in." And having their cousins around at school would be a help, too.

"Of course they will. They're kids. They're resilient. What about you? What are you going to do now that you've decided to stay?"

"I'll start with a job and go from there. I checked a few apps this morning, but none of the postings seemed quite right."

"We don't always get what we want. You'll have to settle for what you can get."

Very supportive.

Sierra turned slightly and hid the eye roll. "How's Rex?"

"Busy as ever at work. When he's not working, he's golfing. He says he needs his downtime."

"We all do."

Amy huffed out a breath. "I'd like to know when it's my turn."

"Don't you have some time when the kids are in school?"

As a stay-at-home mom, Amy should be able to carve out a little time for herself.

"You'd think, but no. I spend Monday, Wednesday, and Friday volunteering at Emma's classroom for two hours. Tuesday and Thursday in P.J.'s. When I'm not in the class, I'm working on organizing the school events, attending PTA meetings, cleaning house, picking up and dropping off Rex's dry cleaning, doing the shopping, paying the bills, and running all over after school for dance class, swimming, music lessons, baseball, and art classes. Not to mention helping with homework and school projects. You'll see, this school is no joke. It demands all your time."

Sierra understood that homework and projects did take a lot of a parent's time. "Why do teachers assign things the kids can't do mostly on their own? Isn't the point of it for the kids to do the work, not the parents?"

"Right?"

"Maybe you should cut back on the extracurricular activities." Sierra wanted her kids to have the opportunity to do whatever they wanted, but they needed downtime, too. Overextending their schedules strained her schedule. Sierra liked balance.

It sounded like Amy had scheduled away all her children's free time.

"They're important to building their character

and making them well-rounded individuals. It will help later in life."

"Yeah, but it's driving you crazy."

"You sound just like Rex. He thinks some of the stuff is too expensive and that the kids don't even like it."

Sierra asked the obvious question. "Do they?"

Amy scoffed. "They don't know what's best for them."

That wasn't an answer.

She went on, "You should see Emma in her little bat costume for her dance recital. She's so cute."

Sierra got it. The pictures would look great on Amy's social media. Everyone would comment and Amy would feel like a good mother.

Sierra tried again. "What do you do for fun?"

"I live for my wine o'clock."

Sierra laughed under her breath. "Your what?"

"That half hour every night after the kids go to bed and I clean the kitchen and have a glass of wine and soak up the quiet." The absolute need for that half hour shone in Amy's eyes, but the sadness that shadowed it struck Sierra as a red flag that something deeper was going on with Amy.

"Where's Rex while you're enjoying your glass of wine?"

"Upstairs reading books to the kids."

Aw. "That's sweet."

A wistfulness replaced the sadness. "Yeah. He always makes time for the kids. Bedtime has always been his time with them because he's at work all day."

"That's really nice. I'm sure they love spending that time with him."

Amy nodded, her eyes going soft. "They do."

If Sierra read things right, Amy wanted that kind of time with Rex. Something wasn't quite right in Amyland.

"Is everything okay between you and Rex?"

Amy snapped her head toward Sierra. "Of course it is. You know how it goes. You have kids and it's all about them. Rex is busy. I'm busy. But we're great. We've got everything we ever wanted."

Be careful what you wish for.

The thought popped into Sierra's head because on the surface everything did seem fine with Amy. But Amy tended to focus on the surface and not look deeper. Everything needed to appear perfect to her sister, even when the undercurrent was sucking her down.

"If you want me to watch the kids one night so you and Rex can have a date night, I'd be happy to do it."

Amy sighed. "I'd have to check with Rex to see what his schedule is like, but thanks."

"Anytime." She really meant it. She didn't want to see what happened to her and David happen to Amy and Rex.

Amy said, "And I can watch the kids if you have an interview or something you need to do."

"I appreciate that." Though Sierra felt reluctant to add to Amy's packed schedule. "Mom said she'd help, too."

"You'll find Mom doesn't spend a lot of time sitting around the house. She's got her gardening club, tennis, lunch dates, hiking club, pinochle, not to mention the country club socials she attends."

"Is she working on husband number five?" Sierra

gave Amy a mischievous grin and tapped her elbow to Amy's.

Amy rolled her eyes. "God, I hope not."

"Why? She deserves to be happy. No one likes to be alone."

"She's got her friends." Amy sighed. "And her admirers." A grin tugged at Amy's lips, but she stopped it before it turned into a real smile. "Losing number four hurt her."

Sierra's heart clenched. "She really loved him."

"She loved them all." Amy paused for a pregnant moment, then asked, "Have you spoken to Dad lately?"

They all loved their dad, but he tended to let time slip away between calls and relied on them to contact him rather than the other way around. Though he was always up for a long chat. He just wasn't one to pick up the phone unless prompted by his new wife.

"Just before I left the Napa area. He seems happy in Arizona with Loran."

"I thought after the divorce he'd be a bachelor forever."

"Loran changed that. They've been married . . . what? Five years?"

"Six." Amy wrapped her arms around her middle. "She's younger than him." Amy let that hang for a minute. "Do you think guys are like that? As they get older, they think about replacing the old model with . . . well, a model."

Sierra chuckled. "Maybe some guys, but not Dad. Loran is only five years younger than him. It's not like he hooked up with some twentysomething."

"I know, but . . . Never mind."

Sierra caught on quick. "Amy, you're beautiful and smart and a great mom. Rex would be crazy to let you go."

Amy stood up straighter. "Of course he would. But he'd never leave me. We're good. Great."

Yes, everything is fine in Amyland.

Sierra checked her watch. "I'm so glad you made time to meet us here today so the kids could play, but I've got to get them home and fed. They start school tomorrow and I want to get them back on a schedule."

"I hear you." Amy whistled at the kids and waved her hand, calling them back from the playground.

The boys jumped off the swings, playfully pushing at each other, saying one or the other had leapt the farthest. Oliver and Emma climbed down from the ride-on rocking bear and dog that sat atop huge metal springs.

Emma ran up to her mom. "Can we get ice cream?"

Amy shook her head and brushed her hand over Emma's hair. "It's time to go to music class before dinner."

"Ugh. Mom. No. I hate violin."

"You just need to practice more and you'll be good at it."

"I hate it!" Emma scrunched her little face into a deep frown and stormed off to the car, climbing in the side door behind P.J.

Amy rolled her eyes. "They're so fun." She hugged Sierra. "Call if you need me to watch the kids after school or whatever."

"Call me about that date night," Sierra countered. She really hoped Amy took her up on it. It seemed like she and Rex needed a night, or two, to reconnect.

Sierra understood all too well how things could turn monotonous and routine in a marriage. Maybe if she'd scheduled a few more date nights instead of avoiding the talk she and David needed to have but always put off . . .

She couldn't change the past. She needed to let it go.

"Mom?" Danny called from beside the car. "Are we going? I'm hungry."

"Yes. Climb in. Make sure Oliver is buckled in his seat, please."

Sierra got behind the wheel, started the car, backed out of her spot, gave a honk good-bye to her sister, who was turned in her seat talking fast to the kids in back in what looked like an argument, probably about Emma not wanting to go to music class. Sierra headed out of the lot and turned toward their temporary home, thinking about what kind of life she wanted here with the boys.

Certainly not one filled with so much to do you didn't have time to really enjoy life. She wanted balance for the boys. And herself.

She thought about her mother and those socials at the country club. She loved that her mom was putting herself out there.

Sierra wondered if she'd ever be ready to try again.

* * *

Sierra stopped at the mailbox, pulling in behind a sleek Mercedes. She stared at the back of the tall blond in a navy suit who got out of the car. She thought he looked familiar, but from behind wasn't sure it was . . .

Mason turned and smiled at her.

She caught her breath at the sight of him and smiled before she even thought about it. "I'll just be a second, boys." She rolled the windows down and got out.

"Hey there, stranger." Mason stood in front of her before she knew it and put his hand on her shoulder. "I was so sorry to hear about your troubles. If there's anything you need, I'm happy to help."

She should ask him about helping her track down the money her husband didn't tell her about, but all she could do was look up at him and wonder how men got so much better-looking as they aged.

"Sierra? You okay?"

She mentally shook herself out of her head and nodded. "Yes. Fine. I'm sorry. I didn't expect to see you here."

"I took over Mom and Dad's place about eight or nine months ago when they wanted to downsize. Dad didn't want to spend all his time tending the land and animals anymore. I didn't want to let go of the ranch."

"You must have some really great memories of that place."

He stared down at her for a long moment. "I do. Sorry to hear you lost your home. You guys doing okay?" He cocked his head toward her boys. "They're huge."

She laughed. "They refuse to stop growing up."

"Kids," he scoffed. "They never do what they're told." Same old Mason. Always good-natured, ready with a warm smile and a joke to make her laugh.

"They're great boys. And we're doing okay. In fact, I just got them enrolled in school."

Mason shook his head. "Ugh. Moms. Always doing what's best for their kids."

She found herself chuckling again. "Well, I did let them have a cupcake after breakfast this morning."

"Mom of the year." His smile made her heart trip over a couple beats.

"It was a bribe to get them to meet their teachers today. They've been out of school for a few weeks now and aren't anxious to get back to it."

"New place. New school. You don't know anyone. Yeah, I get their reluctance."

"Me, too, but they need to take this first step into their new life."

Mason tilted his head. "You're staying, then?"

She nodded, pleased for no reason at all that he seemed happy about it. "I want to be closer to my family. Mom is getting older, I need the help, and though my sisters and I stay in touch, it's not the same as being here all the time."

"I know what you mean. My parents and I used to see each other all the time, but with work and their social life, we don't get together as much." He got a far-off look. "Of course, I avoid them sometimes because of all the 'Why aren't you married yet?' questions."

She couldn't help the quick glance from head to foot and back before she asked, "Why aren't you married?"

He chuckled. "Lots of reasons, but"—his gaze turned to a hard stare—"I guess I've been waiting for the right woman."

Uneasy under his direct gaze, she went around

that statement. "I thought maybe it was because of your job."

"That's what a lot of people think. I see couples in the worst possible situation. They've lost the love and can't communicate anymore. But that doesn't mean I don't think relationships can work. My parents are great together. I want that."

"I love your parents. I was jealous of you."

"Me. Why?"

"You were close with your mom and dad. I sometimes felt like a Ping-Pong ball between mine. They both tried to make everything seem normal and perfect, but when you aren't with one parent all the time, it feels like they don't really know you."

"I try to make my clients see that equal time with their kids is important. Some of them though . . . They don't want to give up custody out of spite, not because it's what's best for their kids."

"Divorce sucks."

"Yep." He held up his stack of mail. "But it pays the bills."

Probably quite well based on what she'd heard about him being in high demand.

"So, Sierra, what are you going to do now that you're back?"

"I need to find a job. I can't afford not to get back to work right away."

"I imagine settling your affairs for the house in Napa is going to take a while."

"I'm probably going to be the loser in the whole thing, too."

He nodded, a half frown tilting his lips. "California. It costs more to rebuild than insurance covers a lot of the time."

"Tell me about it."

"Are you still interested in property management, or do you plan to do something else?"

She tried not to show her surprise that he remembered what she did for a living. "Beggars can't be choosers, but I'd love to get a job doing what I know. I really enjoyed working with clients and renters."

"I might know someone who's looking for help. I could make a call."

The offer touched her deeply. "Oh, well, that's so nice, but I don't want to put you out."

"It's no trouble. I know a lot of people in this town. It's a simple phone call to see if something's available."

Hope surged. A job would solve a lot of problems and eliminate most of her anxiety. "Really? You'd do that for me."

He stared at her for a long moment. "Yeah, Sierra, I'd do that for you."

"Thank you, Mason."

"You're welcome, Sierra." He glanced at the boys again. "When are you going to take me up on my offer?"

She tilted her head and narrowed her eyes in question. "What are you talking about?"

"Bringing the boys over to ride." He watched her for understanding, then added, "Heather didn't tell you."

She shook her head and frowned. "No. I'm sorry, she didn't say anything to me about you." Probably because Heather wasn't the most reliable person when it came to delivering messages.

"I'm not surprised," he said under his breath. "Um, I saw her the other day and told her to tell you that anytime you want to bring the boys to see the horses and go for a ride I'd be happy to have you at the ranch."

"Can we, Mom?" Danny called from the back of the car.

"Horsies!" Oliver yelled.

"Nice, putting me on the spot like that," she teased Mason.

He winked. "I want you to come over. It's been a long time since we went for a ride."

It *had* been too long a time since she and Mason spent time together and she let the giddy feeling building inside her loose. Nothing serious had ever happened between them, but she'd always felt like if they just gave it a chance something could happen.

"Please, Mom." Danny gave her those big puppy dog eyes that made it impossible to say no.

"Are you busy Saturday?" she asked.

"Not anymore." Mason smiled at Danny and Oliver when they both yelled, "Yes!"

"I don't want you to cancel plans or anything."

"It's just a football game. I can record it. Come up to the house at eleven."

Danny leaned over the window. "Are the Patriots playing?"

"They sure are. You like football?"

Danny fell back in his seat. "I used to watch with my dad."

Mason walked over, planted his hands on the open window frame, and leaned down. "I knew your dad."

"You did?"

"Once upon a time we were friends. Every now and then we caught a game together. How about we go for a ride in the morning, you stay for lunch, and we watch the game together."

"Really?"

Mason tilted his head and looked at her. "If it's okay with your mom."

Sierra hadn't realized how much Danny missed watching the games with his father. "I think that's a great idea."

"Will you make chili cheese dip?" Danny leaned forward, his face so earnest and hopeful.

"Yes, honey. Anything you want." Anything to make him feel the connection he had to his dad.

"I want pigs and blankets," Oliver requested.

"Me, too," Mason added, his face just as hopeful as her boys'.

"I expect you guys will keep your room clean and do as you're told until Saturday, including any homework you get this week."

"We will, Mom," Danny assured her.

"Promise," Oliver added to his brother's vow.

"Promise," Mason echoed, making her laugh. "I'll get all my work done so we can spend the day together."

She shook her head, trying to hide her smile. "You're crazy, you know that. You have no idea what kind of mess those two monsters can make of a bowl of chips and chili cheese dip."

He shrugged that off. "I've got a sponge and mop and a leather couch that wipes clean. No problem."

She hoped he meant it. "Okay. We'll see you Saturday."

"I can't wait." He held his fist out to Danny. "See you this weekend."

Danny pounded it. "Yes!"

Oliver leaned way over his seat to fist-bump Mason's hand, too. "Horsies!"

"You can pet all of them and ride one."

Oliver sat back with a huge grin.

Sierra waited for Mason to turn back to her. "You made their day."

"I hope I made yours, too."

"You made me smile. Thanks."

"You're welcome, Sierra." He pulled out his phone and tapped a couple times, then handed it to her. "Put your info in there for me."

She typed in her name and cell number, then handed the cell back to him.

He touched a few more things on his phone and hers dinged with a text in her back pocket.

"Now you've got my number. See you Saturday." He touched her shoulder before heading back to his car. With a wave he drove off.

She watched him go until his car disappeared.

Grabbing the mail from her mother's box, Sierra climbed back into her car thinking about the way she still felt the imprint of his big hand on her shoulder and the warmth spreading through her.

Her heart felt lighter after seeing Mason and how he made her kids smile and excited about something again.

It had been so long since she'd seen Danny that animated that she hadn't even realized how subdued he'd been since his father's death. He hadn't mentioned football at all. But she remembered how they'd watch the games together cheering on their team and letting out long and overblown groans when there was a bad call or their team lost. They ate junk food, had burping contests, and wrestled and laughed together.

The sound of it had filled the house, and she missed it, too.

The fist bumps were supercute, and the looks in her boys' eyes as Mason paid attention to them . . . They needed that kind of male bonding in their lives.

She was Mom. She did her job, loved them with her whole heart, and they needed her. But it wasn't the same as having your dad around, or a man who took a real interest in them.

Mason had invited them over to be a good neighbor and distract the boys after all they'd been through. She appreciated the gesture.

She found herself looking forward to the weekend along with her boys. Maybe they all needed a man like Mason in their life. Someone open, honest, and kind.

* * *

It wasn't until she got the boys settled watching a movie while she made dinner that she remembered to check her text and save Mason's number in her contacts. She stared at the text, enthralled by Mason's words, and jumped when her mother tapped her on the shoulder and said, "The pasta is boiling over." She tore her gaze from her phone to deal with dinner.

But she didn't need to see it to remember exactly what it said and how it made her feel.

Mason: I've missed you. Welcome home. I can't wait to see you this weekend. Sooner, I hope.

Was it strange to feel like she'd been waiting to come back home and realize that maybe he was the reason why? It didn't make sense, but then again with their history, maybe it did in some strange way.

Chapter Eight

Mason couldn't stop thinking about Sierra. Hope and anticipation had been building inside him since Heather told him Sierra was coming home. Those feelings got stronger when Sierra confirmed she planned to stay for good.

If he could contribute in any way to encouraging her to make a life here again, he was all in.

He'd missed her. He thought he knew how much, but it didn't even scratch the surface of how he felt when he saw her yesterday.

Such a simple meeting, but he hoped it led to something more.

He'd let her get away years ago because he'd been too focused on building his career and thinking that she'd always be there for him, that she wasn't going anywhere.

Stupid. Of course someone else saw her beauty and everything wonderful about her and wanted her for himself.

It still pissed him off that David snuck right in there and stole her before Mason made his move.

He wouldn't make that mistake again.

Unless . . . No. Revealing that kind of secret would do no good for Sierra. She'd been through enough. And he didn't know for sure that what he *thought* he knew was even true. Making an accusation like that would only stir up trouble.

And if he was wrong, he could do some serious damage.

Better to keep his mouth shut and his unfounded suspicions to himself.

He walked into the top realtor in town and smiled at the beautiful woman walking out of her plush office to greet him.

"Mason. I'm so happy you called. I can't wait for you to spend all the money I paid you during my divorce on a gorgeous new house."

He chuckled and shook Marissa's hand. "Sorry to disappoint, but I'm here to talk about a job."

Her perfectly sculpted eyebrows shot up. "Handing in your lawyer card to sell real estate?"

"Not a chance."

She held her hand out toward her office past the cubicles where everyone eyed them and answered the ringing phones. "Come. Let's talk."

He followed her into her office, closed the door behind him, and waited for her to take her seat behind her desk before he took the chair in front of it.

She leaned forward and folded her arms on top of the mahogany desk. "You got me a huge settlement and kept my husband from taking my kids. So what can I do for you?"

"Are you still looking for a property manager?"

"I've done several interviews and have someone in mind. I plan to make the offer this afternoon. Why?"

Thank God. He was just in time. "I would like you to consider one more candidate."

"Of course. What's *her* name?"

He smiled, trying not to let on that this was indeed very personal. "Sierra Silva." He didn't use Wallace. He wasn't sure she'd gone back to her maiden name, but he didn't like tying David's last name to her. Not when he thought—

"Does she at least have experience?" Marissa cut into his thoughts.

"Yes. She worked at a property management company in Napa. Her home and place of business burned to the ground in the wildfire."

Marissa lost the knowing smile and turned solemn. "I'm so sorry to hear that. It must have been devastating."

"Her husband passed away almost a year ago. After the fire took everything, she moved back here where she's got family to rebuild her life. She's got two sons to support. They'll be attending the same school as your kids."

Marissa shook her head. "So much tragedy."

"She needs a break, something to go her way. I'm hoping you'll give her a chance."

"Yes. Of course. Ask her to please give me a call. We'll chat, but if you're recommending her, I'm sure we can work something out."

Relief washed through him. "You don't know how much I appreciate this."

Marissa gave him another smile, filled with more understanding than teasing. "You want to make sure she stays."

"I want her and the boys to be happy again."

"You're a good man, Mason. But I know this means something to you."

He tried to play it cool. "Why do you say that?"

"Because you could have simply called me about

this. Instead, you came down here to plead your case if need be."

He sat back and spilled the truth. "She's the one that got away."

A romantic at heart, Marissa simply said, "Then we will give her a reason to stay so *you* can make her happy."

His plan, exactly. Mason stood. "Thank you, Marissa, for doing this favor for me. I owe you."

She waved that away. "We aren't even even, Mason. You helped me keep my business and everything I worked for during the marriage. I may have started with my husband's money, but I made this." She held her hands up to encompass the realtor office. "He never liked me working. But I needed this to fill the hole our awful marriage left inside me."

"Even without his money, I know you would have been a huge success all on your own. He knows it, too."

"If your lady friend has even half the skills I'm looking for, she's got the job, and I'll make it worth her while."

"She's smart, kind, spunky, and driven. She won't disappoint. In fact, I think she'll surprise you." He was really going out on a limb here. He'd taken the safe route in the past, though, and ended up without Sierra. This time he'd put it all out there.

"This side of *you* surprises me."

"I'm not just a cutthroat lawyer, you know. I have a soft side." He used it to be sure the kids involved in the divorces were taken care of properly and got equal time with their parents, so long as those parents deserved it, too.

"Don't let my ex or anyone else's you represent know that."

"Never." He held up his phone. "Expect a call from Sierra shortly. I can't wait to tell her."

Marissa gave him another of those knowing smiles and waved good-bye as he hit the speed dial for Sierra and walked out of the office and onto the sidewalk as the phone rang for the third time and he suspected he'd have to leave Sierra a message instead of talking to her.

"You better have some refrigerator magnets."

He didn't expect that answer. "Um. I have a couple, I think. Why?"

"Oliver wants to thank you for inviting him to go horseback riding by giving you a dozen pictures of horses he drew for you."

The smile hit him with the outburst of laughter that bubbled up from his gut. "Awesome. I don't have enough horse pictures."

Sierra's soft chuckle made his gut tighten. "Well, good, because he'll probably draw you some more when he gets home from school."

"The more the better." He added stopping at the store to pick up some magnets to his mental to-do list. He didn't want to disappoint Oliver by not displaying them.

"Aren't you supposed to be working or something?"

He felt Sierra's nervous energy through the phone. "I've been working on something for *you*. Get a pen and paper and take down this name and number."

"What for?"

"Write this down." He rattled off Marissa's full

name and her office number. "She's expecting your call. She's got a job for you."

"What? She's the biggest realtor in the county, like major successful. Multimillion-dollar listings and famous clients."

"And she needs a property manager. Call her now. She's ready to make an offer to someone else if you don't want the job."

It took Sierra a full ten seconds to say something. "You're not kidding."

He couldn't help the smile on his face. He loved shocking her. "Why would I joke about this?"

"I don't know. But she's . . . huge."

"You need a job, she's got one. Call her."

Another long five seconds passed. "Is she doing this just because you know her? Is she your girl-friend or something and this is a pity job?"

"No. No. And hell no. It is not a pity job. You're exactly what she's looking for. Yes, she's a client. I helped her with her divorce. I knew she needed someone and I'm hooking her up with the best candidate."

"Mason, that's sweet, but you don't know that I'm the right fit."

Yeah, I do.

"I know you're smart, meticulous, good with people, and able to multitask and handle a crisis with a steady hand and level head. You will rock this job, Sierra. I know you will."

Dead silence.

"Sierra?"

"Thank you for the vote of confidence." Her voice was soft and filled with gratitude.

"It's the truth, Sierra."

"It may be difficult to get ahold of references right now."

"The only reference you needed was me. Trust me, Sierra. You deserve this opportunity." Nothing but silence, but he had her full attention. "Did I mention it comes with a huge salary?"

"I'll call her right now." No delay this time.

"Good." He breathed out a huge sigh of relief. "It's going to be okay. The boys are back in school and you've got a job."

"If she likes me."

"She's going to love you." His phone alarm went off. "Listen, I'm late for a meeting."

"Go. I'll make the call and let you know how it goes."

"Promise." He knew she'd get it, he just wanted to hear her tell him all about it.

"Yes. And thank you, Mason. It means a lot that you'd do this for me and put your reputation on the line for it."

"You're a safe bet, Sierra. You're going to do great." He hung up and spent the rest of the day going from one meeting to the next waiting to hear from her. When he didn't by the end of the day, he almost called Marissa to demand she tell him what happened but restrained himself.

* * *

Tired and annoyed Sierra hadn't called him to tell him how it went, Mason drove home, parked in front of his dark and lonely house, dragged his tired self out of the car and up the porch steps. When the automatic light came on and spotlighted the bottle of wine with the bow and card in front of the door, he stopped in his tracks, stared at it, and smiled for the first time since he'd spoken to Sierra on the phone today.

He picked up the bottle, tucked it under his arm, and pulled the card off it. He opened the white envelope, swore he could smell her on the paper, and pulled out the note.

I got the job! Thank you so much!
I owe you one.
Sierra

Smiling, he unlocked the front door, went in through the foyer and back to the kitchen, turning on lights along the way. He set the bottle of wine on the counter, dropped his briefcase on a barstool, and pulled out his phone and typed with his thumb as he tugged the knot on his tie loose.

Mason: Any chance you can come over and share this bottle of wine with me? We'll toast to your new job!

He set the phone on the island counter and shrugged off his suit jacket.

When his phone dinged with a text, butterflies took flight in his stomach. He felt like a teenager waiting on a girl to call.

Sierra: I wish! Bedtime stories with the kids. And I have to be up early for my new job!

Disappointment sent those butterflies dropping dead.

Sierra: Rain check?

And they were resurrected.

Mason: Anytime.
Sierra: Thank you again.
Mason: My pleasure. Good luck tomorrow. I know you'll kill it.
Sierra: You have no idea what this means to me.
Mason: You deserve everything good in this world.
Sierra: I appreciate that. And I mean it. I owe you one.
Mason: I will collect! ☺
Sierra: Gotta go. Boys are waiting. Story time.
Mason: Say hi from me.
Sierra: I will. ☺

Mason sighed, set the phone back on the counter, and went to the fridge. He opened the door and stared at the leftover takeout, decided to pull a frozen pizza out instead, and flipped on the oven to heat while he went and changed into sweats and a tee. He'd save the wine for when Sierra came over and crack open a beer to go with the pizza and his lonely night in front of the TV.

He settled on the couch half an hour later with his pizza, beer, and thoughts of Sierra sitting around a table with her kids and mom having a family meal. He'd like to be included in that homey scene.

He couldn't wait to see her and the boys on Saturday.

Chapter Nine

At the end of a very long second day at work, Sierra fell into the couch, and put her feet up on the coffee table. She leaned her head back and closed her eyes. At last she could take a break, hang out with the kids, maybe watch a TV show after dinner.

"Long day?" Amusement filled her mother's voice.

She opened her eyes and stared up at her mom. "It's only been two days and I'm exhausted." She never expected Mason's phone call to lead to an hour-long phone interview with Marissa feeling out her strengths, weaknesses, and whether or not she was up for the demanding job. She hadn't sugar-coated the workload or sheer number of clients she represented, but Sierra hadn't been prepared for the unrelenting pace. Of course, she had a learning curve. Once she mastered her duties things would be easier. Until then, though, trying to do everything perfectly without making any major mistakes or making Mason look bad for recommending her was exhausting.

"You'll settle in and learn the routine," Dede said.

"I know, it's just I don't want to screw this up. It's a great job. A dream job. And the pay . . . Wow!"

She never expected to find anything that paid so well. Not to start. And now she wouldn't have to rely on her mom to bail her out. She had some financial breathing room.

Sierra didn't mind working her way up, but starting at this level, it came with an expectation that you were the best. She hoped she was up to it.

She already loved Marissa. She didn't want to disappoint her, either.

"How were the boys this afternoon?" Her mother had agreed to pick them up after school for now. They both wanted to give the boys stability and familiarity.

"They were great. I love having them to myself for a couple hours. I get to spoil them."

"If it's too much . . ."

"Nonsense. They're my grandkids. This is why I got old." Her mother chuckled.

So did Sierra. "Thanks, Mom. It makes me feel better to know they're with you."

"Don't forget Heather is expecting you tonight for dinner. You better get a move on."

She forgot her mom had a *thing* at the country club and Heather wanted the kids to come over to play with Hallee so they could get to know each other better.

"I can't wait to see her place."

"It's really cute. You'll love it."

"Don't forget the boys and I are going over to Mason's place tomorrow."

Her mother's eyes twinkled. "I heard he went down and spoke to Marissa personally about that job for you."

Sierra hadn't known that until Marissa mentioned it, saying how out of character it was for Mason to see her in person instead of making a phone call. "I appreciate that he went out of his way to help me. I really needed the job and the income." When Marissa told her the base salary, plus the size of the bonus she could earn for bringing in new clients, Sierra thought it was a joke. But no. The money would allow her to pay off her debt and hopefully buy a small house for her and the boys. Not just yet, but sooner than she thought possible. Of course, her mom would help with the down payment if she needed it, but she hoped to settle the Napa property and avoid having to ask her mom for help.

Dede patted her leg. "I'm just saying he obviously likes you."

"We've been friends for years."

"Timing is everything."

She played dumb. "What are you talking about?"

"You're single. He's single. One and one makes two." Her mom was having too much fun with this. The sparkle in her eyes made Sierra smile.

A romantic at heart, her mother couldn't help herself.

"You're always looking for love."

Mirth turned to a serious look in her mother's eyes. "You deserve to be loved, Sierra. Don't forget that while you're raising your children and working to make a good life for them. You want them to have everything. Don't leave yourself out."

"I've got a lot on my plate right now." She thought about Mason inviting them over for horseback riding and a football game. She deserved to have some fun, something good in her life when for so long it felt like she'd been treading water, just trying to stay afloat in her life instead of really living it.

"This is your chance to reinvent your life. Take it, Sierra. Figure out what you want, what really makes *you* happy. Leave the past behind."

"I'm trying." She really was, but David's odd behavior and that damn loan still haunted her. Maybe once she figured out what he needed that money for, she'd let it go, no matter if it was good or bad. At least, she'd know the truth and be able to move on.

Chapter Ten

"Sierra is having dinner at Heather's place to-night." Amy waited for her husband to look up from his phone.

He didn't. "Are you going over there to join them?"

"*I* wasn't invited. Mom told me about it."

"Didn't you see Sierra earlier in the week for a playdate with the kids?" He didn't glance at her even once.

She didn't see what that had to do with anything. "Why are they getting together without me? Why not make it a big family thing?"

Rex sighed and finally made eye contact for the first time since he walked in the door an hour ago. "Heather's place is small. I'm not sure we could all pack into her place."

"We could have had a barbecue in the backyard."

"Maybe that's not what she had in mind. She hasn't seen her sister in nearly a year. Maybe she wants some time with Sierra, just the two of them."

Amy gritted her teeth and wondered if they were over there talking behind her back, sharing secrets like they did when they were kids.

Rex sighed. "If it bothers you so much, call Heather and invite yourself over to join them."

"Yeah, right."

He eyed her, grinning. "You know you want to. You hate being left out."

"What does that mean?"

The smile disappeared. "You can't stand it. If there's something going on at school, in town, with your family, you need to be in the middle of it."

Her shoulders and neck tensed. "That's not true."

Rex tapped his finger on the color-coded calendar hanging on the pantry cupboard next to him. "Really? There's not a single day on the calendar that you don't have something scheduled. You take on too much. You should scale back, have some time for yourself. Maybe then you wouldn't fall into bed every night exhausted."

Her defenses went up and she attacked without thinking. "It's not like you ever want to do anything with me."

He stuffed his phone in his pocket and pinned her in his gaze, glanced at the calendar, then back at her. "You've made it clear you don't have time for me. When I ask you to do something, it's always P.J. has baseball, or Emma has ballet, some class project, or . . . I don't know, a bake sale that requires you to make a thousand cookies."

"You're the one who plays golf every Saturday and most Sundays."

He held her gaze but waved his hand toward the calendar. "Because my family isn't home. The only time I see the kids is when I'm driving them somewhere you planned, and we don't even do that together. I see more of you on Instagram than I see you in real life."

That stung. She wanted to deny it outright but couldn't. "I want you to be there with us."

"I'm working all week to pay for all the things that take you guys away from me." He sighed and stared up at the ceiling for a moment before looking at her again. "I get they need something to do. But they don't need to do everything, all the time. By the time we finish with Spanish lessons, swimming, and whatever other sport you've got them in for the season, the weekend is gone. It'd be nice to go to the beach or hiking together. Hell, I'd love a whole weekend at home just hanging out playing board games and watching movies and stuffing ourselves on microwave popcorn."

That sounded like bliss. "We could do that."

"When? In the hour between one playdate and a birthday party for some kid in their class they aren't even friends with?"

"All the kids get invited to the parties so no one gets left out."

"That doesn't mean they have to go to every single one. They need to know that family time matters."

Frustrated and at her wit's end, she snapped. "What does that have to do with us going on a date?"

"Time. And the fact you don't have any for me."

"Are you guys fighting?" P.J. asked from the kitchen entry.

"No," Amy said.

"Yes." Rex dared her to contradict him again with a sharp look. "Put your shoes on, kiddo. Let's give Mom the night off from cooking and go pick up burgers."

"Yes!"

Rex waited for P.J. to run to his room to get his shoes before saying, "Something needs to change around here, Amy. You're always telling me to tell you how I feel. Well, I feel left out. I feel like you schedule all this stuff because you don't want to be with me."

"That's not true." She hated that he felt that way.

He glanced at the damn calendar again. "Really? Sure looks that way to me."

P.J. and Emma appeared in the entry, side by side, looking nervous about them arguing in the kitchen.

Emma smiled up at her dad. "I want to go, too."

Rex scooped her up and hugged her close. "Absolutely, princess. I bet you want french fries."

"And a chocolate shake?" Hesitation and hope filled her soft voice.

Amy didn't even bother to try to deny her daughter the sweet treat or Rex a moment to spoil the kids with junk food.

"Shakes all around," Rex announced, as he touched P.J.'s back to get him moving toward the front door. "Say good-bye to Mommy."

P.J. and Emma said in unison, "Bye, Mommy."

The front door closed behind them and Amy felt her stomach drop. She and Rex had had this same argument over and over again the past couple years, but now they rehashed it every few weeks.

She wanted to give her kids everything. She wanted them to experience all kinds of things.

She wanted more time with Rex.

More family time would be so nice.

She looked at her color-coded life hanging on the pantry door and thought about all she'd given up to be a mother. Oh, she loved it. But the satisfaction and joy waned as she lost herself in it. Everything she did was for the kids. She barely had time for herself. She couldn't remember the last time she did something fun just because she wanted to do it.

Sierra got that great job.

When did her own life turn into one endless art project, bake-off with the other moms, and cheerleading for her kids?

Amy wiped her palms down her chic yoga pants. She couldn't remember the last time she put on a sexy dress and heels. Hell, she barely remembered the last time she didn't go to bed in an old T-shirt and flannel shorts, let alone the last time she and Rex spent an hour or more making love.

The last time they had sex, she'd given in to his advances, not really feeling it because she was tired. She'd made sure he got what he wanted and fell beside him, unsatisfied and blaming him for it, when really it was her fault.

She'd just wanted the chore over.

Making love to her husband shouldn't be a task on her list.

The kids' schedule shouldn't be an endless loop of chauffeuring them around and keeping them busy because she didn't know what to do with herself if she wasn't doing something for them.

Rex was right. Something needed to change.

She needed a change.

Chapter Eleven

Heather sat Hallee on her play mat in front of her tower of toys then answered the door. She smiled at the resolute knocks from her sister, and the two other little pitter-patters from the boys' small fists.

She turned the knob and swung the door wide, loving the smiles on all three of their faces as they held their hands up mid-knock. "Hello, munchkins. Was that you pounding on my door?" She gave them a mock angry face, but it only sent them into a round of giggles. Heather found her sister's eyes were full of mirth, too. "Hey, sis."

"Hey. This place is so cute. Away from the road, and you've even got a little white picket fence with the flowers blooming along it."

"Thanks. I got lucky when I found it." She held her hand out toward the living room, hoping her sister didn't see it shaking. She didn't know why she was nervous. Okay, she did, but she shouldn't be. "Come in. Hallee is playing with her toys."

The boys raced past and fell on their knees beside Hallee, quickly picking up toys and engaging her. Heather took a second to watch them and enjoy the moment, seeing her little girl with the boys.

She closed the door behind Sierra, who stood

in the tiny foyer checking out the living room and through to the small kitchen and dining area.

"It's so you. Boho chic with a touch of elegance."

Heather didn't have much, but she made the most of her little space. She loved the wood-framed daybed with the colorful pillows she'd added in green, blue, and a pop of dark pink. They picked up the vibrant colors in the rug. Gauzy white drapes covered the window. Intricate woven baskets hung on the wall in a cluster as art. A simple wood oval coffee table served as a place for Hallee to play with some of her toys and Heather to prop her feet.

She'd added the elegance in the pretty antique chandelier-style lighting. Crystals gleamed and sparkled in the light. A collection of mercury glass candleholders lined the fireplace mantel.

Sierra touched her arm. "I love this place. It seems so perfect for you and Hallee."

"It's just what we needed. Her room turned out so great. I found this beautiful chandelier with golf-ball-sized crystals and she's got a sleigh bed crib that she's growing out of way too fast. I'm going to have to get her a big girl bed soon. I painted the walls a pale lavender and hung these cute butterflies from the ceiling."

Sierra took her gaze from the room at large and focused on her. "The kids seem happy. Show me."

Heather led Sierra on a tour of her house that didn't take more than a few minutes. They ended up in the kitchen where Heather had left two wine glasses on the counter next to a bottle of Moscato.

Sierra stared out the back window. "What a cute little patio. I love how you hung the lights and wrapped them around the tree. It gives the garden you planted out there a magical feel."

"I want Hallee to have a place that feels warm and inviting and fun at the same time, where she can touch things and run around without worrying that she'll break something. And if she does"—Heather shrugged one shoulder—"so what. She's missing something in her life, but my hope is that she'll always feel at home here and know she's loved."

Sierra's eyes went soft. "Isn't there any chance that her father will be a part of her life?"

"No." Heather's heart broke for her daughter. She deserved to have a wonderful father in her life. But it wasn't meant to be.

Heather had been selfish, threw caution out the door, took what she wanted, and her daughter paid the price.

At one time, Heather thought it would work out in some way, but no.

So she'd take the secret of who fathered her child to the grave. She still didn't know what she'd say to Hallee when she grew up and asked about her dad. Right now, it was easy to distract her when she pointed at her preschool friends' dads and said, "Dada."

"Maybe he'll change his mind."

She appreciated Sierra's optimism, but some things were absolute. "I thought there was a chance for us once. But . . ." She shrugged, not wanting to think about the mess she'd made and how it ended.

Sierra rubbed her hand up and down Heather's arm. "I'm sorry. It can't be easy to raise her on your own. But from what I see, you've made a great home for her. She's got you and all of us to love her."

Choked up, Heather swallowed the emotions clogging her throat. "That means a lot." More than her sister knew.

"What smells so amazing?" Sierra inhaled the garlic and tomato sauce smells filling the kitchen, then sighed in pure appreciation.

Heather chuckled. "I call them meatloaf balls." She lifted the lid on the frying pan on the stove and revealed the meatballs simmering in sauce. "I hope the kids like them."

"They look fantastic."

"I'll serve them over rice, if the kids want, with broccoli on the side."

"We'll let them decide. And look at you with the healthy meals, veggies and all. I remember a time when you ate pizza just about every night."

"I worked at a pizza place. Who wouldn't eat pizza all the time when it's free?" Heather picked up the open bottle of wine and poured for Sierra, then herself. She set the bottle down and held her glass up to Sierra. "I'm really happy you're home."

Sierra clinked glasses with her, took a sip, then narrowed her eyes. "I didn't think you were thrilled about me moving back."

"I was just surprised you'd want to stay when you and David had made your life up in Napa. Is it true? You really did want to come back sooner, but David wanted to stay up there?"

Sierra lifted one shoulder and let it drop. "I missed you guys. I wanted all our kids to grow up together. He considered moving back, but then he said he couldn't do it. He loved his job and thought we had a good life up there and he didn't want to change that."

Heather took a bigger sip of wine. "Well, you're here now, and you've got a great new job."

"It's an amazing opportunity. And the money is great. More than I was making at my old job." Sierra glanced around the house. "I can't afford to buy anything just yet, but I'd love a cute little place like this for me and the boys."

"With two of them, you'll need another room. I'm sure once you get your settlement, you'll be able to get something."

"I don't know about that. I was barely getting by. The fire wiped out what little I had in savings paying for motel rooms and basic necessities. I'll get the settlement for the contents of the house, which will help, but the mortgage doesn't go away. And I've got a huge personal loan to pay off."

"Really?" That concerned Heather.

Sierra waved it away. "I'll figure it out. The fire is still so fresh in my mind. The loss. If I hadn't found this job so soon, I don't know what I would have done. Mom has been so great, letting us move in until I can figure out what to do next. It's just so overwhelming."

"I always thought you and David were doing really well." Heather had no idea they'd taken out a big loan. "I wish I could help, but I sunk all my money and then some into this place. My job covers costs and day care and a little extra, but Hallee and I . . . well, we've got what we need."

"I totally get it. Like I said, the insurance will help, but rebuilding isn't an option for me. I need to move on."

"It must be hard to know that the house you and David shared is gone. All those memories."

"I still have the memories. But there's nothing left that I want to go back to. David's been gone almost a year and it's time to settle into my life without him."

The optimistic tone surprised Heather. "Are you thinking about dating again?"

"It's been a long time since I went on a date. It's kind of scary. But also . . . I don't know . . . maybe it's time. I don't want to dedicate everything to raising the boys and miss out having someone in my life to share it with. I'm sure, just like me, you get lonely sometimes."

"It's been especially hard this past year, watching Hallee grow so fast and do so many new things." Heather nodded. "I want to share it with her father, but I can't, so yeah, having a partner, someone special, in my life would be great." She thought about her encounter with Mason at the mailbox. A sexy lawyer would do fine. Someone stable. Someone available and open to a relationship that could potentially turn into a lifetime of memories.

She loved being a mother. She'd love to have another baby.

Mason had never had a family. Maybe he'd like to be a father.

"You're thinking about someone," Sierra teased.

Since Sierra knew Mason, Heather didn't want to give away her secret thoughts. "I've just recently been reacquainted with someone and . . . I don't know. Maybe there could be something there."

Sierra held her glass up. "Go for it, sis. Life is too short."

Heather clinked it again. "Yes. It is. In the blink

of an eye, you can lose everything. Why wait to have what you want."

"Here, here." Sierra took a sip, then glanced in the living room where Hallee let out a big belly laugh as Oliver held up a puppet and made fart noises. "Boys." Sierra shook her head, but a smile tugged at her lips.

Heather soaked up the scene with the boys entertaining Hallee. "This is nice."

Sierra met her gaze. "Yeah. It is. I'm glad you invited us."

"I hope we get to do this a lot more often. I'd like Hallee to really get to know Danny and Oliver."

"Me, too. We better feed them."

Heather, caught up in the moment and her emotions having Sierra and the boys in her home, impulsively hugged Sierra.

"What's this for?" Sierra held her close.

"I'm so glad I didn't lose you."

Sierra squeezed her harder. "You'll never lose me."

Heather hoped Sierra kept that promise.

Chapter Twelve

S ierra parked the SUV in Mason's driveway and tried to wrangle the butterflies into submission with a hand to her belly and a deep breath. This wasn't a date. It was just two friends getting together to watch a football game. Mason meant it as a kind gesture to make her sons happy.

"Can we see the horses first?" Danny asked.

Both boys watched the ones grazing in the nearest pasture. They were beautiful.

She missed riding and the freedom of it.

"We'll see." She opened the car door just as Mason walked out the front door with the ease of a confident man.

Nervous, anxious, and yes, excited, Sierra felt anything but confident. More like self-conscious.

She wasn't the same young lady he knew from their youth. She'd grown up, filled out, and had two kids that made her body dip and bulge in new ways that defied all exercises meant to flatten and tone certain areas.

How did he look the same after all these years?

She stepped out of the car and waved.

"Sierra, you look fantastic. I'm so glad you came."

The ridiculous amount of giddiness that single

compliment shot through her made her feel like a teenager with her first crush.

Did she still have a crush on Mason?

Had she ever stopped crushing on him?

"Thank you again for inviting us." She closed the driver's-side door so Danny didn't hear her. "Danny is really looking forward to this. It means a lot that you'd spend time with him."

Mason brushed that off with a wave of his hand. "I'm happy to have a buddy to watch the game with me. Otherwise, it's just me, all alone in this big house."

She wondered if he spent his nights alone, but didn't dare ask or let her mind go down that road. Not her business.

He'd been kind to help her get the job, but she didn't want to assume he held any interest in her other than being a friend and neighbor.

Mason took a step closer. "And I'm hoping you and I can spend some time catching up, getting to know each other better now that you're back."

"There's not much you don't already know."

"I know the outline. I'd like the details."

"Horsies!" Oliver jumped out the back door and ran for the fence.

Danny ran after him.

Mason let out an earsplitting whistle.

The boys stopped in their tracks and turned back to him. "Not so fast. There are ranch rules you need to learn and follow."

The boys' faces dropped into disappointment at the prospect of new rules to follow, but they stood still and waited to hear Mason out.

"First rule. No going into the pastures or climbing on the fences without your mom or me with you. Horses are big, they may not see you, and they can step on you and hurt you really badly. Second rule, no feeding the horses anything unless I give it to you. They like carrots and apples, but other things can make them sick. Third rule, you always stay within eyesight of me and your mom. There's a lot of things here where you can get into trouble or get hurt. Any questions?"

Both boys shook their heads.

"Okay, then let's have fun. The game starts in half an hour. Who wants to pet a horse?"

Both boys raised their hands and jumped up and down yelling, "Me! Me! Me!"

Mason took Sierra's hand, walked a couple steps pulling her along with him, before he let her loose and caught each of her boys around the belly and picked them up under each of his arms. They shouted in surprise and laughed as Mason bounced them up and down as he walked toward the stables.

Sierra stopped in her tracks and watched them. Her delighted boys. And Mason. Strong. Intriguing. Engaging. Fun. And kind.

He'd known David. They'd been friends once upon a time. Mason knew the boys missed their dad. Here he was, trying to give them a good day and a memory to keep after all the ones they'd hopefully forget.

"Hey, you coming with us?" Mason stood facing her, one wiggling boy under each arm like they didn't weigh him down one bit.

She walked to catch up. "Sorry. I got lost in thought."

Mason set the boys on their feet and took their hands. "I've got a real pretty mare you'll want to meet. And I'm sure Tom is around here somewhere."

She'd forgotten about Tom the cat. "He's got to be pretty old by now. He was old when I last saw him."

"This is Tom the third."

"Excuse me?"

"We named every adopted cat Tom."

"Why?"

Mason grinned like one of her little boys. "You know, Tom and Jerry."

She smiled back at him. "Old school."

"What's Tom and Jerry?" Oliver looked up at Mason, confused. Not surprising. The boys watched cartoons, but they were mostly newer ones.

Mason stared down at Oliver, hands on his hips. "Your education is seriously lacking. If you get bored with the football game, I'll queue up the cartoon on my tablet for you."

Oliver beamed Mason a smile. "O-tay."

They all headed into the stables. Horses greeted their entrance into the darker interior with sweet whinnies that made the boys gasp with surprise.

"They talk, Mama." Oliver's eyes were filled with wonder.

"They're happy to see you, buddy." Mason picked up Oliver and held him close to the beautiful buckskin's head. "Give him a pet down the nose."

Oliver ran his hand down the horse's tan nose, then reached up higher and felt his black mane. "He's soft."

The horse moved his big head closer to Oliver, who giggled. "He likes me, Mama."

Danny stepped close and reached up to pet the horse. He was a bit too short to get a good feel.

"Come down this way," Mason directed and led them three stalls down. He set Oliver on his feet, then swung the stall gate open wide. A beautiful bay mare stepped forward, dark brown coat gleaming. She nudged her nose into Mason's hand, looking for a treat. "Sorry, sweetheart, I don't have anything for you right now, but I'll bring you something later."

"Apples?" Danny asked, remembering what Mason told them earlier.

"She loves green apples."

"What's her name?" Oliver touched her high shoulder.

"Star."

"Because of the white patch on her head." Danny pointed up at it, unable to reach her head.

"That's right. She's a sweet girl. Who wants to go for a ride?"

Both boys raised their hands and bounced up and down on their toes.

"Step back with your mom while I get her out." Mason unhooked the rope across the stable door, took a lead rope from the wall next to the stall, hooked it on Star's bridle, and walked her out of the stall.

He turned to the boys. "Okay. Rules for riding. No yelling or screaming. You'll spook her. She's very sensitive. No kicking. You'll sit on top of her and I'll lead her around the pasture. If you want to stop or get down, you let me know and I'll lift you off her, but no jumping down. You could hurt yourself or fall under her and get stepped on." Mason pointed down at Star's hooves. "See those? They can break your bones if she steps on you. She's a calm girl. As long as you're nice to her, she'll be nice to you. Understand the rules?"

Both boys nodded.

"Great. Who wants up first?"

Oliver ran forward, arms up.

Mason scooped him up and set him on Star's back. "Okay, buddy, you hold on to her mane like this." Mason placed Oliver's hands around two fist-fuls of black hair. "Don't pull or hold too tight."

Oliver nodded.

Mason turned to Danny. "Ready?"

Danny held up his arms.

Mason lifted him up to the horse to sit behind his brother. "You hold on to Oliver's waist and make sure he doesn't slide off."

Danny nodded, looking unsure as the horse shifted under him.

Mason put his hand on Danny's thigh to steady him. "She's going to move a lot while she walks. Move with her."

Danny nodded.

Sierra moved in next to the boys as Mason took the lead rope at Star's head. Mason caught her eye and nodded, acknowledging that she'd walk along-side just in case the boys got scared or nervous or slipped off.

"Here we go." He clicked his tongue and gently tugged the rope to get Star moving.

Both boys' faces lit up with bright smiles when the horse started moving under them and they walked out of the stables, down the driveway, and into the pasture.

"Oh my God. She's so tall." Danny looked over and down at the ground.

Sierra fixed her hand at his waist. "Sit straight up, or you'll fall." Without a saddle and stirrups to keep the boys in place, they needed to focus on staying upright.

Oliver whispered, "This is so cool."

And just like that, the weight of all their troubles lifted off Sierra's shoulders. She smiled up at her boys, who were amazed and filled with wonder, riding their first horse and falling in love with it.

Oliver leaned over and hugged Star's neck. "Can we keep her, Mama?"

"Star is Mason's horse, honey."

"You can come visit her anytime you want," Mason offered. "She'd like it if you did." Mason turned and gave Sierra a *So would I* look.

One part of her hoped she read that right. Another part wondered if it was too soon to start dating again. Maybe she should focus on the boys and getting them a new home. But those were excuses for not putting herself out there.

Truth be told, Mason was hard to resist, especially when he was so kind and sweet to her precious boys.

But that wasn't all that drew her to him. There had been something there when they were younger. So much so that at one point before she married David, she'd had a moment where she wondered if a relationship with Mason was the better choice.

She chalked it up to nerves about getting married. Nothing but cold feet. Everyone experienced it. Second-guessing her compatibility with David just so she could be with another man, one she found intriguing and exciting and sexy as hell. They'd been friends so long, she knew so much about him.

But she'd convinced herself they would only ever be friends because she didn't want to risk losing that bond.

In the end, she'd felt like she and David married thinking the other person fit the image of what they wanted, but down the road they each turned out to be unable to fulfill the other's needs. David didn't think she was spontaneously fun or outgoing enough. She saw David's wild streak—at first so entertaining—as off-putting. He didn't think things through.

They turned into devoted parents but distant partners.

She didn't know when or why they both accepted that was their life, that the spark and fire between them had slowly burned out to ash. By the time David unexpectedly died, she'd been wondering for months if he wanted out of the marriage.

They didn't fight. They didn't disagree. They didn't care enough to do that. They simply lived their lives under the same roof for their children.

Looking back, it made her sad to think he died unhappy and unfulfilled in their marriage.

Still, she wondered if he'd had his foot out the door for a while.

Mason broke into her dark thoughts. "You okay?"

She nodded and smiled for the boys' benefit. "Fine." She checked her watch. "We should head back. The game starts in ten minutes and I've got to get the cooler of food out of the car and some of the things into the oven."

Mason studied her for a moment, then turned Star back to the house.

"Oh, come on, Mom, just a few more minutes," Danny pleaded. "I want to ride by myself."

"Not this time," Mason interjected. "But we'll definitely do this again. Come on, you don't want to miss kickoff."

Mason slowed his pace, letting the boys get every last second they could of the ride before he plucked them both off Star's back and set them on their feet again.

Oliver gave Star's leg a hug and glanced up at Mason. "I like her."

Mason brushed his hand over Oliver's head. "I'm glad you had fun. You can come see her before you go home later tonight."

"If I lived here, I'd sleep with her," Danny announced.

Mason chuckled. "She sleeps standing up."

"Nuh-uh." Danny stared up at the big horse.

"She sure does."

"I'm going to try that tonight." Oliver closed his eyes and wobbled before he opened his eyes again.

"Not so easy, is it?" Mason waved the boys back so he could put Star in her stall. He gave her a pat all the way down her back. "You made those boys' day." He pulled a roll of spearmint candies from his pocket, unwrapped one, and fed it to Star.

He walked out of the stall, secured the door, and held the roll of candies out to the boys. "Want one?"

"Horse treats." Oliver shook his head.

Danny peeled one off. "They're candy. Duh."

Oliver wanted everything Danny had and peeled one off for himself. He hesitantly stuck it in his mouth, then smiled when the sweet, minty taste hit his tongue.

Mason held the roll out to Sierra. "Want one?"

"I'm good. Thanks."

He stuffed the roll back in his jeans pocket, then touched his hand to her back as they walked up to the house. Every nerve in her body flared to life at that simple touch. He didn't crowd her but he didn't remove his hand, either.

She glanced up at him and caught him staring at her.

"I'm glad you decided to come today."

"Me, too. It's been a long time since I saw the boys smile and enjoy themselves this much."

"I liked seeing *you* smile."

"I haven't had a lot to smile about lately."

"Then I'm glad I'm part of why you did."

She stopped and stared up at him as the boys continued toward the house. "What is this, Mason?"

"It's a start to something that seems a long time coming." The words and sentiment rolled off his tongue so easily, like this was as inevitable as he claimed. He took her hand and gently tugged to get her to continue following the boys up to the house.

The warmth of his skin pressed to hers spread up her arm and through her whole body. She didn't pull away like she thought she should, but settled into the moment and the feel of his hand clasped with hers.

It had been so long since Sierra felt connected to someone, since a man touched her. Holding hands with Mason seemed like such a simple thing, but her heart melted at the thought that he wanted to start something with her.

At the end of her marriage, she'd felt undesirable and lacking in some way.

Mason made her feel wanted.

It made her stand a little straighter and feel lighter and giddy all at the same time.

She'd been unsure about coming home, thinking she didn't have anything besides family to come back to that would really make a difference in her life.

But Mason proved her wrong.

She'd wanted to find a way to get by. Mason gave her hope for something more.

Chapter Thirteen

Mason didn't know what to call the feelings running through him. An hour into the football game and he simply felt . . . great. Happy.

Sierra, looking beautiful in her dark pink top, long dark hair falling past her shoulders, stood in his kitchen, pulling a baking tray from the oven. She set it on top of the stove, then looked through the cupboards until she found the plates. She didn't hesitate to make herself at home in the kitchen he barely used.

The boys sprawled on the sofa. Danny watched the game, cheering with him when their team scored. Oliver watched *Tom and Jerry* on his tablet, giggling every so often and completely engrossed in the classic cartoon.

This is what this house needed. A family.

This is what his life needed.

He'd wanted this for a long time.

Once, he'd thought he'd get a chance to have it with Sierra.

If this was the start of his second chance, he'd make it count. This time, he wouldn't let her walk away without a fight.

Only one thing could screw it all up: the secret he'd kept since her stepfather's funeral.

His clients were falsely accused of wrongdoings

all the time. Divorces could cause hurt feelings, and the parties sometimes lashed out, making things worse.

He knew better than to present something without evidence to back it up.

If he said something and it turned out to be wrong, he risked her being angry at him for telling tales. She'd question his motives.

"Mason. You okay?"

He met Sierra's inquisitive gaze and smiled just because having her here made him so damn happy. "Yeah. Fine. Just got lost in thought." He tipped his chin toward the plate of pigs in a blanket. "Those look really good."

Danny took one and tried to see the TV around her hips. "Mom, move."

"Please," she prompted him.

Danny fell back into the cushions. "Please." He leaned over to check out the play on TV and groaned over the incomplete pass.

Sierra set the plate on the coffee table. "I'll get the rest of the goodies."

Mason rose and stood next to her. Close enough to smell her sweet floral scent. He'd missed that about her. She always smelled so good. "Let me help." He followed her into the kitchen, pulled the bottles of root beer and vanilla cream soda from the fridge and out of their cardboard holders, and placed them in the metal bucket he'd left on the counter.

"I love cream soda."

"I remember." He tried to play it off like it didn't mean anything, but Sierra stared at him, getting that he'd stored away a lot of memories and tidbits about her. He didn't know what it was about her, but she made him pay attention.

Maybe if he'd paid attention to his fiancée the way he did when Sierra was around, he'd have made it down the aisle and filled this house with his own family.

"I'm sorry, Mason."

At first he didn't know what she meant, then he caught the remorseful look in her eyes. "We don't need to do this, Sierra."

"I do. I've held on to it all this time. I've wanted to say something to you for so long, I just didn't know what to say."

"You don't need to apologize for being in love with David and wanting to be with him." It sucked. But Mason couldn't change the way she felt. Back then, he'd hoped maybe there was something deeper than friendship between them. Maybe there was, but she'd still picked David. Admittedly, he'd known she would. She and David had been seeing each other for a good long time. So Mason had swallowed his feelings and everything he'd wanted to say to her until it was too late and what little he had said hadn't been enough for her to really believe he wanted her to take a chance on him.

She shook her head. "I apologize for . . . whatever that weird scene was between us. I wanted to say something, then I didn't, and you didn't know what to say to me acting so weird, and then every time we saw each other afterward it was . . . strange. I made it weird."

"Look, I'm not going to deny that I hoped maybe you thought David wasn't the man for you."

"Wait. What?"

Mason thought she knew, but it looked like he'd been wrong. Great. What did that mean for them now? He didn't know, but he continued anyway because he'd been caught. "You and I were always friends, but I hoped we could be something more. David was my friend, but I still hoped you and I . . . Well, I shouldn't have made things more awkward when you were with him."

Her head tilted to the side and her gorgeous dark hair draped down her arm. "More awkward?"

Shit. He hadn't meant to bring this up. "David knew I had a thing for you."

"He did? You did?"

Her disbelief made him chuckle without any real humor. He laid it on the line. "It's more accurate to say *I do*."

Her brown eyes filled with surprise.

"Come on, Sierra, I might have been trying to hide it when you were with David, but I think I've made it clear now that I'm interested in seeing if there's something between us."

"I'm . . . not good at this. It's been a long time since I dated anyone. You and I have history. We're friends."

"And I hope that never changes, but I want more." He took a step closer, drawn by her wide eyes, so filled with disbelief, wonder, and hope, he couldn't stop himself from falling into them.

If they were going to rehash the past, he was going all in. "David knew you and I were friends when he started dating you. Let's just say David and I had a friendly rivalry, always trying to best the other. He got the girl I wanted."

She wrapped her arms around her middle. "Are you saying he was playing some one-up game with you?" Anger and resentment flashed in her eyes.

He wanted to dispel that immediately. "I think he saw what I saw in you and in no time he fell in love with you. You're kind and generous and caring. He was drawn to you just like I was. I was caught up in building my career and I let my personal life slip. I let you get away. I didn't go after what I really wanted and David did."

She raked her fingers through the side of her hair. "I'm having a hard time resolving the past and right now. I wished I'd known how you really felt."

He gave her the God's honest truth. "I want you. That's how I feel right now. That's what I should have said to you back then. Not that it would have made a difference. You didn't feel the same."

Her gaze dropped to the floor and she slid the tip of her shoe along the hardwood. "Actually, I did feel something for you back then."

Blown away, he didn't know what to say. "Seriously?"

She finally met his gaze again. "I just wasn't sure what I thought I saw in you wasn't just wishful thinking."

Mason didn't think, he simply went with his gut, cupped her face, and kissed her, letting all his pent-up feelings and need loose. Her hands gripped his sides and her lips opened to him. He slid his tongue along hers and tasted the same need he had for her.

"Touchdown!" Danny yelled.

Mason certainly felt like a winner having Sierra in his arms.

Sierra broke the kiss and held him away.

He caught the desire in her eyes a second before he turned and caught Danny doing his own version of an end zone victory dance, pretending to spike the ball. Oliver barely glanced up from the tablet.

He turned back to Sierra. "I should have done that that night in the bar."

She chuckled under her breath, a pretty pink blush brightening her cheeks. "And started a fight with David."

"I wanted to start something with you."

She pulled him in a step and laid her forehead against his chest. "I don't know what to do with that now after everything that's happened. I married David. We had a good marriage for the most part."

He wanted to dive into that *for the most part*, but left it alone because he didn't want to talk about her and David. He wanted to talk about them and the here and now.

He cupped her face again and made her look at him. "The past is the past. Let's focus on right now. Do you want to be with me? Do you want to see where this thing between us goes?"

A shyness he'd never seen in her filled her eyes as her gaze fell away, then came back to meet his. "Yes." The whispered word rang loud and clear in his brain.

He brushed his thumbs across her pink cheeks and smiled down at her, his heart light, excitement thrumming through him. "Now we're getting some-where." He leaned down and kissed her softly. "I'm so glad you came back."

She snuggled into his chest and he held her close. "Me, too."

The oven buzzer went off and she pulled away,

but he took her hand to keep the connection between them. "Pick a day that you can get a babysitter for the kids. Let's go out to dinner."

A smile bloomed on her soft lips. "A date?"

He squeezed her hand. "It's long overdue."

The smile went megawatt. "I'd like that."

He wanted to make her that happy all the time.
"I want to spend a lot more time with you." He
squeezed her hand to let her know he meant it and
mentally kicked his ass for not being this open and
honest with her back in the day.

She reached over and turned the incessant buzzer
off, then opened the oven door, letting loose a blast
of heat and the aroma of barbecue pulled pork.

He couldn't help himself. "That smells so good."

"I can't take credit. I picked it up at the Barbecue
Pit. I'm just reheating it."

"I love that place."

"I know." She gave him another shy glance.
"You're not the only one who paid attention."

"Mom, I'm thirsty." Danny spoke around the
chunk of hot dog in his mouth.

Sierra turned to Mason again. "You get that I'm a
package deal, right?"

"Rug rats and all. Got it. They're great boys. I
like having them here. I like *you* here."

She cocked a hip and leaned heavily on one side.
"How come we never got together in high school?"

"Because I was a dumbshit back then."

"You swore." Oliver appeared at his side out of
nowhere.

Mason frowned. "Sorry, buddy, just telling your
mom the truth."

"Are there any grapes?"

"In the cooler." Sierra took Oliver's hand and led him over to it, pulling out the covered bowl filled with green and red grapes. "Do you want a slider to go with that?"

"Yes, please. No slaw."

"I know." Sierra pulled the cover off the grapes and handed the whole thing to Oliver. "Go sit at the coffee table. I'll bring you your sandwich."

Oliver went back to the living room, sat on the floor, set the grapes on the table, and ate while watching some car insurance commercial.

"Are you sure you don't mind them eating in there?"

"It's no big deal. If they spill something, I can have the carpet cleaned." He went to the freezer, pulled out the ice container, and dumped the ice into the metal bucket filled with sodas.

"You sure you want to give them soda? They'll be hopped up on sugar for a couple of hours."

"Relax, Sierra. I don't care if they make a mess, jump on the furniture, and just be rowdy boys. I used to be one, you know."

She sighed. "I just want this to go well."

"It is. It will." He stopped in front of her with the bucket under his arm. "Are you talking about today, or us?"

He loved that she always met his gaze when she had something serious to say. "I don't want to mess this up. You've been so nice, getting me the job, and asking us over here."

"Stop. I didn't do those things so you'd say yes to a date, or to manipulate you into saying yes."

She put her hand on his chest like touching him was so easy now.

He loved it.

"That's not what I meant at all. I'm grateful for the help you've offered, but that isn't why I'm here." She raked her fingers through her hair again. "I appreciate what you've done and I'm so glad we've reconnected."

"Me, too." He saved her from trying to explain herself further when he got that this meant something to her. He mattered. "Let's eat before the boys start chewing on the furniture."

She smiled and went to make up the sliders where she had everything set out next to the stovetop.

He took the drinks into the living room and set the bucket on the coffee table.

"No way. Root beer in bottles. Cool." Danny pulled one out and stared at the cap.

Mason took it, twisted off the top, and handed it back.

Oliver held up a bottle to him. "Me."

Mason uncapped his and handed it back. Both boys took deep sips, burped, then fell into a fit of giggles. Mason took a big swig of his own bottle and burped long and loud just to make them laugh.

Sierra stared at him from the kitchen island, smiling, and shaking her head, but enjoying it all the same.

* * *

The rest of the evening went smoothly. The boys ate too much and ended up on either side of Mason and Sierra on the sofa where their legs touched the whole time but he resisted the urge to hold her hand or hook his arm around her shoulders and pull her into his side because he didn't want the boys to see how close they were getting before Sierra was ready to talk to them about her moving on. The boys loved their father, missed him, and may not be ready for a new guy in their mom's life.

He got that and kept a respectful distance for their sakes.

The game ended with their team winning. Danny jumped up and fist-pumped the air. Oliver was half asleep watching the tablet next to Sierra.

They worked together to clear the food and put everything away. Mason loved that she rummaged through his kitchen looking for plastic containers and appreciated that she stored the leftovers in his fridge for him to eat later in the week. He hoped to spend more time with her and the boys and not eat all his dinners alone anymore.

"Ready to go, boys?" Sierra stood by the entryway with the cooler she'd brought at her feet, holding the kids' jackets.

"Can't we ride Star again?" Danny dragged his feet on his way to get his jacket and gave Mason a pleading glance.

"Next time you come over. It's too late to do it tonight."

"You boys need to get home and take your baths and get ready for bed."

"But Mom . . ." Oliver walked with his shoulders slack. "Please. I'm not tired." The yawn he let loose said otherwise.

"Come on. Say thank you to Mason."

"Thank you." Danny frowned, not making the words sound so appreciative, but Mason got that he wanted to stay and have more fun. He chalked that up to a win for today.

"Thank you, May. Son." Oliver barely kept his eyes open.

"Maybe you guys can come over tomorrow for another ride."

Both boys shot their mom a pleading look.

She eyed him, then addressed the boys. "We've got some errands to run tomorrow, but maybe we can stop by in the afternoon before dinner."

The boys bounced on their toes, excited. "See you tomorrow, Mason." Danny ran out the door to the car, eager to get to tomorrow, it seemed.

Oliver trailed after his brother with a wave good-bye.

"What errands?" he asked, curious about what she had planned.

"My mom is going to see a play. I promised to do the grocery shopping. I also need to get some new work clothes, since everything I owned went up in flames. I'll have to take the boys with me, which means it will take twice as long and require tablet time bribes to get them to cooperate and not have a total meltdown in the dress department." She shrugged and rolled her eyes, looking exasperated already.

"I can watch the boys."

She held up her hand. "Oh, that's nice of you to say . . ."

"I mean it. I don't mind. Drop them off on your way into town."

Her head tilted to the side as she eyed him. "Don't you have your own plans for the day?"

"I'll be doing ranch chores. The boys can help. I'll let them ride again. We'll have fun."

"Mason, I don't want to take advantage . . ."

"You're not. I'm offering."

She hesitated a second, one side of her mouth drawn back in a half frown-smile thing that made him think she really wanted to say yes, but felt she shouldn't.

"Sierra, seriously, bring them over. You'll get your stuff done faster and without the hassle of dragging them along with you. They'll be bored and acting out. At least here, they'll be doing something outdoors and having fun. It's for them, really," he teased, knowing it would really be a huge help to her if he took the boys for a few hours.

"You have no idea what you're asking for."

"A chance to get to know them better, and let them get to know me, too. We know each other, so dating is just a next step for us, but the boys may see me as intruding in your life, or taking their father's place. I don't want to do that. I want them to see me as a friend and someone who likes their mom and wants to make her happy."

Sierra's shoulders went slack. "I don't know what to do with you being sweet like this."

Which made him think David hadn't been all that sweet during their marriage if a simple babysitting gesture made her go all gooey on him.

Sierra went on, "You don't know how much your offer means to me. Things have been really hard lately, but thanks to you, they're looking up." She needed something to be easy and hassle free.

He could do that.

Mason put his hand on her shoulder and kissed her forehead. "I know you've got a lot on your plate with settling your affairs back in Napa and starting a new job here and getting settled again. If I can help, I will."

"You really mean that."

She didn't pose it as a question, but he assured her anyway. "Yes. I do. So drop the boys off tomorrow, go do what you need to do and take your time about it, and I'll see you when you pick up the boys and I'll get to do this again." He tugged her the two steps out of the doorway and into the kitchen so the boys couldn't see them, leaned in, and kissed her, long and deep. He broke the kiss far sooner than he'd like and smiled down at her. "I'm really glad you came over today."

"Me, too."

He picked up the cooler, took her hand in his free one, and walked her out to the car. He put the cooler in back and waved to the boys before placing his hands on the driver's-side open window and staring in at Sierra.

A soft smile made her even more beautiful. "See you tomorrow."

"I'm here whenever you need me," he assured her, then stepped back and waved them all good-bye.

He watched them drive away, knowing they weren't going far, just next door, but wishing they'd stay because the empty house behind him didn't feel the same without them in it anymore.

Chapter Fourteen

Sierra sat at the kitchen island counter listening to the boys upstairs brushing their teeth before she took them to school. She sorted through the envelopes in front of her.

Her mom sipped her coffee, then stared at her over the rim. "I know that frown isn't about Mason. Not after you've come home every day from his place with a smile on your face."

Sierra couldn't contradict her mother's assessment. She and the boys went over every night to help Mason feed the horses and spend time with him. The boys loved it. They were learning a lot about taking care of the animals.

She herself liked getting to know who Mason was now. They were both the same but different, and she enjoyed discovering new things about him.

They'd kept things light this past week because they'd both been busy at work and having the boys around all the time meant they had to be careful about what they said and did.

"Mason is great. The boys love him." Her feelings were growing deeper the longer she spent with him.

Dede said, "What's not to like? He's got a cat and horses for the boys to pet and ride. They like his company because having a big strong man around to let them be rowdy and wrestle is a lot of fun.

And hey, you get to just look at him and kiss him."
Her mother's eyes twinkled with delight. She hadn't
actually seen Sierra and Mason kissing, but it was
a good guess that she was still smiling when she
came home because of it.

"We do more than kiss, you know. It's nice to
spend time with him. I miss coming home and having someone to talk to about my day."

"Have you asked him to help you with your
David problem?"

How could David be such a problem after his
death?

Sierra brushed her hands over the bill in front
of her. She didn't like where her mind went every
time she thought about it. She hated the monthly reminder that her husband kept a big secret from her.

Dede pressed her. "Why are you stalling? If
Mason can figure out where the money is, you can
get rid of that loan and leave it in the past where you
should leave David." Bitterness filled those words.
"If you can't deal with it, let me pay it off and be
done with it."

Sierra appreciated her mother's anger and resentment that David left her carrying the debt. She had
to admit she didn't have a lot of kind thoughts when
it came to David and the loan, but she wasn't one to
bury her head in the sand, either. Still, the thought
of taking that kind of money from her mom didn't
sit right, even if her mom could easily afford it.

"Between David's death, struggling to get by
after he was gone, helping the boys through their
grief while I worked through mine, and losing everything, I'm not sure I can take one more blow.
Our marriage wasn't perfect. I know that. No one's

is. But I don't want to find out it was broken and I didn't even know it."

"Don't blame yourself for something you didn't do."

Sierra's stomach knotted. "That's just it, I don't want to know what he did with that money."

"So you're just going to worry over it, pay it back, and just take it?"

Part of her wanted to, but no, she wasn't one to just let it go. "Who am I supposed to make pay for and answer for it? David isn't here." That really ticked her off.

"It's your decision, but I think this has more to do with the fact you're afraid to ask Mason for help because you don't want him or anyone else to know that David wasn't the great guy and husband everyone thought he was. You don't want anyone, Mason especially, to know that David pulled one over on you."

No, she didn't. "Is it so hard to understand why? I feel stupid and duped and like I didn't even know him if he could do something like this behind my back. He lied to me for months before his death by not telling me he took out the loan. What else was he lying about?"

Her mom thumped the coffee mug on the counter. "That's a very good question. If it were me, I'd want to know so that if something else comes at me out of the blue from his past I'd be prepared. If you know, you can protect the boys. And yourself, Sierra. Who knows what he was into that cost that kind of money."

She'd like to think it was a bad investment, or gambling, though that really seemed unlikely.

David had never been a gambler. Maybe he was helping out a friend and didn't want her to know for whatever reason. Sierra hoped it was something easily explained.

The boys stomped down the stairs and headed for their backpacks by the door. She scooped up the mail, set her mug in the sink, and met her mother's inquisitive gaze. "I need more time to think about it."

She needed superpowers. She'd love to resurrect David and shake some answers out of him.

Instead, she headed for the door to take the boys to school and get herself to work. The boys ran out the door and she turned back to her mom. "I appreciate the push and that you've kept this between us."

"I only want to help, honey. If there's a way for you to recover some of that money, it will make your life easier." Her mother paused, then sucked in a steady breath. "I also think that if you're really hoping to move on with Mason, you should put the past to rest with a clear head and heart." Dede held up her hands and let them drop. "That's my two cents."

In other words, Sierra should be honest with Mason about her and David's relationship. She should trust him to help her with this problem without judgment.

David had shaken her ability to trust. He'd made her cautious. Where her desire was to jump into a relationship with Mason now, she'd cautiously erected a wall between them, using the boys to keep him at a distance and make things uncomplicated.

"Damn. I'm still letting him influence my decisions and get in the way of what I want."

Her mother's eyes narrowed. "What do you

mean? Why wouldn't David let you have what you want?"

She drew back one side of her mouth in a half frown, thinking back to how David subtly manipulated her into doing what he wanted most of the time. "I wanted to move back here. I talked to him about it, but he refused. He didn't want to change jobs or be so close to all of you. He wanted us to have *our* life." As in separate from her family. "I went along because I thought what he wanted was me and the boys."

"And now you're not so sure that's what it was."

"I think something was keeping him in Napa Valley and it wasn't me and the boys." She shrugged. "Maybe I'm wrong." And in that moment, it became clear. "I guess I'll find out."

Chapter Fifteen

Mason stared at the change on his calendar and wanted to smile, but found he was more confused than happy about his next appointment. He walked to his office door and found his assistant at her desk, typing.

"Louise, when did Sierra call for an appointment?"

"This morning. You had a cancellation. She said she's a friend of yours, so I made the appointment."

"Did she say why she wanted to meet with me?"

The object of his inquiry walked in the door.

"Hey," Sierra said, her eyes darting between him and Louise, who couldn't stop looking from him to Sierra like she could see the sparks flying between them.

"I hear you need a lawyer."

Sierra bit her lip, glanced at Louise, then back at him. "Um. Not really, but kinda."

That made him nervous. If she wasn't in need of a lawyer . . . Well, he hoped she wasn't here to break up with him.

Then again, who made an appointment to do that?

"Mason?"

"Yeah?"

"If you don't want to help me . . ."

"Of course I want to help you." A strange sense of ease went through him. She wanted help. She didn't want to break up. And she wasn't here because she'd found out what he suspected but never told her. "Come into my office and tell me what you need."

Louise's gaze bounced from him to Sierra and back. She gave him a knowing look. "I'll hold all your calls."

He waited for Sierra to pass before closing the door on Louise's inquisitive gaze. She'd grill him later. She knew him well enough to know that Sierra, a friend, wasn't here about a divorce.

Normally he'd greet Sierra with a kiss on the cheek or a brush of his hand on her arm in front of the boys. He'd like to kiss her now, the way he did when the boys were distracted and he stole one from her. But she didn't take a seat or look like she came here to make out in his office for an hour. Pity.

Sierra simply stood in front of his desk and stared at him, looking unsure and nervous as hell.

"Do you want to do this standing up or sitting down?" Okay, that sounded dirty even to him.

Sierra raised an eyebrow and dropped into one of the chairs.

He went with her prompt and took a seat behind his desk, keeping this professional. She'd made the appointment. He'd give her his full attention.

Sierra stared at him for a good long moment, then pulled a stack of envelopes from her purse along with a slip of folded paper. She set it on the desk, opened it, and slid the check toward him. "Your assistant said a five-hundred-dollar retainer would do."

He knew she was still short on ready cash, so the five hundred had to be a stretch for her to come up with for . . . whatever it was she wanted him to do for her. Maybe she borrowed it from her mom or Amy.

"I don't want your money, Sierra. I'm happy to help you with whatever you need."

"If I pay you, that means you're my attorney and you can't say anything to anyone about what I'm about to tell you."

That confused him. Didn't she trust him? "Anything you say to me is between you and me. You don't need to pay for my silence. You just have to ask."

"You're mad."

A little bit. "I thought I made it clear what I wanted with you, and it's not to be your lawyer."

She deflated in the chair, her shoulders sagging and all the air going out of her lungs in a loud sigh. "So you won't help me."

"Of course I'll help you. I just don't get why you didn't just ask me about this the half-dozen times you've seen me over the last week instead of making an appointment."

Sierra stood and paced back and forth. "I didn't want you to think I was taking advantage of our friendship."

"I hope we are moving into a deeper kind of friendship where you trust me and know that I'd do anything for you."

She stopped in her tracks and stared at him, looking for something, then deciding she saw whatever it was she needed to see to sit back down and tell him what she needed. "This is awkward. You and

I . . . We're seeing each other now. I don't want to screw that up."

"Hundreds of people have sat where you are ready to end relationships because they couldn't trust the other person enough to have a civil conversation about what they needed and wanted from the other person. So, Sierra, what do you need from me?"

She sucked in a breath. "I need your help to find out if David was having an affair or in some kind of trouble that cost him, *us*, fifty thousand dollars."

He thought she needed help navigating the insurance and red tape on her property up in Napa. He never thought this had anything to do with David.

No wonder she'd been apprehensive to bring it up to him.

Mason fell back in his seat and tried to get his thoughts together and figure out a way to navigate this. He started with the simple question. "Why do you think he was having an affair?"

Sierra pulled some papers out of one of the envelopes and slid them across the desk. "He took out a fifty-thousand-dollar loan nearly two years ago. For what, I have no idea. I didn't know anything about it until after his death and the bank contacted me about delinquent payments I knew nothing about. He had the bills sent to his office, not the house. Once the bank contacted me, I went through the boxes his assistant had packed up and delivered to the house after his death."

"Okay. He took out a loan you didn't know about. Did he use it to pay off debts the two of you accrued during the marriage?"

"Of course I checked that first." Annoyance replaced her earlier trepidation.

"I'm just trying to cover all the bases." He didn't want to dig into their marriage, but she'd come to him for help. This was a can of worms he hoped to avoid. "Did you receive any statements for an account you didn't know about?"

"No. That's what I need you to help me find out. If this money, or even part of it, is sitting in some other account that I can access, I need to find it. Then I can pay off the loan—or at least some of it with what's left." She raked her fingers through her hair, distress and despair in her eyes. "I have been struggling the last year to pay this and the other bills on my own." Tears glistened in her eyes.

David had left her a mess and a mountain of bills. "Didn't he have life insurance?"

She rolled her eyes. "By the time I paid off the funeral costs and credit card debt we had, hoping to make the monthly expenses more reasonable on just my salary, I only had a small amount left to put into school accounts for the boys. My plan was to use part of the survivors' benefits money from David's Social Security to pay bills and transfer what's left into their college funds. Then I got hit with this." She tapped her finger on the loan notice. "The job you got me is a huge help. I make more, so I can afford to pay this, but it's an expense and I have nothing to show for it."

Mason suspected he knew where the money went, but he didn't want to be right. "Did you find any evidence of an affair?"

"His phone is locked. His fingerprint is required

to get into it. Because the phone he used was provided by his company, I don't have the bills for it, so I can't see who he called or texted."

Smart, hiding his conversations and texts from his wife.

Bastard.

"I'm guessing you didn't find any notes or unexplained receipts among his things."

"No. I have no hard evidence that he was having an affair. It makes me sick to think that he hid something like this so well that I didn't even notice. But I think about the two years leading up to his death and I think about how everything had become so stale and routine. As a family, everything seemed fine, but between David and me . . . We lost something along the way."

"You suspect he pulled away because he had someone else." Mason's stomach knotted. The bastard didn't see what he had right in front of him, a beautiful, kind, loving woman.

"I think we drifted so far apart that I didn't see or suspect he was seeing someone else. Like I said, everything seemed fine between us. I knew we needed to spend more time together as a couple, but work and kids took over our lives. We didn't have big, blow-up fights. He mentioned just as much as I did that we needed to get away, just the two of us, but we never did. I don't know how to explain it, except that we were living our lives and it seemed both of us were thinking that as the boys got older we'd have more time for each other.

"I did feel like there were days and weeks where he was preoccupied with something he didn't want to talk about. He went on more business trips the months leading up to his death. The night of the accident, he was driving down south to meet with clients the next day."

Are you sure?

Mason had his doubts.

She answered his unspoken question. "At least, I think that's where he was going. I was so lost in my grief and taking care of the boys right afterward, making sure they were okay, I never asked his boss about it. I just went through the motions each day, trying to get whatever needed to be done, done."

Mason held his hand out to her across the desk. She laid her hand in his and he squeezed to let her know he was there. "You know none of this is your fault, right?"

"I wasn't paying attention. Maybe I just didn't want to know."

"A lot of my clients feel that exact same way. Women and men. They aren't exactly happy in their marriages but there isn't enough strife to end it. There's still hope that they'll find their way back to how they felt when they got together and married. They let things slide. They make excuses, like staying together for the kids. They don't open up about how they're feeling or what they want to change. Sometimes things just fizzle out and they end up here. Other times, someone finds what they need with someone else and they still end up here."

"Is that why you never married?"

"I came close. Once." But his ex felt like he'd been holding out on her. Maybe he had been, because he'd been carrying a torch for the woman in front of him for a long time. And the engagement with his ex ended right after he saw Sierra at her stepfather's funeral.

Sierra showing up here and telling him about this situation made him feel guilty for keeping his secret, even though he didn't know if what he saw was what he thought he saw.

"Mason?"

Jarred out of his thoughts, he met Sierra's inquisitive eyes. "Yeah? What?"

"Do you think David was having an affair?"

"I'm not sure. But I have an investigator who can look into it. He can try to track the money." But if the money led where Mason suspected, he didn't know what he'd tell Sierra. The last thing he wanted to do was break her heart. Or lose her because he'd kept quiet about what he suspected.

Love blinds us all to people's faults. When love fades, sometimes those flaws are all too clear.

He wished for Sierra's sake that she could let David rest in peace with a clear heart.

Instead, she'd been left with suspicions and come to him to clear them up. Mason didn't know if he could do that for her without wrecking the new, fragile feelings developing between them.

He should tell her what he suspected, but he didn't want to accuse a dead man of something he couldn't prove. David wasn't here to speak for himself. And Sierra would only have Mason to take out her feelings of betrayal on, whether he was right or wrong.

"Thank you, Mason. This means so much to me. I've been sitting with this all alone for a long time. I wanted answers, I just wasn't sure how to get them.

If your investigator can find anything out for me, I'll be so grateful."

Mason suspected grateful was the last thing she'd be.

"I'd appreciate it if you kept this between us. My mom knows, but I don't want my sisters to find out. David was your friend. I'm sure you're not thrilled to be investigating him. But I need to know the truth."

How did he get himself into this pickle?

Because he couldn't say no to the woman sitting across from him. Because he wanted her to be happy. Because he'd let her get away once and wouldn't let that happen again.

Investigating David and the money meant it might be that much harder to convince Sierra how much he cared.

"David and I knew each other a long time ago. I know he wasn't perfect. He could be competitive." And go after the girl Mason liked just to see who got her. He had a feeling David learned that winning didn't mean you got what you wanted and he went looking for someone else without thinking about the devastation he'd leave in his wake. "Maybe all this is, is some kind of deal he made that went south and he had to pay back the money or something."

Sierra dismissed that with a shake of her head. "I hoped so, too. But I've come to terms with the fact that I would have found some evidence of that in his papers. I looked for some business proposal or investment. I didn't find anything." She stared at their joined hands. "I think my intuition was telling me he had someone else and I just didn't listen to it."

"You'd be surprised how many wives say that

same thing. You should listen to that gut instinct. I've found based on the number of women who come in here, it's usually right."

"Well, my gut's telling me you're not happy about doing this for me."

He tried to smile but didn't quite pull it off to ease her mind. "I'm afraid that uncovering the truth will only hurt you and that's the last thing I want to do."

"Don't worry. I won't shoot the messenger."

He was afraid she wouldn't be able to keep that promise.

Chapter Sixteen

Sierra stood just as the office door opened. Mason walked in looking fine in a navy suit, white shirt, and blue-and-purple tie. The color made his hair appear even more golden, his eyes a brighter blue. He looked good and had to know it. Every woman still left in the office noticed as they tracked his progress across the entry and through the cubicles to her desk.

Mason stopped in front of her, his eyes diving down her new lilac-colored dress to her sparkly black strappy heels, then coming up to meet her gaze. "That dress is killer. You're gorgeous."

"I was just thinking the same thing about you." That got her a huge smile from him. She was glad for it because things had been casual and guarded between them since she appeared in his office three days ago asking for his help with her David problem.

Mason stepped closer, the woodsy smell of him drawing her in. "I'm so glad we're finally doing our dinner date. I love the boys, but I've wanted you all to myself for a while now."

"I feel the same way. Amy has the kids. They're having a sleepover with their cousins."

Mason leaned in close. "Are we having a sleepover tonight, too?"

She'd thought about it all day, which meant thoughts of him distracted her from doing anything really productive. "If you play your cards right." She was teasing, but she'd planned for this, hoping it would happen sooner rather than later.

"Well, then I'll do my best to impress you with some good food, better wine, and charming conversation."

"All of that sounds amazing, but really all I want to do is spend some time alone with you." It had been so long since she'd dressed up and took the time to make herself feel pretty. Sierra couldn't remember the last time a man paid her a compliment. It had been far too long since she'd been held. Even longer since she'd had sex.

Even more than that, she wanted to feel a man against her, inside her, and all around her. She wanted to feel needed and desired again.

The look Mason gave her went a long way to bolstering her courage and resolve that tonight they wouldn't stop at a few hot kisses while the boys weren't looking.

Tonight was about being a woman again, not just Danny and Oliver's mom. She'd needed that for a long time.

Mason's fingers brushed her face. "I lost you. What's wrong?"

She focused on Mason, the man who'd made it clear he wanted a real relationship with her. A man who'd gone out of his way to make her and her kids feel at home with him and at his place.

"Nothing is wrong. I'm with you." With that, she went up on tiptoe and kissed him right there in her office. The surprise she felt in him disappeared immediately and he took over the kiss, sliding his tongue along hers as his arms enfolded her and held her close.

He'd always initiated the intimacy between them. He seemed to like her taking the lead. She'd have to remember that later.

"Hi, Mason. I see my new employee is more than just a friend you wanted to help."

Mason broke the kiss with a huge smile on his face and turned to Sierra's boss without letting her go. "Hi, Marissa. How are you?"

"Not as good as you, judging by that big grin you're wearing."

Mason chuckled and loosened his embrace of Sierra, but he didn't release her, keeping his arm banded around her waist. "Sierra and I go way back. We've recently reconnected."

Marissa eyed him with a knowing look. "I see that. And I hate to admit it, but you were right about her. She's fantastic. She's brought in three new clients since she started. All of our clients adore her."

Mason squeezed her to his side. "So do I."

Sierra glanced up at him and caught her breath at the wide smile and absolute adoration in his eyes.

"Looks like you two are headed out for a nice evening together. I just wanted to say hi. Have a great night." Marissa turned to Sierra. "I knew you had great taste when you picked out the furniture and decorations to stage the last rental property. Now I know you've also got excellent taste in men, and you must be something special, because I've asked him out at least half a dozen times and gotten turned down flat every time."

Mason chuckled. "I don't date my clients."

"From what I've seen and heard, you hardly date." Marissa gave her another bold smile. "I'm glad you changed that. He deserves someone who knows what a great guy he is."

"I've known that for a long time." She'd nearly canceled her engagement because she thought Mason was a better choice for her than David.

Mason didn't know that though.

He'd asked for a second chance of sorts because he'd let her go. She didn't know that at the time, either, but he'd said as much to her since she'd moved back.

Maybe this was a chance for both of them to get it right.

"See you tomorrow, Marissa." She took Mason's hand. "Let's go."

Mason gave Marissa a good-bye smile and walked with Sierra out of the office and onto the sidewalk. "The restaurant is up two blocks. Mind walking?"

"Not at all."

They started down the street and she couldn't help but smile up at him.

He caught her staring. "What?"

"This is nice. It's been a long time since I felt this light."

He squeezed her hand. "I'm glad. Something feels different about you tonight."

"I guess I want to set aside all the worries and just enjoy being with you."

"You've had a lot on your mind and to deal with since coming home."

She didn't want to ruin the night with talk of

David, but had to ask, "Has your investigator found anything out yet?"

Mason frowned and kept walking without looking at her. "No. Not yet. Something came up on a divorce case and he needed to work on that for me first."

"Of course."

Mason held the restaurant door open for her. "If there's something to find, he'll find it." She walked in and settled into his side when he stood beside her with his arm around her waist in front of the reservation desk. "I just hope whatever we discover doesn't upset you."

"I can't be more upset than finding out he took out a loan and messed with my credit, made it difficult to support the kids, and never said a word about it to me."

"I know the why is important, but sometimes it's worse than the deed itself."

"I'm already expecting the worst."

"Mr. Moore," the hostess greeted them. "We're so happy to have you back. The table you requested is ready. This way." The hostess led them into the dining room and to the right where a private booth was set up with half a dozen tiny candles, a pretty pink-and-white floral centerpiece, a bottle of white wine in an ice bucket, and a dozen red roses bundled with greenery on the table.

Mason picked them up and handed them to her. "For you."

She leaned in and inhaled their heady scent. "Thank you. They're beautiful."

"Like you."

The hostess smiled. "I hope everything is to your liking, Mr. Moore."

"With her here, it's perfect."

Sierra's heart fluttered and melted all at the same time. "Mason, this is . . . wonderful."

"I want you to remember our first date."

The hostess left them alone.

Sierra slid into the booth, followed by Mason.

She set the flowers on the table, brushing her fingers over the delicate petals, and turned to Mason. "My favorite memory of you is when we rode out to that pretty spot along the creek, tied up the horses, and swam in that little pool of water, then laid out in the sun, just talking and being quiet."

"That was a good day. I wanted to kiss you so bad."

"I wanted you to kiss me, but you didn't."

"I was older than you. I didn't want to take advantage."

"You're still older than me," she pointed out, teasing.

"Yeah, but I grew out of stupid and I know what I want now. Back then, I didn't want to mess up our friendship."

"And now?"

"Now I want to grow our friendship, strengthen it, make it better."

Good answer. She wanted the same thing. "I guess when you're young you think it's one or the other. Friends or lovers. But a real relationship is built on that friendship. Everything you add to it only makes it better. Without the friendship, how can you have real trust and intimacy?"

Mason pulled the wine from the bucket and poured two glasses. She took hers and clinked it to the one he held up. "To building on our friendship."

Feeling nostalgic, she reminisced about the past. "I don't know how we got from the cute guy next door who let me come over whenever I wanted to ride horses and just hang out to you being the man who goes out of his way to take my kids' minds off the move, a new school, and missing their father, getting me a dream job, and taking me out to dinner with flowers and candlelight."

Mason settled back into the cushion. "I liked being your friend. You were easy to talk to and be with despite the draw we both felt but let simmer in the background. You liked to have fun and ride and just enjoy yourself."

"And yet, we never got together."

Mason's smile dimmed. "I blame Amy. She tagged along more often than not."

Sierra put her elbow on the table and planted her chin in her hand. "She had a mad crush on you."

"And I didn't want to hurt her feelings. Because you knew she had a crush on me, you never seemed open to allowing yourself to want more between us."

True. "She's my sister. She was in your class at school, and I was two grades behind, so she seemed like the girl you'd want."

"And yet, I liked you. She was . . . don't take this the wrong way, but too high maintenance and fussy and needy."

Sierra frowned and laughed under her breath at the same time. "All true. Poor Amy. That's not very flattering."

"Some guys don't mind. It doesn't appeal to me. She showed off and constantly wanted my attention. At first, it was flattering. But then it got old. You always seemed so secure in your skin."

"Oh, believe me, I went through that awkward stage where I thought everything was wrong with me."

"Amy fussed and complained about all that stuff. If she didn't like herself, how was anyone else supposed to like her?" He held up a hand. "Don't get me wrong, she grew out of it, but at the time, seeing you two together, you were so much easier to be around. I could be myself with you. Amy seemed to have a vision of what I'd be with her that didn't fit who I am. Does that make sense?"

Sierra actually got that very well. It was what she realized about her marriage. She'd built up a vision of what she and David would look like together as a married couple. In reality, they were the same people they'd always been.

"You can't make someone like you, or even love you." She'd learned that a long time ago. "You can try to live up to their image of you, but in the end, you are who you are." In the end, David didn't want her.

"You see me for who I am because we have history. You knew me before I was successful." Mason glanced up, then back at her. "I apologize for this." He cocked his chin toward the man walking up to their table.

"Mason, man, good to see you." The gentleman came right up, hand extended to shake Mason's.

"Allen. It's been a while. I'd like to introduce Sierra Silva. Sierra, Allen. A former client."

Sierra took the gentleman's hand. He glanced down at her other hand, looking for a wedding ring she hadn't worn in more than six months. "I see Mason's untangled you from the dummy who let you go."

Mason took her wrist, drew her hand away from Allen's, and linked his fingers with hers. "She's not a client. She's my date."

Allen frowned. "Lucky you. Disappointing for me."

Mason chuckled. "Last I saw you, you and a beautiful brunette of your own were on your way to Fiji for a couple of weeks to celebrate your divorce."

"And celebrate we did." The gentleman turned solemn. "Listen, I won't take up your time, but my ex is back with more gripes about how I'm not keeping her in the lifestyle I afforded her while we were married and she wants more child support. If Sabrina wants horseback riding lessons, fine, but I want to be the one to take her."

"Got it," Mason agreed.

"Sorry to interrupt your date with this."

"No worries. Make an appointment with Louise, we'll get this settled."

"Appreciate it." Allen gave Sierra a soft smile. "Nice to meet you."

Mason nodded and waited for the gentleman to take his leave. "Sorry. I was hoping we'd have the evening to ourselves and some privacy."

"It's fine. You obviously helped him out of a rough situation."

Mason chuckled. "Allen loves his daughter. He loves his ex. They just can't seem to have a civil conversation anymore. Not that I blame her; she did catch him kissing her best friend, made a scene, it ended up going viral on someone's Twitter. A 'friend' posted a video of the epic yelling match between the two women, Allen standing there dumbstruck not knowing what to do until he ultimately had to physically separate them before the cops showed up."

"Oh man, that sucks."

"I have dealt with so many people who lost their minds in the moment and regretted it almost as soon as it was over. Allen begged his ex to forgive him. She couldn't. Not after he'd embarrassed her in public like that." Mason sighed. "It's too bad, too, because if they'd tried, they might have come out of it stronger."

"And Sabrina wouldn't be caught in the middle."

Mason nodded, looking solemn, then took a sip of his wine.

Sierra went on, "Your job is so complicated and emotionally straining."

"My clients aren't happy to be ending their relationships; the anger is just a mask for the pain. Mostly they're hurt and bitter. They think they want revenge, but what they really want is to be able to move past the pain and anxiety over starting a new life without their partner. Change is scary. Most of them are better off after the divorce, emotionally, but it takes time and perspective to get there."

She squeezed his hand. "It took me a while to get there after David's death. I felt rocked by it. I didn't know how to go on without him. I was his wife. I didn't know how to be a widow and what was expected of me. I just knew I was still a mom and I needed to be there for the boys. But I still needed to figure out how I felt and what I wanted now that my life had changed."

"And then the fire happened and your life is up-ended again."

She appreciated that he got it. "So much is still in flux, but I feel anchored here now."

Mason brushed his thumb against her skin, sending ripples of warmth through her hand and up her arm, spreading out to every part of her body. "I hope I'm part of the reason you feel at home here again."

"It seems like everything in my life has been hard lately. Then you came back into my life and I don't know . . . it just seems so easy to be with you."

"Because we're friends?"

"That part's always been easy. Hiding the attraction in front of the kids is a bit harder."

Mason leaned in close, his breath whispering against her cheek. "You don't have to hide anything tonight." His lips brushed her skin in a light kiss that left her wanting even as every nerve in her body lit up with lust.

Mason sat back and smiled at their waitress. "We need another minute to decide what we want."

Sierra didn't need even a second to know she wanted Mason.

The sexy smile he gave her said he knew it, too.

She took a fortifying sip of her wine, picked up the menu, and tried to concentrate on the words and not every breath Mason took, or the way his arm brushed hers when he opened his menu.

"They do a great steak. The potatoes au gratin are amazing. But you might like the roasted chicken with white wine sauce. It comes with a side of mac and cheese. I know you can't resist that." He knew her all too well.

"I kind of want it all."

Mason turned and locked his gaze on her. "You can have anything you want." He let that hang for a moment and her heart beat faster and her breath hitched when his gaze dipped to her mouth. "I'll get one. You get the other. We'll share." His blazing blue eyes met hers again. "What do you say?"

"Yes. Okay." She had a feeling she was answering a question he hadn't asked, but needed to be answered all the same.

"You make it hard to concentrate."

His deep voice and the thoughts he invoked did the same to her. "You make me think about all the things I've been missing."

His eyes darkened with desire and the sexual tension grew thick and heady between them. She pressed her thighs together to ease the ache of it, but she didn't take her eyes off his gorgeous face.

"You're coming home with me tonight, right?"

"Yep." The word popped off her lips.

He chuckled, humor and frustration all packed into the light sound. "Why didn't I think to just make you dinner at my place?"

To ease the tension and make him smile, she teased, "Well, you can't be brilliant *all* the time."

This time the laugh was straight from his gut and filled with self-deprecation. "Don't tell my clients."

"Cross my heart."

His gaze dipped to the V in her dress. "Your heart is what always drew me to you. Your ability to always be kind amazed me."

She tried. "I imagine your clients don't come to you with a lot of kindness for their exes. I'm sure dealing with their anger and demands all day can get to you."

"I have to say, coming home and seeing you and the boys every night for a few hours erases everything bad from my day."

That touched her deeply and brought a sheen of tears to her eyes. "I appreciate that, Mason. I find myself looking forward to seeing you at the end of the day, too. The second I walk in the door, the boys are asking to go to your place."

"I hope that doesn't change." A suspicious edge tinged that nice sentiment.

She didn't have time to wonder about it, or second-guess why she thought she heard something in his words that maybe wasn't there. The waitress approached the table and Mason placed their order, then refilled her wine glass.

* * *

They enjoyed the rest of the evening, talking about their day, people they knew from the past that Mason was still acquainted with, plans to take the boys on a long ride and picnic over the weekend, and eating and sharing the amazing food.

Sierra loved reconnecting with Mason, sharing a simple but lovely meal, and focusing on each other. He asked questions, trying to fill in the pieces he didn't know about her life in Napa. He didn't shy away from the fact she'd been married to David. He didn't mind that David naturally came up in conversation. In fact, he asked about him, which made it easier to remember they'd once been friends and Mason missed him, too.

In all the time since David's death, she finally found a kind of peace about his absence. Talking to Mason about him settled her in a way that she'd tried to find this past year, but it had seemed so elusive. Now she got it. No one talked to her about David. They all tiptoed around the fact that he was dead. They stopped asking if she was okay or offering condolences because they didn't want to make her sad. But talking about the good times and fond memories of David with Mason made her miss him and, at the same time, lessened her grief.

Mason had no trouble filling her in on his family, either. She asked a ton of questions because she wanted to know more about him. She wanted to know everything about his life now.

"So my dad joined a yoga class after he hurt his hip. My mom thought it was a good idea. She dropped him off, went to run an errand, then came back, walked in to pick him up, and found him bent over with a twentysomething hottie leaning over him from behind helping him with the pose and stretching his hips. She says my dad had a grin on his face and was enjoying himself far too much. She dragged him out of there and wouldn't let him go back."

Sierra busted up laughing. "She knows the lady was just doing her job, right?"

"Mom told him if he went back to her, she'd hire me to represent her in the divorce."

Sierra laughed even harder. "Oh no. I take it he didn't go back."

"Oh, he went back, but to a class that has a male instructor. The guy is very handsome according to my mother. Based on my father's frowns about that, I don't think he likes my mother sticking around to watch the class and stare at the instructor."

Sierra's cheeks hurt from smiling so much. "Oh dear. So I guess you might be working for your father if she goes after the sexy instructor."

Mason shook his head. "I'm staying out of it."

"How is your dad's hip now?"

"Better. He goes to a massage therapist once a week, too. It's helping. He's moving better. He hates being inactive. Worse, he hates that he can't ride the way he used to."

"Do they come to the ranch often?"

"Less and less, but we keep in touch. They're always hounding me to settle down and start a family." Mason rolled his eyes. "Settle down? Like I'm out partying all the time or something."

"It's not easy to find someone. I guess you're more aware of what you want and don't want because of your job."

"Believe me, I've learned that real kindness means more than a pretty face and a fat bank account."

"I've learned that trust and the truth are really important, too."

Mason signed the check the waitress discreetly left on the table during their talk, then turned to her. "The truth is, Sierra, I can't wait to get you home."

She put her elbow on the table, planted her chin

in her hand, and gave him a sexy smile. "Well, what are you waiting for?"

Mason slid out of the booth and held his hand out to her. She took it knowing she was taking the next step in their relationship and a giant step out of her past and into a future she got more excited about each and every time she was with Mason.

Chapter Seventeen

Amy thought she had a plan to keep four kids happy until bedtime but that plan went south the second smoke filled the kitchen and the smoke detector blared through the house.

Distracted with getting the kids to clean up for dinner, the organic pizza she put in the oven had burned to a crisp.

The blaring sound made Danny's and Oliver's eyes go wide with terror.

Oliver freaked and ran out the front door screaming, "The house is on fire!"

Danny followed him at a dead run.

Amy tossed the burnt pizza on top of the stove and ran after them. She found Oliver in the yard sitting in the middle of the lawn with his knees bent, arms tightened around them, crying. Danny stood next to him patting his shoulder, cooing, "It's okay."

She knelt next to Oliver and brushed her hand over his hair. "Sweetheart, I'm so sorry. There's no fire, only a very burnt pizza."

Oliver looked up at her, bottom lip trembling. "Is anyone dead?"

Her heart broke. "No, honey. Everyone is fine." She glanced up at P.J. and Emma standing at her side. "See, your cousins are fine and there's nothing but smoke in the house." She wiped at Oliver's tears with her thumbs. "Come on. Let's see if I have another pizza in the freezer and get that smoke detector to stop that incessant buzzing."

The last tear spilled down Oliver's soft cheek. "It's scary."

Her heart was still pounding. "I know, but it's all over now."

She picked up Oliver, hugged him close to reassure him, and stood. She walked back into the house, scrunching her nose at the burnt smell and smoke still lingering in the air.

"P.J., Emma, and Danny, grab a magazine off the table and wave it in the air and try to get the smoke to blow out the door." She set Oliver on a stool at the counter and picked up the burnt-to-a-crisp disk from off the stove. "I'll be right back, sweetheart. Let me get rid of this." She walked out the back door and went to the trash bins on the side of the house. She dumped the ruined pie into the trash and slammed the lid.

Where the hell is Rex? He should have been home an hour ago.

Of course he picks tonight to leave me alone with four kids.

She walked back into the house and sighed. All four kids were running around, flapping magazines pretending to be helicopters and windmills. Oliver seemed back to his old self. Thank God. The house smelled slightly better, but the smell of smoke would linger for a while.

She kicked the oven door shut, found another pizza in the freezer, tossed it on the counter, and snagged the phone from the charger. She hit the speed dial and waited three rings before Rex finally picked up.

"Where are you?"

A long silent pause on the other end made her stop and think she should have at least said hello first.

"I can't talk right now. I'll call you back in an hour." The clipped tone set her off.

"I'm here with four kids and no backup. I need your help."

"Hold on."

Her patience nearly snapped when she heard his muffled "Please excuse me for a moment. I need to take this," and a woman said, "Sure. No problem."

She got even angrier when it took him another minute to come back on the line.

"What is going on?" he demanded in a hushed whisper.

"Who was that woman?"

"A client."

"You didn't say anything about a business dinner tonight."

"I called you three times today and left you two messages, but apparently you were too busy to listen to them."

She couldn't refute that. After she picked up all four kids at school, took them to the park to play, out for frozen yogurt, got them back to the house to wash up and do homework, then started dinner, she hadn't even looked at her phone . . . until now.

"Can you get out of the dinner and come home and help me?"

"No." He didn't say anything more.

"But I have Sierra's boys here. They're sleeping over. It's crazy. I burned dinner, the smoke alarm went off, and Oliver freaked out."

"I'm sure you've got it covered. I need to get back to my client."

"That's all you have to say."

"We've been over this too many times to count at this point. According to your master plan, the kids were supposed to be at the park carnival thing tonight. I figured you weren't expecting me, since you didn't tell me about it, or even ask if I wanted to go with you."

"Of course we wanted you to go, but there was no way I was taking four kids on my own."

"And you prove my point for me. You thought you'd be doing that alone and changed your plans without telling me a thing."

The anger and frustration in his voice only made her angrier. "So I'm expected to plan your schedule, too."

"I thought we were a family. One that does things together. But lately, you're so busy keeping busy you forget I exist. It took you over an hour to realize I wasn't home at the usual time. Instead of listening to my messages, you interrupt my business meeting and insinuate I'm out with a woman behind your back."

True. Still . . . "It's not like you're hot for me when you get home."

"Most of the time you don't notice I'm even there unless you need me to do something with the kids. It's all I can do to get you to stop whatever you're doing to kiss me hello. It used to be that I couldn't leave or come home without kissing you. Now, it feels like it's just one more chore for you to do. Most of the time, it doesn't make even one of your lists."

True. Damnit. This wasn't all her fault. "That's not fair."

"I'm the first one who'll say no, it's not. I used to have a wife. Now I've got the mother of my kids. You're so wrapped up in that, you don't have time for anything else, including me, and while I get it, I'm tired of it."

That scared her all the way to her soul. "What are you saying?"

"Something needs to change. We've talked about it to death, but you refuse to cut back and spend more time at home. Your priorities don't include me. My needs and wants rank dead last to the kids and their activities and you wanting to make it seem like we've got the perfect life. The photos are great, Amy, but have you ever noticed I'm not in most of them? Where are the ones of us doing things as a family?"

She didn't know what to say.

"We planned tonight as our first date night in God knows how long. Do you remember that?" He didn't give her a chance to respond. "But instead of putting that on your precious calendar, you scheduled yet another thing for the kids to do."

"The park carnival only happens once a year. I thought the kids would love it, but then Sierra asked if I could watch her boys, too."

"That just sounds like excuses to me about how unimportant our date was to you. *I* was looking forward to it. I had a reservation and a plan to seduce my wife. But she wasn't interested. She made other plans. So I made other plans, and I need to get back to them. At least my boss will appreciate my extra effort."

Desperation seized her heart. "Rex, please. Come home, we'll talk about this."

"I've said everything I have to say. You know how I feel. I know you're not going to change. Maybe it's time I did something about it."

"What are you talking about?"

"You're always complaining you have no time to yourself. You obviously don't want to spend it with me, so maybe we fix that and I take my fair share of time with the kids."

She turned her back on the kids who were tearing pages out of the magazines and making them into paper airplanes and tossing them all over the living room. "Are you saying you want a divorce?" She kept her voice low, so the kids didn't hear her say that last word she'd never thought would come out of her mouth when talking about her and Rex. They loved each other. They swore they'd be together forever. They promised that nothing would ever come between them.

"I'm telling you that if something doesn't change *now*, it's not looking good for us."

She stood stunned, listening to the dead line.

He'd hung up on her.

What the . . .

How did this all become her fault?

She glanced at the color-coded calendar.

Green for sports.

Blue for art class.

Orange for music class.

Red for birthday parties. The bold color to help her remember to pick up a gift.

Purple items for the things she volunteered to do: working in the kids' classrooms, school and community events.

She had a rainbow collage of events listed that should have made her life feel full and satisfying. So why did she feel like a bedraggled athlete coming in last at the end of a triathlon every day? She made it through, but she didn't feel like a winner. She didn't feel like she'd enjoyed it.

"Aunt Amy, I'm hungry." Danny stared up at her, his finger in his mouth.

"Don't put your fingers in your mouth. They're dirty."

Danny pulled his finger free and showed her the long paper cut that welled with blood and dripped down to his palm. "It hurts."

Yeah, every accusation Rex lashed her with tonight felt like a stinging paper cut, throbbing in her mind. But when he insinuated they were headed for a divorce and it was all her fault, she felt the dagger to the heart.

Amy fought back tears, her anger and frustration, along with the fear and uncertainty about the future.

She wanted to fix this, but also felt paralyzed, because it all overwhelmed her.

She'd been dealing with those feelings for months. Because she liked everything perfect and organized, trying to untangle her life only made it seem that much harder to do, so she didn't do anything but get through the next marathon day.

Right now, she needed to feed four kids and get them settled for the night.

As always, the kids came first and she came last. She got that's what happened when you had kids.

Most days, she didn't mind. But right now, she'd like a few hours to herself to think about everything going on in her life instead of what fruit or vegetable she'd serve with the pizza and how many bedtime stories it would take to get the kids to go to sleep.

"Can I call my mom?" Danny asked.

Sierra was probably having the night of her life out with Mason at a fancy restaurant that probably didn't even serve chicken nuggets and had linen napkins and fancy cocktails.

Amy desperately needed an adult beverage right now.

"Let's fix that cut. You can call her after dinner." She held her hand out to her nephew and walked with him to the bathroom, leaving the other three loud children tossing paper airplanes trying to outdo one another with the distance they got on their throws.

She didn't feel like she was getting anywhere but older in her life.

Chapter Eighteen

Mason kicked the front door closed, tugged Sierra's hand to get her to turn to him, then took her mouth in a searing kiss that made his heart slam into his ribs, then beat double time. She tasted like wine and honey. Sweet on his tongue. A fire in his arms. She gave back everything he poured into showing her how much he wanted her.

He'd waited so long to have her all to himself and in his arms like this.

He didn't want to waste a second of it. And yet, he had all night to take his time.

She hooked her leg around his thigh, her arms locked around his neck. He grabbed her ass and pulled her in close. About to pick her up and carry her to his bedroom, she jolted and pushed away when her phone rang.

She sucked in a much needed breath and smiled up at him. "Sorry. It's probably the kids calling to say good night."

Reluctantly and with a lot of effort, he let her loose.

She swiped the screen to accept the video call and held up the phone so the boys could see her. "Hey, you guys. Are you having fun?"

"Aunt Amy set the house on fire," Oliver announced.

"What?" Sierra gasped. "Are you all okay?"

"Everyone is fine," Amy yelled. "I burned a pizza, not the house."

Sierra's shoulders sagged with relief. "Sounds like you had some excitement. What else did you do today?"

"All kinds of stuff. I won the airplane-flying contest and ate the most pizza." Danny beamed his mother a smile. "P.J. beat me on the race car game. Emma wanted us to play tea party, but there wasn't anything in the cups, so we went out back and played on the swings. P.J. can go really high."

"You've been busy. I hope you helped Aunt Amy clean up."

"We did. First one to finish their area got to pick the books for bedtime. I won."

"Awesome." Sierra's adoration for her boys and their accomplishments showed in her bright eyes. "Did you brush your teeth and wash up for bed?"

"All done." Danny leaned in close to the screen. "Where are you?"

With nothing but a blank wall behind her, she had no trouble lying. "At home. I'll be there first thing in the morning. We'll have breakfast with Aunt Amy, then come home."

"Can we go riding with Mason? He said he'd teach me to go backwards."

"Why do you want your horse to go backwards?"

"Cuz."

Sierra glanced at Mason. He nodded that he'd take the boys horseback riding. "I'm sure Mason will take you and Oliver riding again. Now I want you to be good boys, be quiet while Aunt Amy reads books, and go right to sleep so you'll be rested and ready to ride with Mason tomorrow."

"Okay." Danny yawned. "You'll be here in the morning. Right?"

"Yes, honey. I'll be there."

"Night, Mommy." Oliver blew a kiss.

Sierra pretended it smacked her on the cheek and smiled. "Night, baby. I love you both. Make sure you thank Aunt Amy for a great day."

The boys waved good-bye and Amy took the phone and turned away from the screen, making sure the boys left. "I hope you had a good night because four kids all going in different directions is chaos."

Sierra chuckled. "*You* said you wanted to keep them for the night."

"Because I don't know how to say no. Except to Rex. Who's pissed at me, by the way."

"Because you offered to babysit the kids?"

"No. Yes. We were supposed to have date night and I forgot."

"Oh, Amy, I'm sorry."

"Yeah, well, it is what it is. So while my relationship is falling apart and yours is heating up, I expect details over breakfast about your fab night because I'm living vicariously through you until Rex decides if he's going to keep me or not."

Sierra stared at her sister stunned, then found her words. "Um, I'm sure Rex just got caught up and said some things he didn't mean."

"Oh, he meant them." Amy waved it all away. "Sorry. I'm bumming you out on your hot date. You're still with him, aren't you?"

Sierra turned the phone so Amy could see him standing next to Sierra.

Amy covered her face with her hand and shook

her head. "Oh god. I'm an idiot. Go back to . . . whatever you two were doing. I've got the kids. Don't worry about anything. See you in the morning." And just like that Amy hung up, and Sierra and Mason stared at each other.

Sierra's eyes filled with worry. "I had no idea she and Rex were having trouble."

"Me, either. She always seems so . . . on it." He shrugged. "I'm sure they'll work it out."

"I hope so."

Mason wanted to erase everything from her mind and bring her back to him. To their special night together. A night years in the making. He wanted her only thinking of them.

"The kids are fine. Amy and Rex will work out their own problems. Tonight, let's focus on us, because I finally have you all to myself. And I don't want to waste a second of it."

Chapter Nineteen

Sierra stared into Mason's eyes, awed by the depth of sincerity and desire filling them.

Had any other man ever looked at her like that?

In that moment, she let any reservations that they were moving too fast fall away. This was Mason. Her friend. The guy she'd nearly called off her engagement for on a flicker of hope they might have something worth holding on to forever.

And now here was the chance to find out.

He held her face in his hands and stared deep into her eyes. "I've been waiting for you and to feel this way again for a long time." His lips touched hers in a soft kiss that packed a punch of longing and need so raw it echoed through her.

She wrapped her arms around his neck, went up on tiptoe, pulled him close, and took the kiss deeper, letting the walls around her heart drop and allowing him and the rush of feelings in.

Excitement.

Need.

And yes, love.

New and blossoming.

Fragile but hardy, with the possibility to thrive if they nurtured it.

So Sierra let go of everything and focused on

them and the way he made her feel. Safe. Wanted. Needed. Important and vital.

A thrill of excitement swept through her as his hands slipped beneath the hem of her dress and brushed up her thighs.

Thoughts about cellulite, unshed baby weight, and pudge flew out of her head the second his hands clamped on her ass and he groaned with pure male appreciation. He effortlessly lifted her snug against him, her legs wrapping around his waist bringing her aching center into exquisite contact with his hard length. She tightened her legs and rubbed against him.

Mason broke the kiss and squeezed her ass. "You're killing me."

"Wait 'til I get your clothes off."

Without a word, he gave her a searing kiss and walked out of the entry, hopefully to his room. Though she didn't much care where they landed so long as he didn't stop kissing and touching her.

It had been way too long since she felt like a desirable woman. It had been too long since her body felt this alive.

And she reveled in it.

Mason clamped his hands at her waist and nudged her off him. Her feet hit the floor and the backs of her legs brushed against the bed. He dipped his hands under her dress again and pulled it up and over her head. The slinky material sailed across the room and landed in a puddle, looking like a pale purple flower on the dark hardwood.

His gaze swept down, taking in her pink lace bra and the matching cheeky panties that she had to admit were well worth the splurge because they made her ass look great. The blaze of heat in his eyes said he thought so, too.

She slipped her hand inside his suit jacket and pushed it down his arms. He shrugged it off while she attacked his dress shirt buttons. He pulled the tie over his head. She took in his broad chest and wide shoulders while he undid the cuffs, took the shirt off, and tossed it.

She swept her hand from his shoulder to his pecs and over his heart. It thumped wildly against her palm. The heat from his skin seeped into hers.

Eyes locked, he sank his fingers into her hair and held her head. "I've wanted this for so long."

"Me, too." Deep inside, she realized she *had* been waiting for this. For him.

They had a connection. She felt it vibrate through him and into her where her hand pressed to his chest. She felt it in the way he looked at her. She couldn't deny that whenever they were in the same room, something drew her to him.

She'd fought it for so long.

They were friends.

That meant something to her.

But this . . . It meant so much more than she ever anticipated or expected.

So she dove in, knowing everything would be different. Better.

They'd be connected in a new way. And she hoped it turned into even more and lasted.

Her heart was ready to move on and find happiness again.

The last of their clothes disappeared in a blur of

hands needing to touch flesh, their lips seeking a tempting taste, and their bodies desperate to be laid out and pressed together. When Mason rose on his hands and stared down at her, his hard shaft sinking into her beckoning core, she felt the depth of their joining all the way to her soul.

He leaned down, kissed her reverently. Time stopped and she took in the moment and branded this amazing feeling on her heart.

Then he moved and she lost herself in the rhythm, the feel of him deep inside her body and soul, remembering what it felt like to be loved and freed and lost in ecstasy and to come back to herself with a man holding her close, safe and protected and loved.

She wallowed in the heady buzz and snuggled into his side, letting the quiet surround her and the newfound joy fill her up.

She pressed a kiss to his chest. "It doesn't get better than this."

"I accept that challenge."

She laughed, loving the sound of his deep, completely satisfied and sated voice, and the assurance he put into those words.

Just as she was about to fall asleep, comfortable and happy in his arms, she found herself beneath him once again, thoroughly convinced that with him, everything just got better and better.

In the morning, he proved it again.

* * *

Sierra was still smiling, every nerve still tingling with the memory of their first night together, when she knocked on her sister's door to pick up her kids feeling like a completely new woman.

In the very back of her mind she wondered, with everything that had happened these last two years, if this abundance of joy would last or whether the other shoe would drop soon.

Chapter Twenty

S ierra stared at Amy and didn't know what to say about her frazzled state. It had been years since she'd seen her sister in complete disarray. Hair a mess, no makeup, her eyes swollen and underscored by dark, puffy circles, she appeared to have smeared pancake batter or butter or both on her black pajama shirt. Her sister didn't usually rub her dirty hands on her clothes. No, she'd have her handy Wet Wipes standing by for such things.

"What happened to you?" Anxiety tightened her gut. She worried Amy was in the midst of some sort of crisis.

Amy's bloodshot eyes narrowed. "I gave up my life to have kids."

Those kids were making a ruckus in another room down the hall.

Amy's gaze bore into her before moving to Mason standing behind her. "Looks like you two had a good night."

Sierra couldn't help smiling up at Mason, thinking of the wonderful night they'd spent in each other's arms and what it meant going forward.

Looking back at her sister, she felt a bit guilty. But not much. It was too hard not to feel this good.

Mason put his hands on her shoulders and squeezed.

"Yeah, you two look cozy now, but that won't last." Amy swung the door open wider, revealing Rex sitting on the couch, a blanket draped haphazardly across his lap as he rubbed the heel of his hand into his eye socket. He was still wearing what looked like yesterday's clothes: slacks and a wrinkled dress shirt. "The party's over."

"Amy, I'm not sure what's going on here, but I can take all the kids out to breakfast and give you and Rex some time alone."

Amy's eyes glassed over and filled with frustration and desperation. "I already made the pancakes." She combed her fingers into her hair, loosening the messy topknot even more. "It's fine. Everything is fine." The desperate tone didn't back up her words.

Rex turned and stared at her. "Everything is a mess." The announcement made Amy pale.

Yes, the house looked wrecked. The kids had done a number on the living room. Toys littered the floor. The coffee table was covered in scraps of paper. A paper airplane stuck out of the leaves of a potted plant by the window. The kitchen looked like a tornado hit it. Frozen pizza boxes lay discarded on the counter. The makings for pancakes and eggs cluttered together at one end. Two pans were on the stove. And the house still smelled like burnt pizza from last night.

To Sierra, it wasn't so bad. Messy to the eye, but easily cleaned up. But this was Amy's house. She liked things in their place. Everything scrubbed clean and immaculate.

Amy herself looked like she was a second away from losing her shit.

Guilt settled in Sierra's heart. She wished she'd

known her sister wasn't exaggerating about the kids running wild. Overwhelmed, Amy had lost control of the situation.

Mason stepped into the house, taking charge. "I'll go get the kids to settle down and make sure they're dressed."

Amy stood immobile by the front door like she couldn't make a decision about what to do next.

The only way to get her sister back on track was to put things back to the way she liked them. Sierra tried to be normal and keep things light. "Morning, Rex. Can I get you a cup of coffee?"

Rex turned and stared over his shoulder but he didn't look at her; instead, he locked eyes with Amy. "Sure. That would be great."

Sierra went into the kitchen, got a mug from the cupboard, poured him a cup, added a dollop of milk like she remembered he liked it, took it to him in the living room, then went back to the kitchen.

Yep. Definitely taking the kids out.

With that settled, she put the kitchen to rights, tucking the food back in the fridge, then loading the dishwasher. She found some plastic wrap in a drawer, covered the bowl of pancake batter, and set it in the fridge for later.

"You can have breakfast for dinner. The kids will love that."

Amy hadn't moved from the entry. She stood there like a zombie staring at Rex's back like she could will him to fix this.

Clearly, they needed to talk.

Sierra could only imagine what was going on in her sister's mind knowing she and Mason walked in on this mess.

Sierra had never cleaned so fast in her life, but at her sister's look of pure appreciation when she finally did take her eyes off Rex and glanced at the kitchen, Sierra felt she'd helped. At least a little bit.

Mason appeared in the hallway entry, four kids lined up behind him. "Everyone is dressed, teeth brushed, hands washed. All the toys have been put away, sleeping bags rolled up, beds made. Let's go eat." He led the kids to the front door. Amy kissed her kids on the forehead as they passed and accepted the thank-yous from Danny and Oliver as they followed Mason and their cousins out to the car.

Rex set his coffee mug on the cluttered table, rose, and walked out the front door in his black dress socks without a word or glance for Amy.

Sierra went to her sister and wrapped her arm around her shoulders. Rex put the kids' booster seats in her SUV, kissed each of his kids, and got them settled in the back. He closed the door and stood with Mason, chatting. Their voices didn't carry, but they both looked serious.

"Do you think he's asking Mason to represent him in the divorce?"

Stunned by her sister's words, Sierra gasped and turned to face Amy. "Did he ask you for a divorce?"

"Not yet. But it's coming." Amy's forehead wrinkled with worry.

"Are you sure? Can't you guys work whatever this is out?"

Amy folded her arms across her chest. "I'm not sure it can be fixed. I've put everything I am into this family." Amy's sad gaze met hers. "I don't have anything left. I do everything I can to make them all happy."

But Amy wasn't happy. Not anymore.

She acted like she'd tapped all her resources and had nothing left.

"Oh, Amy. I feel that same way, too, sometimes. I don't want to wipe one more nose, solve one more problem, make one more school lunch, let alone give my husband the attention and affection he wants and needs. But it will pass."

Amy looked unconvinced.

Work, children, life could really take it all out of you.

But those frustrations were temporary.

Because then you'd have those moments where life filled you up. Your child did something that touched your heart. Your husband washed the dinner dishes, and damn, that was sexy as hell. A song on the radio reminded you of something from your past. Your first date. A dance at your wedding. A long drive you took, just the two of you. The kids made you something special at school and were so proud and excited to present it to you.

Their exuberant laugh made you laugh with them and wish that they laughed like that every day for the rest of their lives.

Your husband kissed you like it was the first time he realized he loved you all over again.

Amy got lost in the storm of life. She just needed to ride it out and find the calm.

Every relationship had ups and downs. They'd work this out and find their way back up to the peak again.

"You and Rex need to take a breath and talk this out."

"We talk *at* each other constantly. Nothing changes."

Sierra took Amy by the shoulders. "Then tell him how you really feel. Tell him you're unhappy. Tell him what you really want him to know. He can't read your mind." Sierra remembered all too well how she wished David would see everything roiling inside her when she needed him to, but he didn't. She wished she'd spoken up. This time, with Mason, she'd do better. She'd make their relationship a priority. "Rex knows you, but you can't expect him to know exactly what's going on in your head. You need to tell him."

Amy's hands came up, dropped, and slapped her thighs. "I don't know what I want." Amy sighed and hugged herself. "I'm tired." She glared at Rex. "I'd like to see him do everything I do for this family. Then he'd know how hard I work, how little time I have for myself."

"Great. Take a day off. Rex is home today. Let him take care of the kids. Go to the spa. I'm sure Heather can fit you in. Get a massage. Have a manipedi. Indulge in doing nothing but letting others pamper you."

Amy didn't answer.

"I'll take the kids to breakfast and have them back in about an hour and a half."

Amy nodded, turned, and walked down the hall toward her bedroom.

Sierra walked out onto the porch and met Rex on his way back to the house.

"How bad is it?"

She didn't really know. "You two need to talk."

"I've talked until I'm blue in the face. She doesn't hear me. She wants everything her way. I get she likes things a certain way, but I'm asking for some compromise and she won't budge." He raked his fingers through his disheveled hair. "I want more time with my family. I don't think that's too much to ask."

"I'm not sure your sleeping on the couch says you want more time with *her*."

"Yeah, well, when I got home last night, she had Emma sprawled in bed with her. I could have put Emma back in her bed, but what was the point. Amy's so exhausted, the last thing she wants to do is work things out with me. In her mind, everything will be fine once the kids are older. I can tell you, things haven't been fine in years. I'm tired of it."

"I said this to her, now I'm saying it to you. Tell her how you feel and what you want. Don't expect each other to know."

"Your sister has her whole life scheduled. I'll see if I can get an appointment." With that snarky comment, he walked into the house and slammed the door.

Sierra didn't take offense. His anger wasn't directed at her. She understood that his frustration got the better of him.

"Hey, sweetheart, you okay?"

She stared up at Mason, so completely taken by his sincerity and that gorgeous face. "I'm great." She touched her hand to his chest and smiled up at him. "I'm feeling a little smug for being this happy and guilty about it because my sister and Rex are having trouble connecting."

"They'll work it out."

"So he didn't ask you for legal advice?"

Mason's head snapped back. "No. He apologized for the uncomfortable scene and thanked us for taking the kids for a little while. He said Amy needed a break, she's just too stubborn to take one."

Sierra shrugged. "That's my sister."

"That's all the Silva sisters," Mason teased. "Stubborn."

She socked him in the gut, her fist striking nothing but lean, strong muscles. "Not nice."

"But true," he teased again.

"Are you sure you're up to taking four kids to breakfast?"

"I know the perfect place. They've got the best pancakes." He slipped his hand around her waist and drew her toward the car. "Plus, I get to spend my morning with you."

"Sweet talker."

He nuzzled his nose into her hair and kissed her head. "I'll be talking you back into my bed later."

"I think I'm going to owe you a nice reward after you've shown such patience and understanding this morning."

He squeezed her to his side. "I can't wait to collect."

Sierra smiled up at him as he held the car door open for her and she slipped into her seat.

Yeah, the beginning was the best part.

And just like that, she spun dreams of a future with him. A future that looked very different from the one she'd imagined with David. Mason treated her like she was exactly what he'd been waiting for. David made her feel like he'd settled for the simple life they'd created together.

She refused to let another man settle for her again. She wouldn't stand for lies. Spoken or unspoken. She wouldn't hide the way she felt or put her needs on the back burner to make someone else happy.

Sierra made sure the kids were all engaged with one another in the back as they passed some kind of cartoon cards back and forth before she quietly asked Mason, "Have you discovered anything about that thing I asked you to look into?"

Mason kept his eyes on the road. "My investigator is working on it, but I don't have anything concrete yet."

An uneasy feeling settled in her gut.

Did she really want to know?

Should she let well enough alone and just be happy with the new life she was creating for herself and the boys?

Maybe. But she didn't think the nagging feeling in her gut would ever go away if she didn't uncover the truth.

Chapter Twenty-One

Amy walked out of the bathroom wrapped in a towel, her hair brushed back off her face, and her skin pink from the exfoliating scrub she'd used in the shower.

Rex sat on the edge of the bed, wrinkling the comforter after she spent five minutes making it perfectly smooth. "We need to talk."

"Later. Right now, I'm going out. You need to take care of the kids today when they get back. I need a day." She sucked in a breath. "I'm taking a day."

Rex nodded. "Great. Fine. Take a day. But we still need to talk about what is going on between us."

Like she didn't know she was putting off their conversation. She hoped to find some calm and perspective at the end of a much-needed massage. This wasn't going away. They needed to work things out. But she needed a minute to get her head on straight.

One horrible thought made it difficult to do that, so she blurted out her worst fear. "Are you having an affair?"

All the air went out of him. His gaze stayed on the floor for a good ten seconds before he looked up at her again. "Is that what you think of me? You think that's the kind of man I am?"

She held her hands up and let them fall to her sides. The knot in her gut tightened. "I don't know what to think anymore. You spend more time at work than you do here."

"Amy, we've been through this. Why should I be here in this house alone when you're constantly out doing something with the kids?"

"Maybe if you were here, we'd stay here, too."

Rex shook his head. "Do you hear yourself? You put this on me. I'm not the one out there trying to impress everyone with how much I do with the kids, how great they are, or how organized I am and able to manage so much on my plate like it's easy."

"It's *not* easy!" She vibrated with frustration.

"I know. But your quest for perfection . . . It's changed you. You used to be fun." He stood and unbuttoned his wrinkled shirt. "When's the last time you had fun doing anything?"

She watched his fingers work the tiny buttons through the holes. Lust for her husband warred with her rising anger. She hadn't felt this way in a long time, but arguing with him, watching him fight for what he wanted and for them turned her on. It gave her hope, even in the midst of feeling like he was putting this all on her. "You get to be the fun parent. I'm the one who disciplines and has to do all the real work."

The shirt hung wide open, exposing his gorgeous chiseled chest. "Is that so? I guess my bringing home the paycheck and keeping a roof over our heads and food on the table isn't real work at all. It's just me being selfish and spending time away from you."

She sighed. "That's not what I mean."

They'd agreed when they decided to have children that she'd quit her job and be a full-time mom. They'd wanted their children to come home to a parent after school and not be stuck at some day care for hours. Financially, it made sense, because day care would have eaten up most of her salary anyway.

Amy didn't mind giving up the job. She just never expected taking care of the kids and the house would take up every waking moment and not leave her any room for herself.

She expected Rex to feel pressure as the sole breadwinner, but she never expected him to feel burdened by it, or that he'd think she didn't appreciate how hard he worked for them.

Rex threw up his hands and let them drop back to his sides. "You resent me for going to work. Then you resent me for not spending enough time with the kids and not paying attention to you. Well, I resent that you use my job as an excuse to make me feel guilty for not being here. I resent that you make your life and the kids so busy you don't have time for me. I resent that you think you and the kids have to be doing something for everyone to see instead of just hanging out together as a family. I resent that when I asked you to spend more time with me, to go out on a date, you volunteered to babysit your sister's kids instead."

Exasperated, she spit out the obvious. "She needed my help."

"She wanted an evening alone with the guy she's seeing. Great. Good for her. But if you had told her we had plans, she would have hired a babysitter or picked a different day. Better yet, *you* could have called the sitter to watch all the kids and made time for me."

"Four kids for one sitter," she scoffed.

"Why not? You have it in your head that you're the only one who can handle four kids. You're the only one who can volunteer in the classroom or organize the bake sale or 5k charity run. You're the only one who can do everything at school and home and for our kids. I'm really not sure what you need me for anymore." Rex stormed past her and slammed the bathroom door. A few seconds later, he turned on the shower.

They were home alone for the first time in months with at least an hour before the kids returned and instead of falling naked into bed, they were fighting.

Amy couldn't remember the last time they made love.

She kind of remembered it had been a pity fuck because she'd been tired but felt like she owed him because it had been so long.

And that was a terrible thought and way to show her husband she loved him.

Now, Rex couldn't be bothered to even notice her standing in front of him naked underneath only a towel. It was like he didn't even see her that way anymore.

He thought she didn't need him.

Well, she needed him to see what she was going through.

It wasn't that no one else could do all the things

she did; it was that she didn't know what she'd do if she wasn't doing those things.

She thought she'd be so happy being a mother.

And she was, except she didn't want to be just a mother because . . . what would she be when her kids didn't need her anymore? They were already getting so big and independent.

She micromanaged their lives, frustrating them because they wanted to do things their way and make their own decisions. Over the last year, she'd seen them trying to rebel against her rigid control. She didn't want her kids to resent her the way her husband did.

With her mind swirling with thoughts and feelings too overwhelming to deal with all at once, Amy dressed quickly, swept her hair into an easy ponytail, and did something she never thought she'd do—she left. She didn't let the guilt get to her that she hadn't said good-bye, leaving Rex to deal with the kids when they returned from breakfast. She didn't let herself second-guess her decision or turn around to do the responsible thing instead of the selfish thing.

It wasn't selfish to take care of herself.

She needed a day. A little time to think without the kids asking her for a million little things or feeling Rex's silence and the distance he kept building between them with his resentments.

She didn't smooth the comforter before leaving their room. She didn't even peek into the kids' bathroom to see what kind of mess four kids left after brushing their teeth. She walked right past Emma's and P.J.'s rooms without even a glimpse to see if their beds were made, toys tidied. Nope. She didn't bother to clean up the living room. She sent her sister a halfhearted silent thank-you for cleaning the kitchen, though the hasty job had left a few crumbs on the counter and the floor needed to be swept. She ignored everything, grabbed her purse and car keys, and left the house, her mind set on what she wanted to do today. And none of it involved cleaning up the mess in her life.

* * *

Heather had everything set up—last minute with little notice—thanks to a phone call from Sierra, when Amy walked in the spa steaming as much as the sauna. She tossed her purse on the counter, folded her arms on top of it, and blurted out, "My husband is an asshole."

"So glad I don't have one of those." The lie came easily, but it sent a wave of regret through Heather's system.

Amy tilted her head the way Sierra did sometimes, making Heather wonder if she had the same mannerism. "Are you really?"

It took her aback for a second. She'd longed to make a life with Hallee's father, but she'd known from the start she probably would never get what she really wanted, even if she deluded herself into thinking somehow, some way it would work out like magic. But magic wasn't real. "Um, I thought we were talking about you."

"Right. Today is about *me*. I want the works." She waved her hands in the air to encompass everything she was asking for but had no clue what that included.

Heather rolled her eyes. "I pulled off a full day of pampering for you. And you can use my employee discount, too."

"Really?" Tears glistened in Amy's eyes. "That's so nice."

"Oh god. You've really lost it if you're crying over a discount."

Amy sucked in a steadying breath. "You know me. I love a coupon."

Heather rolled her eyes. "Me, too." These days it was all she could do to get by on her salary and keep her growing little girl in shoes and clothes. Recently she'd been looking into preschools. She nearly choked on the monthly cost. She'd had a wonderful sitter these last few years at half the cost, but soon Hallee would need to be in a class, working on her primary skills before she hit kindergarten.

Heather reminded herself the exorbitant childcare costs wouldn't last forever but would diminish over time, especially when Hallee spent most of the day in public school and only a couple hours in day care until Heather picked her up after work. But that was a few years off.

She wished she had a husband and could work part-time or even be a stay-at-home mom. She'd love to give Hallee a brother or sister. She'd considered doing it on her own. Why not? She'd been doing just fine with Hallee. Of course, Hallee's father had provided financial support until recently. Now everything was different . . .

She stopped that train of thought and focused on her emotionally drowning sister.

"Come with me. I'll get you set up for your massage. That will relax you and maybe you'll start thinking more clearly about the amazing life you have with Rex and the kids."

Amy's shoulders sagged. "It is amazing. Most of the time. But lately . . ."

Heather hooked her arm around Amy's skinny waist and drew her away from the counter and toward the massage room. "Give yourself a break. There's no contest for raising your kids with the most skills and talents. So what if they can't play an instrument or score a million soccer goals? No one cares if they don't make the swim team."

"I don't want them sitting around the house staring at a screen all day."

"They're barely home at all."

"You sound just like Rex."

She didn't want her sister to think she'd taken sides. "Do you like doing all that stuff with the kids? Do they like it?"

Amy stopped in the massage room, turned, stared at her, and shrugged.

Her sister without words didn't compute. Amy had an answer for everything.

Heather took Amy's purse and set it on the chair. "Strip. Climb on the table. Put the sheet over you. Lie there. Think of nothing. Do nothing. Allow yourself to be quiet and still. Take it in, Amy, and see if you can let things go."

"I won't let Rex take the kids from me."

"From what Sierra said, he wants to spend more time with all of you."

"He was talking to Mason."

"I'm sure that was nothing but two friends catching up."

Amy's bottom lip wobbled. "I'm not so sure."

"Mason knows both of you. If anything, he'd try to talk Rex into making up with you. Everyone knows you two are meant to be together."

"I used to think so, too."

"You're best friends. You love each other. He makes you laugh and you spoil him. You two just work like it's supposed to."

"It used to be so good and easy."

Heather hugged Amy. "You're tired, sis. Take a breath. Relax. Things will get better. You'll see."

Amy sighed. "I hope so."

Heather couldn't help herself. Ever since she'd seen Mason, she couldn't stop thinking about him. "How did Mason look?"

"Good. It's Mason. He always looks great. He doesn't have two wild kids and an upset spouse to deal with."

"Do you think he wants a wife and kids?" Hope filled her heart and made it beat faster. She'd really love a real, grown-up relationship. Mason had always seemed the strong, steady, reliable type. She needed some of that in her life.

Amy found a halfhearted smile. "He sure looked like it earlier."

Heather had heard he'd been spending time with Sierra's boys lately, teaching them to ride and watching them when Sierra worked late. He and Sierra had always had an easy kind of friendship.

Mason might have always been the guy next door, but now Heather saw him in a whole new light. She wanted more than a friend in the successful lawyer. She wanted love. Uncomplicated and real and out there for everyone to see.

Maybe then her family would see that she'd grown up and found a real partner, a legitimately good man.

Wouldn't it be amazing to live on his sprawling ranch, have more kids with him, and have the security being married to a man like him would give her?

She'd thought a lot about Mason since their chat at the mailbox. Maybe she needed to spend more time at her mom's place and "accidentally" run into him again.

Maybe she'd ask him out on a date.

Heather tried to persuade Amy out of her glib outlook. "Rex doesn't want a divorce. You guys will work this out. He's your forever."

And maybe Mason could be mine.

With that thought in mind, she left her sister to her massage, went back to work, and started thinking up ways to put herself in Mason's path. If she wanted a different kind of life, one with a sexy, rich husband, then she'd have to go after it.

It would be so different from her last relationship.

Of course, she got Hallee out of that wild time, where rational thought and consequences meant nothing compared to what she wanted and how she felt in the arms of the man of her dreams.

God, how she missed him. And hated him. And wished for him, even knowing how bad they were for each other.

She couldn't help loving him.

She'd always love him.

But she needed to move on. And this time she'd

play it smart and get what she wanted for Hallee and herself.

A second chance at love.

And no one would keep her from having it.

Not this time.

Chapter Twenty-Two

Mason slid the papers his investigator gave him yesterday into his briefcase and wondered how he was supposed to break the news that they contained to Sierra. He wished she hadn't asked him to look into that damn loan, but he couldn't bring himself to refer her to someone else. Everything had been so great between them. He didn't want anything to mess it up. He didn't want to be the messenger who turned her suspicions into reality and ripped open a wound that might never heal.

David was gone, but the ripple of his mistakes continued to lap at Sierra's life, causing more grief and trouble than she deserved.

David's betrayal would tear a hole in Sierra's heart, make her rethink everything she thought about the man she married. She'd second-guess every detail of their marriage.

Was it real?

How long had David been lying to her?

What did she do now with the information?

What happened when her family found out?

He wished he could keep the revelations to himself and save her the heartache and mess this would create in her life.

Selfish?

Yeah.

It took him this long to finally get the woman of his dreams. They had a real shot at a life together. He wanted it. Bad.

He wanted to marry her. He wanted to be a father to her boys. He wanted to create a life and family with her by his side.

They could be so good together.

They would be, because he wasn't going to let David tear them apart from the grave.

"Hey. The boys are waiting to go down to the stables to ride." Sierra walked into his home office, her gaze going directly to the folders in his briefcase.

He closed the lid and turned all his attention to her and held his hand out. She took it without hesitation, smiled sweetly, then went up on tiptoe when she got close and kissed him. He poured everything he was feeling into the kiss. He wanted her to know how much he loved having her here. He wanted her to know how deeply he cared about her.

He loved her.

He loved her boys.

He suspected she loved him, too.

The night they made love for the first time, he'd felt it in the way she gave herself over to him, the way she held him, the way she made him feel.

He wrapped her in his arms and held her close, needing to feel her warmth and the way she snuggled into him whenever they were alone like this.

She looked up at him, her gorgeous brown eyes inquisitive. "Did you have a lot of work to catch up on this morning?"

"Not more than usual."

"Are you working on a particularly upsetting case?" She studied him, probably seeing the worry about what he knew about David but hadn't told her written all over his face.

"All my cases are difficult, which is why I'm so happy to have you and the boys here to make my day better."

"I'm happy here with you, too. More than I thought possible." Her candor surprised him.

"You mean that."

She rubbed her hands up his chest. "Can't you tell? We spend practically all our free time here."

He loved that they'd made themselves at home. Last night, they'd showed up with shopping bags. The kids did their homework at the table while he and Sierra made dinner. He wished they could do that every day.

"I wish I could spend more nights with you, but . . ."

She needed to be home with the boys. They stole a couple of hours alone this week when Dede took over bedtime with the boys while he and Sierra had a "date." They'd been in each other's arms burning up the sheets. Until she had to go home to her kids.

He took a chance and asked a bold question, knowing he might be pushing things too far too fast. "You feel at home here, right?"

She narrowed her gaze and stared at him. "Yes. Of course. Why? Are the boys making too many messes?"

He shook his head. This wasn't going the direction he wanted. "They're fine. They're kids. Messes come with the territory and they're really good about cleaning up the best they can." He held her hips and tried to get her to understand. "Do you ever think about staying here?"

Her smile dimmed. "I wasn't planning on going anywhere."

Mason shook his head. "No. I mean, do you see yourself living here. In this house. With me."

Sierra's hands clamped onto his arms. "We haven't been together that long."

"We've known each other since we were teens."

"I know. But . . ."

"But what? We're great together. The boys love it here. You love it here."

Her head tilted back and she stared up at the ceiling. "I'm still dealing with the house up in Napa and figuring out what we'll do next."

"Fair enough." He put one hand at the back of her neck and tilted her head back to look at him. "But have you considered making us more permanent and making this your home?"

The wobbly smile and nervous laugh gave him hope. "Mason, I would never presume to think that's what you want."

"That's exactly what I want." He squeezed her hips. "Have you thought about us long term?"

It took her a second to work up the courage to say, "Yes." The shy smile bloomed into a pretty blush on her cheeks. "We've always been friends. At one time, I thought maybe we could be more. But that was a long time ago. Now that we are together, it's . . ."

"What?"

"So much better than I imagined. We have this easy way about us. It's like everything is as it should be. I find myself leaving here and wishing I was still with you. I can't wait to see you every day. I think about you constantly." She brushed her hands up his arms. "When I watch you with the boys . . ." Her eyes turned dreamy and so sincere. "You're wonderful with them. They really love you. The longing and missing their father I always saw in their eyes has dissipated. Don't get me wrong, they still miss him and wish he was here, but now they have you to do things with them and show them how to be good men when they grow up. You filled a void in their lives. And in mine, too."

"I love you. I love them."

She sucked in a surprised gasp and leaned back in his arms, her eyes wide. "Is this happening right now?"

This time, he let loose a nervous laugh. "Yes. I want you to know how I feel about you. I want you to know I'm all in with you, the boys, and *our* life together."

"Mom! Are you coming, or what?" Danny called from the kitchen.

Mason deflated, knowing the rest of this conversation would have to wait. He let loose his hold on Sierra and gave her some space.

She fisted her hand in his tee and held him still, then called out to the boys. "We'll be right there." She locked eyes with him and said the words he needed to hear. "I love you, too. I think I have since the beginning."

He didn't know if she meant since they got together or from back in the day when their friendship had been just as easy and essential in his life as it was now.

"As much as I want to leap into this with you, I have to think about the boys. Their whole lives have been uprooted. They're adjusting to a new place, a new school, and making new friends. I'm not sure they're ready for more."

He opened his mouth to make his case, but she touched her fingers to his lips to stop him.

"I love that you want us to be part of your life *right now.* My heart says yes to all of it."

"But you want to talk to the boys, see where they're at with you and me and moving in here."

"Yes. They didn't get a say in their father leaving, or their house burning down, or us moving back here. Everything has just happened to them. If you and I are going to build a life together, I want them to have their say."

"I'm pretty sure they'll be happy here."

She smiled. "So am I. You're here."

"So are the horses and Tom." The boys loved the animals. Maybe he'd finally get a dog. The boys would love that.

"I think they like you more."

He caressed her face and kissed her softly. "I like *you* more than anything."

Her eyes softened as she took that in.

He kissed her again, knowing she understood how he felt and what he wanted. He could even appreciate that she wanted to do right by her boys and put them first. Too many of his clients never gave a thought to what their kids wanted.

"Mom! Seriously. You're taking forrrr-everrr."

Mason chuckled. "I think they're getting restless."

"When aren't they?" She stepped back. "I forgot to tell you. I got the insurance settlement for the contents of the house in the mail this morning. I planned to use it to get me and the kids a new place, but I guess I'll have to rethink that idea." She gave him a knowing smile, brightening his day even more.

"Put it away for the boys' college."

She nodded and tipped her head. "If your investigator would hurry up and tell me what happened to the fifty grand, I could make better decisions. I've still got the loan, plus the mortgage on the house to pay. Do I rebuild, then sell, or simply sell the property and get out from under it?" She held her hands up, then let them drop, unsure what she should do.

She tapped him in the gut. "I hope you have news for me soon."

He let her walk out of the office without him saying anything about the file in his briefcase and what he knew.

He should tell her. Now.

But he didn't want to ruin the day or have her think back to the first time he told her he loved her and then crushed her with bad news.

He'd waited this long to speak up. It could wait a little while longer. He didn't relish confirming what deep down she suspected about the father of her children. Guessing was one thing: knowing was another matter entirely.

Damn David for being a son of a bitch, for lying to his wife and going behind her back the way he did. He was just as bad as some of Mason's worst clients.

Mason vowed he'd never treat Sierra like that.

It suddenly struck him that if he didn't tell her the truth now, he was lying to her. And he'd never lie to her. He'd love her and the boys and give them the life David promised them but destroyed.

David had been a coward. Mason refused to be the same.

I need to tell her the truth. Now.

"Sierra," he called, walking out of the office before he stopped short and found Amy with her two kids in his living room.

"Look who stopped by." Sierra smiled at him but her eyes held a question.

"I'm so sorry to just show up. I just need to know . . . I have to figure this out," she rambled, then pushed her two kids toward Sierra. "Go with your aunt. I need to talk to Mason alone for a minute." The frantic energy coming off Amy made him wonder what happened to make her rush here to talk to *him*.

This time, he sent a questioning look to Sierra. She shrugged and gathered her niece and nephew into her sides. "Let's go see what kind of snack Mason has in the kitchen."

Mason called after her. "I need to tell you something."

Amy cut him off from going after Sierra. "Please. This can't wait."

"Later." Sierra gave him an apologetic smile and disappeared into the kitchen.

Mason huffed out a sigh and focused on Amy. "What can I do for you?"

"Did my husband speak to you about divorcing me?"

Taken aback, he shook his head. "No." He didn't want the kids to overhear, so he held his hand out toward his office. "Let's step in here and talk about this."

Amy walked in ahead of him, paced back and

forth in front of his desk, then turned to him. "He's planning to leave me. I know he is."

"Did he say so?"

"No. But since the weekend you took the kids to breakfast, we've barely spoken. He spends even more time at the office. He walks in the house, looks around, then just . . . I don't know, goes quiet."

"It sounds like you need to talk to Rex about this."

"I need you to tell me what happens if he wants a divorce. Will I get the kids? The courts side with the mother, right?" She paced away, then spun back around. "He can't take my kids."

Mason had never seen Amy this out of sorts and agitated. "Why don't you take a seat and tell me what is really going on between you and Rex?"

She fell into the chair and folded her arms across her chest, defensive and angry. "I do everything for him. I cook. I clean. I do all the shopping. The man hasn't bought a single article of clothing for himself in years. I take care of the kids. Is that enough for him? No."

"Is that what he said?"

In his practice, he'd learned that often people perceived the other person thought something they'd never said. They put words in the other person's mouth without ever really talking to them or asking how they really felt. Communication was the one thing people forgot to do when things fell apart. So many of his clients would still be together if they'd simply stopped assuming they knew what the other thought and started talking about it. And listened.

People didn't really know how to listen anymore.

They made everything about them. They wanted to be heard.

"He wants me to change the way I do things. He wants me to change my whole life. Like I'm the only one who has to change to make this work."

"What exactly does he want you to change?"

She sat up and shouted, "Everything!" She fell back into a pout and folded her arms.

Mason took a breath and tried again, making this about Amy, not Rex. "What do you want to do?"

She opened her mouth, then shut it. It took her a second to finally respond. "I don't know." She dropped her gaze to the floor, then looked back at him. "That's just it. I'm stuck. I created the life I wanted, but . . ."

"Now it's not working," he guessed.

"Yes. And no." She unfolded her arms and sat up. "I know something has to change, but it's just so much. What if it's not enough?" She went quiet, silently winding herself up again with the thoughts running through her head and making her eyes narrow. "I'm taking the kids. He can see them every other weekend. That's it."

Mason sighed. "Is that what you really want?"

"I want him to realize that my life isn't that easy. I don't sit around all day watching TV and eating ice cream. It takes skill to organize two kids, school, their activities, playdates, homework, managing the house, and getting dinner on the table. I'd like to see him do the grocery shopping. He'd never know what to buy organic and what kind of toilet paper we use. He doesn't have to think about the dozens of things I have on my plate, the decisions I have to make for our home and family. No. He just comes home, enjoys a home-cooked meal, plays with the kids and puts them to bed. You'd think that's the end of my day. You'd be wrong. I've still got to make lunches for the next day, make sure their homework is in their backpacks and not left on the table, put their instruments or sports gear together and by the door so we don't forget it, then clean up the dinner dishes and make sure the house is put to rights before I finally get to go to bed. I'm lucky if I get to watch a whole episode of . . . anything."

"Have you asked Rex to help with any of that stuff?"

"He doesn't know how to do it or doesn't do it right and I have to fix it. I might as well do it myself."

Mason raised an eyebrow. "He doesn't know how to wash the dishes?"

She rolled her eyes. "He loads the dishwasher completely wrong."

"So long as the dishes are in there, does it really matter? You'd get that time back?"

"You sound just like him. Why do I have to change the way *I* do things? Why can't he learn to do things the way I want them done?"

"Have you shown him how you want it done without it sounding like a lecture or that you're criticizing him?"

"Great. Now I'm a bitch for wanting things done right."

Mason held up his hand and shook his head. "No. That's not what I'm saying at all." He tried another way to make her understand. "I find that with most of my clients the one thing they neglect to do is express what they want when things are good. Instead, they let resentments and anger build up and then demand the other person do what they want. They fall into patterns and never take the time to break them by having a civil conversation."

"You want me to go to Rex and explain to him how to fill the dishwasher."

He held his hands out wide. "Why not? If you told him that if he took over that chore in the evening it would free you up to spend time with him, don't you think he'd be open to doing it for you? He knows you. He understands you like things done a certain way. I think if you told him it's important that he does it your way so you aren't anxious or worried about how it's done, you could relax and enjoy your time with him without feeling like you had to do everything yourself."

Her mouth scrunched with uncertainty tinged with anger, but he had her attention.

"I bet Rex could even pack the kids' lunches or do some of the other things, like get their gear together for the next day, if you showed him how you want it done."

She didn't say anything, but he could see the wheels turning.

"If what he wants is more time with you, then put some of the things from your plate on his. Consider trimming some of the things on your to-do list that maybe aren't so important to you or the kids. This is your life, Amy. If you aren't happy and fulfilled doing the things you're doing, let them go. Life is too short to be saying yes to everything only to be miserable doing them." He took the seat next to hers and put his hand on her knee. "You are an amazing mom. Your kids are fantastic. I see how much you love them. I know a little bit about how much work kids can be from having Danny and Oliver here. After just a few hours, I'm exhausted sometimes. But I love being with them, just like I know you love being with P.J. and Emma. You want them to have everything possible. Which is why I know you don't want to divorce Rex and take his kids away from him. You know your kids love and need their father. You love and need Rex. He wants things to change. So change by making him change with you. Talk to him. Teach him how to help you. Show him how to make you happy and less anxious."

"You mean less of a bitch."

"I doubt very much that's how he feels. I bet he wants to make things better for you but he doesn't know how. He's trying to tell you that, but doesn't know how to do that, either. You're wanting something from him but not telling him what that is and how you want it done.

"You guys are great together when you work together. Things have gotten complicated and busy and it maybe feels like things have taken over your life together and you're not really living it."

Tears gathered in her eyes. "Yeah. It feels like that. I try to make time for myself, for him, and it all gets away from me."

"You want to be everything to everyone. I've known a lot of women like you, who find it hard to say no. They take on everything. They are smart, capable, strong women just like you. And I have seen them find a new kind of happiness in taking back their lives."

"You mean after they divorce their husbands."

"Most of the time, yes. But what if you could find that happiness without losing the love of your life?"

They both caught sight of Sierra in the doorway. "He's right, you know. You both want to be together. That's worth fighting for, Amy."

Amy wiped the tears from her cheeks. "I didn't know you were eavesdropping."

"I came to see if it's okay if I take Emma and P.J. down to the stables, but I'm glad I heard Mason's sound advice. I could have used some of that with David."

"You two were having problems?" Amy didn't hide her surprise.

"Every couple goes through periods where things seem off. Most of the time, you right them by reconnecting. Talking. Other times, you let things go and then it seems like this *thing* between you. I get it, Amy. Relationships are hard. Some can't be salvaged. Mom will tell you that. She's been divorced three times. But you and Rex . . . You two can renovate your relationship."

Amy laughed at that turn of phrase. "Renovate, huh?"

"It's been a lot of years. It's time to revise the chore list, redo the one-on-one time you used to make a priority, and gut the schedule that leaves you no free time for yourself. You are important, Amy. Rex wants to make you a priority, he's just tired of trying to catch you coming or going all the time."

Amy wiped away a few more tears, then turned to Mason. "I'll take everything you've said under advisement. I'll talk to Rex. If this doesn't work"—she looked from him to Sierra—"will I get the family discount if I need a lawyer?"

Mason didn't know what to say.

Sierra laughed. "Subtle, Amy."

"Well, you've been kind of quiet about how much time you and Mason have been spending together. I know about the one date, but you've been stingy with the details about how it went."

Sierra radiated happiness. "Mason and I are very happy together. We're talking about plans for the future."

Amy sat up straight. "Seriously? How come I didn't know things were moving so fast?"

"Because I have to consider the boys and what they want."

Amy deflated a bit. "Yeah. I get that."

"So I'd appreciate it if you kept things quiet until Mason and I decide it's time to let the boys in on how serious our relationship is and that we want to make things more permanent."

Amy's eyes went wide. "Wow. Just wow. Like I knew you had a thing for each other, but this is so . . . great. I'm happy for you. Both of you."

Mason stood and went to Sierra, wrapping his arm around her. "Thank you. We're working toward something really special. I want the boys to be happy to be here with us."

"Are we staying here?" Oliver asked from the doorway.

Mason turned to him, then glanced at Sierra, who took over. "We're going for a ride."

"You said that forever ago." With slumped shoulders, Oliver walked to Mason and put his arms up to him.

Mason scooped the little guy up against his chest. "What's up, bud?"

"Can we go now? Ple-ease?"

Mason chuckled and tickled Oliver's softly rounded belly. "Yes. Let's go." He turned to Amy. "Want to stay awhile and let Emma and P.J. ride?"

"Sure."

Sierra put her arm around Amy's shoulders and led her out of the office. "It's going to be okay. You've got this. If anyone can reorganize their life, it's you."

Chapter Twenty-Three

Sierra looked around Amy's immaculate house and smiled. Things looked back to normal in the house even if she and Rex hadn't set their relationship back on the path to bliss. Tonight, she'd give them a chance to talk in peace without their two little ones listening.

"Emma. P.J. Aunt Sierra is here to take you over to Aunt Heather's for dinner."

Sierra loved that she got to spend more time with her sisters and the kids. She'd missed this.

"What time will Rex be home?"

"Half an hour if he isn't still avoiding me."

Sierra brushed her hand up Amy's arm and squeezed her shoulder. "You two will work this out."

Amy huffed out her frustration. "I told the kids' teachers I can only come in two days a week now. I was home today for the first time and didn't know what the hell to do with myself."

"Did you go for a walk? Read a book?"

Amy rolled her eyes. "I reorganized the hall closet."

"You'll get better at doing nothing. Maybe you'll find a hobby or something that you like."

"Easy for you to say. Everything comes easy to you. I always feel like I should be doing something."

"You need to learn to give yourself a break. Instead of organizing closets, meet Rex for lunch. Spend some time reconnecting with him."

"Like you've reconnected with Mason." A knowing twinkle brightened Amy's eyes.

"It seems it was a long time coming. Like it was inevitable. I can't explain it." Sierra checked to be sure Danny and Oliver were still upstairs with their cousins and out of earshot. "He told me he loves me."

Amy did the eye roll thing again. "Of course he loves you. He loved you when you were dating David."

That stopped Sierra's heart and set off an alarm. Mason told her he had had feelings for her for a long time, but what did Amy know about it? "What are you talking about? We were friends, but there wasn't anything romantic going on."

Amy held her hands up and let them drop. "I guess it doesn't matter if you know now, but Mason told me one night before you got engaged to David when we were all out that he wanted to tell you how he felt about you."

Sierra put the pieces together. "And you told him not to say anything."

Amy shrugged. "You were with David."

Anger flashed inside her. She couldn't believe Amy could be so callous about this. "Was this before or after I confided in you that I wasn't sure a life with David was what I wanted?"

"Before. After. What does it matter now?" The question sounded like a plea for Sierra to drop it.

Maybe it didn't matter now. Not after all this time. But still, she needed to know. "When did you tell him I didn't have feelings for him?"

"It wasn't exactly like that. I just never told you he had feelings for you and made it clear that you and David were solid."

Her stomach dropped. "But you knew differently. I told you David and me, we were fine, but I felt like the relationship wasn't as strong as it should be."

"You mean you felt like David loved you but wasn't *in* love with you."

She didn't remember saying it like that, but the description fit. Even now, looking back, it seemed exactly right.

Amy shrugged. "Some people don't get the love of their life."

"You did. Rex is crazy about you."

"Mason is crazy about you."

Sierra thought so, but appreciated that her sister saw it, too. "I've never been happier."

"Everyone has second thoughts when faced with the rest of their lives with one person. Sounds like with Mason, you don't have any." Amy tried to make her focus on now and not what happened then.

Sierra wouldn't let her get away with it. "Exactly. Yet you kept quiet about the fact that I had second thoughts about David because of my feelings for Mason and that Mason had feelings for me. Why?"

"You picked David. It worked out fine. You had two kids and a good marriage. Now you've got Mason. It even looks like he's been waiting for you all this time. Lucky you." It didn't sound like Amy was really happy for her.

"What was it really, Amy? Why keep the secret?" She really wanted to understand why Amy would keep her and Mason apart for no reason.

"Everything was always so easy for you. You had

two great guys who wanted to be with you. David wanted to marry you. After years of just being friends, out of the blue, Mason decides he has feelings for you. While I believed him, I thought that maybe it was possible he didn't want to lose you to his buddy, but he also didn't want to give you what David offered: marriage, family, a good life. So I kept it to myself because I didn't want to see you give up all those things I thought you wanted. You were ready for them. At the time, Mason was married to his job."

Sierra had to admit, that was true. Mostly. She still wondered, if given a chance, like they had now, would Mason have married her back then? Would they have been happy all this time?

"He could have told you about his feelings no matter what I'd said back then. It's clear *now*, the two of you are meant for each other. Is that because you're both ready for each other now because you know what you don't want?"

Maybe.

"I'm sorry if you think I purposely set out to hurt you. I didn't."

Sierra wasn't so sure about that. Amy could be selfish. "It's hard for me to hear that maybe if I'd listened to my heart I'd have been happy with Mason all this time." Maybe David would have been happier with someone else, too.

And then she heard what she'd just said and sighed. "I don't mean that."

She'd chosen David instead of going to Mason and telling him how she felt. She was responsible for her choices and her life.

Amy touched her hand, trying to make amends

for not telling her Mason had feelings for her. "You and David made a good life together. You had the boys. David's death was a tragedy, but now you and Mason have a second chance at forever."

Exactly.

This time, she'd go for what she wanted and not settle for anything less than a truly happy life.

Amy traced her fingers along the gray lines in the marble countertop. She glanced at the front door for like the tenth time, her gaze turning worried as she waited for Rex to return.

This talk with Rex was long overdue. With Amy's ingrained need for everything to be perfect, she had to be worried about this going well and making sure she said and did the right thing to make this better. Despite still being a little pissed Amy kept things about Mason from her, Sierra covered her sister's hand on the counter, stopping her nervous motions before she wore a hole in the stone. "You and Rex want to work this out, which means you will. He wants you to be happy, Amy. We all do."

"Don't you think I want to be happy?"

"I think you need to figure out what makes you happy now. Things change. What we thought we wanted before kids, after kids, at the beginning, somewhere in the middle, at the end, it's not the same as when we started. Allow yourself to let go of what's not working and find something that makes you feel fulfilled again."

"That seems easier said than done."

Sierra squeezed her sister's hand. "Talk to Rex. Figure out what that looks like together."

Amy nodded, then met Sierra's gaze. "I really am sorry. I should have told you what Mason confided in me. The truth is, I was jealous for no reason. You know I had a thing for him back in the day, but he never looked at me the way he looked at you."

"You mean the way Rex looks at you," Sierra pointed out.

Amy found a genuine smile.

Sierra knew Amy's other secret. "You would have preferred Rex and Mason both wanting you."

Amy always had to be the center of attention. She gave Sierra a mischievous grin. "I wouldn't have hated it."

Sierra let it go. She didn't want to fight with Amy or resent her for a past she couldn't change.

"How about you get Rex back and I'll keep Mason and we both just be happy for each other?"

Amy nodded, relief in her eyes. "Deal." Though her eyes clouded with worry as she looked toward the front door again.

"Kids! Let's go." Sierra picked up the tote bag by the front door that Amy had packed with sweatshirts and snacks for her kids. Just in case.

No doubt Heather had everything the kids would need for dinner and a movie tonight.

The four kids rushed down the stairs and headed for the front door just as Rex walked in. "Hey. What's all this?"

P.J. as the oldest led the way. "We're going to Aunt Heather's. Bye." He hugged his dad and ran out the door.

Emma followed up with a hug for her dad. "Bye."

Rex let Emma loose, gave Danny and Oliver a pat on the head as they passed, then focused on Amy. "You're taking the kids over to your sister's?"

Amy held her hands clasped together in front of

her. "Sierra's taking them for a couple of hours so we can talk."

Rex stared at his wife for one long moment, then turned to Sierra. "No Mason tonight?"

"He's got dinner with a client."

"He told me he's head over heels for you."

"I feel the same way."

"Good for you guys. I hope it works out."

"Thank you, Rex. With everything that's happened over the last year, it's nice to have something good in my life. He makes me happy."

"You deserve it."

"Are we going or what?" Danny yelled from the porch.

"And that's my cue to get going."

Amy hugged her and held on for an extra moment before Sierra headed to the door.

Rex gave her a quick hug. "Thanks for taking the kids."

"No problem." She turned to Amy. "I'll have them back at nine."

Rex walked into the kitchen to get something out of the fridge. With his back turned to them, Sierra mouthed, *You've got this*, to Amy, gave her a big thumbs-up, and headed out the door to take four little rascals to dinner.

She hoped Mason's investigator helped her resolve her issue with her deceased husband and she could let the past go and move on.

Chapter Twenty-Four

It took ten minutes to get all the kids to agree on a movie, but Heather and Sierra got them settled in Heather's big bed.

Hallee's eyes drooped as sleep crept in, but she fought to stay awake. Heather would come back in ten minutes and move her to her crib. For now, she let her daughter hang with the big kids. She looked adorable tucked up against Oliver's side as he lay on his back, one knee bent, his other leg crossed over it, swinging.

Danny and P.J. lay down the center, their heads at the foot of the bed. Emma lay across from Hallee and Oliver, with her own little bowl of plain popcorn because she didn't like it salty or drenched in butter.

Sierra tapped Heather's shoulder. "Adult beverages in the kitchen."

Heather stared at all the kids. "Look at them. We need to do this more often."

"So long as you don't mind washing melted butter off your bedspread and sleeping in popcorn crumbs, sure. Let's do this again." Sierra chuckled, but the nostalgia and joy in her eyes said she loved the sweet scene just as much as Heather did.

"We used to crawl in Mom's bed together and watch movies."

"It's been a minute since we did that." Sierra cocked her head and narrowed her eyes. "Is that a Metallica T-shirt sticking out under your pillow?"

"Yeah. David turned me on to them. Remember?"

Sierra's eyes went soft. "He loved them. I surprised him for his thirtieth birthday with tickets. We drove to San Francisco to see them play with the symphony. I don't think I've ever seen him smile so wide or enjoy something so much." Sierra stared at the shirt for a long moment, nostalgia and sorrow in her eyes before she turned and headed down the hall, her head downcast.

Heather sympathized with her sister. David left a hole in all their hearts. Deeper in some of them.

She took in her little girl one last time, so happy to be included and trying so hard to keep her eyes open, then followed her sister to the kitchen.

Sierra handed her half a glass of wine, because kids.

Heather clinked her glass against Sierra's. "To late-night movies with the ones you love."

Sierra sipped, then turned solemn. "The boys slept in my bed for a month after David died. I'd turn on a happy cartoon to chase away their sadness. Some nights, we'd all talk like Scooby-Doo and laugh. Other nights, we sat quietly and just let the tears fall and held each other. I can't tell you how it heals my heart to see them in there with their cousins happy and laughing. They'll remember nights like these just like I remember you, me, and Amy sleeping in our blanket forts trying to scare each other with wild ghost stories."

"You used to scare the pants off Amy with Franny Fright."

Sierra busted up laughing. "One of my best stories."

"I hope you haven't told the boys that one."

Sierra shook her head. "The ones I told you and Amy were far too scary for them. Instead, I made up cute little rhymes about Franny as a mischievous witch. Maybe when they're older I'll tell them the really scary ones. I'll be sure Amy is around when I do." The devilish smile died quickly.

Heather read the heavy sorrow her sister carried. "How are you doing? Today is so hard."

Sierra took a seat at the table and stared into her wine. "I can't believe David has been gone a whole year. It seems my every other thought this past week has been about this day. I knew it was coming, and still, I find myself unprepared to deal with my thoughts and feelings. I miss him. I'm angry he's gone. I wish he was here to see how much the boys have grown. I think about what he's missing all the time. It goes by so fast."

"I know what you mean. Sometimes I look at Hallee and I feel like I can see her growing right before my eyes. She does so many new things, all faster than I can really take them in, and I think if I don't pay attention, I'll miss it myself." Her father missed it all. Heather wished she could change that, but it was impossible. It wasn't all Hallee's father's fault. Heather took the blame for her bad decisions and regretted all the way to her soul that Hallee paid the price.

But she hoped to find a good man to love them. Someone who would love being Hallee's dad. She thought about Mason. She hadn't really stopped thinking about him. But being a single, working mom left little time to pursue a guy who didn't even know she was interested in him.

"I can't believe it's been a year. I can't believe we lost the house, everything of his, and we started a whole new life here."

"Maybe, in some ways, it's better that way. A fresh start for you and the kids. From what you said over dinner, you love your new job and the kids are settling in at school. You said they seem really happy here."

"They are. Part of that comes from being around family. They love it when Mom wakes them up with tickles in the morning. Riding the horses has really given them a sense of accomplishment and confidence."

That was interesting. "So they spend a lot of time with Mason."

"Several nights a week if Mason doesn't have any late-night meetings. He loves having the boys over. His horses like the exercise. Danny is in love with this mare named Goose."

The name made Heather smile. "After the bird or *Top Gun*?"

Sierra chuckled. "I'll have to ask Mason."

"I bet Hallee would love to see the horses."

"You should bring her over tomorrow afternoon. Mason takes the boys riding after lunch on the weekends."

"Do you think he'd mind if I just showed up?"

Sierra waved that away. "Not at all. We'll all be there."

"So it's like old times. You and Mason picked up where you left off." She'd always thought it weird that her sister was better friends with Mason than most of the girls she went to school with.

"In a lot of ways, it seems that way. He's been so great with the boys. They've really come out of their shells around him. I can see how much they miss their dad and Mason is so good about being that guy in their lives who teaches them things and shows them how to be a good man. They need that. They love him."

"I wonder if he thinks about getting married and having kids."

Sierra picked up her wine glass and said over the rim, "He's hinted at it," before taking a sip.

"I wonder why he and his fiancée broke things off."

Sierra shrugged. "People break up for lots of reasons. Mason's been career oriented for a long time. He wanted the relationship to work, but in the end his feelings weren't deep enough. Relationships only work when both people put everything into it. I'm sure you know how that goes." Sierra set her glass back on the table. "Any hope for you and Hallee's dad getting back together?"

Heather gave her the truth. "At one time, I dreamed it could all work out. He'd marry me. We'd raise Hallee together and be happy that we had each other. But . . ."

Sierra's hand covered hers on the table and Heather swallowed the lump in her throat. "But what? What happened? Why doesn't he visit you and Hallee? Why isn't he in her life?"

Everyone always wanted to know *who* he was, not why he wasn't here. The why tore her apart.

"Not everyone gets to keep the love of their life." She was never meant to have Hallee or her father. But she'd loved him with her whole heart and didn't regret the time they shared, only the consequences.

Sierra sat back in her seat. "I'm sorry you lost him, Heather."

They sat quietly, both of them thinking about what they'd lost, the pain and sadness a match, though they'd experienced it all in different ways.

Heather had to live with the choices she'd made, taking what she wanted when she knew it would be impossible to keep and cause so much pain despite the unbelievable joy and love she'd felt and the wonderful gift she'd gotten out of it.

She'd been selfish.

She'd loved and lost and had no one to blame but herself for how it ended. She didn't know heartbreak could hurt this much and cut so deeply.

Tears glistened in her eyes but she didn't let them fall. She didn't expect Sierra to comfort her. Not today. Not on the day she'd lost her husband, the boys' father, the man she thought she'd spend the rest of her life with and had to learn to live without.

Heather understood that kind of pain and wouldn't make this about her.

She didn't deserve that selfish indulgence.

Chapter Twenty-Five

Amy couldn't remember the last time she'd felt this nervous about talking to her husband. If she didn't get this right, it could mean the end of them, their marriage, the family their children knew.

The urgency of the situation tied her stomach in knots.

She and Rex needed to fix this. Now.

Amy needed to be brave and figure out what she really wanted.

Rex sat at the counter with a glass of water, the gold band on his left hand softly tapping against the glass. He did that all the time. The habit sometimes drove her crazy.

Every tap seemed to mark another second of silence.

So she started. "I don't like the way we've been treating each other lately."

He shifted on the stool and stared at her over his shoulder but didn't say a word.

She moved into the kitchen and stood across from him. "I try so hard to make everything perfect for this family."

"You're amazing." His sincerity touched her. "And a little crazy." She'd always loved that sexy half grin.

The smile he wanted from her came easily when he teased her like this. And if they could still find humor in their situation and life, they still had a chance. She hoped.

"You're always telling people how your wife is so great at keeping things together. How much I spoil you and the children and you love it, so I try even harder to live up to that. But then you're angry that I'm trying so hard to make you proud of me and our family."

"Amy, I am proud that I have a kind, caring, loving wife and mother of my children. I'd still be proud if you did even half the things you do for us."

And that was the crux of their problem. "You're angry that we don't spend enough time together."

"I'm unhappy that you seem to go out of your way to schedule me out of the picture. As I said before, it's like the only thing I'm good for is bringing home the paycheck."

Anger flashed, but she tamped it down and gave herself a moment to absorb how he felt. "That's not true. And I'm sorry I made you feel that way. It's not my intention to leave you out or make you feel like we don't want you with us." She sucked in a breath, ignoring the look on his face that told her clearly he didn't believe her. "I've thought about all you've said and how you feel."

"Look, Amy, I've tried to be understanding about your need to be involved in the kids' school and their lives. They're your whole world. I get that. They're mine, too. But I used to be important to you, too." Rex leaned back, his shoulders sagging. "How the hell did we get here?"

"Rex, I hate the way we are now. I want us to

find our way back to the way things used to be." She waited for his gaze to meet hers. "I'm tired." She relaxed her tense shoulders and her arms sagged. "Like all the time. I always feel like I'm rushing around doing things but I never feel like I'm doing them right."

Rex's mouth drew tight. "Amy, you're great at everything. I don't know how you do so much and make it look so effortless."

"It's not. Trust me. It's stressful and time-consuming, and half the time the kids are complaining because they don't want to do a lot of it." She took another breath. "I haven't been listening. To you. To the kids. To my own feelings. So I'm going to sit the kids down with the schedule and ask them what they really want to do and what they can drop."

Rex's eyes went wide. "Seriously?"

"Yes. I don't want them to feel like I'm making them do things. I want them to love what they do. Instead of just signing them up for activities, I'm going to ask them if they even want to do it."

"I think they'd like that. P.J. isn't really into the music thing."

"He hates playing the trumpet."

"Emma seems to like art class."

Amy shrugged one shoulder. "She likes to please. I worry she does it for me, not because she really likes it. But I'm not going to assume that. I'm going to ask her if *she* wants to keep going. The last thing I want to do is turn her into me, someone who can't say no."

Rex eyed her. "Are you going to go nuts with less to do?"

Of course he knew she didn't like to be idle. "When we got married, I really wanted to be a mom. That's all I thought about."

"You're a great mom."

"But I'm also your wife."

His mouth drew back on one side into a half frown filled with sadness. "We live in the same house, but I still miss you."

She knew exactly what he meant. "It's not that we've lost the love."

Rex nodded his agreement. "We've lost the time we spend together. We don't connect like we used to."

"I want more time with you. So with the extra money we'll save on not doing the stuff the kids hate, I will pay the babysitter on date nights. For real this time."

"I'm going up on your schedule?" He eyed the bane of his existence hanging on the cabinet with a teasing light in his eyes and voice, but he was serious.

"I'm getting my priorities in the right order. Bake sales and school plays don't come before you anymore. In fact, I'm putting you back where you belong. At the top of my list."

"Listen, sweetheart, I know the kids need you."

"You need me, too. And I need you. I'm tired of feeling like I'm doing all this on my own." She held up her hand to stop him from unnecessarily defending himself. "I did this to myself and blamed you for not wanting to do everything I set up without asking you about it in the first place. You want to see the kids more, too. You want to make family time a priority."

"Yes. And I want to spend time alone with my wife."

She put her hand over his. "I want that, too. We both deserve more downtime."

"I wouldn't mind sleeping in on a Saturday. Especially if you're in bed with me." The devastatingly handsome smile she hadn't seen in too long appeared and melted her heart.

She smiled back. "That sounds really good." She hoped she could rein in that feeling inside her that she should be doing something. Being lazy and unoccupied with something to do made her antsy.

But doing her husband sounded like a good way to pass the time, too.

"About our sex life . . ."

Rex rolled his eyes. "What sex life?" Again that teasing tone didn't mask the seriousness in his voice.

"I made it another item on my list."

Rex tilted his head and another sorrowful frown took hold of his handsome face. "Pity sex is not sexy. I don't want to be something you check off."

"I know. And I'm sorry. I'd like to work on that, because I don't think we can get back to where we used to be without finding our way back to each other in every way."

"You know, if you tell me what you need, I'll try to give it to you."

She smiled at the innuendo, but Rex remained completely focused, which told her this was important to him. Her happiness mattered. Their marriage mattered.

"Okay. I'd like your help to free up my time and make the evenings more relaxing for me. I'd appreciate it if you'd do the dinner dishes and make the kids' lunches for the next day each night while I get them ready for bed."

Skepticism filled his eyes. "I've tried to help you with chores around the house. The only thing I seem to do right is take out the trash."

"I know. Which is why I'm going to show you how I want the dishwasher loaded." She waited out his eye roll. "Not because you do it wrong, but because I like it a certain way or I get anxious and feel like I have to do it myself."

Rex caught on quick with a nod. "Okay. I get it." A smile crept across his face. "Why don't you make me a diagram?"

Not a bad idea. And though he was teasing her, he knew her well enough to know that was exactly how she'd be able to let go of the chore and let him do it. "I will."

"I'll still read them stories while you relax. I love that time with them."

"I love that time, too. Let's switch off, or do it together."

"Sounds good."

"Once I've got the new schedule finished with the kids, I'd like to go over it as a family. I'd like it if we could do the things that stay on it together, your work schedule permitting."

"I'd like that."

"Okay. I'd like your Thursday nights for our dates."

"You can have any night you want."

"I'd appreciate it if you made the plans."

"My pleasure. It will be my job to wine and dine you." He held his hand out to her.

She reached out, took it, and moved around the

counter, closer to him. "Thank you for understanding. That's exactly what I needed to hear you say."

"You put us all first, sweetheart. Deep down, I think you want someone to do that for you. That's my job. And I haven't done it well these last months."

"I pushed you away."

"I let you because I felt like you didn't need me."

She touched her hand to his cheek. "I always need you."

"I see that now. You pushed me away and filled up the empty space with things to do to fill your time and the hole inside you."

"I didn't mean for it to happen."

"I know. I'm glad we had this talk. I see what's been happening. I hope you do, too, and we can move forward and come back together. I'm really looking forward to having you all to myself on Thursday night."

She leaned in and kissed him softly. "We're alone right now."

He shifted on the stool, wrapped his arm around her waist, and drew her in between his strong legs and up against his wide chest. "What should we do?"

For a split second she thought about teasing and telling him she'd teach him how to load the dishwasher. Instead, she showed him what she really wanted: more of him.

She kissed him with all the intention she had for where she wanted the kiss to lead.

Rex took direction well, even if it was unspoken. He slipped his hands down her hips and grabbed her ass. His lips left hers to travel down her neck and back to her ear. "I've missed you so damn bad."

"Me, too," she said on a breathless sigh.

She missed feeling this way. Wanted. Needed. Like she mattered.

She bet Rex felt the same way and poured everything into loving him.

If they only had a couple hours until the kids came home to show each other they wanted this to work and their love was still very much alive and as deep as it used to be, she'd make the most of it.

She broke the searing kiss, stepped back, took Rex's hand, and pulled him up and out of his seat and toward the stairs. "Come with me."

"I'd follow you anywhere."

"Still?" She smiled up at him, knowing full well he meant it.

"Always."

The mischief came back into his eyes. He tugged her hand, so she walked toward him. He dipped his shoulder and hoisted her over it. She lay like a sack of potatoes down his back. She smacked his ass and laughed because he hadn't carried her like this since they were dating.

"Put me down before you throw your back out."

He smacked his hand over her ass and left it there, the heel of his hand pressed intimately to her sorely neglected lady parts. "Not a chance. I've got until nine o'clock to show you how much I've missed you. I'm pretty sure it's going to take every minute from here to then to prove it to you."

He didn't have to prove anything to her, but the second he tossed her down on their bed and swallowed her giggles with a deep, searing kiss, he made good on his promise.

* * *

In fact, Rex made good on his promise so well and thoroughly, Amy answered the knock on the front door on shaky legs, wearing nothing but her bathrobe.

Sierra stared at her, taking in Amy's tousled hair, rosy cheeks heated by the embarrassment she felt getting caught doing the naughty with her husband, the robe, and her bare feet. Sierra's knowing smile amplified her embarrassment as well as the vixen inside her who was completely satisfied and smug about it.

Sierra's gaze swept over Amy, then met her eyes. "Hello. I remember you."

Amy felt a lot more like her old self than a haggard mom.

"I'm feeling pretty damn good."

Emma stared up at her. "You swore."

"Mommy gets a pass tonight." Rex walked down the stairs in an old worn pair of jeans and a white T-shirt, his hair mussed, too. "Did you have fun with Aunt Sierra and Aunt Heather?"

P.J. yawned. "We had pizza with basil on it. It wasn't bad."

Not a ringing endorsement, but he'd tried something new and didn't hate it. Amy put that in the win column.

Emma hugged her. "I missed you, Mommy."

Amy held her daughter, cherishing the warm feeling in her heart. "I missed you, too, baby. Head upstairs with your brother. Daddy and I will be up to kiss you good night."

Emma trudged up the stairs behind P.J.

"Thank-yous for Aunt Sierra, please."

They didn't stop their ascent, but obediently called out, "Thank you!"

Rex stepped up to Sierra and hugged her. "Thank you for taking the kids and giving Amy and me some time together." He let her loose.

Sierra smiled up at him. "Looks like you two put the time to good use."

Amy shoved her sister toward the door. "Thank you. We appreciate it. Now take your kids home so Rex and I can say good night to our kids and finish what we started."

Rex glanced at her, a gleam and hope in his eyes. "We're not done?"

"*I'm* not done with you."

"Lucky me." He headed for the stairs. "I'll say good night to the kids then. Bye, Sierra."

"Bye, Rex."

Amy stood in the open door as her sister stepped out onto the porch.

"I'm happy for you, sis."

Amy thought about their earlier conversation. "I'm sorry I interfered in your relationship, Sierra. I should have listened to you and told you what I knew about Mason and his feelings for you. I withheld that from you because of my own selfish reasons. It wasn't right. I was wrong. And I'm sorry."

Sierra took a few second to absorb that before she closed the distance between them. "It was wrong. You did it for spite because you didn't want me to have him even though you had Rex and had no intention of doing anything about that old crush. But . . ."

"But?"

"Mason should have come to me if he had feelings and wanted me to reconsider my decision to marry David. Instead of telling you, he should have told me. I was conflicted but I never went to him and said my piece, either. That's on me." Sierra gave her sister a hug good-bye, then stepped back. "Let's leave this in the past where it belongs. Things are different now. We've all changed. I know how Mason feels. He knows how I feel. We're both in a place where we make sense."

"You two seem really great together."

"I feel that way, too, which is why I'm going to start talking to the boys about how I feel about Mason and where I'd like to see us in the coming months."

"Really?"

"Yeah. After everything we've been through, I keep asking myself what I'm waiting for. Why I am waiting at all when time is too precious to waste." She headed down the porch steps. "Stop wasting time, Amy. Rex is waiting for you upstairs."

Amy took her little sister's advice, closed and locked the door, and headed up to the man who made her life so much better in every way because he got her kind of crazy and loved her anyway.

Chapter Twenty-Six

Sierra stood on the porch, holding the boys' hands. Her mother stood beside them as Mason pulled into the yard, the truck cab filled with green balloons. So many that she couldn't even see him through the passenger window.

"What are all the balloons for?" Oliver looked excited for a party that wasn't going to be exactly joyous, even if they were celebrating. A different kind than they were used to, but a way that was necessary and simply part of life.

"We're going to send messages to your father in heaven with them."

Danny's head whipped toward her. "What?" Tears gathered in his eyes.

She released Oliver's hand and touched Danny's wobbly chin. "Your dad passed away a year ago. I thought we should celebrate his life and how much we loved him by sending him our love up into the sky."

A tear trickled down Danny's cheek. "I thought you forgot."

So Danny had been paying attention to the day. She should have known, though he'd been strong and gotten through yesterday without a word. She hated to think of him suffering his sadness in silence. It broke her heart and brought tears to her eyes.

At seven and five, she didn't think they'd remember the exact date. Her mistake. One she'd never make again.

"No, honey. I will never forget your dad."

"But you're with Mason now, right?"

Oh yes, kids paid attention to everything.

She and Mason tried to keep their affection in check around the boys, but she knew they'd caught them innocently touching hands, had noticed the way Mason hugged her good-bye when he really wanted to kiss her, and how he paid so much attention to her.

"I like Mason a lot." She tried to be low-key about it. "We have feelings for each other. We've been friends for a long time, even before I met your dad."

"Is he your boyfriend?" Oliver asked, biting his bottom lip, his eyes filled with uncertainty.

"I suppose you could call him that. Is that okay?"

Oliver nodded. "He's nice."

"So is he going to be our dad or something?" Danny asked, a touch of anger in his voice.

She hadn't anticipated having this conversation today. She hoped to use the next couple of weeks to ease the kids into accepting Mason into their lives permanently. They liked him. They saw him as a friend, but not as Mommy's special friend. Not as the man she loved and wanted to make a life with.

She and Mason hadn't had a chance to get on the same page about this, either.

"Mason wants to be part of our family. He really likes being with you boys. You like doing things with him, too, right?"

Danny reluctantly nodded. "The horses are fun."

Oliver raised his hands as Mason approached the steps with the bundle of balloons in one hand. He caught Oliver in his free arm when he launched himself off the steps and into Mason's chest. "Mom says you're going to be our new dad."

Sierra's cheeks burned with embarrassment. "I said Mason wants to be a part of our family."

Her mom tried to help her out of this awkward situation. "Maybe we should table this for now."

She met Mason's eyes. "Sorry. I know we haven't had time to talk about this."

Mason focused on Danny, who wore a frown, but his eyes were filled with hope. "Well, I know how I feel. You see, your mom and I really like each other. In fact, I love her. I love you." Mason made a point to look at both Danny and Oliver so they could see he meant it. "I don't want to take your dad's place. David will always be your dad. I know he's watching over you both each and every day. I hope he thinks I'm doing a good job teaching you to ride and helping you with your schoolwork and just being here to help your mom take care of you. I know he's with us when we catch a game on TV and hang out with each other. I hope he's happy that I'm with you guys and that I'm here for you no matter what you need me to do and be in your life because he can't be here with you like I know he wants to be. He was my friend. I miss him, too. I wish he was here for you and your mom. I don't want to take his place. I want to make my own place in your lives."

Danny scrunched his lips, then spoke softly. "Sean at school has two dads. They're married to each other, but still . . . He's got two. I don't see why we can't have two."

Oliver hugged Mason's neck. "I like you."

Mason chuckled and squeezed Oliver to his chest. "I like you, too, bud." Mason handed the balloons to her, then took Danny in his arms and looked him in the eyes. "I'm not the replacement. I'm extra."

Danny hugged Mason and his brother at the same time, then shyly backed away.

Her mom dabbed at her eyes with the sleeve of her blouse. "Wow. Um, that was very well said, Mason."

"Thank you, Dede." For the first time, Mason kissed Sierra right in front of the boys. "Hi."

She smiled up at him and Oliver, who stared down at her with a big smile on his face. "Hi."

Her mom waved them over to the porch table where she'd set out slips of paper and colored pencils. "Let's write our messages for your dad."

Danny frowned. "Are we always going to do this for Dad's death?"

It seemed ominous, but Sierra hadn't wanted the first year to pass without them doing something. "Only this year. From now on, we'll celebrate his birthday."

"That sounds better." Danny picked up the green pencil. "His favorite color."

Mason put his hand on Danny's shoulder. "That's why your mom asked me to pick up green balloons. Your dad wore green ties with his suits all the time."

Danny smiled up at Mason. "We gave him a new green tie every birthday. He liked them." Danny frowned again. "They all burned in the fire."

"He drank green beer once and his tongue was all green." Oliver scrunched up his face. "It was yucky."

"The beer or his green tongue?" Mason teased.

"I can't drink beer." Oliver stated that with all seriousness.

Mason tickled his belly. "Silly me. What was I thinking?" He set Oliver back on his feet and handed him the light green pencil. "What do you want to write to your dad?"

"I miss him."

"That's perfect, bud. Let's get on that. If you can't think of what else to say, you can draw him a picture." Mason held his arm out so Sierra could slip in beside him. He held her to his side as they watched the boys write their messages.

Oliver stuck his tongue out a little while he carefully printed his block letters and tried to spell the words correctly.

Danny kept his hand over what he wrote, wanting his message to be private.

She glanced up at Mason and mouthed, *Thank you*. He'd made today easier for the boys. He'd given them permission to never forget their dad even if they were lucky enough to get an *extra* one like Mason.

Mason took a slip of paper and wrote a message, then read it aloud. "David, your boys are amazing. Thank you for bringing them into my life."

Danny and Oliver stared at him for a long moment before they both smiled.

Oliver held up his note. "I drew him a picture of Horse." Oliver couldn't remember all the horses' names, so he just called them all Horse.

"Love it." Mason turned to Danny. "Did you finish yours?"

Danny held up six or seven rolled pieces of paper. "Do you think he'll know what they say?"

"I think he hears everything in your heart."

Danny turned to Sierra. "What did you write?"

She held up the first note. "I love you and miss you every day." She showed him the second one. "Thank you for leaving me the boys so I'll never be lonely without you because I see you in them every day." She wanted Danny and Oliver to know that they reminded her of David. That she'd never forget him because she had them. She wanted them to know she thought about David every day.

She showed him the last one. "I got a great job. We have a new home. We're happy."

Danny hugged her. "He'll be happy to know that."

"That's all he wants for us. I know this past year has been hard. We miss him. We wish he was here. But he'd rather see us smiling than sad for him."

"I'm glad we moved to Grandma's," Oliver announced.

Dede rolled up the slip of paper she'd finished writing. "I just told your father how happy I am to have you all here with me." She tied the note to one of the balloon strings. "How about we send these to your dad?"

Mason helped tie each of Danny's and Oliver's notes to the balloons. Sierra tied her own.

They gave all the balloons to the boys in the front yard.

"One at a time, or all at once. Doesn't matter," she coaxed the kids.

Oliver meticulously pulled one at a time free

from his bunch and let it loose, marveling as each rose up into the sky.

Danny divided the bundles between his hands and let them go together, his hands raised, eyes to the sky as they floated away.

Sierra stood with Mason, his arm around her back. Tears gathered in her eyes. Grief over David's sudden passing, missing what they had, wondering if they'd have fixed things or gone their separate ways, grateful for the time they had, and still suspicious about what he'd kept from her—her thoughts and emotions were all over the place.

Mason kissed her on top of the head. "You okay?"

"It just hits me sometimes. He's gone. He's not coming back. He's going to miss so many things in the boys' lives. And I still have questions about why he needed that loan and if he was hiding something even bigger from me."

"About that . . ."

She turned to him, but Oliver ran over and slammed his little body into her leg and hip.

His arm gripped her leg and he looked up at her. "Mommy, look at them. They're all going straight up to Daddy."

She stared up at the sky with Oliver and brushed her hand over his head, so happy she'd done this with the boys. "I have something else for you and Danny."

"Really? Can I have it?"

"Danny. Come up to the porch." She waved him in from the yard.

Her mom stood on the porch with the two wrapped packages for the boys.

Sierra leaned down and kissed Oliver's nose.

"Grandma has a special present I made for you and Danny."

Oliver took off up the steps to take his package from her mom.

Mason touched her arm. "Sierra, about the information you wanted . . ."

"Did your investigator get back to you?"

"Yes. I didn't want to do this today, but I don't want to keep it from you any longer."

She studied his serious face. "What do you mean 'longer'?"

"I've actually had it for a little while. I just didn't know how to break the news to you."

She didn't like the sound of that. "It can't be worse than what I'm imagining. Just tell me."

He glanced at the boys and her mom waiting on the porch. "Not here. We'll go over it after the boys' ride this afternoon. Maybe Dede can watch them while we talk."

Her stomach tied into a knot. "It's that bad?"

"If I've learned anything in my law practice, it's that secrets are always bad. I wish I didn't have to tell you what I know, but . . . you deserve the truth. I just hope you're prepared to hear it."

"Mom! Can we open these?" Danny called out.

Sierra touched Mason's arm. "We'll talk about this later." She headed for the porch, then remembered what she was supposed to tell him about their ride. "Heather and Hallee are joining us at the ranch later."

Mason stopped in his tracks behind her. "Why?"

She caught herself and turned back to him. "She wants to introduce Hallee to a horse."

"I wish you'd told me about this sooner."

His reluctant tone made her raise an eyebrow. "Have you run out of horses?"

He shook his head. "No. It's just . . . we really need to discuss the information I received from my investigator. But you didn't know, so we'll deal with it later." The postponement frustrated him. He seemed to want to get it over with, but she wasn't so sure she wanted to know given his dire tone.

He touched her back to get her moving up the stairs to where the boys waited at the table, their presents in front of them, hands ready to tear into the packages. "Let's do this and save the rest for later."

Sierra let it go, tried to shake off her worry, and focused on the boys. "Okay, you two, I don't want you to think you're going to get presents every year but after the fire and we lost everything of your dad's I made some calls to our friends in Napa and downloaded what I had and made you these." She nodded for them to go ahead and open the gifts.

They tore open the wrapping paper and tossed it away. Danny and Oliver both stared at their photo books, a picture of each of them with their dad on the cover.

"Our friends sent all the pictures they had of you guys with your dad. Aunt Amy and Heather and Grandma gave me some from family gatherings. I used all the ones I had stored on my phone and put them all together in these books."

Danny flipped through pages, tears rolling down his cheeks.

Oliver simply stared at the cover, his face solemn.

Her mom wrapped her arm around Sierra's middle. "They're gorgeous, Sierra. When you told me what you were doing, I never expected it to turn out like this. It's like a photography book."

"You custom-make them online." She addressed the boys then. "I wanted you to remember all the good times we had with Dad. Now any time you miss him, you can look at these pictures and see his face and remember how much he loved you."

Choked up, she swallowed back her own tears.

The books had taken quite a bit of time to design, but they turned out so well. She customized each one to focus on either Danny or Oliver, though of course many of the pictures showed both of them. But there were lots that were just one of them with their dad and her.

She vowed to make new ones for them every few years, so they had their memories to look at instead of all the pictures simply sitting in the cloud doing nothing for anyone in cyberspace.

Sierra hoped this helped heal their hearts. She couldn't give them back everything lost in the fire, but this had been a way to bring the memories back to life for them.

They were so young. She didn't want those memories to fade away without them having something to help bring them back to life in their minds and hearts.

Danny finally looked up at her, so much sorrow in his eyes. "Thanks, Mom." He clutched the book to his chest. "Thanks."

She hugged him close. "You're welcome, sweetheart." Tears tracked down her cheeks.

Oliver pressed his face into her side. She put one arm around him, too, and held both her boys close.

This had been a hard day. Necessary, but difficult. They needed this chance to remember and keep the healing going and the memories of David alive.

Her phone rang in her back pocket. She let the boys go and pulled out her cell and read the caller ID. "It's work."

Mason moved into her place next to the boys. "Your mom told me about the books. I'd love to see them." Mason and her mom kept the boys occupied while she took the call.

"Hi, Mike. How's the Gilmore place coming along?"

"One of the subs hit the gas line. We're shut down. Emergency services is on the way. We've cleared the area, but we're going to need the owner down here."

"I'll call him and meet him there as soon as I can." She raked her fingers through her hair and silently swore.

Mason touched her arm. "What is it?"

"A work emergency. I need to meet the owner at a property."

"Dede is meeting her friends for lunch. I'll take the boys. Join us at the ranch when you're done."

"Are you sure?"

He squeezed her hand. "It's part of being a family, right? We look out for each other."

The sweet sentiment touched her heart. "You make everything easy."

"It's not supposed to be hard. I don't mind taking the boys. Soon, we'll be together all the time. I hope."

She wondered why he added the last. "You know that's what I want, right?"

"Yes." His excitement shone through. "And I hope nothing changes." That drained the enthusiasm right out of him.

"What would change that?"

"I'm nervous about telling you what I know."

Anxiety tightened her gut. "Nothing David did would make me change the way I feel about you." Her phone buzzed with a text from Mike. She quickly read it. "I need to deal with this. I'll be back as soon as I can, then we'll talk about David." She went up on tiptoe and kissed him quick, gave the boys hugs good-bye, wondering about Mason and the way he spoke about what he'd discovered about David, and questioning if she'd come home to an even bigger problem than the one facing her now.

Chapter Twenty-Seven

Mason heard a car pull up just outside the stables. He hoped Sierra had finished her work emergency early. He didn't like the way they left things.

He'd wanted to be wrong about David, who loved his family. He wanted to believe David would never do anything to hurt them.

But David had hurt them. He'd done something he couldn't take back.

And he wasn't here to answer for it.

Which made it even worse, because Sierra deserved an explanation and an apology at the very least.

A car door slammed.

Mason plucked Danny off the stall door and set him on the ground. "I think your mom is here."

Oliver gave Jezebel's big head a hug. "Bye, Horse."

Mason pulled Oliver off the gate, then swung him around in a circle and set him on his feet. Oliver giggled and smiled so big Mason smiled with him.

He really loved having the boys here. "Let's see if your mom wants something to eat before we ride. She probably missed lunch."

Danny tagged Oliver in the back. "You're it!" He

ran for the open stable doors just as a second car door closed.

Oliver caught up to Danny. Only because he stopped to hug Hallee.

Mason joined them and greeted Heather. "Hey. I forgot you were coming."

Heather touched her hand to her chest, partially covering the cleavage revealed by the one too many buttons undone on her black-and-white plaid flannel. In tight black jeans and boots, she looked ready to ride. "You certainly know how to make a girl feel welcome."

She teased, but he just wanted her out of here before Sierra came home, so they could pick up their conversation where they left off.

But thinking the word *home* made him pause. He wanted Sierra to feel like this was home. He wanted her and the boys to live here. The boys accepted him in their mother's life. But he didn't want to get ahead of himself. He'd waited this long for her. He could wait for her to make the decision about where to live when she felt they were ready for it.

He just wanted to give her everything and make her happy.

He wanted to start each day with her.

And maybe one day, they'd have another child together and give Danny and Oliver a brother or sister. He didn't care which. He just wanted to see his eyes and Sierra's smile on his little one.

He wanted that future so bad.

But it all hung on the secret he knew and had to break to Sierra.

Heather stuffed her hands in her back pockets,

widening the gap in her shirt as her chest thrust forward. "Hallee loves animals. I thought she'd love to see a horse up close and she can play with Danny and Oliver. It's so nice to have Sierra home. I love seeing all the kids playing together."

Mason bit back what he really wanted to say.

Oliver tugged on the hem of his shirt. "I have to pee." He buried his face in Mason's side.

Mason brushed his hand over Oliver's dark head. "Okay, bub. Why don't you and Danny go up to the house and take Hallee with you. There are Popsicles in the freezer. You can each have one." To Danny he added, "Hold Hallee's hand. Help her up the steps. Do not let her out of your sight."

"Got it." Danny took Hallee's hand and walked with her while Oliver ran for the house to use the bathroom.

Mason watched them go, startled when Heather put her hand on his bicep and squeezed.

"It's so nice of you to let us come over and go for a ride. I've been thinking about you ever since we saw each other at the mailbox. I've been meaning to come by, but it's hard to find a spare minute being a single mom and all."

He stepped away, putting a comfortable distance between them. "It must be really hard to do it on your own with Hallee's father out of the picture."

"It is. I hardly have any time to myself." She bit her bottom lip and edged closer. "That's why I wanted to see you. I thought maybe you and I could go out and have some fun."

Stunned, he didn't know what to say or do.

She had to know he and Sierra were seeing each other. Right?

Then again, they'd kept things quiet so the boys could get used to them seeing each other.

Heather closed the distance and put both hands on his chest and went up on tiptoe, her body brushing his, her face inches from his. "It's been a long time and I really want to get to know you better."

His brain finally caught up to what she meant. He took her by the shoulders and gently nudged her away while he let her go and took two steps back.

"This isn't going to happen. Sierra and I, we've been seeing each other."

Heather took a step back, her eyes filled with skepticism. "Really? I mean, you were like brother and sister when we were younger."

"It was never like that and you know it."

"She said she's been coming over to see you, but I thought that was just so the boys could learn to horseback ride."

"It's a lot more than that. Sierra and I have a good thing."

Doubt filled her eyes. "Sierra is just so serious all the time. Doesn't that get boring?" She took a step closer again. "We could be so much more."

Angry she didn't back off when he told her he and Sierra were together, he blurted out, "Is that what you told David?"

The sexy smile died on her lips. She simply stared at him.

He let her know what he'd suspected all this time. "Danny and Hallee have the same eyes." Hers went wide. "Their father's eyes."

They both jumped at the gasp that sounded behind them.

Before Mason even turned toward the stable, he

knew who'd be standing there. He never heard a car because she'd walked across the pasture instead. He instantly knew he'd made a huge mistake in not talking to Sierra about his suspicions before confronting Heather himself. And the look of betrayal he saw in Sierra's eyes now said she blamed him for keeping this from her.

Sierra dismissed him without a word and focused on Heather. "Hallee is David's daughter."

Heather's eyes filled with tears. "I'm so sorry."

Sierra looked so brittle the dust on the wind might shatter her to pieces, but it was Heather's words that set her off.

"You're sorry? Like you were sorry when you stole Miss Maisey when you were four and wanted my baby doll for yourself so you took her? Sorry like when you borrowed my makeup and clothes and never gave them back? That kind of sorry?"

Distress lined Heather's forehead. "I never meant for it to happen the way it did."

"But you did mean to sleep with *my* husband. Were you hoping he'd leave me for you?"

"At first, it was just something that happened."

"At first? So it wasn't a onetime thing? You were carrying on an affair behind my back."

Heather caught herself with a gasp. "It wasn't like that."

Oh, yes it was. And Mason felt every ounce of pain he saw etched on Sierra's face along with her anger.

"You weren't sneaking around behind my back fucking my husband every chance you got? Without protection? For God's sake, Heather, you got pregnant with his child."

"That was an accident."

"Right. You tripped and fell on his dick in the dark and didn't realize he wasn't wearing a condom."

Heather's mouth drew into a tight line. "You're angry. Maybe we should talk about this once you've calmed down."

"This is as calm as I will ever be when it comes to you fucking my husband. And this is the last time we will *ever* speak. Period."

Heather's eyes pleaded. "You don't mean that. Hallee is Danny and Oliver's sister. They deserve to know that and grow up knowing each other."

"Is that right? So you want to tell those two little boys that their father lied to their mother and cheated on her by sleeping with her own sister. Their *aunt*. How do you think that will make them feel about their father? You think they'll think he was a good man?"

"We can explain it in a way that doesn't make them upset with David."

Sierra laughed without any mirth in a nearly hysterical sound. "You stupid bitch. You didn't think about anything but yourself. You just took what you wanted, consequences be damned. You didn't think about how this would hurt me, let alone the children. Tearing up a family didn't even give you pause."

"I didn't want anyone to get hurt. David and I had this amazing connection. He said I made him feel alive."

"Stop talking," Mason warned Heather, knowing every excuse out of her mouth was a dagger through the back and straight into Sierra's heart.

Sierra stood rigid. "No. Go ahead. Tell me how much David wanted you."

"He loved me," Heather whispered.

"Did he tell you that while he was fucking you, then coming home to me?"

Heather looked unsure. "I knew he did. I felt it." Sierra laughed again and it set Heather off. "You don't know what we had."

"No. I don't. Because I was taking care of my kids while you were trying to steal their father and break up their home." Sierra paused, then shook her head and laughed under her breath. "When I arrived, you were surprised I wanted to move back home. You thought David was the one who wanted to move back here and I didn't want to leave Napa. You thought that because that's what *he* told you." She hit Heather with another hard truth. "What did you think he'd do, move us all down here and you two would carry on your affair right under my nose? He didn't want to get caught. He didn't want to lose his family. He didn't want to be with you, Heather. If he did, he'd have left me. All he did was give you excuses."

Hurt, Heather retaliated. "Yeah, well, while you thought he was on a business trip, he was actually with me."

"I got that. Stupid me for believing my husband, thinking that he cared about me and would never hurt me. I knew there was something wrong between us and I didn't do anything about it. I ignored it, because I had faith we'd make it right. And we had a good life despite the growing distance between us."

Heather just stared at Sierra.

"What? Did you think we were fighting like cats and dogs?" Sierra sighed. "You don't know anything about us, Heather. You weren't there when we sat down to dinner and talked about the boys and our day. You weren't there when he played with the boys and put them to bed and spent the weekends hanging out with all of us. You broke a family that could have been saved given some time for David and me to find our way back to each other, because we probably would have. At the core of our relationship we were always friends."

"You put all the blame on me, but he betrayed you, too."

"He did. But you're my sister. I thought that meant something. I would have done anything for you." Sierra's eyes filled with disgust before she closed them for a second. "Just looking at you makes me sick."

"I hoped you'd never find out."

"I bet. How long did you plan to carry on the affair? Until David and I celebrated our ten-year anniversary? Twenty years? Fifty?" Sierra frowned. "No. You were hoping to celebrate all those anniversaries with him. You hoped he'd leave me and the boys and pick you."

"Yes! I wanted him to pick me, but I also knew it would never work out even after we had Hallee."

"Was he there for the delivery? Did he help you pick out her name? Did he paint the nursery especially for her?"

Heather's gaze fell to the dirt.

"No. He didn't. Because he was at home with his family. And now he's not here at all." Sierra gasped and put her hand over her mouth. Her eyes were so wide and filled with an accusation she didn't look like she wanted to speak.

Mason prayed it wasn't what he was now thinking.

Sierra dropped her hands and sucked in a breath and took a menacing step toward Heather. "He died on Highway 1 when it was socked in with fog. He was coming to see you."

The accusation hung in the air, thick and menacing and fraught with Sierra's rage.

Heather wrapped her arms around her middle. Tears cascaded down her cheeks in rivulets. "Hallee got sick. Her temperature was so high. I had to take her to emergency. She had pneumonia. I was so scared I'd lose her, I called and begged him to come. She needed him."

Sierra and Heather stared at each other for a long moment, then Sierra broke the tense silence. "Should we tell the boys you're the reason their father is dead, too?"

"It's not my fault."

"No? Then whose fault is it? David should have been home in bed with me instead of crushed to death on the highway."

Mason turned at the sound of the house side door closing.

Sierra stared at her boys, each of them holding one of Hallee's hands, helping her down the porch steps. That's when the tears fell.

Heather and David deserved her anger.

The kids sparked her grief and sadness.

Sierra brushed away the tears and stared at her sister. "You took my husband. You destroyed my memories of him." She gave Mason a sharp look, then turned back to Heather. "And now I know why David needed that loan. For you. You took money that should have gone to my children. That cute little house you love so much, *I'm* the one paying for it. You just took and took and took and didn't care one bit. Well, let me tell you, I care. I will never forgive you for this."

"Sierra, please," Heather choked out.

"No. You don't get to ask me for anything ever again. Stay away from me and my children. I never want to see you again." Sierra cut off her words before the kids got too close to hear. She closed the distance to the boys and held her hands out to them. "Come with me."

The boys let Hallee loose and took their mother's hands. She turned and headed for the pasture. "We're going home." She directed that right at Mason.

Mason's heart broke and his throat constricted. His chest felt so tight he couldn't breathe. He'd blown this by confronting Heather without telling Sierra what he knew first.

"Sierra, this isn't fair," Heather called out to her as she held Hallee close to her chest and cried.

Sierra didn't even turn around when she shouted, "You should have thought about that when you took what didn't belong to you and killed it."

Heather burst into tears and heaving sobs.

Torn between going after Sierra and trying to make her listen to him and Heather crying all over a bewildered Hallee, Mason chose to save the little girl from her mother and plucked her right out of Heather's arms.

"Take a minute to get yourself together. I'll take

Hallee to see the horses." If he couldn't fix things with Sierra right now, at least he could make a little girl happy.

But damn his heart felt like it had been hit with a sledgehammer. He couldn't bear to see Sierra so upset. He'd explain his part. She'd understand.

He'd show her that no matter what, through good times and bad, he'd be right beside her, on her side, ready to love her through it.

Chapter Twenty-Eight

S ierra tried her best to hide her rage. The boys felt the vibe coming off her and remained watchful as they walked home. They didn't understand why she'd made them suddenly leave, without letting them go for their ride, without even saying good-bye to Mason or Aunt Heather.

But *she'd* said her good-byes. And that was enough for now.

Mason understood exactly what she'd meant when she said they were going home. She meant forever.

Sierra's mind raced.

He must have known, or suspected, something about Heather, David, and Hallee.

That's why he'd put off telling her whatever his investigator discovered.

He'd kept a huge secret from her.

After her husband's lies and betrayal, she wouldn't stand for another man in her life to keep things from her.

If she couldn't trust Mason, they had nothing.

As for Heather, her betrayal cut so deep she didn't think the wound would ever heal. Right now, every beat of her heart pumped out anger and hurt, filling her up to the point she felt like an explosion waiting to happen.

Tears stung her eyes when she thought of David and the last year of their marriage. And she couldn't help but wonder why, if he wanted to be with Heather, did he stay up in Napa with her?

And if he hadn't wanted to be with Heather, why didn't he come clean about the affair and beg her forgiveness?

Lying, cheating bastard.

Her conclusion: he hadn't wanted to face what he'd done, wanted a family with her and the boys and to keep Heather and Hallee on the side. Unable to face the consequences of his actions, he'd simply bided his time, hoping to not have to ever explain himself.

But a secret like that always comes out.

Sierra was surprised Heather kept her mouth shut this long, never revealing to anyone who Hallee's father really was.

And while she wanted to blame her sister for everything—Heather was impulsive, reckless, and always felt like she was entitled to whatever her sisters had—David was equally to blame.

He'd carried on with Heather behind Sierra's back for God knows how long. He'd fathered a child with her sister. He never said a damn thing to her about it. He never voiced even a hint that he wanted out of their marriage.

Of course she knew he'd been hiding something. But he still maintained their relationship. He was the perfect father. They still talked about their days, spent time together, kissed each other hello and good-bye, and yes, they'd had sex. Not as much as they used to, but they'd have a great night and then she'd wake up hopeful everything would go back to the way they were before, but then David would be distant again.

His guilt built a wall between them.

She hadn't known what it was at the time. She'd blamed herself, thinking that it must be something she did—or didn't do—that built the barrier between them.

But it had been David's actions that had ruined them as a couple.

He had doomed them, and he'd known it.

Instead of doing the right thing and confessing and letting her go, he'd hid his dirty deed.

All those months she'd wanted to confront him. Yes, she'd kept silent, hoping things would get better and she wouldn't have to upset the boys by fracturing their family.

But David had torn their family apart the second he slept with Heather.

The boys didn't know the full truth, but they'd felt something off in the house. Just like they felt her dark mood now.

And just like David had done, she was going to have to hide the truth from them, for now anyway.

When she finally got to the house, she found her mom sitting on the porch reading the mail when they walked up the steps. She took one look at Sierra and the smile she'd had for them died on her lips. "What's wrong?"

Sierra walked the boys to the front door, opened it, and stared down at them. "Please go upstairs, wash your hands, then you can have an hour of screen time. I need to speak to Grandma privately."

Danny stared up at her, eyes wide and filled with worry. "Is everything okay? Will we go see Mason later?"

She touched Danny's soft cheek. "I'm sorry, honey, but no. Something happened between us and I need to figure out what happens next."

"I thought you liked him." The concern in Danny's eyes turned to dismay. "Tell him to apologize."

"I wish it were that simple, sweetheart."

"Don't you want it to be okay?"

She put her hand on his shoulder and leaned over to look him in the eye. "I need some time to figure things out." Her anger made it hard to think reasonably and rationally.

Danny's eyes narrowed with frustration that she didn't give him an answer that made sense. If she could make sense of her feelings right now, it would be a lot easier.

She'd asked Mason to find the truth about the money and what David had been doing with it. But now she thought he'd already known. Or suspected it. Either way, he must have known to look in Heather's direction.

Danny took Oliver's hand and tugged him into the house.

She closed the door and turned on her mother. "Did you know?"

Her mother's head drew back at her angry tone. "I don't know what's got you so upset, but I do not appreciate being spoken to that way."

Sierra took a few steps toward her mom and pinned her in a hard glare. "Did you know that

Heather was having an affair with my husband and Hallee is David's child?"

All the color drained from her mom's face and her eyes went wide. "What? No." She shook her head back and forth saying, "No. No, no, no. She wouldn't do that."

"She *did* do that. Again and again and again. She thought David was going to leave me for her."

"Do you believe that?"

"That he was telling her the truth? No. I think he got caught up with her *and* wanted to somehow keep me and the boys. He strung her along, probably hoping he'd come up with some way to fix this."

Dede stood and embraced her. "Sierra, I'm so sorry."

Sierra didn't want to hurt her mother's feelings, but she didn't want to be touched or held right now. And because she didn't want to take things out on her mom, she gently pushed her away and took two steps back, her body tense, her chest aching with the expanding ball of emotions she tried to contain, but wanted to get rid of all at the same time.

"I think Mason knew about it."

"What?"

"I don't know how, or when he figured it out, but I think he suspected they had an affair and that Hallee belonged to David. He never said a word to me. Nothing." She pressed her hand to her forehead. "I think that's why he was reluctant to track down the money."

Dede gasped. "The house. I thought Heather saved up for it."

Sierra sneered. "Their private little getaway.

David would sneak away from us, pretending he had a business trip, and slip right into her bed."

Even more anguish filled her mother's eyes. "Oh, Sierra. I'm sorry. I wish I knew what to say."

"There's nothing to say. David's not even here to defend himself. Not that he could after what he's done. No, he left me to clean up the mess." She paced away, then back. "But you know what, I'm not cleaning up anything. As far as I'm concerned, Heather is just as dead to me as David is. They can both go to hell for all I care."

Her mom touched her arm. "You don't mean that."

She snatched her arm back. "Don't I? This isn't the same as her stealing the keys to my car and taking it out on a joyride. She slept with my husband and had his child and hid it all this time, soaking up all the sympathy we showered on her because Hallee's father wasn't in the picture and poor Heather had to do it all alone." It made her seethe inside to think of all the times she'd tried to soothe and sympathize with Heather. "She played on all of our heartstrings. We went out of our way to help and support her this past year and a half. I've been such a fool." She raked her fingers through her hair. "And to top it off, she's the one who begged David to come see her the night he died."

"What? No. What are you saying?"

"Hallee got sick. Heather panicked. She called and begged David to come. So he made a mad dash to get to her and crashed his car on the highway in the fog."

Her mother pressed her fingers to her mouth and her eyes filled with sympathy and understanding.

"He wanted to get to his sick child. Surely you must understand that."

She fisted her hands. "I'm not some coldhearted bitch. But he might have thought about the children he had at home."

Sierra went on. "Of course he wanted to get to Hallee and make sure she was okay. But it should have never happened because Hallee was never supposed to happen in the first place."

"It's not Hallee's fault."

She knew that but it didn't ease her anger. "Of course not. It's her parents' fault. And now Hallee, Danny, Oliver, and I are paying for their selfish, heartless deeds."

"Isn't there any way this can be fixed?"

She glared at her mom. "Why? How?" She held her arms out and let them drop. "Why would I want anything to do with Heather? So she can stab me in the back again? She was hitting on Mason when I showed up. Hell, she's probably sleeping with him right now." The thought turned her stomach and broke her heart even though she'd heard Mason loud and clear turn Heather down flat.

"I can't imagine Mason would do something like that to you." Dede let her head fall back and stared up at the porch ceiling before looking at Sierra again. "Your sister was always audacious."

"She's a home-wrecking whore."

Anger etched lines on her mom's forehead. "Sierra, that's enough. I know you're angry and hurt—"

"I'm furious. And I deserve to be."

"Of course you do, but you need to take a breath and give yourself time to sort this out."

"Why? So I can go back to paying for a loan that put a roof over *her* head. Should I give her the okay to go after Mason? Why not? She gets everything she wants and doesn't care who she steamrolls over to get it."

"You're right. She's selfish. She expects others to make her life easy. And she gets what she wants. Maybe that's my fault for spoiling the baby in the family."

"We all did. Amy and I took care of Heather. We watched over her. We gave in to her just as much as you did to keep her happy. I helped create the monster, I shouldn't be surprised she stabbed me in the back."

"If you feel that way, then teach her to take responsibility for what she's done."

"How? What can she possibly do to make this right in any kind of way that counts? Can she bring David back so Danny and Oliver have a father again? Can she not sleep with my husband? Can she in any way, shape, or form erase what she did? Can she make me stop second-guessing every interaction I had with David from the time she sank her claws into him? Can she make me feel less like a failure or that I drove him into her arms?"

"This is not your fault. All marriages have issues. That doesn't mean someone cheats."

"No. It opens the door for someone to want something and someone else."

"Sierra, honey, I've divorced three men, including your father, and each time I felt like I'd done something wrong. I took on all the blame. It had to be me. The marriages fell apart because there was something wrong with *me*."

Sierra shook her head.

"I finally realized there's nothing wrong with me. Those relationships ended because we didn't fight to keep them together. David gave up on your marriage. Instead of fixing it, he let the issues between you fester. He made a mistake. Of course you sensed something was wrong, so you were hesitant to keep your whole heart in the relationship. You didn't want to get hurt."

"It was already too late. I just didn't know it." She sucked in a steadying breath. "I didn't want to know it."

"Trust me, I understand. No one wants to know the person they love lied or cheated or simply doesn't want to be with them anymore. Whatever the problems, we want that love to survive. We don't want to feel the pain."

"It's all I feel now. All my memories are tarnished. Can I believe anything he said to me in the end? Was he just placating me, hoping I wouldn't find out? Were we happy, or did we just settle into our life and accept it?"

"I saw the two of you together. You were happy. He adored you and the boys."

"Are you sure? Because if he could sleep with my sister, not some stranger, but someone that close to me, I wonder if he loved me at all?"

The silence stretched while Sierra wallowed in her hurt and pain. Her mom tried to come up with something to say to make this better when nothing would change this.

"This is an impossible situation."

"This is a bad episode of shock TV. I'm trapped in my own real-life version of some sordid talk show where they reveal your sister slept with your husband and your niece is really your kids' half sibling."

"I don't even know how to help you through this." She appreciated her mom's honesty.

"I know you want some magic way to make this all right, that somehow Heather and I can work this out. For the children's sake," Sierra tossed out, because that's what couples tried to do when they wanted to keep things together for the kids.

"Have you thought about what you'll say to the children?"

"How are they supposed to understand this, when I can barely wrap my head around it?"

"They are siblings. I suppose, at some point, they should be told."

"I agree. At some point. But how do I tell my sons that their father was a cheater? How does that news impact them? Will they think it's okay to do that to a woman because, hey, their father did it to their mother? Or will they think it's the worst thing you can do to your partner and that their father is a bad person? No matter what David did, I don't want them to think less of their father."

"The truth is that David was human. He made mistakes. The boys can learn from them. You can make them understand that what David did was hurtful and wrong, but that doesn't mean he didn't love his children, that he wasn't a good father to them."

"He didn't think of what his actions would do to those boys. He didn't think about anything but what he wanted and his own selfish desires. This wasn't a onetime lapse in judgment. He carried on the affair for however long, maybe even up until his death."

"I'm sure Heather can fill in the details."

"I don't *need* the details. I don't want to hear her excuses or apologies. Nothing she says will make this better. Nothing will change my mind about what I think about her now and how I feel."

Dede deflated with a heavy sigh and sank into the chair. "What about Mason?"

"What about him? Am I supposed to trust him when he kept this from me?"

"You don't know for sure Mason knew before he investigated the loan. You love him. Not the same way you loved David. It's deeper. Don't let this come between you. Give him a chance to explain."

She would. But right now, she was mad at herself and the world, and she didn't think anyone could say anything to change that.

"All I know is that I don't want to see her ever again. I don't want to be confronted with what she and David did every time I see her. I don't want to feel this way over and over again."

"Please, Sierra, take some time to let all this sink in and settle before you make any drastic decisions."

"I don't have a choice. I have to think of the boys. I can't just do what I want to do like Heather does without thought to how it affects others. No. I have to be responsible and thoughtful and considerate and decent while she does whatever the hell she wants, consequences be damned."

Her mother allowed the bitter snarkiness without comment. "All I'm saying is take some time. Think about who's at fault and who's not. What's best for your kids?"

Yeah, that last part was the hardest. The boys deserved to know Hallee was their sister. Lies had a way of coming out eventually, and they would have to learn the truth.

She was expected to be the bigger person. But it was damn hard when she was the one wronged in so many ways.

"Would you please watch the boys? I need to get out of here for a while."

"Where are you going?"

"I don't know. Away from here."

"You can't outrun this, sweetheart."

"I know. But I can at least be alone with it for a while and not have to worry about what everyone else wants me to do and how they want me to feel and what they expect me to do to make this all right for everyone. I want to just be mad."

Because being hurt and sad just might break her.

And she didn't want the boys to see her curled into a ball, crying her heart out over a man who broke her heart and a sister who crushed it to pieces.

Chapter Twenty-Nine

S ierra found herself at the ocean, sitting in the sand, staring at the waves crashing on the beach, seagulls screeching overhead, her thoughts a swirl of emotions as wild as the wind blowing her hair back. Tears streamed down her cheeks unchecked. They dripped on her shirt and still she stared out at the wide expanse of water, out to the horizon, and fought the urge to just walk right into the waves and let them carry her away.

She didn't really want to die. What she really wanted was to not hurt anymore. She wanted to erase what she knew from her mind and heart.

She wanted to believe people were good and kind and did the right thing.

David. Heather. They betrayed her. They lied.

How could her sister sleep with her husband?

How could David break every promise and vow and hurt her that way?

If he was that unhappy, if he wanted someone and something else, he should have said so. Ending their relationship would have hurt, but it wouldn't have been this devastating.

Not only had he cheated, he'd done so with her sister.

The thought cut so deep, she couldn't bear it. She hugged her knees to her chest, but nothing eased the pain. Her head pounded with every horrible thought that kept rolling in like the waves, the onslaught of second-guessing all their conversations and everything he did all those months he was seeing Heather behind her back.

Now it all made a horrible kind of sense.

Looking back, she had had her suspicions, but she'd never come right out and accused him of an affair. Part of her didn't want to know. The other part didn't want to mess up the life their boys blissfully enjoyed, not knowing one iota of the troubles facing their parents.

She hadn't wanted to burst their happy bubble. She had wanted to protect them. And her heart.

Ignorance is bliss.

Until you're forced to face the truth.

David did cheat. He lied. He betrayed her and broke their vows.

He left her with a hell of a mess.

She hated David for what he'd done. But David wasn't here. She couldn't yell at him or force him to hear all the terrible things she wanted to say. He'd taken that from her.

But Heather was here. She hated Heather.

She'd have a thousand excuses for her behavior. She'd romanticize their relationship, say it was meant to be, that David's and her love couldn't be denied.

She'd already sworn she never meant to hurt Sierra. But what did she expect would happen when Sierra found out?

And the kids. Oh god, how would she ever explain to Danny and Oliver that their father slept with Heather and had a child with her? They may not understand the ramifications of that now, but they'd understand when they got older.

She hated David for leaving it to her to explain to their children.

Because she couldn't get away with not telling them. Hallee was proof of what happened, and eventually she'd have to be told the circumstances of her birth and that she had two brothers.

What would she think when she discovered Sierra hated Heather because of it?

She sensed her mom wanted to find a way to reconciliation, but Sierra couldn't see past her rage and hurt to a time when she wouldn't feel this way when she looked at Heather.

Just thinking about her brought on a new wave of anger that she had no way of expending. It just built inside her like a volcano, the pressure pushing against everything inside her, wanting to explode.

The salty mist clung to her hair and chilled her skin. She could use a sweater and something hot to drink.

She could use a friend, someone who'd let her scream about all the injustices dealt her these last two years.

She didn't deserve this. She tried to be a good mom, wife, lover, and friend.

None of that mattered to David.

He'd taken what he wanted, their marriage and her be damned.

Her phone beeped with yet another text or voice mail she wanted to ignore. Her mom wondering where she was and if she was okay. Maybe Amy.

Heather probably went to her, hoping to get Amy on her side. Sierra doubted Amy would be sympathetic.

But Amy would be happy to open a bottle of wine and trash-talk Heather and David all night with her. Deep down, Sierra knew that wouldn't really help.

Another beeping notification followed quickly by another. Maybe Mason. He was the hardest to ignore.

She didn't take out her phone. She didn't worry about what they needed or wanted. The last thing she wanted to do right now was make this okay for everyone else while her heart lay in pieces at the bottom of her battered soul.

She laid her head on her knees and let the grief swallow her as the tears came in a torrent she couldn't stop or hold back anymore. She let the pain and grief pour out, but the ache of it never seemed to cease, it just kept throbbing. Even when the tears dried and the hiccups disappeared and the sun fell into the ocean, the grief, the pain, they were still there, claws sunk deep in her heart and mind, unrelenting, just like the waves battering the shore and the wind blowing against her, chilling her to the bone.

Sierra stood on stiff legs, hands numb with cold, and gave one last solemn look at the beautiful ocean and headed back to her car.

The boys were probably wondering what happened to her and why she wasn't home to get them ready for bed. She knew her mom would take care of them, but they expected their own mother to care for them.

She couldn't dwell on her problems forever, but

she'd needed these last several hours alone to think and grieve and be angry and upset without having to explain herself to anyone.

Now, she'd be the adult and mom and gather herself up and forge ahead because what the hell else was she supposed to do.

Life sucked. People disappointed and hurt others all the time. And tomorrow was another day to deal with it all and figure out what she did from here.

The boys deserved the best of her. One day they'd appreciate all she'd sacrificed and given for their happiness.

Being the adult and the mom sucked, because it meant she had to do all the hard stuff so her kids were happy.

After everything she'd been through with David and Heather, she wished there was one person wholly and unequivocally on her side.

Someone who knew all that happened and said, *You deserved better. They suck. Fuck them*, and stood beside her through all that still needed to be done to get her life back on track.

Chapter Thirty

Mason sat on the porch steps waiting for the woman he loved to come home, knowing he had one shot at explaining himself. If he blew it, his whole life's happiness would disappear.

He'd spent far too many years wishing for her.

He'd fix this and make her happy the rest of her life because he didn't want to live without her.

He'd show her every day how much he loved her. She'd never have cause to question how he felt about her and that he was completely, irrevocably devoted to her.

Now if he could only figure out how to make her believe him.

All his texts thus far had gone unanswered. He didn't take it as a bad sign. She hadn't answered any of Dede's calls or texts, either.

The front door opened behind him. He turned and stared up at Dede. "Have you heard from her?"

She gave him a sad frown. "No. Not yet. I thought she'd be home for dinner or at least in time to put the boys to bed."

He completely deflated and hung his head. "She'll be here soon." The assurance didn't ease his mind or heart. It probably did nothing for Dede, either.

"I told you, you didn't have to wait out here."

"I didn't want to intrude."

"Well, they heard your truck pull in earlier and they refuse to go to bed without a bedtime story from you."

He glanced at Dede over his shoulder. "I'm not sure Sierra would appreciate that given how she walked away today without giving me a chance to explain."

"The boys don't know that. They're anxious and worried that their mom isn't here. They didn't buy that she had to go to work, especially after they saw how upset she was earlier. I think you might have a better chance of convincing them she's okay than I did."

He sucked in a breath and let it out, but it did nothing to loosen the band of regret and worry wrapped around his chest, making it hard to breathe.

He couldn't deny the boys or let this opportunity to see them go.

He stood and faced Dede, letting loose one of the apologies he thought he owed. "I'm sorry about how this went down. I wanted to talk to her today about what I knew about David, but after the balloon ceremony this morning and her getting called away to work, I let it go, hoping we'd have time alone after the boys' ride to talk."

"Sierra told me a little of what happened with Heather. I'm beside myself. I don't know what to do. Heather won't take my calls, either. I'll give her time to get herself together."

"Then what?" The bitter question put Dede on the spot, but Mason didn't care. Heather didn't deserve any coddling from her mom. She'd wronged Sierra in the most hurtful way possible. And he'd gotten caught up in her web of lies and deceit.

He had no sympathy for Heather.

If David were alive, he'd kick his ass for treating his wife so callously and leaving her to deal with the fallout of his bad behavior.

There was no good way out of this for Sierra.

She had to live with knowing her husband and sister betrayed her. Worse, she had to explain to the kids and try to do it in a way that didn't make her the bad guy by disparaging their father and aunt. Impossible.

But Sierra had a big heart and she'd try, all the while her heart would be breaking. But she'd suck it up and do right by her children because she loved them enough to take the hit herself.

"Both my girls are hurting."

"Heather doesn't deserve sympathy for what she's done to Sierra."

"David was a part of this, too."

"And Heather is your daughter and you're loyal to her. I get that it's easier to blame David. He's not here to answer for what he did. But you should have seen Heather today, she outright came on to me. She didn't even ask if I was seeing someone. She just thinks she can have whatever she wants."

"Did Sierra hear that?"

"I'm pretty sure she heard the whole exchange. Heather didn't seem to know Sierra and I are *seeing* each other. We've kept our relationship quiet. But she does know Sierra and I have always been close and we were spending time together with the boys at the ranch. Amy knows because she watched the boys while we went on a date, but Sierra never had a reason to say anything about it to Heather other than in a casual way because the boys were always around."

Mason rubbed his hand over his tense neck. He thought about their conversation. "I don't think Heather really likes me. We barely know each other, but I'm a good catch." He didn't say that out of conceit, but because it was true for Heather. "To Heather, I look like great husband and father material. I've shown that I want a family of my own, so she decided to insert herself into my life as the perfect potential wife."

Dede put her hand to her chest. "How did we go from talking about you being a father to those boys this morning to this?"

He held his hands up and let them fall. "It's been a hell of a day." And he hated that he'd hurt Sierra. "I better get upstairs to the boys before they get restless and more worried about their mom."

He left Dede on the porch lost in her thoughts about the day and her daughters and how they were going to fix this. Mason wasn't so sure it could be fixed, but for Hallee's sake, he hoped Sierra was willing to try.

Mason stood in the doorway and stared into Danny and Oliver's room. The night-light between the two twin beds highlighted their faces and solemn eyes. He hated seeing them upset and worried about their mom.

"Hey, why aren't you guys asleep yet?"

"Where's Mommy?" Oliver's bottom lip quivered.

"She'll be home soon."

"Something is wrong." Danny sat up and studied

Mason, looking for any sign that he knew why their mom wasn't here.

So Mason gave it to them straight. "Your mom is very upset right now. She and Heather had an argument. Your mom is deeply hurt and sad. She needed some time to herself to sort out her thoughts."

"She's mad at you, too, isn't she?" Nothing much got past Danny.

Mason wondered if he'd picked up on the tension between his mom and dad when David was still alive.

"I kept something from your mom. I should have told her right away, but I didn't want to hurt her, either. I ended up hurting her anyway because I waited too long to say something."

"What?" Oliver asked.

Danny leaned forward, wanting to know, too.

"That's between me and your mom. I was wrong. I will apologize as soon as I see her." That was the best he could do to show the boys that even adults screwed up sometimes and had to take responsibility and apologize when they did.

Mason moved into the room and stood by Danny's bed. He leaned over and pointed at the books on the blanket. "Want me to read these?"

Danny hesitated a moment, still taking Mason's measure and deciding that he wasn't going to dismiss him yet. He nodded and scooted over so Mason could sit beside him, propped against the headboard.

Oliver jumped out of his bed and climbed up onto Mason's lap, lying down on his chest, his head on Mason's shoulder.

Mason opened the first book and started reading

about pirates and treasure. He got the words out, but his focus was on Oliver and Danny so trusting and sweet, pressed against him.

He loved these boys.

He already thought of them as his own. He wanted a thousand more nights like this with them. And Sierra.

He read one book and then another. The boys settled in and relaxed, their eyes drooping by the time he started book three. They were asleep before the last page, but he read it through anyway, wanting the boys to know he was there watching over them. He settled into the quiet, one arm wrapped around Oliver on his chest, the other around Danny at his side.

Nothing had ever felt this right and poignant and like a wish come true.

If only—

That thought cut off when Sierra appeared in the doorway, fulfilling his thought.

She was finally here.

She stared at him, trying so hard to hide her feelings, but he saw the longing that she wanted this to be their lives and the disappointment that he'd kept something important from her.

Determined to fix it, he gently slipped his arm from Danny's back, letting him settle into the pillow. He adjusted Oliver into his arms and rose from the mattress, laying Oliver in his own bed and settling him under the covers. Filled with love for the boys, he leaned over and kissed Oliver's brow, then turned and did the same to Danny.

With one last glance to be sure the boys were settled and sleeping peacefully, he headed to the door and caught up to Sierra at the stairs. He couldn't help reaching out and brushing his hand down her hair.

She flinched and glanced over her shoulder, giving him a warning glare.

Undeterred, he looked her in the eye and hoped she saw the remorse overflowing from him. "We need to talk."

Chapter Thirty-One

S ierra walked down the stairs, barely spared her mother a glance, and went right out the front door onto the porch.

"It's not fair that you come over here and cuddle with my kids and think that will soften me up." Okay, it had, because, damn, the scene she walked in on was sweet and filled with sincerity because she'd seen the way he held the boys and kissed them good night and it was . . . perfect.

"I came here to talk to *you*. Spending time with Danny and Oliver was a bonus I didn't expect, but they knew I was here waiting for you and wanted me to read them bedtime stories. And you know what, I loved it. I love them. And I love you." He paused.

She stared out at the yard with him at her back, fighting the urge to turn and face him, but knowing she had to because they couldn't leave things like this.

She tried to mentally prepare herself to look at him and not feel anything, but the second she turned and saw the agonizing pain in his eyes she caved and her heart swelled with the love she couldn't deny and didn't want to let go of without giving him a chance. "You lied to me. I asked you to look into the loan, but you already knew what David did with the money."

"No, that's not true. I suspected, but I had no facts to back it up. It would be wrong to make an accusation like that to you, not knowing if it was really true or not. What if I'd told you I thought David and Heather had an affair and Hallee belonged to him and it wasn't true? Do you think I wanted to put you through that without being absolutely certain?"

Sierra sighed. Everything he said made sense. She'd been so obsessed with thinking about David and Heather, what they did behind her back, she hadn't really thought it through.

Mason had been trying to do the right thing, the right way.

"I'm guilty of withholding my suspicions, and yes, not telling you the second the investigator had all the proof to back them up. I didn't know how to tell you. I didn't want what they did to hurt you the way it has. I wanted to figure out a good way to tell you, but there wasn't one. The few times I tried to tell you, we were interrupted. I couldn't just blurt it out with other people around. And I hate the way you found out."

"You mean while watching my sister hit on you."

"You also saw me turn her down flat."

He did. No hesitation. Not even a hint that the prospect of seeing Heather intrigued him.

After everything she'd already lost, Sierra couldn't bear to lose him, too, despite the fact this wasn't completely resolved. "I'm still mad."

"You have every right to be about all of this. But you know in your heart I did plan to tell you everything. I tried to tell you this morning but the timing wasn't right. I told you we'd talk after the boys' ride."

She held up her hand to stop him defending himself further. She remembered all that, it had just gotten buried under everything else for a while.

"Of course Heather picks today to stab me in the back after I spent all that time trying to give the boys a chance to remember their father in a meaningful way."

He pleaded with her again. "I should have told you what I knew sooner, but . . . God, Sierra, the last thing I wanted was to see you like this and know I had any part of it."

"You didn't want to investigate David."

"No, I didn't, because I didn't want what I suspected to be true. But I went ahead with it because you deserved to know the truth."

Mason might be the only person who'd give her the unvarnished truth. "Why did you suspect them?" She stood waiting, afraid to hear the details but feeling like knowing was better than letting her mind torture her with a million scenarios.

"Remember Charles's funeral?"

"You barely spoke to me. You were here with your fiancéc."

One side of his mouth drew back in a half frown. "Feeling like a total ass because the woman I really wanted to be with married my friend. I stayed away from you because I didn't want my fiancée to see how much I wanted you. I guess I didn't hide it well enough because we ended things shortly after that day. I couldn't go through with a marriage to a woman I loved but wasn't wholly *in* love with."

"Mason, you can't tell me that you broke it off with her and stayed single all this time because you were waiting for me."

"Why not? It's true." He shrugged. "I didn't do it consciously. I told myself, one day I'd love someone the way I loved you. I dated. I had short-lived relationships. But that day never came. Until you moved back home. The second I saw you, I knew I wasn't going to let you get away again without my doing everything possible to show you how much I love you." He raked his fingers through his hair. "I blew it today."

She couldn't let him blame himself for something David and Heather did. "No. You didn't."

His gaze came up and met hers. The desperate hope in his eyes softened her heart and erased all the anger she'd directed at him.

"You loved me enough to turn Heather's offer down flat."

"I only want you."

"You confronted her for me about David and Hallee. You made her tell the truth for once."

"I should have spoken to you first, as I planned to, but in that moment I was so angry for you. I couldn't stand there and let her try to do with me what she did with David behind your back."

"How did you come to suspect them?"

"Everyone gathered here after the graveside ceremony. People were packed into the house. You were chasing after the boys, keeping them in line."

"And David was nowhere to be found." After the long car ride the day before, the boys not sleeping in the strange house, having to stand still and be quiet through the long ceremony, and stuffing themselves with goodies when they got back, well, they were acting out. David lost his patience and made himself scarce. Truthfully, their days were filled with those types of outbursts from two energetic boys.

She'd spent most of that day feeling frazzled and resentful that David had checked out on her.

"I saw him with Heather out back sharing a drink and talking. I didn't think much of it. You guys didn't get back often, so I thought they were just catching up."

David and Heather had always had a close relationship. Sierra never thought anything of the way they joked with each other. She appreciated that her husband and sister got along so well, especially since Heather, as the youngest, wasn't often included in her and Amy's outings growing up. The age gap meant she couldn't hang out at the bar with them.

"But you saw the closeness between them."

"I saw a woman flirting with your husband. I expected David to brush it off, take a step back, and go inside to be with you."

"But that's not what happened."

"Heather may have been flirting, but David's the one who took her hand and tugged, coaxing her to leave with him. They started walking across the yard together. Away from the house and the others milling around on the back porch and garden area. Heads together, talking, laughing, they disappeared around the back of the house out toward the pond."

"And the shed out there." Dede had allowed her girls to turn it into a fort of sorts when they were teens. They had a mini fridge, a large rug where they used to sleep in their sleeping bags and tell ghost stories all night, and an old worn leather sofa. It was their hideaway just inside the woods, shaded by trees, and just rustic enough for them to feel like they were in their own world.

And Heather turned it into a lovers' hideaway with *her* husband.

"I couldn't follow them without making it obvious."

"So you're not sure what really happened."

"I suspected, so I waited for them to return. When I saw them, I knew by the looks on their faces, the way they touched hands, trying to make sure no one saw. The way she brushed her hand down her thigh to smooth her skirt and over her hair. David scanned the whole yard, looking to be sure you weren't out there, seeing him return with Heather. I saw the guilt. But I couldn't be sure what he was guilty of. A stolen kiss? More?"

"But you suspected you knew exactly what was going on."

"Yes. And it turned my stomach to watch him go back inside to you and act like nothing happened. He said something to you and you smiled at him. Heather glared at the two of you from across the room."

"After all that, you still didn't think to tell me something?"

"David accused me once when we were all out together of being jealous."

She understood. "He knew you liked me."

"I don't know how I managed to hide it from you all the time, but David saw it. Maybe it's a guy thing. We tend to have radar for other men looking at our girlfriend or wife."

"Do you remember telling Amy that you wanted to tell me how you felt?"

"Of course. I wanted you to know so bad, but she said you were happy with David. You loved him. Telling you would do me no good and probably end our friendship. I didn't want that. I wanted you to be happy."

"I get that, but you should know she also didn't tell you what I told her about you."

He took a step closer, his eyes narrowed with confusion and anger. "What do you mean?"

"I told her that I was having second thoughts about marrying David because of my growing feelings for you."

Mason fell back a step. Eyes wide, he sputtered, "What?"

"My sisters seem hell-bent on meddling in my relationships." Sierra shook her head and pressed on. "Amy encouraged me to stay with David because she thought you were still married to your job and David offered me what I really wanted. Plus, she'd always had a crush on you and she didn't want me to have you."

"Seriously?" Mason rubbed his hand over the back of his neck. "I can't believe she held out on both of us." The frustration in his words matched her own.

"Trust me, I wasn't happy when I found out, either. But here I am, stuck with the aftermath of what my sisters did. Amy's petty interference seems insignificant compared to what Heather did, but both of them changed my life." She pinned him with her gaze. "And you should have told me, not Amy, that you had feelings for me."

He held her gaze. "You have no idea how much I wish I had done just that." He really meant it.

"On one hand I wish I'd made a different choice. On the other . . ."

He nodded, his eyes going soft with understanding. "You have Danny and Oliver."

"Exactly. Now what? What's done is done. I can't change the past or what David and Heather did."

"Everything would have been different if we'd just confessed our feelings."

"Maybe. But we were different people back then. At the time, were we right for each other? Would we have gotten married, had kids, and lived a happy life together?"

"Yes." No hesitation. Just absolute assurance. Mason knew how he felt and what he wanted. "We can still have all of that if you can just forgive me."

"I do forgive you. It's easy to do because you really didn't do anything wrong. You wanted to protect me. That's more than my own sisters ever did for me."

Mason closed the distance and cupped her face in his warm hands. "I love you, Sierra. Let me prove it to you. Let me show you."

"I see it in everything you do, Mason. I let my anger get the better of me earlier despite the fact you'd made it clear you had news for me about David."

"Does this mean we're still together, that you're not going to leave me?"

She placed her hands on his wrists and leaned into his palm. "I don't want to lose you. You and the boys are the only good things I have in my life. I love you." She did. And she trusted Mason. "But I don't know what comes next with all this."

"I want to help you through it. I'm here for whatever you need." He pressed a kiss to her forehead.

"I appreciate that." Unable to look him in the eye and say the next part, she stared at his chest. "I'm just not sure that I can stay here and see Heather and Hallee and not tear open this wound every time I do."

He nudged her face up so she'd look at him. "Don't let her take away your happiness again. If you leave, and we can't be together, I don't know . . . somehow it feels like she wins."

That was the last thing Sierra wanted.

"But if you truly can't live here, then I'll go wherever you want to go."

Stunned by his words, she met his gaze with her wide-eyed one. "Mason. You can't leave your home and your law practice for me."

"Why not? I love you. What good is a job and a home if you aren't with me and I'm alone and unhappy?"

They'd wasted a lot of time trying to build a life without each other, always feeling like something was off or not quite right. They were missing each other and the deep, true love they shared. She didn't want to let go of the way she felt right here, right now, standing with the man who not only would say he'd give up everything to be with her, but meant it.

"Ever since you came back, I spend my days desperate to see you. I think about you all day, to the point I'm distracted on calls and in meetings and people think I've lost my mind. I have. And my heart. Over you. I think about the life we could have together. I think about the boys growing up at the ranch with the horses. I think about us being a family and you and I having more kids."

"Kids?"

"One. At least. Two if you're up for it. However many you want. You can quit your job and be with the kids. Or keep your job. Cut your hours. Take a different job. I don't care. Settle all this other stuff the best you can and be happy with me."

She knew it wouldn't be easy to live with what happened, but she'd find a way, so she could be happy with him. "Okay."

"Really?" Genuine surprise filled his voice. "I thought I'd have to do a hell of a lot more convincing."

"Why? No one has ever loved me the way you do. I want the boys to grow up with a man like you to look up to. I want a husband who thinks my happiness is the most important thing in the world. I want to show you that the love you give me is appreciated by loving you the same way. I want to be ridiculously happy. And maybe part of being happy is letting go of the past and the people who have hurt me."

"I'm not sure you'll really be happy without your sister in your life."

"I don't know if I'm capable of forgiving her. I know I'll never trust her again."

Mason frowned. "Are *we* good?"

"Yes. When I got home tonight, my emotions were raw and all over the place. I was angry and hurt and just a mess. But I pulled into the drive and saw your truck, and though I didn't want to feel anything, a spark of joy burst because you came to see me even after I ignored you. You didn't give up."

"Never."

"Then I saw you with the boys and it was so obvious that you love them. You owned up to what happened and told me the truth about what you knew even though you didn't want to paint a picture of how my husband and sister betrayed me right here at my home, right under my nose, even though I knew they'd been together."

Mason rubbed his hands up and down her arms. "It makes it harder and more real to know the details."

"Yes, it does. It's all part of the same betrayal. I can't escape what happened or how it's changed my perspective of the past and how I feel about David, our marriage, and my sister. Nothing is the same. I'll need time to come to terms with all of it. But I don't need time to evaluate how I feel about you. That is so clear in my mind and heart. David's death, the fire, they've taught me that time is precious. I don't want to waste any more of it or give anyone else a chance to interfere in our lives again. I love you. I want to build a life with you. I won't let anything or anyone come between us again."

"Then let's make it happen."

"Okay." She didn't hesitate to go after what she wanted.

Mason stared down at her with a smile that lightened her heart when she thought nothing would today. "Okay. Where do you want to start?"

"I could really use a hug."

"Come here, sweetheart." Mason pulled her in to his chest and held her close.

She slipped her hands around his sides to his back and hugged him close.

"Best thing that's happened all day." Mason kissed her on the head.

She loved that he tried to make her focus on the good. Right now, she had the best in her arms. And she wouldn't let him go, not for anything.

"It's late. You've had a hell of a day. You must be tired. I don't want to let you go, but . . ."

"Don't." She leaned back and stared up at him. "I don't want to lie in bed alone all night with my head spinning."

"Come home with me. I'll hold on to you." That's exactly what she wanted him to say and do. "I'll make sure you're up and home before the boys wake up. Tomorrow, we'll figure out the rest."

"As long as it begins and ends with you and me, I think we'll be okay."

Mason kissed her softly. "My whole world begins and ends with you."

That beautiful statement wiped away any and all lingering doubts trying to creep in and spoil this reconciliation. Sierra let all the bad get washed away by the wave of love she felt for him.

She'd have to deal with what she knew about David and Heather, but she didn't have to do it alone. Mason would stand beside her. He'd hold her when she needed it. He'd love her through the bad and fill her up with nothing but good.

If he could do that for her today of all days, she bet he'd have no problem making her happy and feel like she was wanted and needed like she did right now every day for the rest of their lives.

She didn't want much, but she refused to live another day without love and trust.

Mason made her feel safe.

He had her back.

He'd lift her up when she was down just like he'd done for her today with his open honesty and heart-warming love.

Chapter Thirty-Two

Heather stood next to the stove in the late-morning light lost in thought until the high-pitched whistle of the teakettle broke into her reverie. That's when she realized the *other* sound she heard was someone pounding on the front door.

She turned off the stove and headed for the loud knocks, ready to send whoever it was on their way.

Her mother stood on the stoop, dark circles under her bloodshot eyes. She'd pulled her silver-streaked brown hair back into a sleek bun, which had the effect of making her look even more tired. "If you slam that door on me, you will regret it."

Heather checked the urge to close the door on the inevitable scolding and refrained from rolling her eyes. "What are you doing here? Shouldn't you be home judging me?"

Dede brushed right past her and stood in the living room. "After what you've done, you deserve a good talking-to from your mother." She glanced into Hallee's room. "Where is she?"

"Day care. I needed some time alone."

"I bet. Your sister is really angry. I taught you better than this."

This time, Heather did roll her eyes. "Please. Four husbands. Don't tell me you never strayed." Their lives growing up had been a revolving door of men coming and going. Dede tried to be discreet with the dating, but they knew what was going on.

"When I was done, I left. I never cheated. I never went after someone who wasn't available. David wasn't free to love you. He had a wife and a family. He was bound to them. No matter how it happened, you knew that and you participated in ruining that marriage."

That hurt, but deep down Heather knew it was true.

"He degraded you. He made you his dirty secret, knowing you two would never really end up together, not with so much standing in your way."

Harsh!

"And you went along with it."

Because I loved him. I thought the time we had together would be enough.

Heather had dreamed about the beautiful life they'd share raising Hallee, knowing it was only a figment of her imagination. Nothing but wishful thinking.

She'd worked so hard to suppress her feelings about Sierra's family, so she could wallow in their love.

Naïve. Stupid. Callous. Scared. Selfish.

She called herself all those things and more. She knew it couldn't last forever, but she never expected things to end with David's death.

"You were the *other* woman. Not *his* woman."

Her heart ached knowing that was true, too.

"You don't know what we had." No one understood how David made her feel, what they shared when they were together.

"Sex isn't love, Heather. It's a thrill. It's temporary."

She knew that all too well. Because the second David walked out the door and went back to Sierra, she felt his absence. All the wonderful feelings inside her dissipated and she wondered if he'd be back. Did he care? Did he really love her? Was the regret in his eyes because he had to go or because he hated himself for cheating on his wife?

"David was married to Sierra. That's a bond not easily broken."

Heather had felt it. Though David was with her, in the back of his mind he was thinking about Sierra. He worried about what would happen if they got caught. He feared losing his boys.

"He had no trouble breaking his vows." That wasn't exactly true. After that first time, she had to push. Every time she asked him to come visit, she had to coax and tempt him. But still he came to her every time.

She'd felt a sense of power in that.

He'd been drawn to her. But he'd also been pulled back by Sierra and the boys.

"So it's true. You went after him like you did with Mason."

She resented how that made her sound. "It wasn't like that with either of them. I didn't know about Mason and Sierra. And David and I had a connection." It had been fragile and tenuous. She'd been careful to never give David an ultimatum because she feared he'd choose his life with Sierra and the boys. Where would that leave her and Hallee?

Exactly where they were now. Alone.

Her mom shook her head in dismay. "Maybe there was something good between you. I hope

David didn't betray his wife and children for nothing. But you can't honestly believe the relationship could hold up to a divorce and the two of you being together after you both destroyed your relationship with Sierra. Did you think she'd happily allow the boys' visitation with their father here with you, the woman who stole her husband and tore her family apart? What do you think the boys would think of you? Of their father? How would they deal with seeing their mother upset and sad and hurt?"

"I never dreamed things would go so far. Hallee was a surprise and a blessing I never expected. The relationship became so much bigger than David and me. But none of that matters now. He's dead. We'll never be together again."

"It matters a hell of a lot to Sierra. It will matter to those boys and Hallee when they learn the truth. Maybe you can delude yourself into thinking it all ended with David's death, but it didn't."

"I don't think that. I'm just saying that I don't get to be with him anymore. He's gone. Sierra got all the sympathy when he died, but I lost him, too. *I* loved him. *I* grieve for him. Hallee will never know her father. She won't have a single memory of him. The boys will. Sierra does. But I'm not allowed to have my feelings or express my grief or even share my memories with anyone."

"Whose fault is that?" The snap in her mother's tone conveyed her anger all too well.

"It's my fault. And David's." She wasn't the only one who did the wrong thing. "We did this." She combed her fingers through her hair and pushed the wild waves back. It made her momentarily think of the way David would do the same thing a second before he kissed her with a passion and desperation she'd never felt with anyone.

She didn't know why he went behind Sierra's back. She didn't care. She had just wanted him. If she could give him what Sierra couldn't, it somehow made her feel like she was the better woman for him.

But he'd never chosen her over Sierra. Not in a permanent way.

When she asked him when they'd finally be together, he changed the subject, distracted her with sex, or simply said he needed more time to figure out a way to tell Sierra that didn't mean he'd lose his boys.

But that was never going to happen.

Revealing their relationship meant the destruction of others.

And now that's exactly what happened.

Sierra hated her. Her mother was disappointed and angry with her. When Amy found out, she'd take Sierra's side. Mason had looked at her with such contempt she still felt the impact of it even now.

Heather folded her arms around her middle, wishing her mother understood. "I never meant to hurt Sierra. I didn't want to break up her marriage. I only saw that David was unhappy." She reconsidered. "He was restless. I felt the same way. None of my dates ever gave me the spark I felt when I was with David. He was kind and funny and paid attention to me. We kept it friendly at first, but I wanted more. And then all of a sudden, teasing turned to serious flirting and the line blurred until I couldn't see it and I found myself in David's arms. I thought I'd get everything I wanted."

"You thought you'd get what your sisters had. A loving husband. Children. A home."

As shameful and deluded as it was, Heather had allowed herself to think that sometimes. "I wanted all those things."

"Well, you got them. Of course, the husband belonged to someone else. The child didn't have a full-time father. And the home didn't include you all happily living together."

"Right. I got what I deserved. Believe me, I know. The guilt eats at me every day. But Hallee doesn't deserve to pay for my mistakes."

"She suffered from day one. It was always going to end this way. You had to know that. Or were you okay giving up your family for a man who'd cheat on his wife?"

She hated that her mom put it that way, but reality slapped her in the face.

Dede didn't wait for an answer Heather didn't really have. "Do you think David would have felt that way? That he didn't care what Sierra, his boys, the rest of the family thought about what you two had done?"

"Obviously he cared. He didn't leave her. He tried so hard to hide what we'd done."

Dede's head tilted to the side. "Did you two stop seeing each other before he died?"

Damn. She hadn't meant to let that slip.

"When I told him I was pregnant . . ."

Dede nodded, filling in the blanks. "Reality hit. He couldn't hide what you'd done anymore. He knew it would eventually come out. He stopped sleeping with you."

Raw pain pinched her heart. "Yes. He said he couldn't do it anymore. He promised to support us, but all the love and affection disappeared. When he looked at me, it was like he regretted every second of our time together." And it broke her heart even now to remember it.

"Guilt is a heavy burden. He wronged Sierra, his boys, even you. And you willingly participated with him. You could put Sierra out of your mind, but he couldn't. Not when he had to go home and face her and his children and their life." Dede frowned. "Didn't you see the toll your affair was taking on him?"

"Yes. Of course I did. I told him everything would be okay. That he didn't have to stay with Sierra if he wasn't happy."

"But he didn't leave her. What ate away at David was that he wanted things to work out with her, right?"

She pressed her lips tight, not wanting to confirm it. Not wanting to feel the hurt that he wanted Sierra more than he wanted her.

"There was no way to fix things. Once she found out about us, she'd leave him."

"And you'd be there to pick up the pieces. I'm surprised you didn't tell her yourself." Her mom leveled the accusation with such conviction.

Heather glanced out the window at the blooming flowers, not feeling as cheerful as them by a long shot.

"You thought about it," her mother answered for her. "Wow. How selfish can you be?"

Very.

But it didn't mean she didn't feel for Sierra, that she didn't feel guilty and rotten about herself for what she'd done. It didn't mean she didn't regret her choices at the same time she cherished her memories of David and that she got Hallee.

"Why does she get everything and I'm left with nothing?"

"Nothing? You have this house. You have Hallee. What have you left Sierra with? A cheating husband. Questions about how he really felt about her and their marriage. She can't even grieve the man she loved because of his betrayals. She has to put on a good front for the boys. She has to preserve his memory for them because she doesn't want her children to know what a bastard their father was to their mother. She has to find a way to tell them they have a sister. That means a talk about how their father had sex with her sister and produced a child. Can you imagine?"

Yes. Because she'd have to have that same discussion with her daughter someday.

"She has to face the whispers and stares from others when they find out the children are all siblings and that her husband cheated on her with her sister."

"I'm the one who will get the worst of that."

Dede glared at her, waiting for Heather to get it. She did. But she didn't have to like it.

"I'll keep my distance."

"Right. Like you won't run into each other. This is a small town. Be realistic, Heather. For once, think things through."

"What do you want me to do? I don't have a lot

of options. I'm a single mom on a fixed income with no support."

"You have a fifty-thousand-dollar payout that your sister has been paying for because you slept with her husband. David took out a loan to get that money. Did you know that? And how do you think that makes her feel to be paying her husband's mistress who happens to be her sister? Did you even think about that when you accepted that money?"

"I didn't know about the loan. I thought he was well off enough to give it to me to support his daughter. What was I supposed to do? The bills from the hospital were piling up. I needed a place for me and Hallee that wasn't some dump in an apartment complex I could barely afford along with day care while I worked."

"Right. So now do you expect your sister to foot the bill for her husband's affair?"

"I expected Hallee's father to do his part!"

"Were you also hoping Mason would make your life considerably better? You barely know him, yet you went to his home with a clear purpose and it had nothing to do with horseback riding with Hallee."

Getting called out by her mom sucked.

"Mason is a great catch. He's never been married. He's been spending all that time with the boys, so he obviously likes kids. I thought maybe he wanted some of his own. He's got a great job, makes lots of money, and Hallee would love growing up on a ranch."

"Except you didn't even ask him if he was seeing someone before you threw yourself at him."

She took her shot. "I had no idea he and Sierra had a thing."

"Really? Then you're the only one who can't see that man is obviously head over heels in love with her."

Frustrated and angry to be the bad guy in everything, Heather rolled her eyes. "Everyone loves Sierra. I got the memo a long time ago."

Her mother fisted a hand and took a step forward, rage rolling off her. "You knew Sierra and the boys were spending a lot of time at Mason's ranch. Didn't it occur to you that something might be going on?"

"She never said a word about it to me when we spoke."

"She kept it quiet because of the boys. She wanted to be sure their relationship was solid before they told the kids."

"Yeah, well, he turned me down flat and outed me to Sierra. Now she's pissed and probably out for revenge."

"What can she possibly do to you that's worse than what you've done to her? What's the point? Nothing will change what you've done. No apology will be enough to erase the hurt."

Heather knew that, but deep down she'd hoped that somehow, some way . . . "So it's a lost cause to even try to make her understand."

"Understand what? You can't expect her to sympathize with you. You certainly didn't care about her feelings or what would happen to her and the boys if David left them."

"I did care. But there was no going back. So what am I supposed to do now?"

"Apologize. Take responsibility for what you did. Ask for forgiveness. Tell her what you hope can happen going forward with the kids and between you and her. Show her that you have a heart despite how you've acted."

Heather didn't know if that would be enough to get Sierra to even look at her again. "Are you going to be mad at me forever, too?" She hated the way her mother looked at and spoke to her. She didn't want to lose her mother's love and support. Her disappointment tore at her heart. If her mom turned her back on Heather, she'd be devastated.

"Mostly I'm disappointed that you'd do this to your sister and her children. You were always spoiled, but that's my fault, though your sisters spoiled you, too. You got away with a lot. But I never thought you did anything hurtful, until now. I hoped you'd see the mistakes I made with men and do better. I hoped you'd see your sisters' happy marriages and want that for yourself."

"I can't help who I loved."

"No. But you didn't have to act on it."

She hadn't been able to stop herself. "I know it was wrong. I'm sorry I hurt Sierra and fractured the family. I'm sure Amy will be just as angry and upset about this as you. I feel terrible that I snuck around with David. I even feel bad for loving him, even though I couldn't help myself." Tears fell down her cheeks. "And I will forever carry the weight of regret and guilt for begging him to help me and Hallee when she got sick and he drove down in the fog to be with us. I never meant for him to die trying to get to us."

Her mother stepped forward and gave Heather a hug she didn't deserve but badly needed. "I know you didn't. It was a tragic accident. Of course you wanted David there to help take care of Hallee in her time of need."

"Sierra blames me for his death." Heather blamed herself, too. But at the time, she'd done what she thought was right. Hallee had needed her father.

"She's angry and hurt and dealing with a lot. Give her time to sort things out for herself. Maybe you two will never come to an understanding, but she will find perspective when she's had time to think. And you need to tell her you are sorry." Dede pulled back and held her by the shoulders. "Heather, take some time and a really good look at what you did and the consequences. You can't go to Sierra and ask for forgiveness until you truly understand the cost of what you did. That includes the fact that David wouldn't have been on that road if not for your affair."

"You said it was a tragic accident."

"It was. But it was also an accident that should have never happened. If you want to make things right, put yourself in Sierra's place. Put yourself in Hallee's, Danny's, and Oliver's places. See this affair from their perspective. Understand how they will see the affair and all that happened. Imagine how they will feel. Only then will you really understand the impact your choices had and will continue to have on yourself and everyone else."

"I don't want to keep punishing myself for loving him. It hurts too much."

"How can you forgive yourself for what happened unless you take responsibility for all of it?" Dede released her and headed for the door. Before she left, she turned back. "You can't hide here forever. You will need to face them. You'll need to look at yourself. I hope you find a way to do that with sincerity and an open heart, knowing that you may not get the forgiveness you want, but that it's the only way you will have a shot at having some kind of relationship with your sister. Sierra loves you. She has been there for you your whole life. You deserve your feelings and hurt and grief, but so does she. And you're the one who caused them. It's up to you to try to make amends."

"I just want to move on."

"That's your choice, too. But think of what it will cost you before you put this in the past and live your life without dealing with this first." Dede never stopped being Mom.

She walked out leaving Heather with *I'm disappointed in you*, and an implied demand that she make better choices.

She should have gone to work today instead of trying to hide and just take a day to figure things out. Of course her mom showed up to hold her accountable. She wanted all her daughters to get along. She wanted them all to be happy.

Heather was pretty sure happiness was a myth.

A picture of Hallee caught her eye and she dismissed that thought altogether. All of a sudden she understood her mother a lot better. Of course she wanted this to all be sorted out and for her girls to get along and be happy. She wanted to go back to holiday get-togethers and birthday parties with everyone smiling and happy for each other.

Heather wouldn't take back what she'd done, but she could accept the blame.

For Hallee, and because she really did love her

sister, she'd do everything possible to make up with Sierra, so they could have some semblance of a relationship where they could be cordial and all the kids stayed connected. They shared David's loss. Maybe being with her siblings would someday help Hallee connect to him through her brothers.

Heather walked back into her kitchen and stared at the kettle. A cup of tea wasn't going to make her feel better. She needed to do what her mother said and dig deep, put herself in others' shoes, and understand that, yes, her feelings mattered, but not more than theirs because she was the one who did the harm.

She knew that. Of course, she did, but she'd been hiding behind lies, omissions, and delusions to keep her secret instead of facing the truth and putting her heart out there to make things right.

Not anymore.

Time to take responsibility and do the right thing, even if it was hard and meant more heartbreak for her.

Chapter Thirty-Three

Sierra leaned back into Mason, loving the feel of his arms around her. Yesterday had been one of the worst days of her life. But she woke up next to Mason with a sense that if she focused on their future, everything would be all right. More than that, she believed they could have a happy life together.

"What do you think?" Mason asked.

Sierra stared at the room that used to be Mason's when he was a teen and lived here with his parents. Since then he'd redone it and turned it into a guest room with basic wood furniture and a queen bed covered in an old quilt. "If we paint and update the pictures and bedding, I think one or both of the boys will love it."

"The off-white walls are kind of dull. Abstract art probably isn't the boys' thing. The bedspread was something left over from when my parents lived here. We'll go shopping. New bedding. They can pick the wall color and decorations. What did you think of the other room?"

Sierra glanced through the Jack and Jill bathroom at the room beyond. "Same. Paint and updates to the bedding and decorations." She glanced up and over her shoulder at Mason. "It's time the boys get to have their own space and make it theirs."

"When do you want to talk to them about us?"

"What do you think about getting the rooms ready first? We could surprise them. We could ask some questions about what they'd like their new rooms to look like in a general kind of way, letting them know I'm thinking of moving us to our own place. That will give them a chance to talk about what they want and how they feel about moving again."

"We'll do it slow," Mason agreed. "Take all the time you need."

She stepped out of his embrace and turned to face him. "I don't need more time to decide what I want, Mason. This past year, I grieved for a man who— You know what? I'm not going there. I'm not going to keep putting energy into my anger and what didn't work. This is my life. If I keep dwelling on what happened and what I've lost instead of what has come into my life and what makes me feel good, then all I'll do is end up sabotaging myself all over again."

"You didn't sabotage your relationship with David."

"Didn't I? I definitely made things worse by not voicing my concerns about us. I let things go. I *hoped* they'd get better. But I didn't do anything to fix it." She thought about all her small attempts to get David to talk, or how she'd tried affection and outright seduction. She'd gotten a response, but it never lasted. "I should have seen what seems so obvious now."

"Do you want to know why I never got married?"

"Why?"

"Because I saw all those couples come through my office miserable and hating the person they once loved like nothing could ever change that. I got engaged thinking the same thing. But then I realized why all those relationships ended, like mine, was because those people didn't feed that love. They let it starve."

That hit her right in the heart. "Yes. That's what happened. We let everything else get in the way of us."

"No matter how hard you'd tried to fix things, once David cheated and lied and spent all that time covering it up, you were doomed. One person can't fix a relationship. One person can't hold it together, but one person can destroy it all."

Mason closed the distance and touched her face. "I'm not worried about us, Sierra. You know why? Because I don't expect you to be someone different when we get married. I know life won't always be easy, but I'll have you beside me to get through the rough times. I want to be there for you, because I want to see you smile every day of your life. I love you. And the way that makes me feel . . . It's something I never want to lose. So I will do everything and anything I can to show you how much I love you every day because I don't want to lose *you*."

She stared up at him. "*When* we get married?"

"Yes. When." He kissed her softly. "But you'll have to wait a little bit for that. I have plans."

She smiled, her heart light because he understood that she needed his open honesty. "Plans for me?"

His eyes filled with desire at her seductive tone. He'd been sweet last night, holding her while she let her mind sort through the anger, sadness, betrayal, and confusion over how this all happened. When the sadness set in and she let the tears fall, he'd buried his face in her hair and whispered soothing words and affirmations that everything would be okay.

And she believed him, because she believed he was the kind of guy who stuck it out. He wouldn't quit on them.

She hadn't stopped loving him all these years. It had lain dormant in her heart, but now that she was free to love him, she wouldn't stop. Not ever. The way he made her feel . . . Well, she wanted to feel this way all the time. It's what she'd been looking for, what she'd missed, what she craved.

And right now, she wanted to show Mason how much she appreciated him for being the man she needed.

"I have plans to keep you here. Plans to make you happy." He slid his hands down her neck, over her shoulders, and along her spine until his big hands covered her ass and pulled her closer. "Plans . . ." He covered her mouth in a searing kiss that sparked every nerve in her body and lit a fire between her legs, especially when he squeezed her ass and lifted her right off her feet. Wrapped in all his strength and love, she held him close and kissed him like her life depended on it.

She wanted to lose herself in loving him. She wanted to feel something good and sexy and hot and let everything else get wiped away.

She was so tired of feeling stupid and taken advantage of and left in the dark.

Mason made her feel desirable and necessary. Especially when he talked about their future and seduced her right out of her sorrows and into his arms like this.

He turned with her in his arms, feet dangling at

his shins, and stopped short of walking out of the spare bedroom door when a car pulled up out front.

His eyes opened and his lips left hers and she missed the intimacy and building need. "Someone's here."

"I don't want to see anyone but you. Preferably naked. And horizontal."

He smiled. "I like the way you think, but it could be Amy with the boys."

"I'm not supposed to pick them up for another hour." But something could have come up and Amy needed to bring them back early.

Mason kissed her one last time, slowly, putting all the promise of more to come in the sexy kiss.

He set her back on her feet and smiled down at her. "You're bouncing back really well."

"Don't get me wrong, I'm still angry and upset. It overwhelms me sometimes. But being with you helps a lot. You take my mind off it. You make me see the possibilities of what we can have together. Something that's honest and built on mutual love and respect."

"I respect the hell out of the way you've handled this."

A car door slammed out front, drawing Sierra's attention to the bedroom window that looked out over the front of the house. She spotted Heather's car and all the anger she'd tucked away this morning came flooding back in a hot wave of rage.

"If you knew what I was thinking right now, you'd think a hell of a lot less of me."

Mason swore under his breath. "What the hell is she doing here?"

"Making things worse." Sierra didn't want to hate her sister, but that's exactly how she felt right now. "I'm not doing this with her."

Mason tilted his head, his face and eyes filled with sympathy. "She's your sister. You can't leave things like this forever. You two should talk."

"All I want to do right now is scream at her." Her whole body vibrated with pent-up anger. "No. She doesn't get to pick the time and place and just expect me to do what she wants. Not after what she's done."

"Absolutely not. I just want you to consider that eventually you two should talk and try to come to some sort of resolution."

"I get that mediating for your clients is a big part of your job, but I'm not ready to come to the table and hear anything she has to say."

"Fair enough. I'll tell her now isn't the time and send her away."

She followed Mason down the hall. "We spent the morning talking about our future, my moving in here with the boys, and she had to show up and ruin it."

Mason ignored the knock on the door and turned to her. "Nothing has changed about all we talked about this morning. That's all going to happen. We will have our life together and no one is going to come between us or ruin it for us."

She deflated. "I'm sorry."

"You don't have to apologize for feeling the way you do. I get it. If it were me, I'd be looking for a fight. You've at least maintained your composure."

"You didn't see my total meltdown on the beach yesterday."

He brushed his hand over her hair and held her head. "I hope you know I wanted to be with you."

She leaned into his hand. "I know. I just needed to be alone for a while."

"You never have to be alone again if you don't want to be."

Heather knocked again, this time softer, more hesitant.

Sierra glared at the door. "I'd appreciate it if you took care of that. I'm going to head over to Amy's and pick up the boys. I'm sure she's got a million questions, and I could use some time with her."

"Your sisters have always been important to you. You guys have always been really close. I'm sorry this is tearing you apart."

"Heather did it all on her own. She crossed a line and I'm not sure I will ever be able to forgive her for it."

"Maybe not now, but for the kids' sake, I know you'll try." Mason had a lot of faith in her.

She grabbed her purse and pulled out her keys. She turned back to him and gave him a half frown. "You're right, but right now, I don't have it in me to even look at her." She went up on tiptoe and kissed him softly. "Thank you for understanding and being so supportive."

"Always." He kissed her again, brushing his thumb across her cheek in a soft sweep as he stared into her eyes. "Bring the boys back here. Let's just spend some time together before we're back to work and life tomorrow."

"Sounds amazing. But you're cooking dinner."

He smiled. "Deal."

They shared another quick kiss, then she turned,

opened the front door, barely spared Heather a look before she said, "No," and walked right past her and to her car.

Heather called after her, "I just want to talk."

Sierra climbed into her SUV, turned it on, and pulled out of the driveway without another thought for her bitch of a sister.

Instead she thought about what she and Mason talked about this morning. She focused on their future, not her messy past.

It may be too fast or too soon to move in with Mason, but she didn't care. She wanted to start the life Mason painted for her this morning with his plans to make her and the boys part of his life permanently.

In her mind, despite what happened with David, she believed that life with Mason would be a happily-ever-after kind of love.

She deserved that.

And she wouldn't let anything get in her way.

Chapter Thirty-Four

Heather stared at the back end of Sierra's car driving away. "She hates me."

"Yep." Mason didn't sugarcoat it at all. "Right now anyway. Can you blame her?"

"No." She sighed and faced Mason. "That's why I came. To apologize. To see if we can work this out."

"Nice try, showing up unexpectedly and forcing her to deal with you." The sarcasm came across loud and clear. "Don't you think she deserves some time to process all this?" Mason shook his head. "Yesterday she spent the morning memorializing David with Danny and Oliver, then she finds out he was having an affair with her sister and her niece is actually her boys' half sister. You expect her to accept all that in less than a day?"

"Can we talk about this inside?"

"I'm not inviting you in without Sierra here. I won't give her any reason to question me, especially when it comes to you."

"I'm not going to do anything. I just thought that maybe you and I—"

"Stop right there. There is no you and I. Sierra and I are together. We are going to be a family. Right now, that doesn't include you."

Heather's heart sank. "She's never going to talk to me, let alone forgive me, is she?"

"Do you blame her if she doesn't after what you did?"

"I'm sorry. I really never meant to hurt her."

"I'm sure she didn't even cross your mind." The harsh statement was unfortunately mostly true. "If she did, you didn't care enough to stop what you were doing."

I couldn't stop loving David.

Heather sighed. "I wasn't the only one who hurt her. David did, too, but I'm the only one everyone is mad at."

"That's not true. She's devastated by what David did to her and their children. He ruined their relationship and marriage. He had everything, but he turned his back on Sierra and what they'd built together."

"He wasn't happy. He wanted to be with me."

"Neither of those things excuses what he did or erases the hurt he's caused. For either of you. Sierra is devastated."

"How do you think I feel? He's gone. I loved him, too. I miss him, too. But I'm not allowed to show that because we weren't supposed to be together."

Mason eyed her. "Do you really mean you weren't supposed to be discovered?"

Yes. And no.

"He wanted to be with me." She kept telling herself that, but couldn't convince herself anymore that it was wholly true.

"He was never really yours. He got caught up in something exciting and thrilling in the moment but it ultimately left him feeling bad about himself and worried that he'd lose everything over something that didn't really mean anything to him."

She wanted to deny that. "I've seen it a lot. A husband cheats thinking it's just sex. It doesn't mean anything. He's got no real feelings for the woman. He still loves his wife. As long as she doesn't find out about it, it's no big deal. But women have intuition. They know their husband better than anyone. Maybe they don't want to see it, but they know. Sierra knew. And David sensed she knew. I bet he even let on to you that she was suspicious of him."

She spoke David's worst fear. "He thought she'd take the boys from him."

Mason dismissed that with a shake of his head. "The courts would allow him visitation and Sierra would never keep those boys from their father because she knows they needed him in their life. I bet what David feared was losing a brilliant, loving, kind, generous woman like Sierra."

"He had me."

"And you gave him a reason to always be in your life."

It took her a second to understand his meaning. "Hallee wasn't planned."

"Maybe not, but she sure did ensure you kept David coming back to you. He was coming back to you the night he died."

True. But . . . "That's not fair."

"No, it's not. Neither is what you did to Sierra."

"I want to make it right." She did, because she'd lost David and she didn't want to lose her sister, too.

"'Right'? What does that even mean? You can't change what you did or that you have a child by *her* husband."

She fell in love with the wrong, right man. She

had a baby with him when he couldn't—or wouldn't, she sadly confessed to herself—be with her.

She never expected to be a single mom.

She never thought she'd lose David.

"I love Sierra, even if I've done a poor job of showing it. I want her to be happy. And if that is with you, then I wish you both the best." Heather sucked in a breath. "I'm embarrassed and sorry about my behavior yesterday. I'm sorry I put you in the middle of me and Sierra. I have a lot of making up to do. It won't be easy, but I want my sister back. I want our kids to grow up together."

"She's still sorting out her feelings. I don't know *if* or *when* she'll be able to consider talking to you or getting the kids together."

Heather appreciated that he'd given up that much, but hated the way he phrased it because it implied Sierra had no intention of keeping Heather in her life. It made her sad and the guilt piled on.

"For what it's worth, I think you'll be great for her and the boys." She shrugged. "That's all I was looking for, for me and Hallee."

"Look for it with someone who isn't already with someone else."

"Good advice." She meant it despite the mirth and sarcasm.

"I hope you take it." Mason sighed. "Look, I don't know if this can be fixed between you and Sierra. Right now, she doesn't want to hear anything you have to say. To her, it all sounds like excuses and empty apologies. She doesn't want to hurt the kids. She won't take it out on Hallee. And she doesn't want her boys to think less of David, or even you.

She's not ready to have that talk with them. Until she is, I'm not sure she'll be ready to hear anything you have to say about it."

"Understandable. I always knew I'd have to explain to Hallee about who her father was and how we fell in love. We both look bad, but I want her to know that despite what David and I did, she was born out of real love. Sierra probably doesn't want to hear that, but it's true. I hope she can find it in her heart to understand I couldn't turn my back on that love and as much as I regret hurting her, I am incredibly grateful to have Hallee."

She didn't know how else to explain it, except that for all the bad she caused, she got something so great out of it.

"Thank you for listening to me and being so good to Sierra and her kids. I appreciate it. If she stays, maybe one day soon we'll be able to . . . well, maybe not settle this, but put it behind us. I really would like Hallee to know her brothers."

"In time, I think Sierra will want that, too. But getting there may take some time."

"I understand." She gave him a halfhearted smile. She hadn't accomplished what she'd come here to do, but maybe this was better. Mason would tell Sierra the details of their conversation. Maybe coming from him, she'd hear what Heather wanted her to know. Maybe she'd think about it. Sierra wasn't mean or vindictive. She'd come around eventually.

I hope.

"Please tell Sierra I'm not giving up, but I will give her some space."

"I'll tell her."

Heather nodded her good-bye and walked down

the porch steps to her car. She'd pick up Hallee from the sitter and spend the rest of the day with her. She needed Hallee's sweet smile and unconditional love to see her through this dark time.

She'd been alone a long time, but she'd never felt this lonely. Her whole family would rally around Sierra. Her mom had already let her have it. Amy probably wouldn't waste any time saying her piece.

Heather had made herself the outcast in the family. She deserved their scorn.

She hoped to earn their forgiveness.

She loved her family and needed their support. Especially now.

Which meant she needed to show them she took responsibility for her actions.

Chapter Thirty-Five

Sierra stood in Amy's kitchen wondering if her sister had been swapped with an alien.

Rex stood at the sink filling the dishwasher. Amy didn't make a single comment, issue a demand he do it differently, or take over the task because no one could do anything like her. Rex appeared completely at ease. In fact, the atmosphere in the house felt different. The kids calmly sat at the island. Danny and Oliver worked on a chore chart. Amy stood between P.J.'s and Emma's chairs looking at a brand-new activities calendar they were filling in.

"P.J., you're green." Amy handed him a green marker. "Emma, you're dark pink."

Emma took her pen. "I only have two things each week."

Amy pointed to the calendar. "Fill in your activities. We'll use purple for the things you and your brother do together."

"Dad is blue, right?" P.J. rolled the marker across the counter to his dad, who stood drying his hands with a towel.

Rex stopped the pen from rolling off the counter with a flat hand and caught Amy's eye. "All set?" He glanced toward the open dishwasher.

Amy checked it out and nodded. "Thank you. Would you mind running it?"

"Sure." Rex turned and took a detergent cube from a tub under the sink, dropped it in the dispenser, slid the lid closed, pushed the dishwasher door up, hit the start button, and turned back to help with the calendar.

The kids finished their part. P.J. had soccer Tuesday and Thursday with a game on Saturday. Emma had dance class on Monday and Wednesday. They both had art class together on Thursday before P.J.'s soccer practice and swim class on Saturday morning before P.J.'s soccer game.

"No more music classes?" The calendar looked far less cluttered with events than the original one still up on the wall.

Amy put a hand on both of her kids' shoulders. "They chose the activities they like the most. We're cutting back so we have more time at home." Amy took the teal-colored pen and wrote Family Time on every Sunday of the calendar, then looked up at Rex. They shared a smile and Rex gave Amy a nod of approval.

Sierra's heart soared that Amy and Rex not only had talked out their problems but were working to make each other happy by making changes in their relationship.

Amy used the same color to write Date Night on every Thursday. This time when she and Rex shared a knowing look, her sister's cheeks pinked.

Aw. Sweet.

They needed more time together.

She and Mason should talk about their schedules and how they were going to work out date night and taking care of the boys. It would be nice to have help getting them to their activities or simply having

Mason there with her to cheer them on at soccer or whatever they chose to do in the future.

Danny had already asked about baseball. She needed to get on that and sign him up. Mason used to play in high school. He could coach Danny at home.

And that thought solidified her decision to speak to the boys about moving in with Mason soon. He'd be such a great father and role model for Danny and Oliver.

Rex stepped around the counter and touched Amy's shoulder, that closeness they used to share back on full display. "Hey, babe, why don't you let me finish this with the kids. When we're done, I promised them a kickball game in the front yard. You and Sierra can sit out back and catch up."

Code for *Go ahead and talk about Heather and the affair.*

Amy gave Rex a quick kiss, ruffled her kids' hair, and went to the fridge. She pulled out an open bottle of white wine and selected two glasses from the cupboard. "Come on, sis, let's talk."

Sierra went to the boys and gave them each a kiss on the head.

Oliver held up his chore chart. "Aunt Amy says I should get fifty cents for each chore, but I should ask for seventy-five and negotiate. I don't know what that means, but I want an allow ants."

Sierra sent her sister a disgruntled frown and glare.

Amy stuck her tongue out at her. "Hold out for the seventy-five cents, kiddo. Mommy can afford it with her awesome job. I bet if you ask Mason for chores at the ranch, he'd pay you a dollar."

Sierra scoffed. "Amy! Really?"

Amy winked at Danny and Oliver and headed out the back door.

Sierra stared at both the boys. "We'll discuss *allowances* later. Be good. Have fun with Uncle Rex."

Rex finished tearing down the old calendar and replaced it with the new one, a satisfied smile on his face when he studied it. "That's more like it."

She bet he appreciated that he had a spot on the calendar now and so did Date Night and Family Time.

"Who's up for kickball?"

All the kids scrambled off their stools and headed for the front door.

Rex caught her arm. "Hey, I'm sorry you're going through this. I had no idea about David and Heather. It sucks. I hope you're okay."

She put her hand over his. "Thank you. I will be."

Rex gave her a half smile and headed out after the kids.

Sierra walked out to the back to find her sister, knowing what she'd just said to Rex would be true one day.

She would be okay. She just needed time to let the feelings come, to reevaluate her life and what happened, and put it into perspective.

One day it wouldn't hurt this much.

There'd come a time when the anger didn't rush in and consume her.

One day it would be a memory that didn't sting so sharply.

Her happiness would overshadow the pain and betrayal.

"So I spoke to Mom this morning after she went

to see Heather. We hate Heather, right?" Amy held up a glass of wine from her Adirondack chair in the garden.

Sierra took the glass, fell into the other chair, stared at the beautiful flowers, focusing on the pretty pink roses, and sighed. "I don't want to hate David or Heather, but they make it damn hard not to."

Amy clinked her glass to Sierra's. "Bastard. Bitch. What the fuck were they thinking?"

Sierra appreciated her sister's outrage. "I don't know." She took a sip of the sweet and smooth peach wine, loving the flavor and crispness. She needed more sweet in her life.

"It hurts." Her chest grew heavy with thoughts of what her sister and husband had done, scenarios of how they carried out their trysts, and how she'd been oblivious to it all. "I think it would be easier if it was some stranger, a random woman I didn't know. But Heather . . ."

"It keeps circling my mind. How could she? Why? How did it even happen?"

"That's the thing. I have some of the details, but it doesn't really matter how, when, why. They did it without thinking about what would happen when they were discovered."

Amy turned her gaze from the flowers, focused on her, and put her hand on Sierra's arm. "They had a child together."

"Hallee." Just saying her name hurt Sierra's heart something fierce. That poor girl. Caught in the middle of all this. The living reminder of how her parents hurt and betrayed Sierra. An innocent child. "I don't know what to do about her. She's Danny and Oliver's half sister. How do I explain that to them?"

"They're too young to understand what really happened. Maybe it's better to tell them now in a simple way. She's their sister. They have the same father. Leave it at that. When they're older and they understand more, they'll ask questions and you can tell them more of the real story."

Sierra thought that might be the best way to handle it.

"But if you tell them, they'll want to see Hallee, which means . . ." Amy let the rest go unsaid.

She'd have to see Heather. She'd look at Hallee and bring back all the hurt.

She didn't want to keep reliving this nightmare. But she also didn't want to punish the kids or keep them apart.

"David and Heather have put me in an impossible position. If I don't let the boys see their sister, I'm the bad guy. If I do, I have to deal with Heather and the affair coming up over and over again for me."

"Well, if you're okay with the boys seeing Hallee, they can have playdates here, then you won't have to deal with Heather. Anyway, David left our sister holding the bag on this one." Amy sipped her wine and looked at her over the rim of the glass. "Do you think if he'd lived, he'd have left you for Heather?"

She'd asked herself that a hundred times. "I don't know. My gut says he wanted to stay with me and the boys. That's why he tried so hard to hide the affair." Sierra shrugged. "Or he just put off telling me, trying to avoid a fight. That's what we did . . . avoid things."

"Been there. Done that."

She studied Amy. "But you and Rex are back on the same page."

"And better than ever. The past week or so has been great. We've found our way back to each other. I feel like I can go to him with stuff now. He feels like I listen to him now." Amy smiled. "I'm trying anyway. We both are."

"The closeness is back."

"Great sex will do that." Amy's bright smile disappeared. "I'm sorry. That was insensitive given what you're going through."

"Hey, I like great sex. I just prefer my husband is having it with me." Sierra couldn't believe she was able to joke about this, but it felt good to find some humor in all the drag-me-down feelings running through her.

"She really fucked up."

Sierra took another sip of wine. "Yes, she did. And the thought of running into her, other people finding out and gossiping . . ." She didn't know if she could take it.

"Fuck them. You know what people are going to be talking about? The fact that you landed the hottest, most eligible bachelor in the state."

Sierra chuckled. "Mason has been a light in all this dark mess."

Amy met her gaze. "And you've been a light in mine. I've missed you. I need you to tell me when I'm turning into a batshit crazy control freak. And"—Amy held up her glass—"who else will have afternoon wine with me?"

"I'm sure Rex would love to sit out here with you sipping wine."

Amy's smile softened into a dreamy grin. "I met him for lunch this week. It was so nice to sit together and have a nice meal and talk about anything but the kids."

"Mason and I really haven't been together that long—"

Amy waved that away. "You've known each other forever."

"Which is why it's so easy to be with him. We know each other. We connect. When I'm with him, I'm really happy. Before I knew about"—she circled her hand in the air to encompass the affair and Heather and David without having to say it again—"I felt guilty that I liked being with Mason so much."

"You felt like you were somehow betraying David." Amy closed her eyes and shook her head, then opened them. "Don't. Even without the affair, David would have wanted you to be happy after he died. He wouldn't have wanted you to stop living your life. He'd want someone for you and the boys. I know that."

So did Sierra, but now all her thoughts were muddled up with the affair and she second-guessed her memories and what she thought David would say and want for her and the boys.

"Since I found out about the affair, I don't feel guilty about seeing Mason anymore. After all, David had already left me before he died. Well, I guess I feel a *little* guilty about being with someone else when the past is so present at the same time."

Amy leaned forward and put her hand on Sierra's knee. "Give yourself a break. David died a year ago.

You grieved. It's okay to move on. Just because you know about the affair now doesn't mean you have to start the process of grieving him and your relationship all over again. The clock doesn't start over. Yes, process what happened, but don't sacrifice the happiness you could have with Mason. If you want to be with him, *be* with him. Love him. Let him love you, Sierra. You deserve it. Don't let them take that from you."

"Mason wants us to move in with him."

"Do it. The best revenge against the ones who hurt you is to live your life, happy and carefree, doing what you love, being with the one you love, and having a great life with your family."

"Heather is part of my family."

Amy sat quietly contemplating the scenery, lost in thought. "I don't know what to do about Heather. I'm angry she hurt you. I want to understand why, but I don't think anything she says will satisfy that question because who can accept that she was simply selfish and heartless? What she did was despicable. But would I judge her so harshly if she had an affair with a married man we didn't know? What if the wife was some other woman? How would I feel then? I'd be upset by her actions, but would I feel this disappointed and disheartened?" Amy locked gazes with her. "It's because she did this to you that I find it hard to see a path to redemption for her. I'm not sure that I can forgive her, and I'm not the one she hurt."

"I feel guilty that this has fractured the family and that it affects your relationship with her and her relationship with Mom."

"She's the one who should feel guilty."

"I can't help it. I thought moving back here would mean we'd all share our lives. Our kids would grow up together. We'd have birthday parties and holidays together. It would be so fun and the kids would take those memories into the future and have that with their kids. The years and distance made our relationships less intimate, but I hoped we'd grow closer again and things would be like they used to be."

"Where we bickered but loved each other." Amy smiled, nostalgia in her eyes along with the humor in that all-too-true statement.

"Yes. We three are so different from each other, but we always managed to get through the rough patches."

"Because we're family."

"Now what?" Sierra asked Amy, because she really didn't know how to get through this, this time. An "I'm sorry" wouldn't fix it. She couldn't look at Heather without thinking about what happened. She couldn't trust her.

"I wish I knew, sis, because this sucks." Amy downed the last of her wine in one gulp. "All I know is you can't let what happened stop you and Mason from moving forward with your relationship. Marry him. Make a beautiful blond-haired, green-eyed baby with him. Live on that ranch and spend every day grateful for your second chance and the happiness you deserve."

Amy painted a beautiful picture of what could be.

No. What *would* be. Because Sierra wanted that life.

And nothing was going to stand in her way of having it. Not even herself.

"I think I'll talk to the kids tonight about moving in with Mason."

"Great idea. While you're at it, pack them up and just show up on his doorstep."

Sierra laughed. "Mason wants to fix up two of the rooms in the house and surprise them."

"See, that's a good man, thinking about making it fun for the boys. He wants them to see that he wants them there. You can't give up a guy like that."

"I have no intention of letting him get away again." But she did want to find a way to put all this other stuff in the past where it belonged, so she could move on with Mason with a clear and open heart.

Amy checked her watch, then settled back in the seat, closed her eyes, and turned her face to the sun. "I've been making myself learn to do nothing but relax."

"Self-care is important."

"I'm not very good at it yet, but I'm trying. Rex and I are taking the kids out to dinner tonight. I don't have anything to do until then that absolutely has to be done."

"I bet Rex and the kids will play for at least another twenty minutes." Sierra settled back in her chair much the same way as Amy and let the sun warm her face.

"It's going to be okay," Amy whispered.

The talk with her sister helped Sierra to settle many of the thoughts running around her mind, but sitting in the silence out in the garden with that whispered promise eased her heart even more. It came with all her sister's love and understanding that there was no easy answer, except to move forward and accept that eventually everything would work out the way it was supposed to because Sierra had people who loved her in her life.

Chapter Thirty-Six

Sierra stood outside the car, the boys ready to go home and in their car seats, and stared up at Mason. "Thank you for dinner."

"My pleasure. I'm glad your talk with Amy earlier helped."

Sierra put her hand on his chest. "It affirmed for me that moving forward is the best way to put the past behind me. I don't want to get lost in what happened, the why, the how, the what-ifs. It's just so overwhelming and disheartening. It takes all the energy out of me. I loved coming back here and watching you and the boys man the barbecue."

"They need to know how to make the perfect burger."

"I think they've got it now, thanks to your expert tutelage." She couldn't help the smile. The boys had hung on Mason's every word and off his arms and back as they tried to wrestle him to the ground while the burgers cooked.

Mason brushed his fingers across her lips. "I love it when you smile."

"You always knew how to make me smile. Now, you do it for the boys."

"They're little monkeys." He stretched his back, pretending he was sore. "I'm getting old."

She tapped him in the gut, her hand hitting rock-hard muscle. The ranch kept him in great shape. "Whatever you say, grandpa."

He locked his hands at her back and pulled her close. "I'm not too old to sweep a pretty girl off her feet." He did just that, grabbing her waist and picking her right up.

She giggled and clasped her arms around his neck. "Put me down."

He hugged her tighter. "You don't mean that."

In fact, she held on and leaned in close, her mouth an inch from his, their eyes locked. "I want you to hold on to me this time."

The mirth in Mason's eyes turned to sincerity. "I won't ever let you go." He kissed her softly, then broke the kiss and stared at her again. "I won't ever give you a reason to leave. I promise, Sierra, you're all I want or will ever need."

Tears sprang to her eyes. She hadn't known how much she needed to hear that until Mason gave her the words. "How can my heart be broken and battered and so full of love all at the same time?"

"Because you care. About me, the boys, your family, and even David and Heather. If you didn't care, it wouldn't hurt so much. And because you use your whole heart in everything you do, including the way you love me. I feel it, sweetheart. I'm humbled by it. I want more of it. I can't wait for you to move in and for us to be a family."

She pressed her forehead to his. "Soon. I promise. I don't want to wait, either."

He kissed her one last time, keeping things relatively tame because they had eyes on them. He set her on her feet, opened the door for her, waited for her to climb in before he looked into the back seat. "I'll see you guys tomorrow."

"Night, Mason." Danny waved.

"Bye." Oliver yawned.

"I better get them to bed. It's back to school tomorrow. Don't work too hard."

Mason remembered the case files he'd brought home and hadn't touched this weekend. "I won't." If she wasn't staying with him, then he'd spend the next couple hours in his office, alone with his files instead of her. "Call me if you need me."

She smiled. "I will. Promise."

When she was home, alone, in the quiet, that's when it was the hardest to shut off the thoughts. He knew something about that, because though he'd get his work done, the rest of the night he'd be thinking about her, them, and what he wanted their life to look like for their future.

He closed her door, waited for her to turn the car toward the main road, and waved good-bye before heading in for the night.

Drawn to the brilliant stars overhead, he looked up and stared in wonder at the sheer number of them. He picked one that seemed to wink at him.

I wish for a long and happy life with Sierra by my side. I want to watch those boys grow up into good men and find someone to love who loves them the way I love Sierra and she loves me. I want all of us to be happy.

More than anything, he wanted Sierra to find peace here on the ranch with him.

* * *

Sierra walked in the front door behind the boys and spotted her mom cleaning up the toys the boys left out. "Mom, I'll do that."

"I'm almost done." Her mother tossed toy cars into the bin and pulled apart the racetrack.

Sierra helped the boys out of their zip-up hoodies and hung them on the coatrack. "Go upstairs and brush your teeth. Change into your pj's and I'll be up in a few minutes to read books."

Her mom finished pulling apart the last piece of the track and tossed the two plastic pieces into the bin. "Lord, it's been a long time since I had to pick up after kids." She put the toy bin next to the other two the boys had brought down from upstairs.

"You won't have to do it much longer."

Her mother gave her a knowing smile. "Is that man of yours getting impatient?"

A smile tugged at her lips. "Honestly, we both are."

Her mom put her hand on the coffee table and used it to help support her while she rose from sitting on her feet. She rubbed at her sore knees before she stood straight. "It's been just as long since I spent that much time on the floor. I hope Mason knows what he's in for."

Sierra listened to the water running upstairs while the boys brushed their teeth. "We talked this morning about turning two of the rooms in his house into the boys' rooms."

"They'll love that. Lord knows he's got the space and then some in that big house." Dede studied her for a moment. "I take it things with Amy went well."

"Believe it or not, she had some great advice. She

made me feel better. She thinks moving forward is the best thing for me."

Her mom nodded. "I agree." Her eyebrows drew together. "I spoke to Heather."

"She stopped by Mason's but I left without really talking to her."

"I hope she apologized to him about her behavior."

"She did."

"I understand your frustration with her, Sierra. What she did . . . It makes no sense, and yet, I understand what she wanted."

"You may want a chocolate bar, but stealing it still comes with consequences."

"She's feeling those consequences. And I understand you need time and distance. But I'd like you to consider something that I hadn't really thought about until I spoke to her. I was so angry about what she did, I didn't think about the similarities you share."

Sierra wasn't sure she wanted to hear this.

Her heart pounded as the answers came to mind and her mother spoke out loud.

"You both lost the man you love. You both have children who will grow up without their father. You both have to explain to them how they are connected. You both have to keep David's memory alive for your kids." Dede held up her hand, cutting off words Sierra couldn't get out her constricted throat anyway. "I know it's the same but different. I just wanted you to think about that. Heather scolded me for not understanding that she has her feelings, too. I guess what I'm saying is that you both have a side. She was wrong to do what she did, but she did love him. Not that that's an excuse, but . . . I don't know. It's so hard to articulate and reason out."

Sierra bit back the anger and focused on her mother and how hard she tried to make Sierra understand that somewhere in all this mess, with a little sympathy and understanding, Sierra could see her sister as a woman who'd loved and lost and who grieved like she had once. Heather faced a future similar to hers and a time when she'd have to explain David to Hallee and how their relationship started and ended. It was a tragic love story that might have ended differently if it had been born of truth and honesty instead of mired in lies and deception.

"No matter how you explain it, what she did was wrong. I know you want us all to be the way we used to be. I just don't think that's possible. But . . ." She took a deep breath and tried to wrap her head around the next words she gave her mother even if she didn't wholly believe in them yet. "One day, I hope, Heather and I can understand each other and love more and hurt less."

Her mom's eyes overflowed with tears. "Yes. I'd like that very much." Dede closed the distance and hugged her close. "Thank you, Sierra, for keeping your heart open to possibility."

Sierra hugged her mom back. "I'm still angry. I still want to kill her. But I feel it a little less today than I did yesterday."

Heather had been coddled and pampered far too long. Not anymore.

Sierra was taking care of herself first this time.

Her mom released her, but touched her hand to Sierra's cheek. "I love you, sweetheart. I hope you know that I want the very best for you."

"I know you do. I know you want that equally for Heather."

"Well, maybe she gets ten percent less than you now."

Sierra appreciated the teasing tone, but knew her mother didn't mean it. And it was okay, because she'd have a hard time not wanting both her sons to be as happy as they could be, either.

"Does that mean you'll miss me when I move to Mason's?"

"I will, but still, it'll be nice to have the house to myself again. I hope my grandsons find their way here often."

"I bet they will." After all, they only had one wide pasture to cross to get here. She smiled for her mom. "And so will I."

"That's a promise, then."

Sierra nodded. "Good night, Mom."

"Good night, sweetheart."

Sierra made it up the stairs just as the boys turned off their bedroom light, leaving the room in shadows, the heads of their beds bathed in a soft glow from the night-light.

Danny held two books on his chest. Oliver sat on Danny's bed, waiting for her to take her place next to Danny so Oliver could sink between them.

"Mom?" Danny studied her, his eyes serious.

"Yeah?"

"Is everything okay? Everyone seems upset about something."

Of course the boys had picked up on the strange vibes. She tried to hide her anger, but they knew something was off.

"You're right. I discovered some upsetting news when we were at Mason's house."

"Did Aunt Heather make you mad?" Oliver played with the ends of her long hair.

"Yes. She did. She took something that belonged to me."

Danny turned on his pillow to face her. "I hate it when Oliver takes my stuff."

Oliver crossed his little arms over his chest. "I do not."

"Yes, you do! All the time."

"Enough. Anyway, it made me angry and I needed to be by myself for a little while to think about it. But then I talked to Mason and I felt better." She wanted to turn this conversation to the future. "He made me think about everything that's happened and all we've lost, and you know what? It made me think of all the new things we can have now."

"Like new Legos." Oliver looked up at her, hopeful he'd get a new set soon.

"Maybe. But I was thinking about us moving into a new place and you two having your own rooms." She didn't give them time to ask questions about where and when. "What color would you like your room to be?"

"Blue." Danny's favorite color.

"Green and orange." Oliver could never pick just one.

"Those are great colors for your rooms."

"We're moving in with Mason, aren't we?" Danny eyed her, a soft smile on his face.

"What do you think about that?"

"It would be awesome!" Danny's smile grew and

brightened his eyes. "He said if I keep working at it, I'll be able to ride one of the horses by myself soon."

"I want to, too, but he said only in the ring and only if he holds the rope. I told him Horse won't run away with me, but he didn't believe me." Oliver scrunched his face, not happy with that at all.

Sierra tried to hold back a laugh. "He's concerned about your safety, honey. That's all."

"I can ride by myself." Oliver frowned far too grumpily for such a sweet little boy.

"Well, if we live with Mason and you get much better at riding I'm sure it won't be long before you can ride Horse all by yourself."

Oliver nodded his approval of that like it would happen when he said so. She let him believe that for now.

Danny fidgeted, trying to dig deeper into the mattress. "Are you going to marry him?"

"He hasn't asked me, but I hope so. I love him a lot." She wanted the boys to know that.

"He watches you all the time. At first I didn't like it, but . . . I like the way he looks at you now."

Mason had won Danny's approval.

It touched her to know her son had been looking out for her.

Sierra brushed her fingers over Danny's hair, understanding completely. "Loving Mason doesn't change that I loved your dad. My heart is big enough to love both of them, just like I love both of you."

It wasn't easy to say that out loud, but in her heart she knew that the love she had for David, the love that created their two perfect sons, was still buried deep inside, waiting for the day when she could look back on it and remember the good times they shared, not just the bad stuff she discovered after his death.

"It'll be fun to live with Mason. He's good at bedtime books. He does voices." Oliver handed her the first book, his eyes already drooping.

"I guess if we move in with him you'll want him to read all the time."

Oliver shook his head. "You can share."

She chuckled. "That's a great idea."

Danny turned his head away.

"What is it?" She waited him out, because Danny had always been the one who took his time.

"Does this mean we won't celebrate Dad's birthday and stuff?"

She brushed her fingers over his hair again. "We will celebrate it every year. David is still your father."

"Mason is extra," Oliver said, then snuggled into her side.

"Okay." Danny nodded his chin toward the book in her hand, ready for the story and to move forward with their life with Mason.

So simple. Easy. Decision made.

She wished being an adult was as easy as being a kid.

Chapter Thirty-Seven

"Are you ready?" Mason wasn't sure *he* was ready for this.

Danny stared down at him from atop the horse. "I've got this."

Mason kept his grip on the horse's bridle and glanced over his shoulder at Sierra, who watched from the other side of the small arena, her phone at the ready to snap a picture. "All right, start at a walk, then you can trot once around the circle." Mason's heart raced, but he let loose and stepped back so Danny could kick his mount into a walk.

Danny glanced at Mason, making sure he'd really let him go on his own. "I'm doing it." He sat straight in the saddle, the reins loose in his hands, and moved with the horse.

Mason let out his breath, relief swamping his system. So far, so good.

"Go, Danny!" Sierra cheered, taking a picture.

Oliver stood beside her waiting his turn. Big brother got to go first. Oliver wasn't happy about it, but Mason hoped one day he'd have a little sister or brother who wanted to do everything Oliver got to do first.

Mason had plans to make Sierra his wife. But first, he needed to make sure the boys were okay with it. If their questions about when they were going to move in said anything, they were ready to be a family, but he had to be sure.

The last two weeks had been quiet. Normal.

When he was home alone in the evening, he worked on their rooms. Sierra bought the boys new bedding and desks. He took care of the painting. Next on his list, he wanted to tackle the bathroom.

For that, he had a contractor coming this week. He also wanted to do something for Sierra to make the house feel like hers, too. She mentioned how much she loved the kitchen in her old house, how cheerful and soothing she found it, with its pale green walls, white counters, and dark cabinets. He had the dark cabinets, but the granite counters were earth tones, gold, brown, tans, that wouldn't go with a bright pale green. So he'd ordered new countertops, and also a bigger sink, because she complained how small his was when the boys generated dirty dishes at an astronomical rate. He'd also asked the contractor to build a raised garden bed off the kitchen door so Sierra could plant a vegetable garden like she used to have in Napa.

They were little things, but he hoped it helped her understand that this was her house, too. He hoped it allowed her to feel free to change things to make the house hers.

They were taking their time while working toward making a life together happen.

Mason liked the thoughtfulness behind how they were doing this, but he really wanted Sierra, Danny, and Oliver moved in and settled with him as soon as possible. He'd waited a long time for a wife and family. He wanted it now. His excitement and enthusiasm grew each day.

And today, after the promised horseback riding with the boys, he planned to take them to get one of the things he needed to make Sierra his.

Danny kicked the horse into a trot, kept his balance, back straight, reins loose, wearing a big smile that lit up his face. He was a natural. Soon, he'd be riding like he was born to the saddle. They'd all be going on family rides.

It made Mason think of all the times when they were teenagers when he'd found Sierra haunting the stables, spending time with the horses, ready to go out with him at even a hint that he wanted to ride.

Something about having her near just always felt right, and now having them all here made him happier than he'd ever been.

Sierra walked up beside him as he kept a close eye on Danny. "You look pleased."

"He's doing great."

"You taught him well."

"I always knew I wanted this." He indicated Danny up on the horse, Oliver hanging on to the fencing, cheering on his brother, and her right beside him. "I just didn't know how much."

She smiled up at him. "I didn't know what I was going to do when I moved back, except the abstract, find a place for me and the kids. I never imagined it would be this place. With you. I didn't dream that big. You've helped me to allow myself to want more."

He put his arm around her waist and drew her to his side. "From now on, it's you and me. Let's always dream big."

She snuggled into his side. "This is great already."

Oliver ran up to them. "My turn."

Mason picked him up and settled him on his hip. "You ready?"

Oliver nodded.

Mason was ready, too, for a life filled with moments like this.

"Danny, rein him in and come to a full stop."

Danny gently pulled the reins, bringing his horse to a halt. He patted the horse's neck, then leaned over and hugged him. He sat up straight, keeping hold of the reins. "That was awesome!"

Mason approached and set Oliver on his feet next to the horse, then said to Danny, "Dismount like I taught you."

Danny swung his leg over the back of the horse and dropped to the ground. He pulled the reins over the horse's head and stood next to him, holding the horse still.

"Very good."

Danny beamed him a smile, pleased with the praise. "You can do this," he encouraged his brother.

Mason took the reins from Danny. "Help your brother mount." He'd taught Danny how to help Oliver into the saddle. Mason could pick him up and settle him atop the horse, but he wanted the boys to learn to work together.

Danny cupped his hands. Oliver grabbed the saddle, one hand on the front, the other on the back, put his foot in Danny's hands, and pushed himself up, laying his belly over the saddle, then swinging his leg over the horse and righting himself in a seated position. He clutched the pommel and held on. "Got it."

"That's great teamwork."

Danny adjusted the stirrups so Oliver's feet rested in them.

Mason pulled the reins over the horse's head and handed them to Oliver, who adjusted them in his hand like he'd been taught.

"Ready?"

Oliver smiled and nodded, his focus straight ahead.

Mason made a big show of letting go and holding his hands up. "You're on your own."

Sierra snapped a photo.

"Walk him around the circle," Mason coaxed, holding his breath but confident Oliver would ride as well as his big brother.

Oliver lightly tapped his heels into the horse's side.

Mason chose Kit for his mild temperament. Still, putting one of the boys on him and letting them loose put a knot in his stomach. If something happened, he'd never forgive himself.

But Oliver rode like a champ. He kept the pace slow, happy to just be in the saddle and on his own.

"I'm doing it." Oliver pulled the reins gently to the left to make the horse turn along the circle curve. Not that he really needed to—the horse had to follow the fence—but Oliver was doing great. Mason couldn't be more proud.

They gave Oliver a good ten minutes to ride circles around them. His smile never wavered.

"Does this mean we can ride out in the pastures with you on our own now?"

Mason planted his hand on Danny's riding helmet and stared down at him. "One step at a time.

Oliver isn't quite ready. You both need a little more practice. But soon."

Just as he said that, Oliver got tired of slow circles and kicked the horse into a nice trot. At first his eyes went wide with surprise, but then he laughed and enjoyed the faster pace.

Sierra took a video, then looked up at him. "What were you saying?"

"They're fearless."

"You gave them the tools and training to know they can do it."

He gave her a worried look. "We're in trouble with them. You know that, right?"

"I think we can handle it."

He hoped so. Because if anything happened to one of the boys, he'd be devastated.

This is what it feels like to be a parent.

It hit him all at once. He'd accepted that the boys came with Sierra. He welcomed them in his life. He thought of them as his. But for the first time it really hit him what that meant. A lifetime of worry and hoping that they had safe and happy lives.

Sierra looked up at him and read his mind. "Scary, right? You want everything good for them, but there's so much that could go wrong, so much that you can't control. Including that they're their own people and have a mind and will of their own."

"Can we lock them up until they're at least thirty?"

She laughed. "They're good kids. Discipline and boundaries. The rest is just hoping they use their heads and hearts."

Oliver brought the horse around in front of them

and reined in like he'd been riding forever. He turned to his mom with another big smile. "Did you see?"

"I saw it all, baby. You were fantastic."

Mason felt like he'd lost at least a year off his life worrying about the boys, but he had to admit, they rode well and followed all his directions and rules.

He was so impressed with Oliver, he plucked him right out of the saddle and swung him around. "Excellent job." He grinned down at Danny. "You, too." He set Oliver down next to his brother. "I think this calls for a guys-only lunch in town."

He'd already spoken to Sierra about taking the boys for a couple hours. Time enough for her to decorate the boys' rooms with all the things she'd bought for them.

"Yes!" the boys said in unison, then turned to their mom. "Please."

"Okay, but you need to go up to the house and wash your hands before you go."

The boys took off for the house.

With an arm around Sierra, Mason took the horse's reins and walked with her and Kit back toward the stables. "We're so close to really making this happen."

"The boys are going to love their new rooms."

"I mean everything. You and me. A life together." She smiled up at him. "I can't wait."

* * *

Mason had no intention of making her wait long. Mostly because he was impatient to make her his wife.

Danny and Oliver demolished a cheeseburger,

fries, and shakes. Chocolate for Danny. Vanilla with caramel sauce for Oliver.

Mason finished his burger, but he'd barely tasted it with his stomach tied in knots and filled with butterflies. "So, guys. I thought we'd stop at a store before we head home and buy your mom something."

Danny sucked on the straw, but with barely any shake left, all he did was make loud gurgling noises. "What?"

Oliver stared at him, waiting patiently for the answer.

Mason dove in. "I love your mom. You know that, right?"

Two dark heads bobbed across from him.

"We've talked about us living together and being a family."

"Mom said soon, but so far nothing's happened," Danny pointed out.

"Right. Your mom and I are working on it. But I want to make sure your mom knows moving in means a lot more than just us sharing a house."

Both boys' heads tipped to the side, their eyes filled with questions.

"I want her to be my wife."

"She said you guys might get married." Oliver stared at him, letting him know they'd covered this and to get on to something new.

"I'm going to ask your mom to marry me, but before I do, I wanted to make sure that you're both okay with that."

"I'm pretty sure that's what she wants." Danny abandoned the empty shake and pushed the glass away. "She smiles a lot more now. So that's good."

Oliver nodded his agreement at that assessment of their mom and Mason's relationship.

He'd obviously stressed about this talk a lot more than needed. The boys were happy their mom was happy. They liked being with him. Sierra and he had laid the foundation for the boys to know this was coming and they accepted it because they were all happy being together.

"Do you guys want to help me pick out a ring?"

Both boys sat up straighter.

Danny's eyes filled with excitement. "Really?"

"What kind?" Oliver asked.

"A sparkly one."

They slid out of their side of the booth, ready to get the job done. He thought about asking Amy to help him with the perfect ring for Sierra, but he wanted the boys to be a part of everything they did, including getting engaged.

Mason tossed some bills on the table to cover their lunch and the tip and ushered the boys out of the diner and across the street to the jewelry store. He'd gotten several recommendations from the ladies who worked in his office as well as a couple clients. The place was pricey but they were known for their custom designs. He wanted Sierra to have something special.

The boys walked along the cases, checking out all the pieces.

"May I help you?" the woman behind the counter asked, smiling at him and keeping an eye on the boys.

"I'd like to see your engagement rings."

Her smile widened. "Of course. They're at the

end." She waved her hand toward the back of the store and walked along with him that way. She stopped in front of a case filled with diamond rings in all kinds of shapes and sizes. Some simple. Others ornate and ostentatious.

The boys flanked him and stared into the case.

Oliver looked up at him. "Very sparkly." He pointed at a ring that had about thirty diamonds. It was huge. "That one."

Mason inspected it for a moment, then scrunched his lips into a half frown. "I see why you like it. It's got a lot of sparkle, but I think your mom might like something simpler." He glanced at the saleswoman. "She'd probably like something classic, but . . . pretty." He didn't know how to explain it.

Danny pointed to a set of three rings. "That one."

Oliver stared, too. "Yes. That's it." He leaned down and pressed his face to the glass, then looked up at Mason. "Get that one."

The woman opened the case and pulled out the three rings stacked on a cylindrical holder. Mason loved the classic round diamond solitaire, but the two bracketing bands really made it special. The gold had been molded to look like a twining vine set with four blue diamond-shaped sapphires on each band.

"It's a three-carat certified diamond. Marquis-cut sapphires in the bands. The set together is classic, delicate, and very pretty with that standout diamond." She turned the dangling price tag. "The GIA certification details as well as the price."

He expected the hefty price tag and didn't even blink or hesitate when he realized he could buy a car for the amount of the rings. If he'd been here alone, he'd have picked this set for Sierra. That the boys picked it, too, for her made it even better.

He thought he might have to steer the boys to something that would suit Sierra, but they knew what their mom would like just as well as he did.

Oliver seized Mason's hand and pulled it down so he could inspect the rings up close. Danny hovered over them, too.

"Are they good enough for your mom?"

"She'll really like it," Danny confirmed.

"Very sparkly." Oliver touched his finger to the diamond, then moved Mason's hand so the diamond caught the light and sparkled even more.

Mason glanced up at the clerk. "We'll take them."

"A beautiful choice. She'll love it." The woman looked at both boys. "You guys have great taste. That's my favorite set."

The boys stood taller, pride lighting their eyes.

"Thanks for your help, guys. I couldn't have done this without you. I really wanted to be sure I got your mom the very best."

"I can't wait to give it to her." Oliver clasped his hands at his chest.

Mason handed the rings along with his credit card over to the saleswoman. "Um, listen, buddy, we need to keep this a secret for a little while. I want to ask your mom to marry me in a special way."

"When?" Danny asked.

"I was thinking next weekend." The house would be done and ready for them to move in. He wanted his ring on Sierra's finger when that happened so she'd know he meant for them to be together forever.

"Do you guys think you can keep a secret that

long? No hints. No telling her what we bought, or that I'm going to ask her to marry me."

Danny and Oliver both looked a little reticent about having to wait but they nodded.

"I'll need your help with the proposal, too."

That perked them up.

"You think you can help me surprise her?"

Both boys nodded, their heads bouncing up and down with their renewed excitement.

Mason signed the sales slip.

The clerk opened the beautiful wood box, revealing the three rings inside, cushioned in white velvet. "Congratulations."

He smiled, knowing that Sierra's yes was a given, but still nervous about making the proposal perfect for her.

The woman placed the box inside a small white bag with the jewelry store's logo on it. "I hope you have a long and happy life together."

Mason held the bag by the strings, took both boys in hand, and walked out of the store with them beside him, excited to give Sierra the rings they'd picked for her and so ready to start the rest of his life with her.

Chapter Thirty-Eight

Sierra met her mom at the bottom of the stairs. Something in her eyes made Sierra suspicious.

"Is everything okay? Where are the boys?" They were supposed to go horseback riding with Mason before they surprised the boys with their redecorated rooms.

"Today's the day." Her mom looked both happy and sad about them moving into Mason's house.

"We've been talking about it for weeks. Mason says all the work is finished at his place, though he hasn't let me come over and see any of it this past week."

"It'll be a surprise for all of you." Dede touched her arm. "You've been so resilient. I'm amazed at how well you've managed to deal with everything. I know it hasn't been easy, but I see how hard you try to stay focused on what you want and the future."

"It's the only thing I can do. Being with Mason makes it easier to let it go and move on."

"He makes you happy."

Sierra didn't understand the trace of a question in that statement, but it was easy to reassure her mom. "Yes. So happy. I see him with the boys and I fall deeper in love with him. He's made us a priority in his life." Mason still worked hard, but now instead of spending late hours at his office because he didn't have anything pulling him home, he was happy to find a work-life balance for himself.

Her heart melted every time she saw him and his eyes lit up. Then he'd give her a wide smile and kiss her like he hadn't seen her in forever.

She loved talking about their day over dinner and how they traded off reading stories to the boys at night. They'd done that here at her mom's place this past week, but she imagined them doing it at Mason's from now on.

The ranch would be their home.

And she couldn't wait.

"Mason loves us. I'm excited about our future. So are the boys. They light up around him. They even mimic him." She smiled to herself. Every night Mason stood to clear his plate from the table and the boys did the same thing and followed him into the kitchen. Mason rinsed his plate and put it in the dishwasher. The boys followed his lead and did the same.

They looked up to him.

They wanted to be like him.

She loved that.

With Mason, everything seemed easy and possible.

"I just want you to be happy." Her mom searched her face for any sign she had second thoughts about moving in with him.

"Mom, I was happy when David and I moved in together and started our family. With Mason . . . I wish I could express how joyfully blissful I am. I think about him and I smile. I see him and all I want to do is hug him and kiss him and just be with him. When we talk, I know he's listening and wants to know about my day and what I want and need in my life. From the start, he's talked about *us*. It's not about him or me, but what *we'll* do going forward. How we'll raise the boys. The life we'll share."

"That's how it should be."

"After all this business with him investigating David and learning about Heather, I know I can count on him to have my back and stand beside me. I know that if we disagree or he does something I don't like, he's willing to talk it out, apologize, and make things right." Sierra appreciated his openness so much. "I know that if we hit a rough patch, he'll speak up about what he needs and that we'll talk it through together. He's seen so many relationships fall apart. He knows how devastating David's betrayal was for me. Our relationship is different. It's better. When Mason is happy, I'm happy."

"Then you're truly fated."

For some reason, that sparked a memory from the past. Something she'd forgotten, but suddenly wanted to share with Mason. It shifted something in her heart and eased the sting of what David had done to her.

"Where are the boys? We need to get going."

Dede checked her watch. "Mason picked them up twenty minutes ago and took them over to the ranch to get the horses ready for your ride."

Mason taught the boys all about chores and caring for the horses.

"Strange. I told him last night we'd head over together."

Dede shrugged and looked away. "He must be anxious to have you all there together today."

Sierra had spent the morning packing up their rooms while her mom kept the boys occupied downstairs with breakfast and cartoons.

"Well, I'm headed over there. We'll be back later to pick up the bags and boxes." They'd use Mason's truck, because they'd accumulated a lot of new stuff since arriving.

Excited, Sierra's belly fluttered with anticipation. She couldn't wait to merge their lives together. She wanted to be his partner in every way, and that included finally being together every night. She wanted to wake up with the man of her dreams every morning.

She couldn't think of a better way to start and end her day than being with Mason.

"Go. Have fun."

Sierra took a step toward the door, then turned back and wrapped her mom in a huge hug. "Thank you for everything, Mom. For being my sounding board, welcoming us home when we had nowhere else to go, and understanding that I need time when it comes to Heather."

"If I could erase that from your heart, I would."

"I know. Thank you for all the support. I appreciate it even when I'm stubborn and try to do everything on my own."

"I'm always here when you need me."

"I always need you, Mom, even when I make it seem like I can fix everything on my own."

"Stubborn is right." Her mom hugged her tighter anyway.

"I love you, Mom."

"Oh . . ." Choked up, her mom gulped. "I love you, too, sweetheart." Her voice shook with the emotion-filled words and Sierra's heart grew two sizes too large for her chest.

She sucked in a deep breath, released her mom, gave her a smile, and headed for the door. "See you soon."

"Enjoy today. Take it all in."

Sierra raised a brow at how she said that, but thought it good advice and headed out to meet her guys.

She smiled at the thought and moved a little faster to get to the ones she loved.

Chapter Thirty-Nine

Mason's gut had tied itself into a knot so tight he could barely breathe. He kept a close eye on Danny riding alone beside him. Sierra rode on his other side with Oliver seated in front of her. The two of them looked sweet riding together.

He offered to have Oliver ride with him, but the little guy wanted his mom today.

The boys had helped him set up this surprise. They kept glancing at him, their smiles and excitement evident.

Mason hoped Sierra attributed it to the fact they were headed to the creek where the boys loved to fish and splash in the wading pools.

He'd been waiting for this day a long time. He'd never been more nervous in his life. He wanted to give Sierra something amazing and wonderful.

The creek came into view. Danny reined in his horse and dismounted just like Mason taught him. The horse cropped grass and remained docile with Danny holding the reins.

Mason dismounted and plucked Oliver from his mother's lap. "This is going to be so good."

Mason appreciated the little guy's enthusiasm and optimism.

"What is all this?"

Mason gripped Sierra's hips and lifted her right off her horse, drew her body to his, and let her slide down him until she stood close in his embrace. "A celebratory picnic."

Her gaze left the blanket spread out under one of the huge oak trees with the food basket and cooler to meet his. "What are we celebrating?"

"Us." He took her hand and drew her toward the creek.

Danny had already tied off the horses' reins to the bushes like Mason had shown him earlier in the morning when they rode out to set everything up while Sierra packed up their stuff. Tonight, they'd all sleep under the same roof for the first time.

Mason couldn't wait.

But first, he needed Sierra to answer one question.

"Do you remember this spot?"

"We came here all the time when we were in high school. We'd skip stones and just hang out listening to the water. I poured out all my secrets to you."

"We share some history." Mason drew her to a stop in the shade next to the rolling creek, the cascading water gurgling over rocks next to them, and took her hands in his. "I'm looking forward to us making more together."

Danny and Oliver appeared on either side of him and stared up at their mom. She glanced down at them.

"What's going on?"

Danny pulled out his hand from behind his back and showed Sierra the small white box.

Mason explained. "This represents our past."

Danny flipped the lid open on the box and revealed the charm bracelet Mason had had made for her. "A horse for all the rides we took together. A diamond for all the nights we spent staring up at the stars and talking. Whether it was in the back of my truck, out in the pasture, or right here, those are some of my best memories."

Sierra's eyes misted with tears. "Oh, Mason."

"And a daisy."

She laughed. "For all the times you picked a wildflower and plucked the petals off in exactly the right order to land on *he loves me not* for whatever boy I had a crush on."

"Even back then, I wanted to keep you all to myself. I was just too stupid and focused on other things to see that what I really wanted was right in front of me."

A single tear slipped down her cheek.

Oliver drew his surprise out from behind his back.

Mason held Sierra's questioning gaze. "The bracelet is for the past. This one is for the present."

Oliver pulled the lid off the white box and revealed the set of keys on a heart-shaped key chain.

"Keys to *our* house."

She smiled and pressed her lips together as her eyes glassed over again. "I can't wait to make it our home."

"Tonight will be the first night of the rest of our lives where we go to sleep and wake up together."

Both boys heads turned up to him.

He glanced at both of them. "Did I forget to tell you you're moving in today?"

The boys looked to their mom for confirmation. She nodded. "That's right. We are."

"Yes!" the boys said in unison, their big smiles conveying their excitement.

Mason squeezed Sierra's hands to draw her full attention back to him. "Before you do and I show you the surprises I have for you at the house, there's one more thing I want to give you." He slipped his hand in his front pocket but didn't draw it back out just yet. "This one is for our future." He pulled out the wood ring case, used his thumb to open the lid, and held it out in his palm as he sank to one knee.

Sierra gasped, put her fingertips to her lips, and stared from the ring to him to the ring and back again. "Mason."

"I love you. So much that it fills me up and I feel like I can't possibly feel this much for one person. Then you smile at me and that feeling gets bigger and my whole world gets brighter. I want to build a life with you. I want a lifetime of memories filled with you and our children."

Her head was already bobbing up and down, but he kept going because she deserved to hear it all and have him ask the question.

"I want you to be my one and only. I want you to be my wife. Will you marry me?"

She kept nodding, tears falling down her soft cheeks, her lips trembling when she said, "Yes!" She leaned down and kissed him. "Yes." She kissed him again. "Yes. Yes. Yes." She kissed him for one long moment.

He stood, pulling her into his arms and kissing her more deeply.

The boys cheered and gave them bear hugs, their little arms around his and Sierra's legs.

Mason managed to step back, take her hand, and put the diamond engagement ring on her finger.

"Where's the rest?" Oliver checked the box in his hand.

"The other part is for the wedding day." Mason took Sierra's hand and kissed her knuckle right above the ring. "Do you like it?"

"I love it." She stared at the diamond.

"The boys helped me pick it out."

Her gaze shot to his. "Really?"

"I got their permission to ask you, then we went shopping."

She chuckled under her breath. "That's really sweet."

"We're going to be a family," Oliver announced.

Danny took his mom's hand and checked out the ring again. "It looks really good. Wait 'til you see the rest. It's awesome."

Relief hit Mason in a wave. Sierra said yes. The kids were excited about them getting married, and Sierra looked happy that he'd pulled off the proposal and included the kids.

"When are we getting married?" Oliver asked.

"Not *we*," Danny scolded Oliver. "*They* are getting married."

Mason ruffled Danny's hair. "It's definitely we. My commitment to your mom is a commitment I make to you, too. We will be family." He hugged the boys to his sides. "I, for one, can't wait."

Sierra kissed him again. "Me, either."

Oliver wriggled away and handed Sierra the box with the keys in it. He ran off to the picnic. "It's time for cake!"

Danny handed over the bracelet and ran to catch up to Oliver.

Sierra raised an eyebrow. "I thought you brought lunch."

"I was told that a celebration required cake." He tilted his head to the boys pulling the cake out of the cooler.

Sierra laughed. "Absolutely."

Mason took the bracelet out of the box and fastened it around Sierra's wrist. He brushed his fingers over her skin and stared deeply into her eyes. "Were you surprised?"

"In the best way." She linked her fingers with his. "I knew we'd get here, I just didn't expect it to be today."

"Why not today? You're moving in. I wanted you to know I want it to be forever."

She turned into him. "I never doubted you wanted me."

He looked into her eyes. "Always."

He kissed her softly, then she backed away, pulling him along with her. "I can't wait to show you how much I love you tonight. In our bed." She shook the keys in the box.

Mason suddenly had second thoughts about bringing the boys with them for the proposal. He'd love to lay her out on that blanket and make love to her under the tree.

But the boys smiled at them and he decided this was good, too.

This would be a memory all of them cherished.

* * *

Sierra held her hand out to her mom to show off the gorgeous engagement ring. Mason had really outdone himself. She couldn't wait to see the wedding bands the boys kept talking about while they ate cake and drank sparkling cider by the creek.

It truly had been a wonderful proposal, filled with poignant moments. Mason had put a lot of thought into it and her gifts.

Her mom touched the charms on the bracelet. "This is lovely, Sierra."

"Mason wanted to remind me of the past we share. It was really beautiful."

Her mom looked from her to Mason, standing right behind her, his hands on her shoulders. "I wish you both a lifetime of happiness together."

"Thank you, Dede."

Sierra touched her fingers to Mason's hands on her shoulders. "Mom. If you don't mind watching the boys for just half an hour before we take them to Mason's—"

"*Our* house," Mason corrected.

An uncontrollable smile spread across her face. "Yes. Our house. I wanted to show Mason something out by the pond."

"Sure, honey. Take your time."

"Thank you." She took Mason's hand and tugged him toward the back door.

"Why are we going to the pond?" A sparkle in his eyes hinted at what he hoped they'd be doing by the pond.

"It's not what you think."

His face fell in disappointment, but he rallied. "Are you sure?" He stepped behind her, took her hips in his hands, and kissed the side of her neck, nuzzling his nose in her hair.

She leaned back into him. "Come on. You'll see." She grabbed his hand again and pulled him along.

They made it to the garden gate before Mason slowed his pace. "Sierra, why are we going out there?" He meant the place where David and Heather snuck away to so long ago.

Funny how it felt like a lifetime ago now.

It was hard to be mad when she felt so excited and happy and hopeful.

"It's not what you think. There really is something I want to show you. I didn't remember it until this morning when I was talking to my mom. And then you proposed and now it seems even more important to show it to you."

Mason reluctantly went along, holding her hand all the way to the pond. She stopped near it and stared out at the two ducks floating in the water.

"How many summer days did we spend out here?"

"A lot. Amy strutted around in her bikini."

"How many times did she pretend to have a leg cramp so you'd help her out of the water?"

Mason chuckled and shook his head. "She tried, I'll give her that. But I always preferred hanging out with you."

"Funny how we never took it further back then."

"Maybe we always knew there was time and we'd be together eventually."

Sierra's heart sped up. "I think you're right. And I can prove it." She grabbed his hand and led him to the shed they used as a little cabin. She didn't hesitate to push the door open and step inside.

Memories assailed her as she stared at the board games stacked on a bookshelf, the old afghan and mismatched pillows on the worn leather sofa, the blue-and-cream braided rug on the floor they had sat on during countless card games, bowls of snacks spread around them.

But it was the dozens of pictures they'd tacked up on the walls over the years that caught and held her attention.

Sierra spotted the one she remembered this morning and walked over to it, Mason right behind her. She plucked the old Polaroid from the wall, the tack still stuck in the top. She turned to him and showed him the picture of the two of them sitting on the small dock that stretched into the pond that they used to jump off all the time.

They were sitting so close together their shoulders and arms touched. She was looking up at him and he was looking down at her, both of them smiling.

She traced her finger over the picture. "I don't even remember someone taking this shot of us."

They'd often been lost in conversation together, avoiding everyone else, happy to just keep things between the two of them.

"It could have been taken any number of days."

He bumped his arm to her shoulder. "We spent a lot of time together. I'd bring my friends out here. You and your sisters would have yours. It was always a party. Nothing wild. Just fun."

"I really loved our friendship. I had my sisters, but somehow you were always easier to talk to and be around."

"Probably because I was an only child, I liked

hanging out with you guys. It was better than being alone at the ranch. And you liked doing everything I liked to do."

"But there's something else that's special about this picture that I remembered this morning. Even back then, I think I knew we'd always be together." She turned the picture over and showed him what she'd written on the back. Inside a big red heart she had written Sierra + Mason.

"I don't know why I wrote it like this. We were just friends, but I knew I loved you. Not the way I do now. It's so much bigger now, but still . . ."

He linked his fingers with hers. "We laid the foundation. Now we're both ready to build on the love that started all those years ago."

"You get it. I know it's sappy." But she didn't care.

"No, it's not." He tapped the picture. "Sometimes we wish for something and feel like it will never come true. Maybe that's how you felt when we didn't take things to the next level back then. But here we are back together and getting married."

Her smile came fast and filled with joy. "We're getting married!"

He tapped the photo. "Because Sierra plus Mason equals a whole lot of love." He kissed her then, drawing it out, letting her feel how much he loved her.

He broke the kiss and stared down at her. "I'm glad you showed me this. After Amy told me you weren't interested before you married David, I thought I was the only one who harbored feelings from back then. I know now that wasn't true, but this just really seals it for me."

"I always knew what I wanted, but I guess we both had to experience what didn't work so we could really appreciate what we have now."

"That's a great way to put it."

She hadn't exactly wasted that time. She had the boys to show for it, and she'd never regret her relationship with David for that reason alone.

And maybe it was a little petty, but she found it fitting to know that David and Heather came here to this little hideaway and carried out their betrayal and all the while this picture hung on the wall with her wish clearly stated on the back.

Standing next to Mason, his ring on her finger, a future of happiness on the horizon, Sierra found it easy to let go of the past. Life had led her to this home when she was a teen and she'd found her first friend in this new place with the boy next door. When circumstances turned her life upside down and took everything but the boys from her, she'd landed here again and found that friendship with the boy who'd turned into a very good man was even more necessary. And the love she'd harbored for him all these years was free to grow and fill her up like nothing else she'd ever had in her life.

Sierra tacked the picture back up on the wall.

"You don't want to take that with you?"

"It'll be here waiting for me if I need it." Just like Mason had been here waiting for her all these years. "Let's go home." She took his hand and walked out of the shed, leaving her hurt behind, knowing she had everything she needed to be happy.

She had her boys.

She had Mason.

Chapter Forty

Sierra woke up with Mason's big body plastered to the back of her, his arm draped over her hip, and his face buried in her long hair. A sense of all-encompassing contentment filled her up. She'd have liked to spend the rest of her life just like that, nestled in Mason's arms, feeling that much love and joy at just being with him.

It had been that way for the past two weeks.

The boys had settled in without any apprehension. They loved their rooms and pretty much took over the rest of the house like they'd always lived here. Mason didn't mind at all, but he'd made it clear his office was off-limits.

They'd found a routine that worked for all of them.

Mason left early for work each morning, using the extra hour in his office before any of the other staff arrived to catch up on paperwork or go over his cases for the day. Sierra dropped the kids at school, then went to work. When their schedules permitted, she met Mason for lunch since they worked so close to each other. Mason picked the kids up right after school on Fridays, saving them from going to after-school care. He took the boys horseback riding before Sierra got home.

Mason cooked Friday to Sunday. Sierra did the cooking during the week.

She loved that they found a rhythm and everything synced so easily.

Seeing Mason embrace the new structured chaos in his life and enjoy it so much made her feel safe and secure. Mason took on her and the boys with enthusiasm.

Sierra now sipped her coffee in the kitchen Mason had redone just for her.

Not only had he welcomed them into his home, he'd made it feel like theirs, too.

"What are you thinking about?" Mason walked in and went to the sink to wash his hands.

The boys chatted down the hall in their bathroom doing the same after helping Mason feed and water the horses.

"I'm standing in our beautiful kitchen thinking about how much I love living here with you."

Mason shot her a surprised and exuberant look. His smile made her heart melt. "Everything about this place has changed. Especially the feel of it."

She knew exactly what he meant. This was a big place for a bachelor to live in alone. Now, the house had a family. It was cozy.

It felt like home. A place where they laughed and loved and shared their lives.

Mason dried his hands, hung the towel from the oven door handle, then closed the distance between them. "You look amazing in that dress." His gaze skimmed down to her toes and back up again, momentarily stopping at the deep V in the pretty wrap dress she'd chosen for the engagement party her mom was throwing them in half an hour. The simple white dress had tiny pink flowers sprinkled over it. It felt feminine and flirty.

With Mason's hot gaze sweeping over her, she felt sexy and desirable.

She placed her hands on his chest. "I thought you might like it."

Mason traced his fingers along her shoulder and settled his warm hand on her neck. "Are you ready for today?"

She heard what he didn't ask in that question. "I asked my mom to invite Heather and Hallee to the party."

His eyebrow shot up. "You did?"

"I listened to your argument, thought about it, and decided you were right. I can't ignore her forever. What she did doesn't erase the fact we are family and at some point I need to accept that the boys have a sister they should get to know better."

"And you and Heather need to have a real talk about what happened. It's not good to keep your feelings all bottled up."

"I know. I heard you, Counselor. I'm not sure today is the day to do that, but as you said, I don't want to look back and miss having everyone together to celebrate with us." She wanted to see if she could be in the same vicinity as her sister and not want to kill her. "If nothing else, this will make my mom happy. It's the least I can do, since she's throwing us the engagement party."

"Wait until she finds out we're getting married in less than three months."

Sierra felt the nervous butterflies in her stomach. "We have so much to do in such a short time." The ocean view boutique hotel she fell in love with had a cancellation and because the owner and Mason were friends, they got first dibs on booking the date.

They planned to keep the guest list to family and close friends, but on Mason's side that meant a lot of people because of his status in the community. She didn't mind. Not when it meant she'd be Mason's wife.

"We have a lot to celebrate."

They sure did. Besides their upcoming wedding, Sierra had sold the property in Napa for a better than decent price to a developer thanks to Mason's brilliant negotiations on her behalf. Most of the insurance money she'd received went to paying off the loan and setting up college funds for the kids, but she invested the property money and set aside a chunk in savings for a rainy day.

Going forward, she and Mason would combine their funds. Mason's income far exceeded hers. He'd told her she could quit her job or scale back her hours. Whatever she wanted to do. He had no problem supporting them. At first, she'd balked at the thought of not working. After what David had done to her financially, she wanted to know she had the money if something happened. But then she reminded herself that Mason wasn't David. He didn't hide things from her. He didn't lie. She trusted him.

So she talked to her boss and scaled back her hours to thirty a week so long as she was available by phone for emergencies. After the wedding, her new hours would take effect.

And who knew, maybe she'd quit altogether when a new baby came along. Talk of marriage had sparked talk of expanding their family. They planned to start right after the wedding, and Sierra couldn't wait. She wanted another child. Mason loved the boys, but he dreamed of a child of his own. She wanted to give him one. Maybe two.

"You've got that sweet smile again."

"This year we'll celebrate our wedding. Maybe next year we'll celebrate the birth of our child."

Mason's hand brushed down her arm and swept over her hip. "I can't wait."

"A few months ago, I had nothing left of my old life. The boys and I came here with next to nothing. We have a whole new life and it's wonderful and so full I couldn't ask for more."

"I didn't know how much I was missing in my life until you came back into it. I can't help but feel like this is how it was always meant to be." He kissed her softly.

"Kissing again," Oliver announced to Danny who followed him into the kitchen.

"Aren't we supposed to leave now?" Danny finished buttoning his white dress shirt.

Oliver had also changed into his party outfit.

The boys looked great in their black pants and white dress shirts.

"I guess I better get dressed." Mason kissed her on the forehead and gave each boy a shoulder squeeze on his way out.

She smiled at Danny and Oliver. "How lucky are we?"

They both stared back at her, wondering what she meant, but deep down they understood. In the years to come, with the life she and Mason would give them, they'd understand.

Home is where you are always loved and welcome.

Chapter Forty-One

Dede wanted the party to be everything Sierra and Mason deserved for this happy occasion. So far, the guests seemed happy, the food and drinks were plentiful, and everyone gathered in small groups to chat on this beautiful sunny day.

She checked her watch. Almost time for the cake and a toast to the happy couple. The caterer was already setting out the plates and forks.

The poster by the cake table caught her eye again. She loved how Sierra had blown up the old Polaroid of her and Mason sitting on the dock when they were teens. Amy had snapped a new picture of the pair in the exact same pose. The poster showed the two pics side by side. They'd grown up, but their smiles—and the way they looked at each other— were the same.

"Thank you so much for the party, Mom. It's beautiful."

Dede encircled Sierra's waist with one arm and used her other hand to point to the poster and the old photo. "Those two belonged together."

"It took us a while to get here, but we're really happy."

Dede turned and faced Sierra. "Thank you for including Heather and Hallee. I know it's hard, but

I think it's important for both of you to keep a connection no matter how tenuous."

Sierra put her hand on Dede's shoulder. "I mostly did it for you, Mom, but I also wanted to see if I could do it without making today about the past. And I can. Today is about me and Mason and our love story." She held her glass up toward the poster, the past and future represented. "I want to keep looking forward, not back."

"I hoped you'd feel that way."

Sierra glanced over at Mason talking to his friend and neighbor, Luke Thompson, with Oliver hanging on Mason's back, his chin propped on Mason's shoulder. "Look at him. At them. How could I not be happy today?"

"I just want you to know I know it's there under all the good and I appreciate that you're strong enough to bury it and appreciate what you do have, not what you lost."

"Maybe it's callous . . ." Sierra frowned. "Or maybe it's just my way of coping, but what Mason and I have is so much bigger and better than what I had with David. Don't get me wrong, it wasn't all bad."

Dede touched Sierra's hand. "I've been married and divorced three times, sweetheart, I know what you mean. The love you have for Mason is different from what you felt for David. It's okay to feel that way. It's okay to celebrate it without feeling like you're disparaging David's memory and what you had with him before it went bad."

"I don't feel bad. I've gotten to a place where I can hold on to the good and not let the bad steal the joy from that. We loved each other. We had two children together. That's worth holding on to fondly without letting the bad taint it."

"Good for you, Sierra." Dede hugged Sierra again and whispered her wish, "Maybe in time, you'll be able to do that with your sister."

* * *

The caterer waved her mom over and Sierra took a minute to appreciate her mom for being the rock she needed and the thread that tied Heather, Amy, and Sierra together.

"I know you invited her, but are you ready for me to ask her to leave?" Amy pointed her wine glass at Heather, who walked back into the garden area from the path that led to the pond and shed.

It made Sierra think of how Heather and David snuck off there. Anger flared, but the sad look in Heather's red-rimmed eyes drew sympathy from what she thought was her hardened heart.

Sierra thought about her trip back to the shed with Mason and how the memories came back and filled her with all the emotions she'd felt then and now for him.

Heather missed David. She'd loved him. They'd had a child together.

If David hadn't been Sierra's husband and she saw her sister in this state over a man she'd loved and lost, how would she feel?

She'd sympathize. She'd want to comfort and console her sister.

No one had done that for Heather because David had been Sierra's husband.

What they did was wrong, no doubt. It caused a lot of damage.

Heather deserved to feel terrible for what she'd done.

But for the first time Sierra put herself in her sister's place. Heather mourned David. She missed him. She wished for him.

Sierra felt all those things when he died and she was just a widow, not the wife of a philanderer. That's who David turned her into after she grieved and found out about what he did.

That's not who David was to Heather.

"I need to talk to her."

Amy scoffed. "You're not seriously going to forgive her for what she did."

Sierra met Amy's disbelieving gaze. "She's been carrying the weight of what happened for both her and David."

"Because she deserves it."

"She knows that. But I can't keep feeding this anger. I'm working harder at hating her than I am on forgiving her. Maybe if I did it the other way around, this pit in my stomach every time I think about her would go away, because I don't want to hate my sister." It hurt her heart to shut her sister out like this, to think such terrible things about her, to wish bad things for her. She couldn't do it anymore.

Amy sighed. "I know what you mean. It's hard. She left me a message last week asking if I'd call her with the name and number of a good babysitter. I don't know if she didn't want to ask me to watch Hallee for her, or she wants someone as backup, or what. I want to see my niece. I want her to know that I'll always help with Hallee and that if she's really in a bind, I'm here."

"That's just it. You and Mom got sucked into our drama. I'm sure Heather feels like it's us against her because of what she did. I don't want it to be that way. I don't want Mom to feel like she's stuck in the middle of us for the rest of her life, like she can't support both of us without feeling guilty or disloyal to either of us. As a mom, I feel for her, because I don't know that I could do that with Danny and Oliver."

"Me, either. P.J. and Emma have their squabbles. I help them work it out. Mom can't fix this with forced apologies and making you two talk it out. This is a deep kind of hurt. Talking about it will only hurt more."

"Maybe the only way past this is through the hurt." Sierra grasped Amy's arm. "Thanks for being on my side, but I want you to know it's okay to have her back, too."

"You're a kinder person than I am. I don't think I would have worked my way through this the way you have and gotten to a point where I could even contemplate talking to her, let alone trying to work it out."

"I feel like if I don't try, I'll regret it. If David was still here, I'd want to find a way to at least be civil with each other for the kids' sake. The least I can do is give my sister the same courtesy for the same reason."

"When you put it like that, yeah, it makes sense." Amy bounced her gaze from Sierra to Heather and back. "We do a lot for our kids." Amy hugged her, then gave her an encouraging smile.

Sierra walked toward Heather, stopping briefly to clasp hands with Mason who'd stood by watching her and Amy quietly talking alone. He had to know the gist of the conversation and where she was headed. He gave her a reassuring smile and let her move on toward her sister.

Heather sat alone, her head down, holding a drink she hadn't touched. Her head snapped up when Sierra approached the table and took the seat across from her.

"Uh. Hello."

"Hi." They had to break the ice somehow. Inane greetings seemed a good way to start, but Sierra wanted to make this as quick and painless as possible. "You hurt me."

"I know." Heather looked her in the eye, hers filled with remorse and pain. "I'm sorry."

Sierra took that in and let it settle in her heart. "I believe you."

"You do? Why? After what I did . . ." She shook her head. "I can't take it back."

"I sincerely doubt you'd want to." Otherwise it wouldn't have continued after the first encounter. And then there was Hallee.

One side of Heather's mouth drew back in a half frown and tears glistened in her eyes. "I don't know what to say to you."

Because they weren't meant to share the details. Those memories belonged to Heather. Sierra didn't need to pile on to the hurt by hearing all the sordid specifics.

"I was just talking to Amy."

Heather glanced over at their sister spying on them from across the yard. "She hates me, too."

"No, she doesn't. And I don't want to hate you, either. But you made it damn hard not to. You're my sister. I used to clean and bandage your skinned knees and push you on the swing and talk to you about boys and kissing. I'm pretty sure I'm the one who gave you the sex talk."

Heather's cheeks pinked. "Mom's idea of a sex talk was telling me not to do anything you and Amy were doing."

They shared hesitant smiles and it felt like it cracked the shield Sierra put between them to keep Heather away. "I suppose we should have taught you to be careful who you fall in love with."

"I'm sorry, Sierra. I never meant—"

Sierra held her hand up to stop her. Heather's mouth snapped closed. She deflated, her shoulders sagging.

"I don't want to hear any more apologies. What I told Amy was that if you were David, I'd make an effort to be civil. That's probably the best I can do right now. The kids deserve at least that much from us. I don't want to necessarily tell them they're siblings right now. But I don't want to keep them apart, either."

Heather's gaze went to Emma and Hallee out on the lawn, rolling a soccer ball back and forth between them. Danny and P.J. sat nearby eating a bunch of grapes from the fruit plate they served earlier.

Sierra sighed. "I don't want them to miss birthday parties and holidays together because you and I can't be in the same room with each other."

"I don't want that, either. I've been trying to figure out a way to make things up to you in some way. I didn't want to do this today, but I went to my boss and applied for a promotion that I deserve but probably would have gone to someone else because I tend to think everything will be handed to me, and that's not how things really work."

Sierra had pointed that out to her.

"I told my boss that I deserved that position. I'd earned it. I did half the work already without being paid." Heather stared down at the table, then met Sierra's gaze again. "I want to provide for my daughter and give her the best life I can. I want her to know that I worked hard to better myself. And I'm working on it."

"What does this have to do with us?"

"I want you to know I'm working on being a better me. And that starts with standing on my own two feet, taking responsibility for what I've done, and finding a way to pay you back for the money David gave me. So I got the promotion I deserved and the raise that goes with it, so I could get a loan to pay you back half the money David gave me." She shrugged. "I didn't do it for the whole amount because I believe David should support his daughter."

Sierra reluctantly agreed with that.

"I'll get the check to you this week. I didn't know he took out the loan. I didn't really think about him taking money away from you and the kids." Heather sighed, her eyes filled with regret. "Let's face it, I tried really hard not to think about you."

Sierra appreciated the honesty, even though it stung.

Heather kept going. "I will never be able to apologize enough or make this right, but if you're willing to set this aside, at least for the kids, then I'll follow your lead on how you want to handle getting them together and how and when we tell them the truth."

"Hallee is too young to understand. The boys might get the concept, but they're still too young to grasp the gravity of what having a sister means. Maybe when Hallee is old enough to understand the concept of siblings we'll tell them. Until then, let's stop rehashing what happened and live in the moment. We can be civil. Who knows, maybe one day we can even be friends again."

Heather pressed her lips together, eyes watery, and nodded. "Thank you. It's more than I deserve."

"No more talk like that, either. All the energy I poured into being angry, all the energy you put into thrashing yourself over this, it's not good for either of us."

"Why are you doing this now? Or at all?"

"I'm about to get married to a man I really, really love. I have a chance to have the life I always wanted with a man who only wants to love me back and make me happy. The last thing I want to do is carry this with me and let it drag my heart down. I don't want to carry this weight with me into something that is so . . . perfect."

Heather gave her a sad smile. "I'm happy for you."

Sierra stood and stared down at her sister and gave her the truth. "I hope one day I'll be happy for you, too." She turned to go and spotted the kids playing Duck, Duck, Goose on the lawn. She smiled when Oliver goosed Hallee and the little one jumped up and tried her best to chase Oliver, who was faster and steadier on his legs than the toddler. Hallee lost, but the sweet grin on her face said she didn't care. She started around the circle of kids, touching each of their heads, saying *Duck* each time.

Sierra hadn't put a lot of thought into the wedding details, but one thing she absolutely wanted was all the kids to participate. Danny and Oliver would share the duty as best man to Mason. She'd ask Amy to be her matron of honor. But Emma and Hallee would be adorable flower girls. P.J., though older than the rest of them, would still make a great ring bearer.

She turned back and found Heather staring at the kids, too, a single tear rolling down her cheek.

"I'd love it if Hallee was a flower girl in my wedding."

Heather's surprised gaze shot to hers and she gasped.

"I'll get her a pretty dress. *All* the kids will be included."

Including Hallee in her life seemed an easier way to move forward. With Heather, she'd need to take baby steps to rebuild the trust that had been shattered. It would take time. Maybe they'd never get back to what they had, but Sierra would try to find peace with what happened and with her sister.

She left Heather and went back to Mason and their celebration, content she'd not only salved the discord with her sister but made wedding plans that amped her anticipation for their big day.

She couldn't wait to get married and look back on it knowing she'd done her best to leave the past behind and start fresh with the man she knew would be her perfect partner.

Chapter Forty-Two

Sierra stood at the back of the ballroom in her gorgeous white wedding gown feeling like a princess. The wedding coordinator handed her the bouquet. The heady scent of white roses filled the air. The simple bouquet complemented the lavender hydrangea, pink peony, and white spider mum bouquets decorating the tables at the back of the ballroom and the aisle leading to the temporary stage in the middle of the dance floor.

Mason stood there with Danny and Oliver waiting for her grand entrance. They all looked dashing in their black tuxes. P.J. stood just inside the door holding a white satin pillow with the rings tied to it. He tugged at the collar of his dress shirt.

Amy stood next to him wearing a gorgeous fuchsia A-line chiffon off-the-shoulder dress, looking spectacular. She brushed P.J.'s hand away from the offending collar. "Stop fidgeting."

Emma and Hallee stood behind them in their matching pale pink dresses with the tulle overlaid skirts and, tied around their waists, fuchsia satin ribbons that matched Amy's dress. So sweet and cute.

The florist handed them each a basket filled with pink rose petals.

Hallee spotted her and ran over, the basket

bouncing against her side. She set the basket down and grabbed fistfuls of her beaded wedding gown. "Pretty."

Sierra stared down into Hallee's beautiful hazel eyes. For the first time, she allowed herself to really see the resemblance to Danny's eyes and she saw David in the little girl. There was of course a hint of her sister in Hallee's pert nose and bowed mouth.

Hallee threw her arms around Sierra's legs. "Auntie. Pretty."

Sierra's eyes teared. She patted Hallee on the back, then dipped down and traced her finger along the curve of Hallee's sweet face, admiring her dark curls that always seemed to be in disarray. Just like Heather's. "You look like a princess in your dress, too."

Hallee spun around and almost toppled over with the momentum, but Sierra caught her waist and kept her upright.

"It's time to start," the wedding coordinator announced.

P.J. started out first.

Sierra touched her fingertip to Hallee's nose, making her smile. "It's your turn, sweetheart. Go with Emma."

The girls followed P.J. down the aisle tossing flower petals into the air and watching them fall in disarray on the white draped aisle.

Amy took the edges of Sierra's dress, pulled and shook it out, then let it drop. "Gorgeous, sis."

Sierra smiled, but a pang in her heart made it stop before it hit maximum wattage. For a heartbeat she wished things were better between her and Heather. She'd excluded her from all the wedding preparations. She hadn't even included Heather in picking out Hallee's dress.

She'd needed the space and to keep the preparations and wedding happy and all about her and Mason.

"Don't tell me you're having second thoughts." Amy studied her, then glanced over her shoulder as the girls stepped up on the stage, making it Amy's turn to go.

"Not at all. Mason is my future." She waved Amy to go. "Hurry up. I want to kiss my husband."

And later, she'd thank her sister for letting Hallee be a part of the wedding and attending despite how frosty things were between them. Maybe it wouldn't be the same as it used to be, but they could definitely be better than this.

Amy glided down the path, turning her head slightly to give Rex a sexy smile on the way. Sierra had no doubt they'd make it to their rocking chairs on the porch watching their grandkids play in the yard.

The wedding march started. She didn't hesitate to take her place in the double door entrance and paused to take in the smile on Mason's face when he saw her. She took him in, standing with their sons, and that smile. The connection they shared drew her right to him.

She felt the stares from their avid audience of friends and family, but she only had eyes for the man who stepped forward and held his hand out to her. She took it and stepped up onto the stage.

"God, you're beautiful." Mason gave her a soft kiss.

Sighs erupted in the audience along with a few woots from the guys.

Mason smiled down at her, then gave his neighbor and buddy Luke, who'd become certified online to perform their ceremony, a sheepish grin.

Luke teased him. "Give me five minutes and you can kiss her all you want."

Everyone burst out with laughter.

Sierra handed her bouquet to Amy and took Mason's hands and lost herself in his steady, loving gaze and the simple ceremony. His declaration of love and devotion along with the promises he made filled her up. She didn't hesitate to give him back all he'd given her and before she knew it they'd exchanged rings and said, "I do," and Luke pronounced them husband and wife.

Mason kissed her again, taking his time, the cheers washed out by the sheer joy emanating from both of them.

"I give you Mr. and Mrs. Moore."

Hearing that felt so right.

Everything about being with Mason felt like it was meant to be.

Amy handed her back the flowers.

Sierra and Mason faced their friends and family as husband and wife and she couldn't smile big enough to convey the happiness bursting out of her.

They'd planned their exit for the photographer to get an amazing shot.

Emma and Hallee led the way with Danny, Oliver, and P.J. next, Amy at the side behind them, and she and Mason following them all back down the aisle, smiling for the pictures she knew would be amazing and capture the moment.

They left their guests to find their way to their tables for lunch while she, Mason, and the wedding party took more pictures in the hotel's amazing gardens.

Twenty minutes later, they rejoined their guests to rousing applause and she and Mason took to the dance floor for their first dance. The kids joined in, making everyone smile again.

Mason danced with her mom and she danced with his dad, then she danced with her boys together before dancing with her dad while Mason danced with his mom.

They finally took a break to eat and chat with guests.

She spotted Heather sitting quietly by herself, the other guests from her table on the dance floor. Heather looked so alone. It should make her happy to see her sister get a little of what she deserved, but it didn't. It made her sad. She didn't want to feel this way today of all days. She wanted everyone, including Heather, to be happy and celebrating.

She didn't have a solution that would bring her and Heather closer but she'd think on it later. Right now, she wanted to live in the moment and wallow in her happiness.

Sierra let it all go for now and enjoyed the rest of the reception by her husband's side. She pulled Mason back out onto the dance floor for a slow song and found peace as they swayed to the music.

When it came time for them to leave for their honeymoon, their guests lined the exit and stairs to the waiting limo.

Sierra stopped and kissed her boys good-bye. "Be good. We'll call you tomorrow and send pictures." She looked forward to spending the next week in

Hawaii at a luxury resort, soaking up the sun, and working on a brother or sister for the boys.

She intended to spend every second with Mason, not just getting through the days, but living them to the fullest for the rest of her life.

She hugged her mom. "Thank you for always being there for me."

"Be happy."

"Done. I couldn't get any happier than I am right now."

Amy stepped away from Rex's side and pulled her in for a hug. "I'm so glad you moved back home."

"Me, too. See you when I get back."

Mason let loose the boys, who practically strangled him with their hugs. He waved good-bye to her mom and sister and his family, then they finally made it down the steps under a rain of flower petals to the limo. She glanced over her shoulder to toss the bouquet, but spotted Heather standing with Hallee in front of her.

She squeezed Mason's hand. "Give me a sec."

He glanced at Heather and nodded.

Sierra walked up the two steps, smiled down at Hallee, then handed the bouquet to her sister. She leaned in close and whispered something for her sister's ears only. "I hope this brings you good luck and you find a man who is all yours and who loves you the way Mason loves me." She meant it. They both needed to move on.

Tears slipped down Heather's cheeks.

"Mom has the kids while we're gone, but I bet they'd love a sleepover at Aunt Heather's." Maybe they weren't ready to hang out like they used to, but the kids loved being with each other, and that shouldn't have to change.

Heather wiped away a tear, found a smile, and nodded. "I'd love that."

Sierra rejoined her husband, light of heart and filled with hope for the future, knowing no matter what, she didn't have to face anything alone again.

She had her family, the boys, and Mason.

Author's Note

Sierra loves reading her boys bedtime stories, but her favorite ones are the ones she tells about Franny Fright. When she was young, they were frightening tales she told to scare her sisters. But now, they're fun . . . and just a bit scary.

Here is just one of those tales . . .

FRANNY FRIGHT

Franny Fright took such delight
In making things go bump in the night
A clink and clang from her boa chain
A boo and ooh like a scary ghoul

Franny Fright plays her tricks
On the little ones she picks
Tickling toes
And chilling their bones

You'll hide under the covers when Franny Fright
*   hovers*
Squeaking floors
And slamming doors
Your delightful screams Franny Fright adores

So when the sky is dark
And the moon is bright
Watch out for Franny Fright

Acknowledgments

I am so grateful to the Avon Books/William Morrow team for all the support and enthusiasm for all the stories I bring to life. And I do mean team, because the books aren't finished and in readers' hands without the editorial, marketing, publicity, sales, and all the other support staff that have a hand in every book.

A very special thank-you to my amazingly talented and patient editor, Lucia Macro, for always diving deep into every story and making sure, in the end, it's the best it can be.

To my hardworking agent, Suzie Townsend, who takes care of business and has my back. I'm so lucky to have you as a friend and partner on this amazing journey.

And of course, thank you, readers, for picking up my books, giving me your precious time and attention, and spending time with my characters. I know I put you through a lot, but in the end, I promise you'll always find a happy ending.

Reading Group Guide

1. The novel is about the secrets people keep from one another. Discuss whether some secrets should remain just that—secret—and the kind of damage that secrets (revealed or not) might do to relationships.

2. What do you think might have happened to Sierra and David's marriage if David had lived?

3. As a reader, are you able to forgive Heather? Why or why not? Do you believe Sierra should forgive her?

4. Amy seeks perfection, especially "public perfection." Discuss the ways society today encourages this often false façade. Do you think it's harmless fun or damaging?

5. Why do you think the author chose to begin the novel the way she did? How do you think it sets the stage for and later reflects the rest of the book?

6. The Silva sisters' father is mentioned only in passing, but do you think their relationship with him—or lack thereof—might influence

their current relationships with the men in their lives? How do you think their mother's idealism combined with bad romantic choices have also affected the sisters?

7. The author made a choice in making Mason a divorce attorney. In what ways does Mason's profession inform his views on love and marriage?

8. Mason unconsciously waits for Sierra for most of his life. Is this sort of love possible in reality?

9. Heather makes a choice when she has an affair with David. Do you think she truly loved him or was she acting out of jealousy? In what ways does her rivalry with Sierra affect her actions?

10. Do you feel Amy's actions in warning Mason off Sierra when he confessed his feelings for Sierra to her were vindictive? Or did Amy act out of concern, actually thinking that Sierra had made her choice?

*Next month, don't miss these exciting
new love stories only from
Avon Books*

The Chase by Lynsay Sands

For Scotswoman Seonaid Dunbar, running away to an abbey was preferable to marrying Blake Sherwell. No, she'd not dutifully pledge troth to anyone the English court called "Angel." There was no such thing as an English angel; only English devils. And there were many ways to elude a devilish suitor. This battle would require all weapons, and so the chase was about to begin.

You Were Made to Be Mine by Julie Anne Long

The mission: Find Lady Aurelie Capet, the Earl of Brundage's runaway fiancée, in exchange for a fortune. Child's play for legendary British former spymaster, Christian Hawkes. The catch? Hawkes knows in his bones that Brundage is the traitor to England who landed him in a brutal French prison. Hawkes is destitute, the earl is desperate, and a bargain is struck.

Four Weeks of Scandal by Megan Frampton

Octavia Holton is determined to claim the home she grew up in with her late father. But she discovers the house is also claimed by one Gabriel Fallon, who says his father won the house in a bet. They make a four-week bargain: Pretend to be engaged, all the while seeking out any will, letter, or document that proves who gets ownership. But soon they realize their rivalry might lead to something much more intimate . . .

REL 0522

NEW YORK TIMES BESTSELLING AUTHOR

JENNIFER RYAN

THE ME I USED TO BE
978-0-06-307367-8

After serving time for a crime she didn't commit, Evangeline returns home to discover her late father has left her responsible for the family's failing ranch, her mother blames her for her father's death, and her brothers want her out of their way. Her only ally is Chris Chambers. The cop who put her away is sure she took the fall for someone else.

LOST AND FOUND FAMILY
978-0-06-300351-4

For years, Sarah Anderson has hidden the truth about her late husband's lies from their children and his mother, Margaret. When Margaret forces Sarah to bring the boys for a visit, she has attorney Luke Thompson investigate Sarah's past. What he finds is a truth very different from what he's been led to believe: Far from being cold and unloving, Sarah is devoted to her boys.

SISTERS AND SECRETS
978-0-06-307181-0

There's nothing more complicated than the relationship among family, and the Silva sisters—tragedy-touched Sierra, seemingly perfect Amy, and free-spirited Heather—are no exception. As their secrets are revealed, each realizes that there is more to their family than meets the eyes . . . and forgiveness may be the only way to move forward and reclaim true happiness at last.

JRY2 0522

NEW YORK TIMES BESTSELLING AUTHOR

JENNIFER RYAN

THE RETURN OF BRODY McBRIDE
978-0-06-230602-9

Former bad boy, now-decorated Army Ranger Brody McBride is home on a mission: Find the woman he never should have left behind and right the wrong he did eight years ago. But Brody is shocked to discover that, along with the heartbreak, he left Rain Evans with something infinitely better than she could have imagined: two beautiful daughters.

FALLING FOR OWEN
978-0-06-266806-6

Attorney by day, rancher by night, Owen McBride made it his mission to help the innocent. But when a client's abusive ex-husband targets Owen, and his gorgeous neighbor Claire gets caught in the crossfire, his feelings turn anything but professional. The mysterious beauty awakens something in him, and he'll do anything to keep her safe.

DYLAN'S REDEMPTION
978-0-06-269144-6

Jessie Thompson had one hell of a week. Dylan McBride, the boy she loved, skipped town without a word. Then her drunk of a father tried to kill her, and she fled Fallbrook. Eight years later, her father is dead, and Jessie reluctantly goes home—only to come face-to-face with the man who shattered her heart. A man who, for nearly a decade, believed she was dead.

JRY1 0618